flecks
of
GOLD

Alicia Buck

Bonneville Books
Springville, Utah

I would like to dedicate this book to my family, who put up with reading painfully small increments of my story every week but kept enthusiastically asking for more anyway. Thanks to Jan Hirschi for her initial edit, as well as to Valerie Buck for subsequent edits. They helped me so much, and my book wouldn't be even half as good without them. I want to especially thank my husband who was my constant sounding board throughout the whole story process. Nothing would have been possible without his support.

ISBN 13: 978-1-59955-389-4

LIBRARY OF CONGRESS CATALOGING-IN-PUBLICATION DATA

Buck, Alicia.
Flecks of gold / Alicia Buck.
p. cm.
Summary: Mary Margaret discovers that she is from a magical kingdom and that her golden eye color is a sign of royal blood.
ISBN 978-1-59955-389-4
1. Fantasy fiction, American. I. Title.

PS3602.U2623F57 2010
813'.6--dc22

2010011209

Published by Bonneville Books, an imprint of Cedar Fort, Inc., 2373 W. 700 S., Springville, UT 84663
Distributed by Cedar Fort, Inc., www.cedarfort.com

Cover design by Angela D. Olsen
Cover design © 2010 by Lyle Mortimer
Edited and typeset by Heidi Doxey

Printed in the United States of America

10 9 8 7 6 5 4 3 2 1

Printed on acid-free paper

Prologue

I was falling, crashing through golden light so bright that even with my eyes closed my eyelids lit up like a movie screen. My elbow ricocheted off the brilliance, sending a piercing zing through my arm and snowballing my body into a wild spin. There was no way to tell whether I was dropping or being propelled forward like a bullet down the barrel of a gun. I slapped and spun, nauseated and bruised. What did I care? She was gone. Taken. My world, consisting once of just me and Mom, had crumbled, and I was willing to do anything to snatch it back, even mimic the frightening conjuration I had seen him create before he vanished.

Chapter 1

I flipped the page in the magazine Joe had left at our house and shook my head. Why a cop with the temperament of a pit bull would be interested in movie stars mystified me. Mom came over from the kitchen to squeeze in by my side, granola bar in hand.

"This baffles me." She hit the pages of the magazine with the granola bar, and crumbs fell on my lap. I glared, but she smiled, her cheeks dimpling and her eyebrows raised mischievously. I couldn't resist her—I laughed. Mom's blonde curls mingled with my straight dark brown hair, her pale face leaned in next to my dusky olive cheek to see the pictures more easily, and we chuckled together over how obsessed some people were with the detail of actors' lives.

There was a sharp rap on the door, and then Joe walked through the entryway without waiting for an answer. My body tensed. Mom felt me stiffen and smiled nervously before prying herself from the chair to give Joe a hug.

"What a nice surprise. I didn't expect you until tonight," she said happily, if somewhat warily.

"I got off work early. Is there some reason I should have called ahead?" His voice sharpened with insinuation.

Mom's shoulders hunched. She seemed to shrink from her confident height of five-five to just five feet. "I said it was nice," she said in a small voice.

"Well, I know." His shoulders relaxed, and he switched from sullenness to blustery mirth. Mom breathed out a sigh while I hunched deeper into the easy chair.

"Joe, I meant to ask you. Mary and I have looked all over the studio and through the other rooms, but we can't find that painting I did of the girl playing in the sand. Have you seen it lately?" She looked around the living room as if the painting would suddenly appear.

Joe slid his eyes sideways and then snapped, "How should I know?"

"No reason." Mom backed off quickly. "I was just hoping you could help me. You know how I misplace things, but I need to find it soon. That buyer I told you about wanted the painting before the end of the week."

I gritted my teeth, galled to see Mom go from careless joy to insecure wariness, but that was nothing new when it came to Mom and her boyfriends.

"I've been working all day. I don't want to spend hours going through this mess for one painting." Joe's eyes were slits, but I thought his exasperation seemed fake. I looked around our tidy living room with the neatly stacked canvases and snorted. He shot a glare my way.

Mom retreated again. "You don't have to help if you don't feel like it. I'm sure Mary and I will find it." I gripped the magazine tightly, struggling to keep in my angry words.

Joe narrowed his eyes at me, but before he could comment about me wrinkling his favorite magazine, the phone rang. Mom picked it up just as Joe reached for the receiver.

"Fiona Underwood speaking," she answered brightly with a nervous look at Joe. Both Joe and I watched as Mom's concerned look faded. She flicked a quick glance down to the floor and then back toward Joe before turning slightly away. "Yes. Is that so? I see. No, no, thank you for calling me. I appreciate it. Good-bye." She returned the phone to the receiver slowly but didn't turn back immediately.

"Who was that?" Joe demanded.

"That was Arthur Stippens. The buyer I was just talking about."

Joe stiffened, his look turning belligerent.

"Where's my money, Joe?" she asked softly, her eyes full of betrayal.

My mouth dropped open, but Joe's hostility didn't dissipate. His shoulders cocked back. "I try to do you a favor, and this is how you thank me?"

Mom looked uncertain. I was afraid she would fold, so I blurted, "Then why didn't you tell Mom about what you'd done when she asked where her painting was?"

He glared at me before turning back to Mom with a big smile. "I wanted to surprise you tonight, but fine, I'll just give you the money now." He pulled out his wallet and handed over four hundred dollars.

Mom's eyes stayed on the money in her hand for several moments before she looked up. She flicked her gaze to my tense face and must have seen something there that swayed her.

"Where's the rest of it?" Her voice was firm.

"That's it." Joe smiled, but his voice was hard. I watched to see if Mom would back down, but her eyes didn't drop.

"Arthur said he paid one thousand dollars, so give me the rest."

"You couldn't have gotten a thousand for it, and you know it," he snarled.

"You're right. I wasn't going to get one thousand. Mary negotiated one thousand two hundred." She spoke softly but firmly. "That's our money. Give me the six hundred dollars, and then I think you'd better go."

A vein on Joe's neck pulsed angrily as he clenched his fists. I sat on the edge of the chair, ready to spring if he made so much as an aggressive gesture toward Mom. His fists uncurled and his lips turned up in a cocky hook. "No, I don't think I will." He folded his arms and leaned against the wall. "You're making a big deal out of nothing. I was just helping you."

"You didn't have my permission to sell my painting, and you weren't going to tell me about it or give me the money. You are not the man I thought you were. Please just go."

"I didn't need your permission. We're a couple. Couples share things."

"Please leave now." Her voice wavered, but her chin didn't drop.

Joe took a step forward, and Mom started trembling. I dropped the magazine and rose from the chair to move next to her. Joe stood up straight, but I was still a good three inches taller than his five-seven frame.

He cast a challenging glance at me before edging around to Mom's unprotected side. He twined his fingers through her smooth blonde hair. "Or what, you'll call the police? I don't think you're quite getting the picture here. I'm a cop. All my friends are cops. What do you think will happen if you call the station?" He twirled his finger around a lock of Mom's hair.

I wanted to punch the air right out of him and stepped forward, but Mom touched my arm.

Joe gave me a mocking look before he continued. "My friend Benny will answer the phone. I've told him about you. He agrees that family problems should be kept in the family." He jerked on the hair in his fingers, and it ripped out. She let out a whimper, and I could see a new fear in her eyes.

I snapped. I hadn't taken ten years of karate for nothing. My vision narrowed until the room disappeared and all I could see were the buttons of

Joe's shirt. All I could think of was my desire to hit him so hard that his solid body would defy gravity and fly. A flash of golden lace lit up behind my eyes. Then there was a click inside my brain as the image shifted slightly, changing somehow. I connected with his abdomen, and Joe flew. He smashed into the wall eight feet away.

Mom and I gazed at him, stunned. I'd heard of extreme situations giving people unusual strength, but my blow had flung him almost the entire length of the room. It reminded me of action movies where they use wires to yank the stuntman off the ground to make the hero's hit more impressive.

The golden light behind my eyes wasn't really new. Gold was always popping up at the edge of my vision when I looked at things slantwise, but I'd never felt that click before, that shift. Mom and I stood in a stupor. I looked at my arm and knew that it wasn't capable of such power.

Despite the force of the blow, Joe rolled to his feet more quickly than I would have expected. He was a cop, after all. I guessed he was used to getting knocked around. He bulldozed across the room straight for my gut. I wrenched myself to the side and tripped him with his own momentum.

My nerves buzzed with adrenaline and fear. I didn't know if I should hit him while he was down or grab Mom and run. Then Joe sprang to his feet, hatred smoldering in his eyes.

"You'll pay for that," he snarled.

My heart bucked in my chest. I watched his body closely for what he might do next. He lunged with a left jab, and my arm moved to block, almost before I could think about what I was doing. Gold blazed in my skull in a web work of lines. Then something inside shifted, and I punched. The air whooshed out of Joe, and he sailed across the room. He crashed into the wall and slid to the ground, breathing raggedly. I dared a glance at Mom and saw her backed against a corner, hand over her mouth. Her eyes flicked fearfully beyond me, and she made a small squeak. I turned to see Joe on his feet across the room, pointing a gun at my head.

"I should shoot you right now. If it weren't for . . ." He trailed off and suddenly looked fearful before recovering his sneer. "Don't ever try that again, girl, and stay out of my business from now on." He shoved off from the wall. The show of languid nonchalance was ruined, however, by a wince of pain. "I need a drink. I'll be back later." He paused by the door to grab another one of my Mom's paintings. "Don't do anything stupid, or I promise I'll hear about it."

Mom rushed to my side as soon as the door clicked shut, and I noticed for the first time that she was clutching a heavy paperweight in one hand. "Are you hurt?" she asked.

"No, I'm okay." Tears rolled down her face. We held each other for awhile in shock. She cried herself out while I fumed. The strangeness of what I had done made me uneasy, so I concentrated on my anger.

Mom had gone through a lot of lousy boyfriends throughout my life, but no one had ever tried to hurt us physically before. After Mom's tears dried, we sat in silence on the floor, staring at the advertisement on the back of Joe's magazine. It was a real estate promotion for Tucson, Arizona.

"How many months are left on the lease for the apartment?" Mom asked suddenly. It was no surprise to me that Mom had lost track of how long we'd lived in our Portland apartment. Days, weeks, years had no meaning to her, so I kept track of all our expenses.

"We've been on a month-to-month lease for awhile now."

"Good. I think we need to leave. I know not all the police in Portland are Joe's friends, but I don't want to risk it."

I reluctantly nodded. I wanted to see Joe go down, but neither of us knew what kind of support he had at the police station. "I'll call the manager and give him our notice," I said.

"I don't care about losing money for the rest of the month. We need to go now." She looked around as if unsure of where to start.

"Look in the phone book under movers while I call to cancel our utilities," I directed.

Mom hired some people to pack up and move for us. She offered to pay them extra to come in an hour, and we rushed to pack a few days' worth of clothes and toiletries so that we could help load boxes by the time the men came.

"Where are we going to go?" I asked, closing a box of living room junk.

Mom grabbed the People magazine off the coffee table as the movers lifted it. "Here." She jabbed her finger at the sun-filled picture in the ad.

"Okay. I'd better call the number and see if they can start looking for something while we're driving there." I spent the next hour trying to sort out living arrangements for sunny Arizona.

Two days later the screen door of a tiny red and pink brick house slammed shut behind me as I hefted my backpack higher on my shoulders and headed to my first day of school. The sun was out, dispelling the slight chill of night. The morning's warmth startled me, and it hit me again how little I knew about Arizona. Cactus arrangements were a popular yard design at the houses I passed. I found only a few plants that looked at all familiar.

A strange bush with tiny, orange, egg-shaped fruits caught my eye, so I picked one to examine it. It had a smooth outer skin and was about the size of a salad tomato.

"They're called kumquats," a voice said over my shoulder. I jumped, lost my footing, and backed up quickly to recover my balance. The voice belonged to a tanned guy with dark brown hair who looked about my age. He wore slacks and a letterman's jacket that almost matched the blue of his eyes. He was handsome and he smiled invitingly. The thought of Joe flashed through my mind.

"Thanks." I turned to walk quickly toward school.

"Wait."

A whoosh went through me like a cool blue blanket of weblike fibers. It covered my mind, stopping thought, and spread through my body in a chill. My feet halted of their own volition.

"Sorry, I didn't mean to scare you like that. I just saw you looking at that kumquat and thought you didn't know what it was. It's actually pretty strange that any are left on the bush so late in the season."

He caught up, and I started moving again, bombarded by foreign wisps of fanciful thoughts. I shook my head to dispel the strange feelings.

He nodded toward the fruit I still held. "You don't have to peel it or anything. Just pop it in your mouth. Kumquats are good, though they're kind of sour. You'll have to tell me what you think. By the way, my name is Kelson. What's yours?"

"Mary Margaret." The two-word version of my name sprang out of my mouth as if summoned. I scowled at the sidewalk and tried to fight a completely out-of-character desire to tell this good-looking guy all about myself. I couldn't help but like his name. It was distinctive, much better than mine. I'd never understood why Mom, so creative and non-traditional in so many ways, had fallen in love with such a boring name. We weren't even Catholic.

"Mary Margaret. I don't know why, but it seems to fit you."

I almost snorted, but I didn't want to look *too* unfeminine.

"Are you going to school?" he asked. Part of my mind couldn't help but note how completely obvious the answer to his question was. Did he think that I walked around wearing a backpack simply to examine kumquats? But the greater, fog-filled part of my brain wanted to impress him. All sorts of silly words flashed through my head. Thankfully, before I could open my mouth and embarrass myself, he spoke again. "Do you want to walk with me the rest of the way?"

I was afraid to answer in case one of my nonsensical thoughts popped out, so I just nodded and concentrated on putting one foot in front of the other.

"Come on now, you don't strike me as the kind of girl who's shy. Give me something to work with here." He increased his pace to keep up with my staccato steps.

I combed my brain for something neutral to talk about. "Have you lived here very long?" I finally muttered.

"Have *I*? I think the real question is, 'Where are you from that you don't know what kumquats are?' "

"Oregon."

"Really? What's that like?"

"I liked it. It's a lot greener than here." I stopped, realizing I sounded juvenile.

"That would be really strange. I've lived in a desert my whole life. The only green here is cactus, desert brush, and transplanted trees. You must be having a hard time with the heat. How long have you been here?"

"Two days."

"Oh, was it you who finally took that ugly pink house? I saw the moving van. I live on the corner, two houses away."

"It isn't so bad on the inside," I said, feeling protective of the tiny house.

"I'm glad. I can never look at that thing for long—hurts my eyes."

"It's not like it's fluorescent pink," I snapped. I instantly felt horrible for being rude.

To my surprise, Kelson laughed. "Whoa there. I didn't realize you two were so attached." He smiled teasingly. "I won't say anything else about your house."

I flushed and resolved to watch my tongue. I was prone to speak before thinking and only afterwards would I realize that I'd been abrupt, tactless, or rude. I felt terrible later, but it was like demolishing a house only to realize afterward that you were just supposed to paint it.

We walked in silence for a while, and I was grateful. With my churning emotions, silence was safest, but it was still pretty uncomfortable. I held back a sigh of relief when we finally reached the school.

"Well, it was nice meeting you, Mary Margaret. See you around." Which probably meant, "I might see you, but don't expect me to talk to you."

"Yeah, see you. Thanks for the kumquat thing," I said, holding the little fruit up like an idiot.

"Right. Tell me what you think." He waved a final decisive good-bye.

I berated myself for my complete cheesiness. What was up with me this morning? So I'd never been the world's most popular kid. Even if I was a bit of an outcast, I'd never had this much trouble making small talk before.

I went to the office and got my schedule, then headed to my first period class—chemistry. I found the room a little before the bell rang. Two girls in designer outfits were talking and laughing near the back of the class. Several boys drooled openly over them. The back was my favorite place to sit, so I approached the seat next to the girl with perfectly styled blonde hair wearing a tight, blue v-neck shirt and black pants. She looked up at me. I felt a twinge of regret for not choosing my outfit more carefully. My jeans were two years old, and my green washed-out shirt and old jacket hung on my body like a limp rag.

"This seat is saved." The blonde girl eyed my towering height as if it disgusted her.

"Sorry." I smiled tightly, looking into her eyes.

She recoiled. "Wow, Suze, take a look at this girl's freaky eyes." The rest of the students in the room turned to look. I dropped my gaze and quickly sat down a few seats away.

"Seriously, they're like tiger eyes or something. It's scary, and she's like ten feet tall," the girl continued loudly.

The bell rang, shutting the blonde up, but I kept my eyes cast down through the hour to avoid curious classmates trying to snatch a glimpse of the one-woman freak show. After awhile I felt the other kids' eyes drift away and ignore me again. I noticed that no one ever came to sit in the "saved" seat. I slouched in my chair and simply endured, wishing I'd put off coming to school.

After class I went up to the teacher to ask him what I needed to do to catch up.

"I'm sorry," he said in an oddly high voice. "I didn't even see you. You should have said something."

"It's okay." I was used to being overlooked. Sometimes I felt like it was almost magical the way my giant, tiger-eyed self could go unnoticed.

The teacher gave me my assignments, and I glumly left the room.

I was glad when it was finally lunch. English hadn't gone well either, and my nerves were on overload. A traitorous part of me was angry with Mom for choosing pond scum as a boyfriend, but the bigger part of me knew it wasn't her fault. I really didn't feel like being rejected again, so I sat down at an empty table near a corner of the lunch room.

I was wallowing in a small, but beautifully decorated pity party, complete with imaginary streamers, so at first I didn't hear my name.

"Hello? I'm talking to you, Mary Margaret," someone said.

I looked up, startled. "What? Oh, uh, Kelson. I didn't hear you."

"Yeah, I got that. So can I sit here or what?"

"Sure." I felt confused, but Kelson just plunked down, a sigh escaping his lips. A fresh wash of unfamiliar, worshipful thoughts swooped into my head.

"Today's been horrible. My teachers must have conspired to assign a dune full of homework for the same day. I think they want to see if they can make us have a break up."

My brow furrowed at "break up." Was that a funny new way of saying break down? And what about the "dune" thing? Maybe he was a writer.

Then my cynical thoughts dulled and drifted away. "I've wondered if teachers tell each other when they're going to give tests so that they can all do it on the same day," I said. That wasn't too bad. I'd managed to refrain from gushing, but I wondered why I was even concerned about what I said to Kelson. I didn't do boys. I would talk to the occasional guy in an acquaintance kind of way, but I'd never been interested in pursuing a boy, no matter how cute—or rather, *especially* if I thought he was cute.

"Yeah, I mean, it's not like I can study all the time," he said.

"Hmm," I said, sorting out my thoughts. Kelson was just a normal person. I could handle this. I'd never let crushes affect my behavior before, but the romantic blue-hued feelings were hard to ignore.

"Sometimes I wish I were magic and could just stop time long enough to get caught up with everything. Do you ever wish that?" He looked at me intently.

I started to grin like a loyal puppy, caught myself, and merely curved my lips courteously. I fought against agreeing with him, even though the swirling cacophony in my head wanted to. "I'm actually glad there's no such thing as magic. The world has enough complications as it is."

"Are you sure?" The tide of romantic thoughts receded, and I could almost swear I saw a calculated look in his eyes.

"So, I didn't see you in any of my classes this morning," I said.

He grinned. "No. What classes did you have?"

"Chemistry and English."

"Oh, well I had P.E., then chemistry. What do you have this afternoon?"

I checked my schedule. "American government, then art."

"Great! I have government too. We can walk together."

He kept giving me an intense stare that thrilled and unnerved me at the same time. I needed a break from that intensity, so I told Kelson I had to stop at the bathroom for a minute and would meet him at the stairs.

I wanted to relax, but I was caught in the most unusual jumble of sensations. Kelson was gorgeous. I felt irresistibly drawn to him, which was what was freaking me out. I was not the kind of person to be overcome by good looks. In fact, I didn't trust most men as far as I could throw them. Something had overridden my carefully cultivated safeguards, and I didn't like it one bit.

As I turned these thoughts over in the bathroom, I remembered the kumquat, still in my backpack. Swinging the bag around, I pulled it out, rinsed it off in the yellowed sink, and looked up into the cracked mirror, scrutinizing myself. I had to have gotten my hair from my dad. No one on Mom's side had chocolate brown hair.

As I bit the kumquat, juice squirted onto the corner of the bathroom mirror. A sour taste hit my tongue almost as strong as a lemon, but then sweetness spread through my mouth, leaving behind a pleasant aftertaste.

The taste reminded me of my confused emotions about Kelson. He seemed so sweet, but there was this indefinable feeling I got around him, like an aftertaste, that I couldn't tell if I liked or not. But why was I so determined to find something bad in the one good thing that had happened today? I shook myself and went to meet him at the stairs. When I approached, he smiled, and I chided myself for being so suspicious of every man alive.

We reached American government, and Kelson sat next to me near the back. Despite the teacher's theatrical outbursts, it was hard to concentrate on the lesson. Kelson's presence next to me felt palpable, like a firm pressure on the side of my body.

I was glad to leave that class and head to art. If art couldn't make me relax, nothing could. The smell of wet clay, turpentine, and paint hit me as I walked in. My shoulders loosened. No one talked to me, but in art I didn't care. I simply took up a piece of paper and began to draw what the teacher instructed, losing myself in the detail of the skull that sat on the table in front of me.

Like Mom, I considered myself an artist, but I was pretty sure no one saw their art the way I saw mine. When I lost myself in my subject, it was as if there was another hidden element, just out of reach. When I drew, I not only saw lines and shadows, but a different shape at the edge of the subject. It was more than imagination. It was a view that was beyond simple sight, a pressure like what I'd felt when sitting next to Kelson. It was something I knew I could grasp if I only had a key to understanding how. Whenever I contemplated this second sight, I felt slightly silly, but it was hard to dismiss it as my imagination when I saw the golden patterns so often.

The bell rang sooner than I expected, and I wondered why my other classes couldn't have gone by as quickly. As I transferred piles of homework from my locker to my already overstuffed backpack, I noticed Kelson with a group of guys in blue letterman jackets. Short-skirted girls in tight shirts dripped off the boys' arms like jewelry.

I studied Kelson covertly. He looked so at ease, so normal. His jacket was slightly different from the other guys, and I briefly wondered why. A sappy urge to walk over and say hello floated through my head as I watched, but when I looked away, I was gripped by a strong desire to flee his presence and feel like myself again. I strode quickly out of school, ready to get home and complain about the day to Mom. I'd walked about a block when I heard someone approaching from behind.

"Mary Margaret, wait up," Kelson said. A whoosh of warmth, which somehow made me picture a blue-white mist, spread through me. It was pleasant, but my stomach clenched in reaction, and I turned around slowly. Amorous thoughts swam through my brain.

"Hi. How was your first day of school?"

"Fine." I stuffed my hands in my pockets.

"You must have a lot of stuff to catch up on."

"Yeah, but I don't mind. I don't have much else to do. So what's your letterman jacket for?" I asked, trying to divert the conversation from me.

He hesitated, and I had a funny impression that he was trying to think of an answer. "Swimming," he finally said.

"That's cool." Thinking of follow-up questions was difficult with my head full of Kelson's blue eyes. I tried to clear my mind. "Why is your jacket different from the other guys at school?"

"I didn't really letter in this school. Actually, I just moved here awhile ago."

"Oh, where did you come from?" I asked, trying to concentrate.

"Iberloah." He gave me the strangest look, curious and mischievous, and so intense I looked away. "Have you heard of it?"

"No. It sounds really unusual. What state is it in?" I thought that it sounded more like a foreign name, but Kelson didn't have a hint of an accent.

"It's a small town in Mitiga—ah, I mean Michigan. No one who doesn't live there even knows about it."

I looked away, finding it easier to think that way. I'd never heard of the town, but Michigan was no desert. Hadn't Kelson said earlier he'd lived in a desert his whole life?

"Do you swim?" he asked out of the blue. It took me a second to change gears.

"A little. I was kind of on a team in middle school."

"Maybe we could go swimming sometime." His grin now looked almost hungry.

I shivered. "Maybe." Something was bugging me, but it was like a ball of knotted yarn in my head.

We reached my house and stopped in front of the cactus garden.

"Well, I'll see you around."

"Yeah, thanks."

Watching Kelson walk away again triggered the memory of the sour sweet aftertaste of the kumquat. Unease accompanied me into the house.

Mom wasn't home, and I found a sticky note on the fridge reminding me that she'd be home by 5:30. I'd forgotten that she'd gotten a job. I was happy she'd found something so quickly, but a job at the Bernard Packing Company didn't seem like a good fit. I wondered if she'd worn one of her long beaded shirts. They were her favorite, but if she was moving boxes they might get caught. I put my disappointment aside and settled down to do pointless English worksheets.

Mom didn't come home until six. The dinner I'd made was cold, and

I was considering calling the number on the fridge when she walked painfully through the front door.

"Are you okay?"

"Yes." She sat down on the recliner with a groan. "No. I didn't think it would be so hard. My arms feel like jell-o, and my back aches, and look," she warbled miserably, holding up the end of her beaded shirt. Several strands had been torn out.

"Oh, Mom, I'm sorry. Maybe you shouldn't wear a beaded shirt tomorrow."

"I don't think I have any," she said helplessly. I could tell that her exhaustion was making her melodramatic.

"You can borrow mine. Why don't you eat and then head to bed early?" I microwaved a plate of shepherd's pie and took it to her in the living room.

"So today was your first day at a new school. How'd it go?" She tried to put energy into her inquiry.

"I'll tell you about it tomorrow. Just go to bed, okay? I don't want you collapsing on the job."

"All right, but I want to hear all about it tomorrow."

I cleaned up dinner and then went to curl up in the easy chair. By the time I started reading my chemistry textbook my eyes were drooping. Without realizing, I drifted off to sleep, the book sliding from my fingers to the floor.

Chapter 2

When I woke, a wild orange rose with pink tips rested atop my homework on the coffee table. It was already wilting from lack of water, and its fragrance tickled my nose. I was surprised that Mom had gotten up so early. I just hoped she would fare better at her job today.

I quickly dressed, shouldered my backpack, and lurched through the door. Kelson was walking slowly past my house when I came out.

"Hey," I said.

"How's it going, Mary Margaret?"

"Fine, I guess." Talking to him seemed easier now. The pressure I had felt yesterday was still there, but less intense, like a phantom touch compared to the strong push from before.

"So why'd you move here in the middle of the school year?" Kelson asked.

"It's because of this guy," I said. "It turned out he was only dating my mom to steal her paintings, and then he threatened us. Anyway, we moved here because we weren't sure what else to do."

I wanted to pull the words back into my mouth. *Why did I tell him that?* When we reached the school, I still felt disconcerted.

"Well, I'll see you around," he said.

Right. No comments, nothing. I'd said too much, and I could tell he just wanted to escape. Part of me was glad, but another part, one that was growing alarmingly fast, was miserable. I tried to wipe away my feelings as I went to my first class of the B-day schedule. It was called adult roles, and I was only taking it to learn some budgeting skills so Mom and I wouldn't starve. Scanning the room, I was shocked to see Kelson waving at me. I wondered why he was in the class.

I hesitated before sitting next to him, but there was nothing else I could do. If I sat somewhere else, he'd be offended, and so far he was the only person who'd been nice to me.

The class was intriguing, but I could tell Kelson was bored. He kept glancing at me like he wanted to talk, but I buried my nose in my notebook.

He caught me on the way out of class. "So, Mary Margaret, where are you off to next?"

Did he always have to use my full name? "Computer graphics."

"Hey, really? Me too. I'll walk with you."

We arrived just as the bell rang. The only free computers were across the room from each other so Kelson and I separated. I felt like I had a split personality. I wanted to get away from him, but I also wanted to be near him. Every time I saw him, I felt a sweep of warm fog and my stomach flipped. When the bell rang, Kelson came up to me, smiling.

"You want to go to lunch?" my mouth blurted without my consent.

"Yeah, let's go."

We sat down at an empty table in the corner of the lunchroom, and I started to relax. Kelson started talking about the wonders of modern technology, and even though I thought it was a little strange—after all, Michigan wasn't exactly stuck in the Stone Age—I was glad I could sit there and just nod when expected.

After my next class, medical anatomy, I got lost looking for calculus, so when I walked in I was too flustered to do anything but sit down quickly. Then I felt a swell of warmth. I looked up, and there, sitting across from me, was Kelson. I felt confused, thinking he shouldn't be there, but as I looked into his eyes, I couldn't remember why his presence would be strange. A soft blanket enfolded my mind, and I felt flushed and giddy. It was hard to concentrate with Kelson's presence dominating my thoughts, and I shook my head several times to clear the fog, but it didn't work. As soon as the bell clanged, I rushed out of the classroom

I almost ran to my locker, but I wasn't fast enough. Kelson was waiting for me right outside. At the sight of him, I felt my knees give way a little, and the fog rushed back.

"Hi," he said.

My brain refused to come up with any words, even "hello." I just couldn't look away from his crystal blue eyes.

"Walk with me?" Even though it was formed as a question, it was a command. He held out his hand, a smile playing on his mouth. I watched in astonishment as my hand reached out and grabbed his. We started walking, and warmth spread up my arm.

I wondered idly, as the fire extended from my hand to my entire body, if I would succumb to heat stroke. I couldn't seem to form an intelligent thought. Every time I started to wonder why Kelson was so interested in me, my thoughts would switch to the pomegranate bush we'd just passed or the size of the cracks in the sidewalk. By the time we reached my house, I could barely see my door, much less think that I should walk through it.

"Can I come in?" Kelson asked.

I started to say yes, but stopped. "No." I flushed in embarrassment as he jerked back, looking surprised. "The house is still a mess, and I have to do a lot of homework, so I don't think it would be a good idea. I'm really behind." I shut my mouth, realizing I was starting to ramble.

He studied me but smiled after a moment. "No problem. You wanna walk to school with me tomorrow?"

"Sure. See you tomorrow." I slid into my house, shutting the door and then leaning against it, taking deep breaths. The strange mishmash of emotions and thoughts started to clear immediately. It was strange how confused I became around Kelson. It wasn't like me at all, and though I felt practically euphoric near him, a twinge of fear laced through me now that he was gone. It was like I lost control whenever he was near.

I wandered into the living room and slumped onto our plaid couch without noticing Mom sitting on the recliner. She looked up from her romance novel.

"Hi, honey, had a hard day?" Her sky-blue eyes scrunched in concern, and she put her book down to come give me a hug. I buried my head in her shoulder, feeling her silky hair against my face and smelling her reassuring scent of oil paint, turpentine, and lavender. Then it occurred to me that she shouldn't be here.

I pulled away. "Why are you home?"

"Um." She looked away. "Well, it seems I'm not quite cut out for the job."

"What? What happened?"

"I tripped and fell onto a stack of boxes. Everything inside broke." She shrugged, but her eyes looked miserable.

"Still, it was an accident. They can't just fire you."

"They didn't. I decided it was best to resign before I broke anything else." Her lips curved in a small smile.

"Oh well, it was a horrible job, anyway. We'll find something better for you."

"Of course we will. With my Mary on the case, anything is possible. Now, enough about me. Let's talk about you. I want to know everything."

I told her about my classes, but I didn't want to talk about Kelson. By the time I finished, Mom was outraged at the amount of homework I was expected to do. I just laughed. It was nice to have someone on my side.

I tried to tell Mom about Kelson at dinner, but I couldn't form the words. Finally, I just asked her if she'd worked on a painting that day. I listened half-heartedly as she told me her plans to paint a desert landscape. Though I couldn't seem to tell Mom about Kelson, I couldn't get the thought of him out of my head. I yearned to see him while at the same time I dreaded it. I'd never felt this mixed up before.

"Tell me about my dad," I said suddenly. I had no idea what had prompted me. I'd never dared to ask Mom about him before, but I wanted to know what he'd been like. Had she felt the same fog in his presence that I felt around Kelson?

Mom looked as surprised by my question as I was. She recovered, though, and smiled sadly. "Your dad looked a lot like you. He had dark, wavy hair that he wore to his ears. His eyes and skin were like yours, but his eyes had a little brown at the edges. We met in college. I was trying to lug a huge canvas back to my apartment, but I kept dropping it every few steps. He came to my rescue, helping me with the canvas all the way back to my place. We started talking, and he told me he'd been touring the campus to see if it was right for him. After meeting me, he decided it was. So he enrolled, and we started dating.

"Your father was a wonderful man, though a little odd at times. It took awhile to get used to him, but he was very sweet. H constantly did things that made me feel special, and he was grateful for the simplest things. I guess his kindness rubbed off because he always made me feel like I was more somehow, like I was worth something." Her face fell, and I guessed she was thinking of Joe.

"Five months after we met, we were married and two months after that I got pregnant with you, only . . ." Her voice trailed off, and she looked so sad. I felt sorry that I was making her relive this, but I'd never really heard the whole story. I couldn't help myself.

"It sounded like you were both really happy. What happened?"

"I don't know." She sighed and looked up from the table. "I've never understood what happened. Two and a half months after we got married, we were living in a basement apartment and going to school. The last day I saw him, it was morning, and I felt really queasy again, though at the time I didn't know it was because I was pregnant with you. Your father tried to cheer me up by giving me a rose from the bush outside. He promised that he'd cater to my every whim when he got home from classes. Then he gave me a kiss and walked out the door."

Mom spoke in a daze. "That was the last time I ever saw him. When I got home that evening, he wasn't there. I thought he'd decided to study on campus. After ten o'clock I knew something was wrong. It was too soon to call the police, but I didn't sleep all night. I reported him missing as soon as I could, but the police never found him. I've always wondered if maybe something happened to him . . . but, no. He just left. A week later I found out I was pregnant."

Her eyes focused again, and she reached for my hand across the card table. "Darling, I want you to know that when I found out I was going to have you, I was so glad. Knowing you were coming, that I would have a bit of him with me still, it kept me going when I just wanted to roll over and quit. Your father may have left me, but he gave me one last gift. You are the best thing that ever happened to me."

I was crying, and Mom's eyes looked suspiciously bright too. "Cuddle?" she asked, holding out her arms. She was sitting on a cheap folding chair that wobbled, and I eyed it dubiously. She grinned, and I decided to chance fate, sitting as delicately as possible in her lap as she hugged me. The chair groaned and popped, and Mom and I held our breaths and then laughed.

Chapter 3

he next morning Kelson was waiting for me outside the house. Seeing him, I felt like I was getting brain freeze. My knees went weak, and then, to my utter embarrassment, they gave out, and I plonked to the ground. My head felt dizzy, so I rubbed my temples. It didn't help. Kelson's hand touched my shoulder, and I looked up in surprise. The warm fogginess emanated from his touch.

"Here, let me help you."

I put up my arms, and he lifted me as if I were a whiff of cloud. I almost toppled down again in sheer surprise.

"You're strong." I immediately wanted to hit myself; I sounded like a lovesick cow. I must have looked it too because he smiled and shrugged.

"It was nothing. You're thin."

I am not! Not that I'm fat or anything, but I'm a bit too big in the hips to be called thin. It's especially hard for someone five feet, ten inches to be waiflike. I let his comment slide, however.

After he lifted me, he kept my hand and wouldn't let it go. Each step we took toward the high school seemed to take less and less effort. The sharp contrasts of the landscape became more indistinct, and I thought of the phrase "floating in the clouds." Did other infatuated people see the world in the same fuzzy focus?

We reached the school, and I found it difficult to release Kelson's hand until he dropped mine.

"Well, see you later," he said. Then when I didn't move, he grinned and made a shooing motion. I jerked into a walk. "Think of me," he said over my shoulder as I stumbled away, and suddenly all I could do was think of Kelson—Kelson's dark hair, Kelson's blue eyes, Kelson's smile.

The rest of the day was a blur, and the center of the blur was Kelson. The only half-lucid part happened in art. Instead of finishing the skull that we'd started, the teacher said we were free to draw whatever came to mind, no matter how silly or nonsensical. An urge hit me, and I started drawing pieces of something without really being aware of the whole. As I drew, the fog that had been threading in and out of my mind all day started dissipating. I saw streaks of gold at the edge of the paper, and the world came into better focus.

When the bell rang, I realized that I had been concentrating so much on the little details of my drawing that I wasn't even sure what it was. Looking down I saw that it was Kelson, only it wasn't the Kelson I knew. This person was much older. Though his features were no less handsome, his skin was darker, making his ice-blue eyes more poignant. They blazed with coldness and cruelty. I quickly looked away toward his mouth only to see a parody of the triumphant smile I'd spied so often. Now, however, the smile looked grotesque rather than charming. It was the first time I'd ever concentrated totally on the golden edges in my mind while I was drawing rather than on the paper. The result made me shiver. I stuffed the picture into my art cubby and left. My thoughts, which had been sluggish at best, now moved like quicksilver.

I hurried to my locker, stuffing my homework into my bag, and mashing the papers into a crumpled ball. I just wanted to go home, alone, without having to worry about what I had just drawn and how much it confused me. I didn't want to see Kelson again until I had time to think.

But a block away from school I heard rushed footsteps. "Mary Margaret."

I felt myself turning. The boy I faced was confident and charming, not the kind of guy I usually talked to, but certainly not sinister. The fog that had cleared seeped back. I shook my head, but it was hard to hold onto the image of my drawing when the handsome young Kelson stood beside me.

"Did you think of me today?" he asked. I nodded dumbly. Words were beyond me.

"Good. I am glad things are going so well. Only the finishing touch left, yes?"

I didn't know what he was talking about, but I nodded like an idiot. I was probably smiling like one, too.

He grabbed my hand. "You can never be too careful." He grinned.

I couldn't speak the whole way home.

"Well, I'll see you later," I managed when I reached my door. I wanted to get away so I could think.

"Are you forgetting that you invited me to come over today?" He leaned in so that the only think I could think about was his body close to mine. I'd been upset about something, but the fog had obscured my worries. I couldn't remember why I'd wanted to be alone.

"Of course not," I heard myself say. "Come in."

Mom wasn't anywhere in sight. I sighed inwardly, not sure why I was feeling uneasy.

"Why don't we sit down?" he asked.

I sat abruptly, barely catching the couch on my way down. It was as though I didn't have control over my own movements. I lifted my arm to see if I could. It swung up with no problem, and I watched it in fascination. Kelson sat down close to me, and I immediately forgot about my arm. He took hold of the forgotten limb and lowered it to my lap but didn't let go.

"You are quite right, Mary," he said as if we'd been talking. "We must finish things now. Look at me." I had been studying his jacket; there was something about it that was strange. The fabric shifted from beat-up cotton to a silkier shininess, and then back again. What was going on? I wanted to keep studying his jacket, but at his words, my gaze shifted to his eyes. I tried to look away, but our eyes locked before I could get a hold of myself. The ice blue of his irises was sharp, piercing, but everything else around the room was becoming fuzzy.

"You like me, right?" Kelson asked with a little grin. My head bobbed yes. "Do you like me enough to give yourself to me?" His grin became an affected shy smile.

My neck muscles clenched, and the fog cleared briefly from the shock of his question. "What do you mean?" I managed through the thick muddle in my mind.

Kelson looked down as if embarrassed, and then his eyes locked with mine again. "I mean, I really like you, Mary Margaret, and I want you to be with me. Will you give yourself to me?" His eyes bored into mine, and I could hardly think. Nothing made sense. I hardly knew this guy, but the romantic fog urged me to acquiesce no matter what the consequences might be.

My mouth opened to say yes, but something tugged at my memory. I stopped. Thinking rationally was like moving through sludge, but the eyes I was staring into reminded me of the edge of a memory. A picture was overlapping reality, and then I saw a flash of the drawing I had done in art class. It vanished, but the eyes I stared at did not change from the hard, cold eyes I'd drawn. I jerked my gaze away and stood up quickly, bashing my shin into the coffee table.

"I hardly know you," I stuttered. It was so hard to speak.

"Just say it!" he shouted, standing up and grabbing me by the shoulders. My head snapped back to his face, and I saw rage there. He must have seen my fear because he loosened his grip, and his anger vanished.

"I know *you*, Mary Margaret. I know you deserve to be with someone who treasures you. If you were mine, all would bow to us. You'd never have to worry about anything. You'd be sought after by millions, have all you ever needed, and never have to live in squalor again."

What was he talking about? It was all so strange, and so confusing. The fog drew me to his words, despite their absurdity. Say yes, it whispered. Say yes and let go of all your worries. Why couldn't I think straight? A knot of annoyance rooted itself firmly in my thoughts, ignoring the fog that tried to push it to the background. *Why should I say yes? Who asked him to take my worries away?*

"Why?" I managed to breathe out.

"You need me, Mary Margaret. You need me to take care of you. Just let go. Let me take care of everything for you so you don't have to struggle anymore."

My annoyance rose. *Need him? Ha!* Who had been taking care of Mom and me since I learned to read and use a phone? Me. I refused to be categorized as helpless. How dare he waltz in here and ask me to give myself to him after knowing him only three days? What kind of weirdo was he anyway? Of all the kooky people I'd met in my life, and there had been plenty, he was at the top of the list. As my thoughts churned, the fog thinned, then disappeared. The room sharpened, and golden threads wrapped around the edge of my vision. I stood back from Kelson and firmly removed his hands from my arms. "I don't know what kind of strange fantasy world you're living in, Kelson, but I think you should leave."

Kelson stared at me in disbelief. "But you aren't even trained!" he blurted. "How did you . . . ?" His eyes narrowed, making them look even more like the eyes from my drawing. I shivered.

"It doesn't make a difference. I will have you one way or another. You see, you are much too important a piece to be left here."

Piece? What was he talking about? Things were going from bad to worse. What kind of man-curse did Mom and I have on us? If Kelson was anything like Joe, I knew he might be on the verge of getting violent. I had to think. What could I do to get him out of my house? A physical attack probably wasn't a good idea if I could avoid it.

"Um, maybe we can talk about this tomorrow at school. I have a lot of homework, you know, and my mom might come home any minute with her boyfriend."

Kelson laughed. "You still don't understand, do you, Mary Margaret? I'm afraid you won't be doing homework anymore. I must get back to Iberloah, and you, my dear, are coming with me."

"You want to take me to Michigan?"

"Surely even you have guessed what is really going on here. What I really am."

"Yes, you're an insane guy, acting out your delusions." I could have hit myself. It probably wasn't smart to enrage him right now.

"I suppose it would seem that way to you, living in this world," he mused. His fingers rubbed his chin. "Suppose I just show you—watch closely."

He held out his hand, palm up. One second it was empty, but the next instant a globe of bright blue light hovered above his cupped palm. I took a step back and felt the wall pushing against my backpack. I slid sideways, trying to get as far away from Kelson as possible. His light was a trick. It had to be. Had he come to my house earlier and set up something? I looked for a camera, a string, anything, but I saw only the ball of light resting slightly above his hand.

The funniest part was that in his light I'd seen an image of a blue pattern that looked a lot like the gold webs that were always at the edge of my vision. The pattern had flashed clearly in my mind the instant before he made the ball and now lingered in my thoughts, its duplicate appearing behind my eyes in gold. I twisted slightly, mimicking what he'd done; suddenly, a ball of golden light sprung up in front of my face, and I stared. I couldn't believe what I'd done. I had felt the energy it took to create the globe of light. It was unnerving, and I quickly undid what I'd done. Kelson's light was gone now as well, and the room suddenly seemed full of shadow.

"Very good." He looked genuinely surprised and maybe a little worried. "You are gifted. I will have to watch myself. Come now, Mary Margaret. It's time for us to leave." He extended his hand to me, but I backed into the corner. I was more frightened now than when I'd thought Kelson was just your average obsessed stalker. What could he do? Could he make me do things I didn't want to? He almost had earlier, but I'd stopped him somehow. What if this time I couldn't stop him?

"Stay away from me." My voice shook. I had to get out of the corner, get past him somehow. My eyes flicked to the front door. If I could just get there.

Kelson caught my look. "Don't try it. Where would you go? No one knows you. Your mother doesn't have a boyfriend. In fact, didn't you come here to get away from Joe?"

"How did you know his name?" My stomach plummeted.

"I know a lot of things about you, Mary Margaret. Joe was a crude way to get you to come to me, but effective. Wouldn't you say?"

"But, you . . . . How? And how did you know we would come here?" My brain refused to process this new and terrible information.

"How did you come to think of Tucson? You didn't happen to see an ad on a magazine, did you? I'm glad it didn't strike you as odd to have a real estate ad on the back of a gossip magazine. I was a little worried it wouldn't work, but here you are, just as I wished."

It didn't make sense. Nothing he said added up rationally.

"The path in this place is the most thin," he continued. "The journey is rough, even for our kind. It would be impossible in Oregon. I suppose it has to do with similarities and symmetries, but I won't bore you with the details. We need to go."

Our kind? I wanted to scream from the absurdity of it all. I had to get away.

"Come, we're wasting time."

Panic gripped me. Then I heard the door opening. Kelson turned toward the sound.

I had to warn Mom, but my mouth was too dry. I swallowed hard. But it was too late. She was already in the door, and Kelson moved swift as a cat to intercept her.

"No! Leave her out of this," I said.

"Actually, I had thought to take both of you, anyway," Kelson said.

"What's going on here?" Mom's arms were full of grocery bags, so she didn't even try to free herself from Kelson's grip. She didn't know to be afraid, but a glimmer of understanding quivered in her eyes. *Break away,* I thought at her. *Run for help.* But Kelson was already escorting her further inside, shutting the door and standing in the way of escape.

"You're just in time, Fiona. We were about to leave. I'd be delighted to take both of you. In fact, in some ways you may be more useful than your daughter. Take my hand, Mary." It was a command, and now that Mom was there, I didn't dare refuse. I walked to him slowly, trying to think of something I could do. Mom looked confused and alarmed. Her eyes brimmed with questions, but she remained silent. *Be ready*, I beamed at her as hard as I could. She nodded ever so slightly.

I extended my arm, fist closed, to Kelson. He took my wrist as I hoped he would. In the moment his hand closed over my arm, I jerked down hard and struck up with my left hand. My palm connected with his nose, but I didn't hear the hoped-for crunch that would've meant I'd broken it. He staggered back and let go of us. Mom dropped her bags, and we ran for the back door. My backpack bounced on my back.

I didn't see Mom stumble.

"Mary," she gasped. I turned and saw Kelson gripping Mom's arm fiercely. "Go! Get help," she said. Kelson tried to reach past her to grab me, but Mom twisted, hampering his movements.

He grabbed her tightly around the waist, arms locked to her sides. "Fine, one then. I'll be back for you later, Mary Margaret." There was a flash of blue pattern, and then blinding light. I looked away, shielding my eyes. When I looked back, both Mom and Kelson were gone.

Chapter 4

Mom! I ran back through the hall. They couldn't have just disappeared. Kelson must have dragged her through the front door. But when I reached it, the smashed eggs on the floor were undisturbed.

When Kelson vanished, I'd seen another pattern flash in my head. This one had been far more complex. I hadn't really been paying attention, but I thought, if I tried, I could reconstruct it. It was my fault that Mom was taken. I had to get her back. I didn't care if I blasted myself into oblivion trying to mimic the pattern Kelson had used. I closed my eyes, trying to remember all the twists and curves of the blue pattern that had flashed through my head. There were one or two points I wasn't sure about, but I pieced together the structure anyway. When the golden threads looked as good as I could get them, I twisted as before . . .

. . . and found myself tumbling, crashing through golden light. It was too bright to open my eyes. It felt like going down a tube slide, but without the pull of gravity to keep you sliding on only the bottom. I tucked myself into a ball to lessen the effect of my painful bouncing back and forth, regretting the stupidity of trying to copy something I knew nothing about. I felt like Alice down the rabbit hole, but without the reassurance that this sensation would ever cease.

Just as I felt myself blacking out, the brilliance vanished. My body crashed one last time, and I slumped to my side. I took a deep breath, then coughed as I choked on disturbed dirt and the pungent smell of urine. A cacophony of sound assaulted me, but I was too dazed to make sense of it. I sat up and looked around.

I was in a small hut of some sort. A few rays of sunlight filtered through a door at the far end. After my eyes adjusted I saw feathered bodies lining the sides of the structure, fluffing their feathers in perturbation—chickens. The squawking suddenly made sense and seemed far less sinister, but I was anything but calm. In fact, I felt swamped in fear, real fear unlike anything I'd ever felt before. My mind refused to accept what had happened.

"I've knocked myself out," I muttered. "I'm just having a really weird, smelly dream. I'm dreaming of chickens because I slipped on the broken eggs and knocked myself senseless. That's it. It has to be."

I pinched myself hard, yelping as I realized I was already bruised there. The rest of my body protested as I tried to stand. "It isn't real. This isn't real," I mumbled.

I was having trouble breathing through the haze of dust, hay, and bird defecation floating in the air, so I limped for the door. I slammed the door shut behind me as fast as possible in case a pecking chicken was chasing me. The bright light outdoors shocked my senses all over again. I jerked my arm over my eyes, squinting.

My vision cleared, but I kept blinking, trying to make the hallucination in front of me disappear. It didn't. I'd traveled somewhere . . . else. I gazed stupidly toward a group of funny, square, flat-roofed houses that looked to be made of mud plaster. The problem wasn't the houses, though they looked primitive. The problem was the fact that I was in a desert, only it didn't look the same as Arizona's desert. There were no saguaros, and the ground was a dun color rather than the nondescript Arizonan dirt. There were little, scraggly bushes here and there. The road leading to the village was hard-packed earth where nothing grew.

There was no mistaking this place with the greenery of Michigan; the funny pattern thing had made me go somewhere, but it certainly didn't look like the place I had wanted. I felt a sob build in my throat, and my backpack's weight doubled. Landing in a chicken coop was a blatant clue that I'd most likely remembered Kelson's pattern wrong. The barren landscape confirmed my suspicions. Where was I? Where was Mom?

There was only one way to find out. The chicken coop was next to a house set apart from the main clump of squat buildings. I shuffled toward the dirty building with trepidation. There was a wooden door in the front, and I wondered where the wood had come from. I could see no trees. My thoughts dwelt on trivial things, shying from the deeper mystery of where I was.

A timid rap on the door was all I could manage, and I stood back, almost hoping no one would be home. What could I say? *Hi, I just dropped here from a golden vortex. Would you mind telling me where I am?* That wouldn't go over well in any country. If I still couldn't believe this had happened, how could I expect anyone else to?

I was still trying to think of a plausible story when the door opened and I saw the most amazing person I'd ever beheld. She had dark milk-chocolate skin that was accented by a thousand little wrinkles. Her hair was snow white, but the most startling thing were her eyes. They were pure emerald green. She wore loose white trousers and a long cotton shirt slit to her waist on each side. Over the shirt was a bright green vest with a diagonal neckline. A five-inch-wide length of green cloth began at the top of the neckline and hung down her back. The whole ensemble struck me as a cross between Indian and Arabic, but not distinctively like either. She studied me while I studied her, and then she bowed slightly.

"Hello, um, my name is Mary and I was with ah . . . my tour group, but got lost awhile back. Could you tell me where I am and where the nearest phone would be? Because you see, I . . ."

The woman held up her hand. "Eya coshim," she said and gestured for me to enter. *Oh no*, I thought. It was worse than I'd feared. What language had she spoken? It hadn't sounded familiar at all. I paused on the threshold, unsure if I should enter, but she was holding the door politely for me. I took a deep breath and stepped forward.

Inside, a wall divided the house into two rooms. The floor was covered with rugs of colorful and intricate circles and curlicues. I was again reminded of a mixture of Arabic and Indian design. The woman gestured to me to sit, so I dropped to the floor since there were no chairs anywhere. I was tense, ready to jump up again if I needed to. She sat down across from me, her mouth curving in an easy smile, and I felt the muscles in the back of my neck beginning to loosen. There was something about the smile combined with the crow's feet around her eyes that seemed wholesome and unassuming.

I flashed a tentative smile back and looked into her eyes instead of keeping my gaze on her torso. Her head snapped back, and her smile wavered, so I quickly dropped my head, watching her thin frame closely for any aggressive signals. For all I knew, this land could have stories about demons with golden eyes.

She touched my hand, and I darted a glance up to see her smiling again with an apologetic look on her face. She pointed to her chest.

"Ismaha," she said.

"Mary." I pointed to my own chest.

She nodded and pointed to a large bowl full of water. "Eshin?" She mimicked washing her face. I flushed in embarrassment. I probably looked like a wreck. *Landing in a chicken coop was not good for my clothes,* I thought, looking down at my dropping-spattered jeans. My T-shirt had a big splotch on the right side where I'd landed on the floor of the coop. I put my hands up to feel my hair, and discovered a big rat's nest where hair should've been. My face went hot. Why hadn't I thought to check what I looked like before knocking on the door?

I crouched over the basin, my sore body protesting the awkward stance, and scrubbed my hands vigorously before washing my face. I also tried running my fingers through my hair, but my fingers caught in snarls, and I gave up after a few strokes. As I washed, Ismaha sat in silence, looking slightly away from me as if to grant me some dignity. When I was done, she looked back at me and smiled more broadly.

"Dora." She nodded once. I guessed that meant good or better, but I couldn't be sure. This was going to be one heck of a communication challenge. How could I get her to understand what I needed? It seemed impossible, but I took a deep breath. "Where am I?" I gestured all around me, trying to indicate more than just the house.

She looked a little confused, then I think she understood what my strange motions meant. "Iban ou Iberloah."

My mouth dropped. Iberloah? Then I *was* in the right place. Except, where was Mom? I jumped up. "Have you seen my mother? She's about five-two with long blonde hair. She's probably being held by a man with dark brown hair and blue eyes." I tried to indicate Mom's height, then I tugged my own hair and pointed to a blondish part of the rug to show the color. The woman looked at me curiously, but I don't think she understood what I was trying to convey. I gave up and started for the door, determined to search for Mom if I had to knock down every door in the village.

Before I reached the door, however, Ismaha gently took hold of my arm. I looked at her. "I have to go. I have to find my mother." She held up a hand in a motion that clearly stated, "Wait." She then pointed at her mouth, then at me.

"I don't have time to learn how to speak your language. I have to find my mother now, before Kelson goes somewhere else with her, and it's too late." I wanted to leap out the door and start my search, but I didn't want to be rude after her kindness to me. Ismaha pointed to my hair and the blonde part of the rug, and then gestured to indicate her village. She shook her head.

"But she has to be here. She just came not long ago. How would you know if she isn't here?" It was so frustrating that she couldn't understand.

She shook her head again sadly, and I suddenly knew that she *had* understood. Mom wasn't in this village. Landing in a chicken coop rather than exactly where Kelson and Mom were was indication enough that even though I was in Iberloah, I still wasn't where Kelson was. I'd gotten the pattern wrong. But Kelson had mentioned living in a desert his whole life before contradicting that by saying he was from Michigan. He'd also said he lured Mom and me to a desert because of similarities. I wasn't in the exact place, but I felt cheered at hearing the name Iberloah. Ismaha had said it was Iban ou Iberloah. Did that mean Iban was near Iberloah, not in it? My head bowed. "I have to find her," I whispered.

Ismaha raised my head and again pointed to her mouth, then to me. Her brows were wrinkled in sympathy, and I felt tightness in my throat that was perilously close to becoming a sob. But I swallowed it and squared my shoulders.

"Yes, let's get started." My mouth pressed to a determined line. I would learn the rudiments of this language as fast as I could so that I could find Mom. I was still confused about where I was, though. If Iberloah wasn't really in Michigan as Kelson had said, then what country was I in? It was definitely a third world country, but which one? I would have to ask Ismaha as soon as I learned a few words.

Ismaha and I sat across from each other in the middle of the main room. She lifted and lowered her hand palm down in a gesture that seemed to say, "Don't worry. Stay calm." She then stared at the space between us, and I noticed green threads forming in the air. I recognized it at once as the same kind of pattern magic that Kelson had done. I tensed, but Ismaha continued to sit calmly, placing each strand in the air with exactness, glancing to me to make sure that I noted where they fell into place. When she was done, she looked at me and indicated that I should study the pattern. I did so, but I already had the pattern memorized. It was complicated, but not nearly as complex as the pattern that had dropped me in her village.

She waved at me to imitate her. It took me only a second to figure out how she'd made the pattern appear in the air rather than just in her mind.

My golden pattern jumped to life next to her green one the next instant. She looked a little surprised. Next, she pointed to the part of the pattern that I could sense was the nexus of the whole. It shifted, and the pattern flashed for an instant, slightly different than before.

She indicated that I should copy her. I twisted in the spot she had shown, and this time I felt more in control than when I'd copied Kelson's blue pattern, for I could see and feel where I was pulling, rather than just using my intuition. I waited for something to happen. Nothing did, and I was afraid that this time I'd done something wrong.

"That is our language's lacing. It is often used during negotiations with other countries," she said. It was the oddest thing. I understood what she said to me, but the words weren't English. They sounded strange, yet familiar at the same time, and the different sentence structure felt awkward. I noticed my mouth was hanging open, and I shut it with a small snap. Ismaha grinned.

"How is that possible?" I asked. The words coming from my mouth felt off, but Ismaha seemed to understand them.

"Many things are possible if you know how to see them," she said. "My language makes a pattern just as everything does. When those patterns are discovered, we can change them, which then changes the properties of objects."

"I think I understand," I said, not really sure if I did. I was slightly distracted from the flow of my thoughts by my voice producing previously unknown words.

"Now, why don't you explain to me what you were so emphatic about before. You seemed to be looking for someone, but I'm sorry to say no one has come to our village today other than you."

"I'm trying to find my mother. She was taken by this boy—I mean, man. I mean, I think he's really an older man, not the teenager he seemed to be. He has the same kind of magic you showed me, and he wanted to take me too, but Mom stopped him. He did this huge, complicated pattern when he disappeared with my mother so I tried to copy it and follow him, but I must have gotten it wrong because I ended up in your chicken coop instead, and now I don't know what to do. You said that this is Iberloah—or is this just near Iberloah?—which is where he said he wanted to take me, but he said it was in Michigan, and this is definitely not Michigan. Where are we, anyway?" I sucked in a huge breath, having hardly breathed during my ramble.

"I do not know this Michigan you speak of. This is the country of Iberloah."

"Country? I've never heard of a country called Iberloah. Is it a really small one in Africa or something?"

"I am sorry, I do not know Africa either, but Iberloah is not small. It is the largest country on the continent," she said.

I didn't want to be rude by refuting her, even though she was obviously wrong. Since we weren't really getting anywhere, I tried a different tactic. "Okay, so about how many miles wide is Iberloah, and where are we located on a map?" Oddly enough, when I said "miles" it sounded like the English word. I had expected "Michigan" and "Africa" to sound the same as English, but not "miles."

"I do not know what you mean when you say 'miles.' We measure our distances by kenars. One kenar is about 1,000 paces of a normal-sized man. Iberloah is 950 kenars wide at its shortest point."

That explained why the word "miles" hadn't translated, and I wondered how many other English words wouldn't translate. I calculated the differences of measurement quickly. Her description of Iberloah's size didn't make sense. There were several countries as small as that in Africa, but the name Iberloah didn't even sound familiar. "Do you have a map?" I asked. I knew once I saw a map, everything would make sense.

"You're lucky. Not many people in this village have maps. They are too valuable. But I've saved one from my days of travel. I will get it for you." She went into the other room and came back holding a thick rolled-up parchment. I helped hold the edges while she carefully unrolled it. What emerged confused me more than her earlier statements about Iberloah.

The map showed a continent unlike any on Earth. I had seen some of those old-looking maps that weren't exactly accurate. This one looked like an impressionist painting of those really old maps. The land mass was an unfamiliar blob of strange proportions and was much smaller than Africa. Different countries were outlined, Iberloah being the biggest country shown on the land mass. A huge river flowed through the middle of Iberloah southwest to the sea, and Ismaha pointed out that the capital, Ismar, was located where the river met the sea. She pointed to the squiggly marks that made the word "Iban" and told me that we were north of Ismar by about 500 kenars. I had a horrible sinking feeling that I would have to get to the capital before I'd find anything like an airport, and though I wasn't a whiz at calculating distances in my head, I figured that even though 500 kenars was less than 500 miles, it was still a long way to hike. I hadn't seen any cars, and I doubted that I would.

I must have looked really troubled because Ismaha asked, "What is wrong, Mary? You seem displeased by my map."

"Oh, I'm sorry. I'm just really confused." I suddenly remembered my backpack. I had my American government book in there as well as medical anatomy, chemistry, my notebook, and a ton of random worksheet papers. I shrugged off the bag and felt as though my shoulders would float away. I hadn't realized how much my bag was weighing me down. I unzipped the top and rummaged. I pulled the gov. textbook out and opened the hard front cover. On the inside was a map of the United States. I turned it around and shoved the book toward Ismaha.

"See this? This is my country. Have you ever seen it before? Do you know where the nearest airport is or where I could find a phone?" I stopped short at the sound of "airplane" and "phone," which came out in English.

Ismaha didn't seem to hear me; she turned the pages of my book reverently, and studied the many pictures. "This is amazing. I've never seen its like. Where did you get it?"

"I had to buy it for class." I shrugged and flipped the pages to the back to the map, pointing. "Have you ever seen this country before?"

"I have never seen any of those countries nor that continent. I am sorry, but you must have a very poor mapmaker. There are no continents on Esa like that."

"It's only one country, and not even the whole continent is shown on that map, but that's not the point—" I stopped, struck by something. "Esa?" I asked.

"The world, all the continents reside on Esa."

"You mean Earth, right?" "Earth" came out sounding just as foreign as "phone."

"I don't know the word 'Earth,' " she said.

I couldn't understand why that word hadn't translated. I was pretty sure she meant the same thing, but a terrible suspicion was encroaching on my thoughts. It was too much. Traveling from one place to another in a vortex was far-fetched enough. There were limits to what a girl could blindly accept.

"Ismaha, would you say you have a good knowledge of the world? I mean, you said you'd traveled before. Did you only travel in Iberloah or did you go all over?"

"I've traveled to many places outside my own country."

"Did you ever run across places with cars, or airplanes, or even telephones?" The words all came out sounding English.

"I am sorry. I do not know these words. What do they mean?"

"Um, cars are these machines that take you places. Well, you have to drive them, but they can get you to places a whole lot faster than walking or even riding a horse." I didn't go any further in my explanations. I felt the strangeness of my words, and Ismaha's look confirmed what I suspected.

She shook her head. "What you speak sounds like a dream. There are no such things in any of the countries where I have traveled."

"I don't believe it," I whispered. I couldn't accept that no technology had touched this part of the world, and I refused to believe I had ended up not only in some other country, but on a whole different planet. My reasoning wasn't making much sense, considering that I had just zipped from Arizona to who-knew-where in the space of a few minutes, but I couldn't abandon all faith in the laws of physics. Ismaha was just ignorant, that was all. She was probably bluffing about all her "travels." I was confident in the thought that the modern world extended almost everywhere. There weren't many places on Earth that hadn't been infiltrated by the Peace Corps or anthropologists or something. I would just have to find them.

"You've been really kind, and I'm very grateful, but I have got to go." I stuffed my book back in my backpack and slung it on my shoulders.

"Where will you go without supplies? The nearest village is 30 kenars away," she said.

She made sense. I needed supplies, but I didn't know how to get them. Maybe Ismaha would be willing to help somehow, though I didn't want to bank too much on that. The only food I had was a smashed granola bar in my backpack's front pocket. Just thinking about it made my stomach rumble. I hadn't eaten lunch in school, and that'd been ages ago. Despite the bright sun outside, my stomach told me that dinner time was hours past. This day had been the longest one in my life. My insides clenched and growled again, this time loud enough for even Ismaha to hear. I blushed.

"There is no need for you to leave yet. Come, I will give you something to eat." She stood, went to the funny, round-shaped hearth, and stirred the coals into life. She swung the pot hanging over the fire away from the coals, a thick, cloth mitten over her hand. Lifting the lid, she smelled the substance within and replaced the lid.

"You are fortunate. It is almost done."

I caught a whiff of the soup, and my mouth watered.

She glanced at me and added, "Do not be concerned. I only wish to help."

I slowly sank back down onto the rugs, feeling awkward. Waiting for the food to finish cooking took only a few minutes, but my appetite was suddenly uncontrollable. I clutched my stomach in an effort to make my rumblings less, but it only grew louder. Finally, she got out two clay bowls and dished out the soup.

"Thank you." I closed my eyes for a second in heartfelt thanks, and then dug into the strange stew. I had no idea what was in it, but I would have eaten anything at this point. After I had inhaled nearly the whole bowl, I looked up to see Ismaha watching me curiously.

"You are far from home." It was a statement, not a question. I nodded anyway. Her words were a trigger, and I instantly felt on the verge of tears. Adrenalin had kept me going so far, but now my stomach was full, and fatigue seeped into my aching body. I sagged and concentrated on counting in threes—my usual method of keeping my eyes dry since I would rather die than be caught crying in public.

Ismaha tactfully tried to turn my thoughts to more constructive matters. "Do not worry. I think you must go to the king with your problem. He is a good king and will help you if he can, especially if I write a letter to him saying he must."

"You know the king?" I asked incredulously. This village didn't seem like the kind of place where someone who knew a monarch would live.

Ismaha smiled. "I live humbly now, but once I was quite famous." Her green eyes twinkled mischievously.

"What were you famous for?"

"Why, for my skills as a magician. Not everyone has the talent that you and I have. I am very glad that you have the gift also, or our language lesson would have taken a lot longer. You would have had to give me your permission to switch your own language lacing, and we would have had to work that out the hard way."

"Why would you have had to ask?" I was completely fascinated. My body forgot how tired and sore it was in my eagerness to find out more about this new power that had disrupted my entire existence.

"There are rules to everything. For example, I could not do any lacing that would change your inner self without your consent. No magic can impede free choice."

"But at school I couldn't think of anything but Kelson, even though I didn't really want to," I burst out before thinking.

"Tell me of this 'Kelson.' "

I explained the events of the past three days, and Ismaha sadly nodded. "Unfortunately, there are some magicians who try to twist the natural laws as far as they can be twisted. Kelson wasn't directly changing you; he was trying to influence you to choose the change. Did you ever really try to think of something else besides Kelson?"

I blushed. "I guess I didn't really try to stop thinking about him most of the time, but there were a few times I got him out of my head."

"Good. From what you have said, Kelson was putting the first stages of an enchantment on you. Though you are still free to choose, the first stage of an enchantment seeks to befuddle your mind to sway you into giving your will to the magician. Once that is done, your free choice is lost forever. Well, I shouldn't say forever because there is always a way to choose, even in so dire a situation. It takes great inner strength to break such a terrible enchantment." She paused. "That, or a really strong reason, such as a deep love, or something of that magnitude. Bound-will enchantments have rarely been overcome."

"Oh." It was a relief to know that there would be no more mind control or anything else without my permission. "Kelson tried to get me to say that I would be his before he took my mother, but I said no." I had come very close to acquiescing though. Now that I knew what would have happened, I shivered. Then my thoughts shifted. "What kind of things are possible with these magic lacings?"

"Everything in the world has a pattern: living things, nonliving things, even concepts can have a pattern to them. When you know these patterns, you can change them in some ways. Take, for instance, this thread." She plucked a string from the end of a tasseled rugs and held it up. "Most people have to be shown the pattern for each object, then they must carefully memorize it before being able to change that pattern. I gather you knew nothing about lacings before you came here?"

I nodded.

"Well, I showed you how a pattern is taught to a student when I made the language lacing. It is difficult to draw most lacings because they are three dimensional and are often too complex to be seen well on paper, so a teacher must project the lacing for his student." Slowly another pattern of green lines appeared. This one was much simpler than the language lacing, and I was able to copy her with no hesitation. She studied my pattern with care.

"You are quick; most students have a hard time forming an unknown lacing. Do you ever see snatches of a golden image when concentrating on an object?"

"Yes!" It felt wonderful to know that my strange inner vision had not been a figment of my imagination. In my weaker moments, I had wondered if it was one of the first stages of insanity.

"I would like to try something with you, if you don't mind. Concentrate on the paper of this map. Try to catch those hints of gold that you see within your mind to see the pattern of the paper."

I looked hard at the old parchment as if I were about to draw it, but this time I actively sought out the golden threads I had only ever noticed on the edge of my vision. It was kind of like looking directly at a sunspot behind closed eyes. If you looked directly at the sunspot, it moved out of view, but if you looked slightly to the side, it stayed where it was and you could study it. Instead of just a funny yellow splat, I saw the paper's magical pattern. It was amazing.

I was so excited, I turned to other things in the room to see if I could discover their lacings. It was kind of like getting the hang of those "Magic Eye" pictures that you have to look at cross-eyed to see. At first, it was difficult for me to see the 3-D images, but once I got the hang of how to focus my eyes, I could breeze through them. It was the same with seeing lacings. Ismaha cleared her throat.

"Sorry, I got a little carried away. I never knew such a thing was even possible."

"Show me the pattern of the paper."

I formed the pattern before her, and she studied it for flaws.

"You are blessed. There are not many who can discern a lacing without first being shown. Most magicians must study for years to learn just a few of the many millions of lacings there are to know in this world."

"How many see it like I do?" I asked.

"Only one or two every few generations see as clearly as you. There are more who can see parts of the pattern, not the whole."

I wondered why I, who was from somewhere far away, would have an ability that few here had. It was a little scary. I still didn't know exactly what I was dealing with here. So I could see patterns—what help was that? Sure, Kelson had inadvertently shown me where to tweak the lacings he'd made, and Ismaha had shown me purposefully, but there were many joints and lines on each pattern. What if I twisted the wrong part? Would I accidentally blow myself up?

"How do you know what part to change in a pattern to do what you want? How do you know what will happen?" I asked.

"Ah, that is a part that may give you a bit more trouble. Though you can see lacings more clearly than many, the magicians who study the patterns for years are also more able to determine which patterns are similar, which can connect, and which, if changed, will cause disaster. Teachers also show the students as they learn." Ismaha again held up the thread. "You have seen the string's pattern, and the paper's pattern. What can you determine about the two?"

Oh great. I felt like I was in some surreal high school class. I sighed and studied the two different patterns. They were both fairly simple, but the paper was more complex with extra swirls and cross weavings, so I studied it longer than the thread. I noticed that there was a section of the paper lacing similar to the thread's and told Ismaha this.

"What else?" she asked.

I looked again, but my eyes were starting to sting. I just wanted to sleep. It had been a long day, and my brain was on overload. "I don't know," I said a little sharply. I immediately felt bad about my outburst. Ismaha had been nothing but nice to me, but I just couldn't handle any more today.

"You are tired and have a long journey ahead of you. Sleep now and I will help you get the things necessary to travel to the king on the morrow," Ismaha said.

"You've been so kind, but I couldn't ask you to do more. I don't have anything to pay you with," I protested weakly.

"We'll discuss that tomorrow. I hope you do not mind sleeping on the floor here. I have only one bed, and my old bones will not allow me to sleep on floors any longer."

"No problem. I'm a regular granola babe." The words "granola" and "babe" didn't translate. Ismaha gave me a strange look, but before I could reword my statement, she shrugged and went into the back room.

I curled up on the floor rug and stretched one arm over my Jansport backpack. It gave me an sense of comfort to touch it, as if my green school bag were the only thing left of my childhood and my old comfortable sense of home.

I dreamed of golden patterns. They floated before me; some merged and made new patterns. Others morphed by themselves or disappeared completely. I kept trying to figure out what it all meant. It was like the math dreams that I sometimes had where I kept struggling to calculate an answer, only to have the original problem become confused.

I woke near dawn, my bladder uncomfortably full. My arm ached from acting as my pillow, and my hip felt more bruised than ever.

Ismaha showed me a small metal pan to use as a toilet, and then retreated back to her room. I stared at it for a moment, perplexed. I won't go into details but I will say for that one moment I was jealous of what boys have that girls do not.

When I finished, I called Ismaha back. I stood directly in front of the pan in an attempt to avoid further embarrassment. But Ismaha went straight to it.

"Watch," she said. She looked at the urine, then a flash of green went off in the back of my head, and it was gone. Even the acrid smell vanished. I reviewed what she had done and noticed what part of the pattern she had changed to make the urine disappear. Quite a useful trick, I thought. It would certainly cut down on disease if others could do it too.

"Did you see the lacing of what was done?" she asked.

"Yes."

"Good, then let's get you ready."

We walked out of her house. The chickens were out and pecking at the ground. There were villagers out now as well, even though the sun was just rising. The village was bigger than I initially thought. After a few houses, the road sloped steeply, revealing a lot of buildings and activity.

"The view is deceptive from your house," I said.

"I don't like to feel crowded."

We headed to an open market. Many of the stalls were just opening, but everyone we met seemed glad to see Ismaha. They gave her friendly waves and hellos while eyeing me with curiosity. I stared covertly back, remembering Ismaha's reaction to my eye color. But it was hard not to gape at the villagers. Everyone had varying shades of skin from a slightly darker olive than mine to a deep sepia, but hardly anyone had brown eyes. All the people I saw had eyes that were different shades of blue or green. The colors were startling against their rich skin tones.

Ismaha moved us briskly from one stall to the next, getting a blanket, food, and water. She bought me an outfit similar to hers, but with fewer hanging parts. I measured the blue pants against my legs to see if they were long enough. They weren't, of course. I was about half a foot taller than everyone around me.

The beige shirt was sufficiently large, however. It was loose in the arms and looked like a long peasant shirt. She bought me a vest to go with the shirt so it wouldn't flap all over the place. The vest was blue with neat circular designs sewn into it. The neck fell diagonally, like a karate gee top, and buttoned on the side.

Finally, Ismaha bought me a small knife. By the time we finished, I was worried. How could I possibly pay her for the supplies? Why was she helping me so much?

We stacked our purchases in her main room, and Ismaha turned to me. "Now we will discuss payment," she said.

"But . . ."

She held up her hand. "You said you have nothing, but you showed me a great treasure last night."

"All I showed you was my book."

"Exactly. May I see it again?"

I unzipped my bag and handed her the government textbook.

"I will take this as payment if you will allow it," she said.

"But it's not even in your writing. What good will it do you?"

"You have already forgotten our lesson from yesterday. There is a pattern to everything. I will simply have to study your writing to find out what it's pattern is."

"How long will that take?"

"Years probably. Unless you are willing to help me." She smiled, and I couldn't help smiling back at her.

"I'll see what I can do." I took the book. I opened the text to a random page and stared at the words. Nothing happened. I looked up at Ismaha in confusion.

"Seeing objects is different than discerning the lacings of concepts. Concepts are much more insubstantial, and harder to contemplate in a pattern. Try reading the writing while concentrating on the pattern of the language's sentence structure."

I looked down again and read a little of the page. It seemed odd to me, and I wondered if that was because I was speaking with a different cadence and rhythm now. However, the strangeness of it helped me to see the pattern after a page of reading, and I was finally able to project the lacing for Ismaha to view and memorize. She looked at the golden pattern intently from several angles, then produced a copy in green.

"Wonderful! You have given me a great gift. I thank you." She headed to the back room and came out after only a moment holding a folded letter sealed with a green wax blob. A design had been pressed into the wax. I peered closer and saw the design was a tree.

"Get this to the king when you reach the city, and he will help you." I took the letter, unzipped the bigger front pocket of my backpack, and slipped it in.

"And this will help you find your way to Ismar." She handed me the rolled map that she had shown me the night before.

"I can't take this. Didn't you say that maps are rare?"

"Yes, but I do not need it. I no longer travel."

I grinned at her and saw her lips quirk in response.

Ismaha distracted me from my gratitude by pointing out that she thought I would attract less attention in the native garb she had bought, so I changed. After donning the unfamiliar shirt, pants, and vest, I turned to my backpack. It was a little looser than before without the huge government book, so I stuffed my dirty clothes in the book's place.

I considered leaving my chemistry and anatomy books with Ismaha as well, but decided that if she had found the books amazing, maybe someone else would too. I was also loath to part with anything that connected me to home.

Ismaha had bought me another pack that I could sling over my shoulder. I stuffed the travel supplies into it, put everything on, and staggered. Traveling would be difficult, but at least I was wearing my running shoes.

"I wish you a safe journey," said Ismaha.

"I owe you so much. I may never be able to pay you back for your kindness, but I won't forget it," I said. I was surprised to find myself sad to leave. I hardly knew Ismaha, but I knew I would miss her.

Shopping hadn't taken long. It was still morning, even relatively cool. I strode down the village road, crossing the market now in full swing. Vendors yelled to me as I passed, but I ducked my head and walked more quickly. Now that Ismaha wasn't with me, I felt unexpectedly shy. Everything was so strange.

There were no industrial sounds. People gibbered loudly. The dogs I saw were dirty yellow and yipped strangely. Children ran around the village half naked, and several sported large lizards on their shoulders that hissed when the children dipped low to the ground. The adults wore colorful clothing in a strange style that mashed together Arabic, Japanese, and Indian clothing.

Wares in the market stalls reminded me of European antiques, but none of the objects exactly matched any design I'd ever seen. Most women had strands of their hair partially braided back from their face. Their hair flared out in the back, hanging free. All I had been able to manage was a messy ponytail trailing halfway down my back, secured with a leather strip—which was how most of the men wore their hair, minus the messiness.

Though I was glad when I passed out of the village, the sight of so much open desert distressed me. I wondered if I should've waited until the evening to travel. I'd read somewhere that evening was the best time to walk when in a desert, but maybe it didn't matter if you had enough water. The sun was already warming the top of my head, and the landscape was dauntingly open around me. Ismaha had said the road went straight to the next village, so I walked hesitantly over the hard-packed dirt road.

At about noon—I couldn't be sure of the time because my watch had stopped—I knew I was going to be in trouble. My body ached from the weight of my loads and from my now-colorful bruises. The sun beat at me with a relentless fervor. Sweat ran down my face, but my mouth felt like sand. I took a break to eat lunch. I considered throwing my books onto the ground along with my random papers. But I wasn't totally desperate yet, so I decided to wait and see how long I could stand carrying them.

The road stretched endlessly, wavering heat mirages always just ahead. I trudged forward, longing to rest, but overruling such desires by thinking of Mom with Kelson. What had he done with her? What had I done wrong when I tried to follow him? I attempted to recall the pattern he had made, but I still couldn't understand what I'd missed, so I gave it up.

Instead, I studied the lacings in the objects I passed. Rock, bush, lizard, spider, funny-looking insect, and so on. I even caught a hare's pattern before it vanished in the underbrush. It was actually fun. I tried to quiz myself on the lacings I'd seen, but that was problematic since I had to find the object again to double check the pattern. I still didn't have a clue what good knowing these patterns would be, but the only other thing to do was feel hot, sore, and generally miserable.

Chapter 5

I was getting really good at seeing patterns in the things around me. In fact, I started to get bored of the same bushes and bugs, so I tried to think of other ways to see patterns. I got out all the food in my bag to look at their lacings, and then started sneaking glances at the things that passers-by carried.

By dark, I was still walking. My swift stride had turned into a halting shuffle. My feet were killing me. I considered just dropping where I stood instead of reaching the village, but there was too much traffic, so I put one foot in front of the other, hoping to see the village over the next rise. It took several rises before I actually saw it, but when I did, the sight was spectacular to my travel-weary eyes. It was certainly bigger than Iban. Lights shone in the buildings, which were at least two stories high. From the hill where I stood, the town looked like a huge maze surrounded by tall walls. I was afraid that once I got into the city I would get helplessly lost.

Despite my slow shuffle, I was soon surrounded by buildings. A few people still traveled on the road, though I guessed it had to be something like 10 PM. All I wanted was to find a bed. I stopped a passing man and asked where an inn would be. He directed me quickly and then hurried off, leaving me more confused than before. I walked the way he had first pointed, hoping a light would descend, telling me the right path to follow. But no heavenly beacon showed up to light a trail, and I found myself in a very dark, narrow alleyway.

I looked around in confusion and tried to retrace my steps, but I kept twisting into dirtier, more rundown paths. There were fewer lights here, and I started to get the heebie-jeebies. If this were a movie, I'd get jumped from behind any second now. I tried to hum the *Jaws* theme to make myself laugh, but the sight of two disgustingly dirty men killed the amusement like a snapped stick.

The men advanced with sickening smiles. I glanced quickly behind to see if I could run that way, but found I had unconsciously backed myself into a dead end. While they were still a few feet away, I sloughed the bags off my shoulders and shifted my feet to a fighting stance. If I could maneuver them toward the wall, I would abandon my packs and run like a wild thing.

Despite my height, two against one wasn't good odds, and I wasn't stupid enough to think that I could incapacitate two men without getting hurt. Besides, I'd never actually harmed someone on purpose before. When I was sparring in the karate dojo, I wore pads and controlled my strikes. The only other time I had hit a person with full force was when I'd punched Joe. But that time I hadn't been stranded in an unknown desert and forced to walk loaded up with supplies all day. My arms and legs felt wobbly with exhaustion and fear. I summoned what was left of my strength.

"Can I help you with something?" I attempted to mold my face into an unconcerned expression, but my lips trembled a little. They didn't answer, just took up positions on either side and slid closer. *Well, okay, I knew that wasn't going to work.* When they were only two arm lengths away, I took a deep breath and yelled, "Help!" at the top of my lungs.

That put them in motion. I sidestepped the man with a dirty gray shirt while kneeing him in the groin, always a good place to start. The green-shirted man grabbed my arms, but I wrenched my wrists from his grip and struck up with both fists into his face. He staggered away, and I was distantly aware that hitting him had really hurt my knuckles.

The man I dubbed Gray came up more cautiously this time, and I circled with him, trying to keep an eye on the other man at the same time. Gray rushed in suddenly, swinging frantically at my face. I blocked him easily, but lost track of the man in green, who came up from behind to bear-hug me. Green caught one of my arms, and Gray took advantage of this by grabbing my other arm and hitting me in the face. The world exploded and spun for what seemed an eternity before I recovered enough to fight back.

Green's smell was nauseating. My foot swept back to kick him in the groin, and then slammed down on his feet. But as he loosened his grip, his partner struck me again on the other side of my face. I saw light, then blackness, then a hand descending toward my nose. I wrenched to the side in time for the blow to strike my shoulder, but I was having trouble focusing.

I kicked at Gray and ripped my arm free from his grasp. I was going to loosen Green's grip again when he suddenly dropped away from me to the ground. Surprised, I tripped over him. Gray was about to use my imbalance to kick me over when another man came between us and caught Gray's foot mid-kick and threw him to the ground.

Seeing his partner unmoving on the ground, Gray scrambled to his feet and scuttled quickly away. I wasn't sure yet if I should be grateful or try to fight this new man, but he spun away to check Green's pulse, and then straightened and turned back to look at me. I was stunned to note that he was about as tall as me, if not taller. Everyone I'd passed on the road had been shorter.

I couldn't see his face clearly, but the weak light accented his high cheek bones and defined jaw line. He wore the strange desert garb in a color too deep to discern in this poor light. My shoulders tensed when I noticed a sword hanging at his side.

"Are you hurt?" he asked.

I felt like a truck had run over me, but I wasn't going to admit it in case he was trying to put me off my guard. "I'm fine. I just need to get to an inn, sleep it off. Thanks for your help." I gathered up my bags but put them loosely on my shoulders so I could quickly shrug them to the ground if I needed to. Then I walked away, keeping a wary eye on him. I tried hard not to limp. Nothing was twisted, but my exhaustion from the fight and hiking all day made my gait hard to control.

"Wait, let me at least show you where an inn is. This is a dangerous part of the city. Many thieves dwell here," he said.

"And why are you here?" I asked before thinking better of it.

"I heard your call for help," he said simply.

"Oh. Well, thanks for coming. Look, I'm really grateful, but I don't know who you are, so I think I'll just find my own way."

"Do I look like the kind of person who would associate with the likes of that?" He straightened his shoulders indignantly, waving at Green.

I looked closely at him again. His desert garb fit him perfectly. His dark hair was pulled severely back into a ponytail, and he held himself with practiced grace. Okay, so he didn't look like common riffraff, but it was hard to see his face in the dimness of the alley.

"All right. Please show me where to go." I gestured for him to go first. Despite his rescue, I wasn't about to have my back to a stranger.

He led the way, scanning the street as he went. My gut twisted in worry. My eyes kept twitching to the shadows and then back to the man leading the way. Soon, however, we turned onto a street that was much wider and cleaner. More lamp lights lined this road, and I felt immeasurably better.

My rescuer seemed to relax as well. He turned and asked, almost suspiciously, "Why were you in that part of Cibar?"

I blushed. I was so tired that I blurted out, "Look, I've never been in this stupid maze of a town before. Every turn just got me more lost." I stumbled a bit over nothing and had to concentrate on my footing.

"We're almost there." His voice was soft, almost kind, but I wasn't in the mood to feel grateful for sympathy.

I could hardly think straight, and my face was on fire with pain. The rest of me didn't feel too hot either. *Blasted desert,* I thought irritably. "I want to take a bath and put ice on my face and knuckles. I doubt I'll find either of those things in this third world country." I realized too late that I was muttering my thoughts out loud.

"What are you mumbling?" the man asked.

"Nothing."

"What is a third world country?" he persisted.

"*This* is a third world country," I exploded, gesturing around me. "This unsanitary dump with no plumbing, no electricity, and no blasted cars. Do you realize that I could get to your stupid capital in less than three hours if I just had a car?" Many of my words hadn't translated, and the man looked confused, so I stopped my tirade with a sigh. "Sorry, I'm not at my best right now," I apologized. He had apparently determined that it was safer to stay quiet.

We reached an inn, but it was a moment too late to save what remained of my dignity. My body was in shock, and I stumbled on the inn's steps, then folded up in a heap in the middle of the doorway. The man picked me up easily, and I wondered if all men from Iberloah were extraordinarily strong. It wasn't simple to pick up a girl as tall and solid as I was, but he carried me into the inn and sat me down on a cushion near the wall. I leaned back and groaned when he touched my face lightly.

"This will bruise badly if not helped," he said.

"I doubt you'll find any ice in this . . . this place," I finished lamely, too exhausted to find a word foul enough to express my disgust.

"We do not need ice if I may have your permission to create a lacing to heal your wounds."

I sat up quickly against the wall and stared at him full in the eyes. The inn's common room was well-lit, and I jumped in surprise to find that the man's eyes were bright purple with a cluster of gold flecks shooting out from the center. My eyes must have shocked him as well—he inhaled sharply and muttered something unintelligible. I looked down again quickly.

"You're a magician?" I asked. There was a bite to my words.

"Yes." He had recovered his graceful poise.

"Well, don't try to put an enchantment on me. It won't work. I know how to fend you people off now," I bluffed.

His shoulders rocked back as if from a blow. "I would never participate in such foul practices."

I risked a flick of my eyes to his. He looked furious. I recoiled, sliding along the wall further away from him, guessing I'd just put my foot in my mouth. I didn't want to find out if he was offended enough to hit me. He knew how weak I was and how helpless.

Then he spoke. "Wait, forgive me. I did not mean to scare you. I'm merely angry that such magicians exist." He touched my arm lightly where one of the thugs had hit me.

I winced. To cover my pain, I said, "I wasn't afraid. I was just readjusting my position on my pillow, thank you very much." I looked defiantly back into his eyes, hoping the gold would unnerve him. It didn't. He stared back, lips twitching as if he were trying to suppress a laugh. *The nerve!*

"If you don't mind, you can just show me the lacing, and I'll do it myself." I glanced at him, but he simply nodded and showed me the pattern between us one strand at a time, as Ismaha had done. His lacings were a bright purple, and I finally realized that a person's eye color determined his thread color. Or maybe it was the other way around. I was too tired to care.

I looked at his pattern for a second. "Which one do I tweak?"

"Tweak?"

"Um, which strand do I change to heal my cheeks?"

He nodded and pointed to one of the strands. I quickly created the pattern in my head, twisted the thread, and felt an immediate release of pain in my right cheek.

"That's wonderful," I said, sighing. "What's the next one?"

He showed me the pattern for each area that had been wounded, and which thread to change to correct my injuries. *Now this is useful,* I thought contentedly when I'd finished healing my bruises and cuts. The magic had made me even more tired, but I started to wonder at its other possibilities.

I thought I could probably also get rid of my soreness if I could figure out the right patterns and which strand to change. But that was where I was blocked—I still didn't know how to figure out which part to change without someone showing me.

Through the euphoria of less pain, I noticed that the man still sat next to me, watching my face intently.

"Thanks, Mr. uh . . ."

"Breeohan Irat Ahasan." He gave a slight bow of his head. Wow, I was going to have to ask him to repeat that one about a million times before remembering it. "And you are?"

His name had been so long, I decided to give my full name for competition's sake. "Mary Margaret Underwood." It didn't sound as impressive. "Well, thanks for dropping in to lend a hand." I stood, swayed a little, and then steadied. He stayed sitting, so I moved off to find the innkeeper and bargain for a room.

The innkeeper flatly refused to take anything but money when I tried to bargain some of my goods for a room and food. My heart sank down to my well-worn running shoes. I was too tired to go anywhere else, afraid that I might get lost again. I sat heavily on a pillow, rubbing my eyes as if that could squeeze out a plan. My elbows thunked on the low table, and I rested my heavy head in my hands.

The sound of footsteps made me look up. It was the purple-eyed guy. I'd forgotten his name already.

"Is there a problem?" he asked.

"No, I'm fine, thanks," I lied.

He sat down across from me, and I sighed, exasperated.

"I wondered if you might have something to trade with me. I tried to find a present for my sister today, but found nothing." He looked nonchalant, but I realized that he must have overheard my conversation with the innkeeper.

An ironic smile spread across my face. "I may have just the thing. You seem to be a man of fine tastes." I flashed a cheesy grin, though the effort was difficult. "Would you by chance be interested in a book?" I heaved my backpack to the table and ripped the zipper open. After some thought, I pulled out my chemistry textbook and handed it to him. He looked just as awed as Ismaha had, carefully taking each page by the edge and turning it.

"I can even show you the pattern to translate the text, if you want, but I can't show you which part to change."

He looked up sharply at this last statement, and returned to gazing at the colored illustrations. I felt a Cheshire smile spread across my face as he examined the hard cover. Bree-whatever looked to be about twenty, but he struck me as a scholar. After all, hadn't Ismaha said that mages had to study patterns for years before doing anything useful?

"So what'll it be? Do you want it?"

"Yes." His breath came out in a sigh of obvious longing.

"Do you think your sister will like it?"

"My sister?" Confusion clouded his face, and then he remembered. "Yes, my sister will love this."

"So she loves reading too?"

"Yes," he said too quickly.

"What's her name?"

He hesitated, obviously trying to think. "Avana."

"Ha, you don't really have a sister, do you?" I couldn't help but snicker.

"No." He looked ashamed, which surprised me. I immediately felt chastised.

"I'm sorry. You've been really nice, and I keep harassing you. You don't have to do this for me." I felt like a heel.

"I want to." He looked at me intently, but then dropped his gaze. "I mean, I would really like this book and the lacing pattern if you will sell it to me."

"Sure. What'll you give me for it?"

"Would sixty shem be enough?"

I didn't want to flaunt my ignorance, but I didn't think the guy would take advantage of me after going out of his way to help. "How much is that?"

"Where are you from?" he countered.

"America. Do you know it?" I asked longingly.

He shook his head, and my rising hope crashed down with a dull thud.

"It's far away from here." To my horror a tear slipped down my face. Boy, was I useless when exhausted. I quickly wiped it away. "Sixty shem will be fine. Here." I showed him the pattern to change the writing one golden strand at a time as he had done for me, though I thought it would be a lot less of a hassle if I could show him the whole thing at once. He looked at it carefully and nodded.

"I will remember." He reached into his relatively small pack, and took out a sack of coins, then counted out sixty. I had no idea if he was giving me the equivalent of sixty dollars or sixty cents.

"How much is a room, do you know?"

"Do not let him ask more than one shem for a bed and some breakfast in the morning," he said. That gave me a better idea of how much Mr. Purple Eyes (and man, did he have nice eyes) had paid. I suspected that he'd overpaid me by a lot.

"Thank you." I glanced at his face. He appeared incredibly curious. He didn't ask any more questions, however, so I rose and paid the innkeeper for a bed and breakfast.

The bed was lumpy, but I didn't care. I fell asleep almost instantly. When I woke up, the sun was shining through the shutters of the room's one window. I wondered if I'd overslept. Thoughts of Mom goaded me into action, and I found that my muscles felt surprisingly less sore than yesterday. I tied my knotty hair back as tightly as possible and reluctantly slung my bags onto my shoulders.

Downstairs, I dropped to a table and found that breakfast was a horrible slimy soup that tasted like earthworm. It was an unappealing beginning to the day, but I doubted these people had ever heard of cereal. As I ate, the purple-eyed guy approached me. I couldn't decide if should be glad to see him still at the inn or wary.

"May I sit?" he asked.

"Sure."

"I was thinking. As we talked last night you mentioned getting to the king's city. Am I correct?"

"Maybe. Who wants to know?" My lips curved to soften my words, but I felt a nervous flutter lurch through my middle.

"I am going there and thought we might travel together. Two traveling abroad is always safer than one."

My stomach turned. I put my spoon carefully on the table, and took a deep breath. "I got lost once. It won't happen again. I'm not usually stupid enough to get in that sort of situation, and I know you're just trying to be nice, but I really don't need," *or want*, I added silently, "a big strong man to protect me." I realized the speech sounded childish, but my pride smarted from my misadventure, and the fact that he seemed to think I was helpless did nothing to balm the wound. Nor did it restore my faith in men.

"I didn't say you were."

My brow arched. I still felt out of sorts and guilty at the same time, and I didn't dare open my mouth.

"We are going the same way; we might as well help each other."

It *would* be nice to have someone to talk to, but did I want to put myself in that position? I looked up into his purple eyes. They reflected nothing but earnest goodwill. I felt no wash of giddiness as I had with Kelson. Finally, I sighed, relaxing my rigid stance. "All right, but I have to warn you—I won't put up with any funny business."

He looked confused again. "You don't like jokes?"

"No, I mean . . . Oh, forget it. Are you ready to go?"

He nodded, and we walked out of the inn into the stifling dry heat of the day. It must have been later than I thought; yesterday hadn't been this warm until near noon. I wouldn't admit it to Bree-something, but I was secretly glad he was there to guide me out of the city and onto the road. It baffled me that I could be so good at patterns but so terrible at direction.

He and I walked together in silence for awhile, and I had a sickening flashback to another walk not too many days ago with another man. This tall stranger in a dark green gee-like top and loose purple pants had been nice so far, but thoughts of Kelson were a good reminder that I couldn't totally trust him. He didn't seem like Kelson, but that didn't mean anything. I was obviously just as bad a judge of men as Mom. I couldn't afford to let my guard down. The sword strapped to his back added to my anxiety. I kept checking my brain for any hint of the fogginess, but it remained clear, and after a few hours I started to get bored of walking in silence.

"So why are you going to the king's city?" I asked.

"I live there. I'm going home."

"Why did you leave?"

"Do you always interrogate those who help you?" he said. I started to say no, but then thought for a moment. I had asked Ismaha a lot of questions too. It was actually amazing that I was talking so much. Maybe my need to find Mom was superseding my usual desire to avoid awkwardness.

"Yes."

He laughed. "You are an unusual girl, Mari."

Ha! He didn't remember my name either. "It's Mary, don't worry about remembering the rest. What was your name again?"

"Breeohan."

"Do you go to school in the king's city?" I asked.

"Not any more. I passed the magician's trial this summer."

"What does that involve?"

"You have magic, but you know nothing of the magician's trial?"

"Where I come from, magic doesn't exist."

Breeohan stopped walking. "That's impossible. Magic exists everywhere. Every country on Esa has people who wield pattern magic, and every continent is aware of it."

"How would you know? You're a little young to have traveled the whole world."

"I have read of other's journeys," he said, sounding defensive.

"To every corner of the world?" I asked incredulously.

He blushed. "Well, no. But I've read of many places and have talked with other magicians about the prevalence of magic in the world."

"Well, it isn't on my continent." *Nor any of the others that I know of,* I thought uneasily. "I don't know why I have this pattern magic."

"When we get to the city, you will have to show me your country. I have a world map there."

"That would be great," I said, hoping Breeohan's map might prove I was still actually on Earth.

At about noon (I hated never knowing exactly what time it was) we stopped to eat. I fanned myself with one of my English worksheets. I felt gritty, soaked with sweat, and just generally disgusting. I hadn't bathed in days, and it was torturous. My hair was greasy and still ratted, despite repeated attempts to comb it with my fingers.

I looked at Breeohan. He was a little sweaty, but otherwise looked immaculate, as if he'd bathed that morning. It was strange to see him dressed so much like an Arab, but with differences that made it obvious he was from somewhere . . . else.

Breeohan caught me staring, and I looked quickly away. He might look exotic to me, but I knew I looked terrible, and I didn't want him scrutinizing me.

"When did you arrive in Iberloah?" he asked.

"Three days ago."

He looked at me disapprovingly. "You could not have gotten here three days ago. The nearest sea port is about 450 kenars away, and the nearest river port 350 kenars."

I guess it did sound unbelievable, but I didn't know what to say. I doubted that he would believe me if I told him that I'd landed in a chicken coop after going through a terrifying golden tube, so I didn't say anything to defend myself.

He let it drop. "We'll reach a stream by early evening. I thought we'd stop there. It would be impossible to reach the next town tonight. It's 60 kenars from Cibar."

I perked up at the word *stream.* Water! I could wash myself. I could at least scrub parts of me, if it was really small. Suddenly my remaining hunger couldn't compete with my desire to be clean. I stuffed my food and water back in the bag. "Let's get going, then."

Breeohan wasn't done with his lunch, but he put his bread away and got up. I strode off at a brisk pace but slowed down a little to let him catch up.

"How big is this stream?" I asked eagerly. "No, wait, don't tell me in case it's too small to be much good. No, you'd better tell me so I can prepare myself for the worst."

He laughed. "It's not as bad as you fear. It is about ten paces wide and deep in some parts. But don't worry, you will not need to know how to swim to cross it."

"Do you know how to swi—" I stopped short, painfully reminded of Kelson's letterman jacket. He'd said he'd gotten it for swimming.

Breeohan glanced over at me, but I stayed silent. He answered my unfinished question anyway. "The capital is by the sea and a river outlet, so I do. But many from the inner desert are never near deep water. They have no need to learn."

"Do you have swim teams?" I asked, trying to see how much Kelson had made that up.

"What's that?"

I wondered how much background study Kelson had done on my country before approaching me. At least now I knew why he'd gone on and on about the marvels of modern technology. What I still couldn't understand was why he hadn't brought heavy artillery with him to accomplish whatever he'd been trying to do. My only guess was that the trip might have ruined the stuff. After all, my watch and calculator had stopped working.

I walked faster, thinking of what Kelson might be doing to Mom. Was she okay? If he'd hurt her, I would never rest until I found him and brought him to justice. I noticed vaguely that Breeohan had been watching the changes of expression cross over my face. I breathed hard from speed walking, and Breeohan caught my arm to stop me.

"What's wrong?" Concern reflected in his bright purple eyes.

"Have you ever heard of a guy named Kelson?" I stopped, realizing I didn't know his last name. "He can do this pattern magic stuff, like you, but I think he's older." I thought of the picture I had drawn of him.

"I'm sorry. I know of no one by that name. Why do you want to know? Are you seeking him at the king's city?"

"I doubt very much that he'll be there. Unless . . ." I didn't know anything about Iberloah. What if Kelson had been a mage for the king and was acting under his orders? If that were true, I couldn't trust the king to help me. I looked suspiciously at Breeohan. What if he knew too? What if he was sent to bring me to the king since Kelson had failed? I shook myself. *Get a grip, Mary. The world does not revolve around you.* I was becoming suspicious of everyone, but it seemed unlikely that Breeohan could have anything to do with the plot against Mom and me, even if the king were involved. I felt like I was in a suspense movie surrounded by plotting enemies. That thought made me laugh. But one thing was sure, with no phones and no Internet, communication would be much more difficult here. There was no way Kelson could even know I had followed him to Iberloah.

"What is your king like? Do you know him at all?" I asked abruptly.

"You keep asking me questions and never answer mine. I will not answer your question until you answer at least one of mine."

"Which one?"

"Why did you look so worried? Who is this Kelson?"

That was two questions, but I decided I might as well tell him what had happened. If he didn't decide I was crazy, maybe he could help somehow. "I'm worried because this man, Kelson, kidnapped . . ." that word sounded strange. "He took my mother against her will right from our home. He did this huge complicated pattern and disappeared. I tried to follow by copying what he did, but I got it wrong and ended up in Iban instead of where he went. So now I'm going to the king to see if he'll help me find her. Can you tell me whether he's the kind of king who will help?"

"Wait. I've never heard of a pattern that will allow a person to travel quickly from one place to another. It isn't possible."

"It *is* possible because I did it. Ismaha said there was a pattern to everything, even concepts, so don't be mad if I don't think you're the ultimate authority on what can and can't be done."

"You know Ismaha?" He looked stunned. I realized that Ismaha really was famous, after all, at least among other magicians.

"I met her after crashing into her, uh . . . land." I didn't want to tell him exactly where on her land I'd been dumped.

"Is this traveling dangerous? Does it hurt?" he asked.

"Now who's asking all the questions and not answering them?" I teased.

"Everything that comes out of your mouth is so outlandish, it cries for questions."

"Ha, I could say the same to you."

We smiled at each other, and I felt my previous tension ease. There was something in Breeohan, like in Ismaha, that made me trust him.

We walked for awhile, each in our own thoughts, then Breeohan said, "It is a strange story you tell. Why would this Kelson want to abduct your mother?"

"I don't know. I think I was really who he wanted the most, but don't ask me why. He said he was going to take us both since she was useful to him too, but I got away, and he got frustrated so he took her and said he'd come back for me." I scuffed the ground with my running shoes in frustration. I should've done something. I should've saved her somehow. It should've been me instead of her.

"Well, the king will help if he can. He is a good king, though he worries his people since he won't marry and produce an heir."

"I get that. I wouldn't want to be forced into marriage if I was the king. Who wants to marry a complete stranger? It's gotta be tough for people in that kind of system."

Breeohan walked silently beside me, looking thoughtful, so I let my thoughts wander. We reached the stream in the early evening, and I saw that it might be possible to immerse myself in some places. The water was clear and inviting, and I seriously considered jumping in with my clothes still on. I knelt in the sand at the side, dipped my hands into the cool liquid and splashed my face, rubbing vigorously. It felt wonderful, but it made me yearn for a full bath.

I peeled off my sneakers and dusty socks so I could dip my aching feet into the refreshing water. I decided I'd better wash my socks while I was at it, so I rubbed them together under the surface, wishing for soap. Breeohan appeared at my side as I rubbed at my now dun-colored socks.

"Here, use this." He handed me a bar of soap. It smelled sweet, like flowers, and I laughed. Who would have thought someone like him would use flower-scented soap?

"So, was this soap for you or do you have someone special you were going to give it to?" I asked as I lathered the socks. I looked up and saw him blush. "Ah ha! So there *is* a girl that you wanted to buy presents for, just not your sister. Am I right?"

"It's for a friend of my family."

"Does her name, by any chance, happen to be Avana?"

Breeohan looked startled. This was fun.

"You used that as your sister's name. Remember?" I couldn't help but smile at his discomfort.

"Yes. I thought I would bring her something from my travels, but the book really was for me. She wouldn't be interested in it." He sighed.

I wondered if Avana was a beautiful airhead. Men always seemed to go for beauty rather than brains. "Well, good luck figuring out how to translate my book. You might like chemistry. It's all about the patterns that electrons make around the atom and how they bond with other atoms to make more complicated patterns." I stopped for a second, considering whether this strange lacing magic was somehow connected to atomic structures. *It might be distantly related,* I conceded, *but if each object's pattern was its atomic structure, the patterns would be far too complex to memorize.*

Breeohan looked at me strangely again. I knew that most of what I'd just said hadn't translated to his language, but I didn't want to explain in more detail. I wasn't a whiz in chemistry, and I didn't want to just spout off some bogus explanation.

"You'll learn about it when you can read it. Now would you mind trotting off somewhere for awhile so I can take a bath?" I waved a dismissive hand at him.

He gave a low, and I thought, mocking bow. "I will gather sticks for a fire."

"You promise you won't peek or anything?"

He gave me the disapproving look I was becoming used to. "Never."

"Okay, sorry." He could he be touchy sometimes. It made me feel more confident about actually dipping into the water, though.

I waited until I couldn't see him anymore before stripping off my dust-caked clothes and carefully feeling my way to deeper water. It was heaven. I soaped myself all over three times with the perfumed stuff. I even used it in my hair, wishing I had shampoo and conditioner. I didn't want to be caught in the water when Breeohan came back, so I washed at hyperspeed.

Looking at my clothes reluctantly, I decided that I would don my jeans and shirt so I could wash the native garb. The jeans and shirt were dirty too, but even a chicken coop hadn't made them as dirty as traveling. I was washing the native clothes when Breeohan came back.

He stared at me, taken aback by what I looked like now that I was clean and wearing different clothes. I cleared my throat and felt color rise to my cheeks. He'd been staring long enough. It was fascinating to watch a blush race up from his neck to his clean jaw and high cheek bones, transforming his milk chocolate skin to a brown red.

"I've never seen such clothes. Do all your people wear such strange pants?"

"Yes and no. It depends on whether you're a jeans and T-shirt kind of person. Would you like to take a bath?"

"If you wouldn't mind."

"Sure, I'll just find some rocks to lay my clothes on."

I grabbed my soggy clothes and walked barefoot over the sandy ground, watching out for prickly plants.

"Mary." I stopped and turned. "You won't peek?" He smiled mischievously at me.

"Never." I bowed even lower than he had.

"Such a bow is treason if done to any but the king," he said, but he smiled.

"I'll remember that," I said, and then walked away.

Chapter 6

took my time finding rocks for my clothes, not sure when it would be safe to come back. But after a while of sitting around doing nothing, I decided he'd had time enough.

"Yo, Breeohan, are you done yet?" I called from a distance.

"Yes. I wondered if you would ever return."

I came closer and saw him sitting in front of a fire, getting out food.

"Well, excuse me for thinking that you might want a long bath."

His skin looked a shade lighter than before, a light milk chocolate, and his wet hair was tied back in a tight ponytail. I still had mine loose, so it would dry faster. He wore a different outfit, and I wondered how he could fit so much stuff in one bag.

I sat next to him on the big rock, noticing that he didn't smell like flowers. He did smell good, though. It was nice to smell clean after so much dirt and body odor. Breeohan was putting various food bits in his small pot before he settled the pot within the fire's coals. I took out a piece of stale bread, gnawing on it without much enthusiasm, despite my hunger. I yearned for American food. What I wouldn't give for a cheeseburger.

"Don't you have any travel rations you could cook?" he asked.

I shook my head. All I had was smoked meat, stale bread, and some chewy stuff that I suspected was dried fruit.

"Why don't you share your bread with me, and I will share my stew with you," he said.

"Okay, but you're getting the bad end of the stick. The bread's stale."

"You speak very strangely. What is it like, where you are from?"

"Well, we don't have a king in my country. It's a democracy. We vote for a representative to decide what action is best. If enough individuals don't like what that representative has done, they can elect a new person when that guy's time is up. It's a government 'for the people, by the people, and of the people,' " I said dramatically.

"So the citizens of your country actually determine what will happen?"

I shrugged. "Mostly. What's it like to have a king?"

"He makes the decisions, but he does take a vote from the counselors on major problems. There is a counselor from every region, so that all may have a voice."

"Are there nobles?"

He nodded.

I continued, "I've never understood how that works. What makes one family noble? Their relationship to the king?"

"That and individual struggles for position through marriage." Breeohan scowled at the pot in the fire.

"How weird. What about the people who aren't lucky enough to be somehow related to the king?"

"They are merchants or artisans or whatever they want to be." He sounded bitter.

"And what are you?"

"A magician." He looked at me with an expression that clearly said he didn't want to talk about it. Maybe he had been thwarted by a noble. Maybe he was a poor noble and didn't have much power to do anything but look pretty.

Breeohan got the pot out of the fire and produced two spoons.

"I only have the one pot, so we will have to share."

"Wow, no offense, but have you been sick recently? Do you get cold sores? Have you kissed anyone who may have a disease of some kind?"

He looked offended. "I have not been sick, and I haven't kissed anyone." After a moment he asked, "What are cold sores?"

I sighed. "Oh, never mind. I'm sorry if I offended you." I paused. "Do you mean you've never kissed anyone at all?" I couldn't help but ask.

He blushed, caught. "It is not proper to speak of such things."

I was surprised. Breeohan was almost too good-looking for me to be comfortable around. The thought that he hadn't ever kissed anyone both reassured me and made me shift uneasily. "Don't be embarrassed. I think it's admirable. Not many of the boys my age at home could say the same thing. I've never been kissed." The last sentence popped out of my mouth without permission. I wanted to pull it back but instead kept my expression nonchalant.

Breeohan looked surprised, and I laughed at the absurdity of it all. "You may be shocked to learn that I don't talk to people often."

"You? Silent?" He laughed as well.

"It's true, but I can't afford to be a complete recluse now. I have to find my mother." My face fell, and I picked at my shirt.

"Well, with that outfit, those strange shoes, and that unusual bag of yours, you will have a hard time avoiding notice here."

"That's okay. I'm used to being a freak," I said, thinking of the girl from my chemistry class.

"I'm finished with my portion of stew. You can have the rest if you think it won't harm you."

"I said I was sorry," I mumbled, grabbing the stew and spoon. It needed salt, but I was too hungry to care.

I rolled out my blanket, but wasn't able to fall asleep. I kept thinking of Mom, of Kelson, of impossible plans that would allow me to find her, of the hopelessness of it all. A tear rolled down my cheek, but I made no sound.

In the morning we packed up quickly and started walking again. My hip felt sore from sleeping on packed dirt, but I was becoming more used to taking long strides. I didn't ache as much as before. The day passed quickly, and I searched for patterns in objects as I went. I was staring at my fingers, trying to determine their lacings when Breeohan asked what I was doing.

"I'm finding my finger's lacings," I said, a little embarrassed at being caught, though I didn't know why I should be.

"You see that clearly? You can see the whole lacing?"

"I guess, but I don't know what to do with the things once I see them. How did you learn which line to change to do whatever you want it to do?"

"I was taught, and I practiced."

"How long did it take you to learn?"

"I have been learning lacings and other subjects for ten years, since I was ten."

So that made him twenty. I wondered how hard it would be for me to catch up to someone my age in pattern magic. That was, of course, if I ever learned it. I had too many things I was already worrying about. I didn't need to add magic training.

"I could teach you how to manipulate the lacings as we travel, if you like."

I hesitated. All this magic stuff was strange and a little scary to me. But if—no, *when*—I faced Kelson again, it would be better for me if I knew how to use the magic he could wield with such ease.

"All right. Where do we start?"

"To every change on any part of a pattern, there is a reaction of some kind."

I gathered that. That's why I hadn't dared experiment with the delicate strands on my own. I didn't say this to Breeohan, however. I just looked at him expectantly.

"You can start to anticipate what strands will cause what reaction after you have studied many lacings and can see what parts are similar or dissimilar in each pattern. Sometimes that will not help you, however. That is why lacings' reactions must be passed from master to pupil."

All right already, I thought. *Get to the action.* The term "master" made me uncomfortable, and I wanted to start *doing* rather than *talking* about it.

I didn't have to wait long, however. He was soon showing me several patterns of the things around us and projecting what I could do to them by tweaking certain strands of each lacing. It was amazing. Breeohan showed me how to make a twig unbreakable, how to turn sand into glass or rock. I was starting to see what kind of things were possible with this lacing magic, but the pure scope of possibilities boggled and frightened me. I had to stop after awhile. Changing patterns took energy, and by noon I was spent.

Breeohan sat calmly on a rock while I wheezed next to him. I glared. "Why aren't you worn out?"

Breeohan took out some rations while I stared at his graceful poise jealously. "I have been practicing for years and have built up endurance."

"Show off," I mumbled. He smiled serenely.

By late evening Breeohan and I reached the next village. I was glad to see that it was smaller than Cibar. There was no chance of getting lost, even if I was separated from Breeohan. The inn we found was as clean as I supposed any place in this primitive country could be, and I didn't choke too badly on the food. At least it wasn't slimy, which was a big plus. There was an awkward moment when the innkeeper looked at us slyly, flashed this icky, knowing grin, and asked if we wanted a nice room with a big bed.

"Do you see a ring on this finger? No! So you shouldn't assume—"

Breeohan broke into my speech since I guess he saw that the innkeeper was confused. "We need two separate rooms," he said.

"What does a ring mean?" he asked after the innkeeper stalked away in an offended huff.

"Oh, I didn't think of that," I said, embarrassed. "In my country, a ring on the left hand's third finger means that you're married."

"In our country one shows that he is wedded by wearing a band on the left wrist. I wondered myself if you were married." He looked pointedly at my watch that I still wore despite its uselessness. I blushed deeply, quickly unclasped the watch, and stuffed it in my backpack. It was disorienting, not knowing anyone's cultural system, and I was getting tired of always being confused.

The next morning we headed out before the sun had risen fully. The air whispered with a cool breeze, but I knew it would soon change to a hot wind that would squeeze the moisture from my skin.

"So, wristbands show if you're married. Is there anything else I should know about before I go and stick my foot in my mouth again?"

"What does that mean, 'stick my foot in my mouth'? It sounds painful." I glanced toward him to see his brows drawn together. He looked frustrated and confused.

"It just means that I made a mistake, spoke without knowing what was going on. I'll try to steer clear, I mean, stay away from colloquial phrases, but I'm not sure if I'll manage it very well."

"I would not wish to point out things of which you might already be aware, but I did notice that you do not observe the going down of the sun in the evening, nor do you thank the sun in the morning."

"Is that what you were doing when you touched your forehead and swept your arm up before? Is that a cultural or a religious thing?"

"Both. The sun is God's banner, reminding us of his daily presence in our lives. That is one reason why it is better to travel during the day, for God's presence in the night is much dimmer. Day is a time of bright truth where dark things cannot hide." He spoke simply, with no trace of doubt.

"So if I don't salute the sun will I get in trouble?"

Breeohan ran his hand over the strap of his bag, back and forth before answering. "In a way, you may have trouble. You could be labeled as a blasphemer. That would not be too bad. But if you are accused of being a worshiper of Baleel, the dark one, that would be serious. Worshipers of Baleel are hanged, and the citizens may not bother to give you a trial before they kill you for fear of a curse."

I shivered, though the sun was now high and the air was like a fiery blanket. "I guess I'll salute the sun from now on. Thanks for the tip."

For the rest of the day, Breeohan taught me new lacings. The patterns were starting to get a little jumbled in my head, so he quizzed me until I wanted to scream and had to ask him to stop before I bit his head off.

That night we slept in the open, and the next morning I saluted the sun with Breeohan as it rose.

The following day saw us walking resolutely in the baking sun as Breeohan taught me new lacings and what to do with them. I started to guess which strand could be tweaked before Breeohan showed me, and he'd tell me if I'd guessed correctly or if I would have blown us up. It seemed I was gaining endurance in walking and manipulating lacings at the same rate. My legs were less sore, and I was able to change about twenty lacings before I had to call it quits.

Breeohan admitted he was shocked at my progress.

"What can I say? I'm an A student," I said.

Breeohan didn't ask what I meant. He just shook his head, and muttered something that sounded suspiciously like, "Why even try . . . crazy ranting."

I grinned slyly. "It's killing you, isn't it?"

"Of course not," he said stubbornly, gaze fixed on the road.

"You don't want to know what an A student is?"

He kept striding forward, looking down the road, and I just waited.

"Oh, very well! What is an A student?" His breath whooshed out, and he glared at me before his twitching lips gave him away and he smiled.

I told him all about my school and classes, changing the words if they didn't translate so that he could understand.

"I'm tired of talking about me. Tell me about you. Do you have any brothers or sisters?"

"I have no siblings, and my mother lives near the palace. The wind flew over my father many years ago."

It was my turn to be confused. "What does that mean?"

"He is gone." He seemed to struggle with trying to explain, as if he had been perfectly clear in the first place.

"Did he leave you? My father left my mom and me too. Just up and vanished without even telling her he was running off."

"I'm sorry, but that's not what I meant. He has gone with the wind."

I felt like giggling at his inadvertent Scarlet O'Hara reference, but then I finally got that he was saying his father was dead, which sobered me instantly. "Do you miss him?"

"I hardly knew him. I was at school, and meetings between us were formal."

"I've often wondered what it's like to have a father," I said.

"You don't remember your father then?"

"He left my mom before I was born. In fact, she says he didn't even know she was pregnant with me. Don't get me wrong, though. My parents were married. He just left before she found out about me."

"I'm sorry."

"Oh, it's okay. Mom and I do fine by ourselves. I take care of her." I stopped, realizing that I had failed to protect her from Kelson. I had brought him into our home. If that was taking care of Mom, I should be fired.

Breeohan must have seen my face fall. "It is not for the child to take care of the parent, but the parent to care for the child until the child is young no longer. Then the role is reversed."

"Hey, who're you calling a child?"

"It's an old saying." There was a slight smile on his face which I regarded suspiciously. "I was simply trying to tell you that it wasn't your fault, Mary."

"But it *is* my fault. I was the one who fell for his enchantment trick and let him waltz right into our house. Ismaha said I could have stopped the enchantment any time if I'd really wanted to, but I was weak and foolish."

"Enchantments are sly things. Even a fully trained mage could fall under the influence of one if the caster is subtle enough about it."

I knew he was just trying to make me feel better, but I appreciated the effort. "I bet you'd never fall under an enchantment, or something similar, say . . . feeling befuddled over a girl." I smiled playfully at him, thinking of Avana.

He blushed as I had intended. Really, he was just too easy.

We got to a town that night, and after a salute to the sun, we headed to our different rooms. The next morning's salute creeped me out when I noticed several villagers scrutinizing my movements. I was glad Breeohan had instructed me.

Walking was easy today. My muscles bunched and slid without any soreness at all. I also noticed that my legs looked a little leaner, a bonus I was happy to observe. On top of all this good news, I was able to perform fifty lacings before I had to stop for the day. It was time for a little fun.

"So tell me about this Avana girl. Is she everything that is lovely and wonderful? Do you swoon at the sight of her? You do blush a lot, but somehow you don't seem like the swooning type."

Color flooded Breeohan's neck and cheeks. "I do not swoon. Only feather-headed females swoon."

"Well, well. I guess there are some attitudes that stay the same no matter where you go. It's nice to know how you feel about women. Maybe I should go warn this Avana girl to keep her distance for her own good," I softly mocked, though I felt a true twinge of misgiving.

Breeohan's aloof pose crumpled. He raised his hands as if to ward me off. "That's not what I meant. I was only talking about the silly girls who do it for attention. There really are women like that, believe me. I've had to catch them before."

I couldn't help the laugh that shot out of my mouth. "You really had to catch someone? I thought that only happened in romance novels."

"More than one lady has fallen conveniently into my arms when I was trying to make an escape. In fact," he turned to me with a wily curve on his lips. "I seem to remember you falling at my feet not too long ago."

I stopped dead and folded my arms. "I did not swoon. My legs were wobbly, and I was resting them for a moment. I didn't ask you to pick me up."

Breeohan looked over his shoulder at me but kept walking. Finally, I had to drop my arms and run after him or be left behind.

"You never told me about Avana," I panted when I'd caught up.

"There's nothing to say."

"Your flustered expression says otherwise," I goaded.

"She's just a family friend, as I said before. Show me the juno bush lacing."

My eyebrow rose, but I flashed the lacing. "What made you decide to buy her soap as a gift?" I continued relentlessly.

"Mother told me to get her something. Can we please change the subject?"

"Okay. So is she younger or older than you are?" I looked up at him innocently. He scowled and strode ahead of me while I laughed.

Chapter 7

The next morning Breeohan announced that we were only three days away from the king's city. We'd slept in a little canyon he called the Klio Wadi that reminded me of the Grand Canyon, but smaller. His words echoed as he spoke, and I had the silliest urge to call out "hello," so I could hear how many times the greeting came back.

"Does water ever run through this place anymore?" I pretended to look interested in the dry stream bed, but really I was counting how many times I heard "anymore" repeat. Only four times. I searched my mind for a possible lacing that could create the echo. I found I couldn't help but look for lacings in everything. It was like the time I became addicted to Tetris. When I was twelve years old, I'd played that game every waking moment. At night I'd dreamed about how to fit the blocks in place. Finding lacings was quickly becoming just as addictive, but I knew it would be much more useful.

"Hello," I said quietly, trying to see the pattern. I thought of sound waves, and . . . *ah ha, there it is!* Breeohan raised his eyebrows at me.

"I just wanted to find the pattern," I said defensively.

"And?"

I showed him. After our first day of lessons, we had both stopped doing the line-by-line thing. It was obvious to me that he didn't need the slow method, so now we showed each other whole patterns to save time.

"I can't wait until you meet the magician masters. They won't know what to do with you."

I felt troubled. "Breeohan, I'm not sure I want to meet your masters. In my country, all people are equal, despite one being the teacher and the other the student. The way you refer to your 'masters' makes me nervous.

I'm already having enough trouble accepting the fact that I'll have to deal with nobles and a king."

"Don't worry, the term *master* is simply one of respect to a teacher."

"That's reassuring," I said. "Just don't expect me to call you 'master.' "

"I wouldn't dream of it." He smiled his familiar mocking smile, and I gritted my teeth. He always seemed to be laughing at me.

"What's so funny?"

"I'm sorry. I was just imagining what you might do when you appear in court."

"Imagining what a fool I'll make of myself?"

"No." He didn't sound very convincing.

"Well, do you know anything about how to behave?"

"I might."

"Then would you teach me?" I grumbled.

"On one condition. You call me 'master.' I am, after all, teaching all of this to you without any payment."

" 'Wouldn't dream of it,' huh? Well, dream on, buddy." I packed up my blanket and stalked off down the narrow ravine.

He caught up to me and lightly grabbed my arm to make me look at him. "Wait, I'm sorry. I forgot that you don't like jokes." He was laughing.

I didn't feel like explaining that when I'd said no funny stuff, I'd been referring to something completely different.

"I am not going to call you 'master,' " I said, annoyed at his laughter.

"I know. I don't want you to. I just wanted to get you back for teasing me. You do it to me often enough."

Okay, so that was true. I started to slow my walk to its normal long stride. He was right—I could dish it out, but I sure couldn't take it. I needed to learn how to loosen up a little.

I was about to apologize when a deafening yell echoed all around us. Breeohan and I dropped our bags and turned toward the walls of the little canyon, backs together. Breeohan had his sword out in as little time as it takes to sigh. My hands clutched into fists, empty, and I hoped the thugs wouldn't be well-armed.

They emerged from the rocks like lizards from a crevice. Their garb blended well with the red of the canyon walls. The thugs must have been waiting for the next idiots to walk through. It was a perfect set-up for an ambush. I counted seven of them, but I didn't want to miscalculate in case more were hiding.

Their faces were painted light brown and red to give them better camouflage. As they ran toward us, I thought of U.S. Army men and was glad that this country didn't seem to have any guns. We certainly wouldn't have lasted long against hidden snipers. I doubted our chances now. It was hard to stay positive when seven men in war paint were charging toward me, yelling like wild animals.

I focused on the rock-strewn streambed in front of the nearest attacker and twisted just as the man's foot reached the sand. A rock sprang into his path. He tripped. I knew it wouldn't stop him, but I couldn't think of what else to do. Another attacker passed the fallen man, coming uncomfortably close. I manipulated a wind lacing and a fierce breeze whipped dirt into his eyes. He reeled back, trying to protect his face with his sleeve.

Too late I realized that another man had come up from the side. He grabbed my arm, and I struck without thinking. The now familiar flash of golden pattern sprang into my mind, and the man flew back just as Joe had a few weeks ago. I finally realized that I'd unconsciously changed the air pattern to push the man away with much more force than a mere blow. I couldn't dwell on my discovery because another savage-looking thug was swinging a club at my head.

The only pattern that came into my head was one for old brittle wood. I changed his hard solid club to old wood, and raised my arm in defense. The club splintered against my arm and fell in pieces. I was out of ideas, so I hit the man with the same air-enforced blow as before. He flew back several feet, landed with a thud on a rock, and didn't get back up. I winced.

It was hard to tell what Breeohan was doing, though I knew he was swinging his sword at several of the men. It looked like the best weapon any of them had was a club. In my moments of reprieve I changed their tough clubs into brittle wood. I saw Breeohan's sword shatter one of the thick weapons. The attacker looked shocked, but Breeohan hardly paused.

I couldn't see what he did next because I was distracted by the man I'd tripped. He had a bleeding scratch on his cheek and he was coming toward me like he was ready to murder me. He must've been the leader because he had a long broadsword clutched in his hands.

He swung, but I dropped and rolled, springing up again on his left. I was trying to think of a plan, but things were happening too fast to remember patterns, much less do something with them.

My attacker roared at me, and that gave me an idea. I yelled back, sounding as unearthly as I could, then I manipulated the echo pattern I'd discovered so that my strange and frightening cry echoed all around the men, hounding from all directions. The effect worked better than I'd predicted. I even got a little chill from the banshee sound echoing around us.

Our attackers certainly looked spooked. They paused in their fighting. Breeohan's head twitched around nervously. I cut the echo off abruptly and whipped up the sand in the canyon with a strong wind, bringing up my arms to cover my eyes and mouth. I could only hope Breeohan was doing the same. The wind cut off at my command, and I hid my mouth behind my dusty arm.

"Get out of my wadi," I said. The words bounced around in a hissing whiplash.

The men ran in terror through the crevice that Breeohan and I had come through that morning. I waited until I couldn't see them anymore before I went to check on Breeohan. He was covered in dust and sand. I had never seen him so disheveled.

"That was impressive," he said, looking up at me.

"My mom always said I was a drama queen." I flipped my hair back jauntily, but there was a sudden lump in my throat. "We'd better hurry in case they come back."

Breeohan nodded.

We traveled quickly and came out of the canyon onto upper ground at about noon. The wide main road stretched before us by evening. Taking the shortcut through the canyon had been Breeohan's bright idea, but after being attacked I'd decided that even if there was another short cut, we should stick to the open road. The desert rolled around us in a wave of sand and brush. I was still biting down on gritty dirt. I felt smelly, sand-encrusted, and just generally disgusting.

It was slightly mollifying to see Breeohan covered in dirt too. His clothes had taken a beating from my sandstorm. They fell less gracefully and seemed to have soaked up the reddish brown sand like a sponge. Both of us had a red tint in our clothes that I doubted would ever come out.

"Will we reach an inn tonight?" I asked, a little whine sneaking into my voice. I tried to sound more cheerful. "A bath would be wonderful if we could get one."

"We will not reach another town by nightfall. We'll have to go as far as we can, then wake early to reach the next town by nightfall tomorrow."

I was glad when we were able to lie down for the night, but I found it hard to sleep. I kept imagining that our attackers would come back.

The next day was a blur of gritty, hot, painful walking. I was sore all over again. I kept reviewing the attack in my mind. Twice now I had been assaulted by men in this country. I was tired of being dirty, overheated, and attacked.

I was limping by the time we saw the town lights. Breeohan had noticed and wanted to stop and heal me, but I was too focused on visions of soap and clean caressing water to listen. I just kept walking, eyes fixed on the town. All the buildings looked the same, and I still hadn't figured out the lacing for the Iberloahan writing, so I couldn't read the signs.

Breeohan overtook me and led the way down the town road. He cut down an alleyway, saying it was a faster route to the inn. Immediately misgivings plagued me. Hadn't I just made a pact with myself to never take one of his "faster routes" again? And, just like a tragic play, as we turned the corner leading out of the alley, three beefy guys swaggered toward Breeohan and me.

"You and your dumb shortcuts," I hissed. To the men I said, "Look, I'm really tired. Could you just take my bags and leave me alone? I mean, robbing someone doesn't necessarily have to include injury, right?" I held out my leather bag, hoping they wouldn't notice my Jansport. I was still really attached to the thing and didn't want to lose it.

Breeohan gave me a funny look, but I gave him a shrug to convey I was serious. I was too tired to fight.

One of the men, built like a weight lifter, slouched forward warily. He seemed a little familiar, but I thought that maybe the experience of being attacked several times was making me dissolve all my attackers' faces into one big conglomerate. *Whatever, just take the stupid bag,* I thought impatiently.

"You the magician?" the weight lifter asked Breeohan.

Breeohan and I exchanged glances, and I wondered if two attacks in two days might not be a coincidence after all. The snick of metal sounded as Breeohan slid his sword from his scabbard. Muscleman stopped moving forward. He signaled his mates to proceed instead. Unlike our previous attackers, these guys had swords. The swords curved in a moon-shaped arc, much thicker and slightly shorter than Breeohan's. The thugs' swords looked like they could snap Breeohan's weapon in half in one stroke.

Breeohan was not fazed, and I felt bad for wanting no part in the situation. "Fine," I grumbled. I couldn't just leave him to fend for himself. I dropped both packs against the cracked wall of the building to my left. "Please, there must be some sort of misunderstanding. We aren't the people you're looking for. We're simply traveling salesmen. Can I interest you in some amazing wares?"

Breeohan gave me another look of confusion. The poor boy had probably been in a constant state of confusion since meeting me.

The thugs looked a little confused as well, but Mr. Weight Lifter said with unexpected sharpness, "This man has purple eyes. He said the magician would have purple eyes."

He? I had no idea who the man was referring to, but I realized my bluff wasn't going to work if they already knew who we were. I went to stand beside Breeohan, shifting into a fighting stance as I wished heartily for a big weapon. A tough stick to combat the swords would have been nice, but I only had a knife. Never having used a knife for anything other than cutting food, it wasn't my weapon of choice.

"Step back, Mary. I don't want you getting hurt. They're only after me anyway," Breeohan said.

"I may not have a sword, but I have other skills."

"Which you could use best without distractions."

"No time to argue." And there wasn't. The men were upon us.

Breeohan swung upward and caught one of the beefy men's swords with his, then his steel clashed with another man's sword blow. The third man came for me, and I had to admit that with no sand around, I was unsure of what to do. Figuring out amazing defensive moves with this new magic ability was really difficult when I had no time to think. I made a mental note to come up with some magic defense plans for the future, if I had any future.

I noticed that my attacker wore sandals that laced up his ankle. I pictured the wind lacing and untied his shoes, then bonded the leather together. He fell with a crash and his sword clattered. I summoned a wind to slide the sword closer to me, then snatched it up. It weighed down my arm. I doubted I'd be able to do anything useful with it despite all the years I had studied with a samurai. My "sword" in karate class had been wooden, much lighter than this thick solid metal.

Sandal guy tried to tear his laces apart, but I had bonded them well. One of the men fighting Breeohan left him to come to me. Breeohan tried to stop him, but the other combatant swung, and Breeohan had to refocus his attention. My new attacker slashed with such lightning speed, I could barely follow his movements. I blocked his blows clumsily. My muscles ached as I forced the sword into the defensive positions I had learned in my safe dojo a million miles away from this grungy, sweltering place.

Our swords locked. Despite my height advantage, I knew the man was going to kill me. I sensed the knife in his other hand and could do nothing to stop his sharp thrust. Pain ripped through my side. Black threaded the borders of my vision. I fought it off, clanged free of his long sword, the knife still buried in my side. I couldn't think clearly. A knife was sticking out of my middle, but I knew that I couldn't black out, or I would be dead. I swung my sword to the other side just in time to stop the man's killing sweep.

"Breeohan." I meant to yell, but it came out in a whisper. He was suddenly at my side, sword clashing with brutal force against my assailant's blade. Skilled as the thug was, Breeohan was faster, which was probably why the man had come after me in the first place. Breeohan moved with the sure grace of a hunting cat and the speed of a falling guillotine. I wasn't sure what happened. The world was turning black at the edges and closing in to the middle.

I sank to my knees on the cobblestones. Though I knew that I shouldn't remove the knife until something could be done to staunch the bleeding, the pain was like nothing I'd ever experienced. I'd never even broken a bone, and now a weapon was protruding from my side.

I concentrated as hard as I could on remembering something pleasant and hit upon the time Mom and I had bought hot fudge sundaes and stayed up all night watching chick flicks, laughing at the sappier moments together. It was better than thinking about my current pain.

"Mom." Tears leaked from my eyes.

Fingers brushed my arm. "Mary, can you heal yourself?" someone asked.

"I can't, I can't." I said the words through gritted teeth, my concentration fully focused on not fainting.

"Mary, you must give me permission to heal you. I can't do it otherwise."

What had he said? It was hard to hear the man through the pounding of blood in my ears. The world was turning dark, and I decided to let it fade. Perhaps then the pain would go away.

"Mary!" The person holding me shook my shoulders hard, and the black receded slightly. "Look at me," he said, turning my head toward his. "You must give me your consent. Please, Mary, just say 'yes'."

Alarm bells went off in my head. *Kelson.* The memory of cold blue eyes flashed to the surface of my mind. *I have to resist him, have to get away,* I thought in confusion. "No, no. I won't let you take her," I whispered. I shook myself, trying to get out of Kelson's grasp, but a wave of hurt ran through me. Gasping, I stilled.

"It's me, Breeohan. It's Breeohan. Kelson is gone. Please, Mary, please trust me." The voice sounded full of emotion. I tried to look at his face. Purple eyes stared intensely at mine. "Please, Mary. Trust me."

There was no guile in those purple eyes, only worry so intense it smote me inside. Not blue eyes, purple. Breeohan. "Yes, heal me. I trust you, Breeohan." That was all I could manage to say before the world closed in on me.

Chapter 8

I felt light behind my eyelids but didn't want to open them. My body was still tired, but my brain started processing images. Swords, thugs, a knife in my side. This thought woke me fully, and I quickly moved my hand to feel my left side. No pain struck me, and no bandages pressed my skin. There was a soft mattress under my back, and I looked around to see stucco gray walls and an open window across from the bed, letting in a warm breeze.

"So you're finally awake."

I turned my head to see Breeohan sitting at the side of my bed on an actual wooden stool. This was the first time I had seen any sort of chair anywhere in Iberloah. It gave me hope for better things.

"What happened?"

"You were stabbed. I healed you."

"I gathered that. Did you, um, take out all those guys by yourself?"

"Yes."

I was careful not to ask if they were dead. "So how does this work? Could you heal me whenever you wanted now, or do you have to ask permission every time?"

"Once permission is given, there is no need to ask again."

"That's a scary thought. Could you do anything besides heal me?"

"No. You only granted me leave to heal you, nothing else."

"So in an enchantment, the magician tries to get permission to do whatever he wants with you?"

"Yes." After a moment, he added, "You can tell me that I am no longer allowed to heal you, and then I won't be able to."

"Could anyone do anything harmful with the permission to heal?"

Breeohan considered for a moment. "I can't think of anything, but I have never tried to think of any way to twist that grant. Would you like to take back your consent?" He sounded a bit defensive.

"No. I told you I trusted you. Well, I think I did." My memory was a bit fuzzy.

"You did." He smiled, and his smile was warm. It lit up his face, and I noticed for the first time that he looked tired and worried.

"Why are you tired? Didn't you just heal me and then sleep?"

"It was a little more complicated than that. I wasn't sure about all the lacings involved in your wound. I had to move carefully so that I wouldn't make the stab worse or kill you by accident."

"Ah-ha, so you *could* kill someone if they gave you permission to heal?"

"I suppose so." He looked thoughtful. "But then again, maybe I wouldn't have been able to kill you after all, since I only had your consent to heal you. I didn't think of that last night, though. It would have saved me a lot of worry." He looked sullen. "How do you think of these things?"

"Maybe I just see this lacing stuff with a different perspective than you because I haven't lived with magic my whole life." *Or maybe I just don't trust anything I don't fully comprehend,* I added silently.

"Oh, here. Eat this." He thrust a bowl of gooey brown soup at me. I didn't really want to chance it, but Breeohan looked so expectant that I reached hesitantly for the spoon he offered. It tasked like runny meatloaf. I like meatloaf when it's solid, but soup meatloaf doesn't quite cut it. I ate it anyway because I was hungry and Breeohan was watching, but I tried to will my taste buds to stop working.

I still felt weak. How much blood had I lost? The thought hit me suddenly that without Breeohan's magic, I would be dead.

"Breeohan, I don't think I thanked you yet for saving my life."

"No, you didn't, but I knew you would come to it eventually. You're welcome." There was an odd sort of silence between us then. I couldn't think of what to say, and Breeohan looked rather uncomfortable as well.

"Well, I'll leave now so that you can get some more sleep." He quickly got up, almost knocking over the stool. He grabbed it before it fell, and then strode out of the room. It made me smile to see Breeohan acting ungraceful, and I briefly wondered why, but then felt too sleepy to think anymore.

The next time I woke to urgent needs, so I reluctantly levered myself out of the cozy bed. I was still uncomfortably dirty and greasy, but was glad Breeohan hadn't done anything other than heal my wound. On standing, I noticed that the blister on my foot was also gone. After relieving myself in the chamber pot by the bed, I got rid of the evidence. My shoes were in the corner with my bags, so I pulled them on. I ached for a bath, but when I found the innkeeper, he said he could only sell me a pot of water for washing. I went back up to my room and tried to think of a lacing that would clean me completely.

I thought of myself clean, remembered as hard as I could what it had been like at home when I could take a real shower with soap, shampoo, and conditioner. It had to have a pattern, but it was hard to find a lacing from only a memory. I had to refocus in a sense, but it finally appeared. I was so dirty I almost didn't care if I accidentally blew myself up by tweaking the wrong lacing string. I focused on the one that seemed right to me, twisted . . . and felt the dirt, smell, and griminess fall away into nothing. It was as if I'd just taken a shower at home. I felt indescribable relief. Next, I used it on my jeans and shirt as well as my Iberloahan outfit. Cleaning the native garb did not make the knife hole disappear, however. I tried to remember how they had looked when they were new, hoping to find a way to restore them to that state, but finally I realized that they had probably been used when Ismaha bought them for me.

Well, I've certainly bought my fair share of new clothes in my life, I thought. I decided to remember my own clothes when they were new, to see if that would help. The thought gave me a wrenching longing for home. I took a deep breath to calm myself. Crying wouldn't do any good. I needed to concentrate on finding the pattern for new clothes to distract myself from maudlin thoughts.

I found the pattern while remembering my jeans crisply pleated and dark blue on the store shelf. One strand of the pattern blazed more clearly than the rest, so I concentrated on my jeans, and jerked that line. Suddenly my jeans lay on the bed, as stiff and dark as when I'd first bought them. I did a little jig. *I'll never have to buy jeans again,* I thought, but then stopped dancing abruptly as I remembered that I might never *be able* to buy new jeans if I couldn't get back to civilization.

Fixing all my other clothes to their original newness made me feel much better. The Iberloahan garb fell neatly on my body, and my hair was snarl-free for the first time since reaching Iban. The cleanliness lacing left it fresh and straight, as if I had blow-dried it, and I could almost smell the rose scented conditioner I used at home. But that was probably just my imagination.

My newfound cleanliness gave me the courage to go downstairs and roll the "what kind of food will I get this time" dice. Clean, I could face anything—even soupy meatloaf. In the common room I looked around for Breeohan but didn't see him until he stood up and waved from a corner table. His ability to go unnoticed reminded me of my own strange ability to not attract attention if I didn't want to, and I wondered if that had something to do with lacing magic as well.

Thinking of magic made me think of the attack, and for the first time since waking, I considered the significance of the lead thug's words to Breeohan.

"Why were those men looking for you?" I sat down next to him as if we had been in the middle of a conversation and I was simply resuming it.

He looked kind of stunned. "You look . . ."

"Clean?" I helped.

"Yes, but no. You look . . . nice." He glanced around as if he couldn't remember where he had put something. "Uh, do you mind if we fade into the background before we start discussing things?"

"Okay." We sat there, trying to act like pieces of furniture, not worth notice. I thought for a minute, remembering what I'd done before if I wanted to be ignored. The pattern I must have instinctively used in the past sprang to life. I twisted a strand and saw the hint of gold flash in the back of my mind.

"You never cease to surprise me," Breeohan said.

"I try." I showed him what I'd done, and he copied me, becoming hard to see. We weren't really invisible, just chameleonlike, blending with the area around us. "So why are people after you?" I asked.

"I have no idea. I don't have any enemies that would want me dead. At least, I thought I didn't. I couldn't ask the men who attacked us; I was too busy with you."

"Sorry," I said, hoping that meant he hadn't actually killed anyone.

"Don't be. It was me they were after. It was my fault that you were injured. I'm starting to wonder about our attack in the canyon as well. Do you think they could have been connected?"

"It's possible. I thought I was just imagining things, but one of the attackers from last night looked familiar to me. So let's assume that the two fights *were* connected. The first guys failed to catch you, so they sent a message somehow for the next group or something. That's possible, but I still don't see why. Are you sure you can't remember any enemies with major grudges?"

"That isn't something I would likely forget. We will just have to stay inconspicuous until we get to the palace and can consult with the king and other magicians. He didn't ask if my name was Breeohan, just if I was a magician."

"Are there many people in Iberloah with purple eyes?"

"No, it's a less common color."

"So their attack could have been more than a random act of violence against magicians," I said.

"Yes. I know of only one other magician with purple eyes."

"Any with golden eyes?" I asked, curious.

"There are certainly a lot of magicians and non-magicians with a bit of gold in their eyes, like mine for example. But no one has eyes quite like yours." Though it was hard to focus on Breeohan's expression, he sounded strangely evasive.

"Are my completely gold eyes a sign of evil or something? Why did both you and Ismaha jump when you first saw them?"

"It's a little hard to explain. Do you mind if I wait to tell you until we're safely out of town?"

"Fine. We should go as soon as possible, but could I get a little food first? Ever since you healed me I've been ravenous. I guess I need a lot of energy to replenish my red blood cells." I knew he was aching to ask me what red blood cells were, but I discarded my "ignore me" pattern and signaled a waitress. Breeohan was forced to remain silent as a girl came over looking puzzled, probably wondering why she hadn't noticed me before.

"What would you like?" she asked politely.

"What do you have?" She rattled off a list of foods I'd never heard of before. I decided it'd be safest to just get bread.

After she left I was startled when Breeohan said, "I will get my things and meet you in your room. I think it is safest if I stay less noticeable."

"I'll be there as soon as I can." I had to watch closely to see the ripple of movement he made against the chair as he got up and left.

When the bread arrived, I headed quickly for my room. I didn't see Breeohan, so when he spoke, I nearly jumped out of my sneakers.

"Don't do that," I said, angry.

"Sorry." He was laughing.

"Yeah, you'll be sorry when I turn you into a newt," I mumbled.

"I wouldn't put it past you to figure out how, though it has never been thought possible before."

"Don't worry, you'd get better," I said, thinking of Monty Python. It was really annoying to not have anyone understand my jokes. They weren't all that funny anyway, so it didn't matter, but I suspected my jokes made Breeohan think me very odd.

"Let's go," I said in exasperation as Breeohan tried to explain that if I did somehow figure out how to turn him into a newt, he wouldn't actually be able to get better unless I turned him back or he did. If he still had his power in newt form, that is. And I wouldn't be able to do anything like that at all, unless he gave me permission. We left the room, with Breeohan still trying to analyze my joke, walked quickly out of the inn, and almost ran into two huge, dirty fellows bristling with weapons.

"Watch it," one said.

I looked up quickly into his face, shocked to recognize one of the attackers from the canyon. It was hard to stop the gasp, but I managed to turn it into a cough. I snapped my head down and swiveled around the two men.

"Sorry," I mumbled, head bowed. I quickly strode away, aware of their eyes on my back, afraid that at any moment they would recognize me as the girl in the canyon and jump me. I didn't slow down until I turned a corner, out of sight. I wondered where Breeohan was. My chest tightened with worry and fear of ambush, so the touch on my shoulder made me yelp.

"Shhh. It's just me. You had better make yourself unnoticeable. I guess there's no question now that the two attacks were connected. Take my hand so you don't lose me and get lost trying to find the way out."

"Hey, it was one time," I said, annoyed. I quickly became unnoticeable and grasped his hand. It was weird to hold hands, and I was glad we couldn't see each other very well and that my face was hidden. His hand was calloused and warm, but not sweaty, and I felt a little tingle in my chest as he led me through the winding city streets.

Get a grip, Mary, I thought. *You're acting like a kid. No wonder Kelson had such an easy time bamboozling you.* The thought of Kelson brought me back to my senses. I firmly smashed the tingling in my fingers and chest and simply followed along beside Breeohan, thinking of Mom and rescue.

Once outside of the city, I dropped Breeohan's hand like a hot potato.

Breeohan was silent, and I started to worry that I wasn't walking with him anymore.

"We should keep the unnoticeable lacing for awhile," he said just as I was about to shout for him.

My breath whooshed out. "That's fine. Let's go then." I started walking down the road.

"Wait, Mary. We might lose each other."

I hesitated, feeling a strange desire to feel warmth and callouses. I beat the thought away. "Not if you start talking. Who wants you beaten up or dead?" I had to swallow. No one I'd ever known had died, much less a friend. I didn't want Breeohan to die either. The thought made my chest tighten.

"I already told you. I can't think of anyone."

"Look, I think it's time you tell me a little more about yourself, Breeohan. All I know is that you're a wizard, twenty years old, an only child, and your mother lives near the palace. Does that mean you're a noble?"

"Yes."

"Well . . ." I waited for a moment. "Doesn't that mean that you're the heir when your mother dies, or do you do it differently here?"

"That is how it's done."

"Okay then," I said, starting to get annoyed by his reticence. "I'm sure that means someone could want you 'gone with the wind' if that meant that he or she could inherit instead. Unless only men inherit here, then it would be a he."

"Both men and women can inherit."

I was really regretting that I couldn't see Breeohan's face well. I hated not being able to read his expressions as he talked. After two minutes of silence, I couldn't stand it anymore.

"Fine," I said, "if you don't want to trust me, that's your decision. Maybe it would be better if we split up, anyway. I'd feel safer on my own than with you where I could get attacked at any moment for a reason I have no way of knowing because you don't trust me enough to talk about yourself."

"I was just trying to think. Don't be so riohoka."

"So . . . what?"

"So easily offended, led off course from true understanding."

I counted to ten slowly. "Okay, Buddha. Do you think you could possibly process your thoughts out loud, so that I can understand the situation?"

"I was thinking that perhaps we should part and enter the capital city separately. If those men are looking only for me, then that would be the best strategy for you. But the men in the wadi saw you as well, so perhaps it wouldn't help to split up. Although, the two you ran into didn't seem to recognize you. And there's also the chance that they're after *all* magicians, so parting would then be futile and dangerous."

"Breeohan," I said, my voice oozing impatience.

He must have heard the warning in my tone, for he continued, "I don't understand why anyone would want me dead. I *am* a second cousin to the king, and the closest one in line to the throne, but the person under me is Aria, and she has never shown any interest in ruling. She cares only for music. She would never give up her study of lost musical forms for ruling."

I was so stunned, I stopped walking. The ripple of Breeohan's movements disappeared. "Are you joking? There's no way I've been traveling with a prince."

Breeohan came back to me. He shed his chameleonlike lacing, and I could see his face clearly. "Would you please drop your lacing, Mary? I want to see your face."

I did so, reluctantly. If he was lying about being an heir, I didn't want him to see how confused I felt. I didn't think it was a very good joke.

"I am not a prince. Well, technically you could say I'm the prince since I am next in line to the throne, but I'm not the king's son. He's not even my uncle. The direct line of rule has had some bad luck. King Verone is the last child of King Kree. It's all a little complicated, but the end result is that for many years now, I have been expected to rule when the king dies. I wouldn't have to if the king would marry and beget an heir, but he seems determined to stay unwed. He has named me as his heir."

"I've been casually walking around with royalty?"

I must have looked stunned because Breeohan responded with a slight edge to his voice. "Don't act like this, Mary. I am the same person as I was before. It shouldn't make a difference that I'm royalty."

That snapped me out my stupor. "Whoa, there, ego-boy. Just because I've never actually met anyone royal before doesn't mean I think you're any better than I am. Because you're not. In case you didn't understand from my previous explanations of my country, we believe all people are created equal. That means royalty or not, I am not going to bow or scrape the ground, worshiping you. So you can just get off your high horse right now."

My speech didn't have the effect I thought it would. I wasn't sure, but I saw what looked suspiciously like the beginnings of a smile on Breeohan's face. I turned quickly and started walking down the road. Breeohan made a funny coughing noise that I suspected might actually have been laughter before he caught up.

"If what you say is true and you are the next person in line to be king, then you're crazy to think that there isn't anyone who wants to kill you. Where did you grow up anyway, Never-Never Land? I may not be from a country ruled by monarchs, but I know history, and people are always trying to dethrone kings, kill off heirs, and do whatever they have to do to gain power. It is a universal truth that not many people can handle power without becoming corrupt and wanting more power."

"*I* don't want to be king. It was thrust upon me. I had no choice in the matter."

"Didn't you? Can you honestly tell me that you weren't allowed to decline?"

"It's complicated." His voice didn't invite questions, but I went on.

"So, if this Aria girl doesn't want to rule, who does?"

"I don't know. The royals at court are often condescending and happier with themselves than with anyone else. I have to know all of them, but I don't know many of them well. Still, I can't imagine any of them being capable of such treachery."

"Well, someone is, noble or not, and you aren't giving me a good idea of who, so I guess we'll just have to see who looks guilty when we get there."

Breeohan laughed. "One thing I know. If one of the aristocracy is trying to kill me, you won't see any guilt on his face. Nobles are masters at hiding emotions."

"You don't seem to be all that great at hiding your emotions."

Breeohan blushed, proving my point.

"I've spent most of my life around magicians, not nobles. My mother thinks that I haven't tried hard enough to master the skill of masking emotions. She says I will always get taken advantage of because my face is as clear as stream water."

"People will trust you more, though."

"I hadn't thought of that," Breeohan said. We walked awhile in thoughtful silence. "We'll reach the capital by nightfall," he said suddenly.

"When do you think we'll be able to see the king?"

"It depends on how busy he is, but I may be able to get a private audience fairly quickly, considering all that has happened. I'm sure he will want to know about the attacks." He was looking thoughtfully at the ground, so he started when I grabbed his shirt and spun him toward me.

"And my mother. I know you have a lot on your mind right now, Breeohan, what with your kingly future being threatened, but my mother is out there somewhere with some lunatic, and that means everything to me. Don't forget her." My heart felt tight in my chest. I knew I was angry at Breeohan now because for one moment, I too had forgotten my real purpose. I'd exchanged my concerns about Mom for worrying about Breeohan. *What a fickle daughter,* I thought savagely.

"I haven't forgotten your mother, Mary." He spoke so softly, I felt horrible for blowing up. "I was also speaking of the attack on you and your mother."

"Oh." I felt even worse.

"Your very presence in this country is a mystery. And so are you."

I was still thinking about Mom, so I was a little confused. "I'm what?"

"A mystery." He smiled mischievously.

"I am not. I'm even easier to read than you are," I retorted.

"I don't know. I can't seem to figure you out. You behave so strangely sometimes. Are all people where you come from like you?"

"Maybe a little. But I guess I am a little odd, no matter where I am." I thought sadly of all the times I had been shunned as a little kid. I hadn't liked playing dolls and dress up, and strange things happened around me. After a while even my best friends had faded away. I saw now that those unusual occurrences had happened because of my magic ability. Though it explained things, assured me that I wasn't actually crazy, I was still sad for all those times I'd felt like a scary character in a sci-fi movie.

"Well, I think I ought to warn you about a few things before you go and put your arm down the serpent's hole."

"Oh yeah? Like what, Teacher?" I still wasn't going to call him "Master."

"For one, there are many types of bows that you will have to learn. It is important that you get the depth of the bow right so as not to offend. You have given me a bow before that should only be given a king, do you remember?"

"I remember. I'll save that one for him."

"Good. The problem we will have is your rank, where you fit in comparison to the other nobles."

"That's where you and I see differently. I think I'm equal to even the highest of kings." I gave a little flourish with my fingers as I imagined royalty might do.

"We could say that you are a visiting princess. That way, no one would dare take retribution on you if you made a mistake."

"Who would believe that? I'm just a high school student."

"A what? Oh, never mind, you're probably right. You don't act anything like royalty, even though you look it. But then the king doesn't act very royal sometimes, either. For that matter, neither does the training general, and he's a prince. You know, you remind me of them in some ways. They are just as confusing at times. They, however, just seem enigmatic, whereas you—"

"Don't even say it."

"Anyway, I know it sounds far-fetched, but not many of the nobles in court have traveled far, and even fewer have a thorough knowledge of geography. Your strange ways might be the very thing to convince them that you are a princess."

"Aren't princesses usually rich? We won't exactly arrive in a limousine, surrounded by bodyguards. Presentation is everything, and I look like a beat-up traveling salesmen. What if someone asks how I got here?"

"Though I didn't understand half of what you just said, I think I understood your main point, and I have a plan."

"In books, whenever someone says they have a plan, it always turns out disastrous," I said. The sun was sinking, and I thought I could make out distant buildings in a city ten times larger than any we had come to yet. From far away, I could almost imagine that I had really just been wandering in the Arizona desert and was coming up on a real city. The lamps weren't nearly as bright as electric lights, but my wishing made the illusion seem possible.

"Trust me. All you have to do is act like you own the world, and I will do the rest." He started walking faster, and I had to convince my tired feet to pick up the pace. He donned the chameleon lacing again, so I followed suit.

Chapter 9

As we neared the huge buildings of the city, my Arizona illusion vanished. The buildings were coarsely made. The dun-colored cobblestone road looked nothing like asphalt. The smell of garbage and smoke bothered my nose, making me wish for a breeze. And the sight of a pack of dirty kids hunkering down in an alley killed all my happy memories of air-conditioned, pest-free houses.

Breeohan grabbed my hand and led me down the alley past the children. They were so busy squabbling for what looked like a rotten piece of meat that I thought they wouldn't have noticed us even if we'd been shouting. I found I was wrong, however, when my foot kicked a rock. They stopped fighting immediately, looking around for the source of the noise. Their expressions of mingled fear and ruthlessness made me shiver, and I hurried past before they searched the alley more thoroughly.

"Don't those children have any place they can go?" I asked.

"There are orphanages, but many children slip through the sand. Some might consider children on the streets better off than those in the orphanages," Breeohan said.

He stopped at a beat-up door in an alleyway, and I wondered what we were doing in such a grimy place.

He knocked and then said, "He may not be here," as if I would understand.

We waited in tense silence. I was just about to suggest that no one appeared to be home, when the door opened a crack. Breeohan dropped his lacing. I held my breath and slid further out of sight.

"Who is it?" asked a voice that reminded me of scraping rocks on gravel.

"Don't tell me I have been away so long that the sand has changed my face, Rafan."

The door opened wider, revealing a dirty young man who looked to be Breeohan's age. His hair was tangled and his clothes torn, but the dirt made his blue-green eyes stand out all the more. He grinned at Breeohan, reminding me of a naughty kid who had just pulled off some tremendous prank. I stepped into a deeper shadow.

"Breeohan, you look awful. Just back from the magician's trial?" His voice was suddenly less deep, but it still sounded like sandpaper. I cleared my own throat as if I could fix his.

"I think you'd better take a look at yourself, Rafan. Why are you dressed so disreputably?" Breeohan asked.

"Come in, and I will tell you about it." He gestured for Breeohan to enter. Breeohan looked all around but didn't see my still form in the shadows.

"I'm not alone. Mary? Rafan is an old friend from school."

"Mary? I never thought I would see the day when you would bring strange women to my door," Rafan said, winking.

I knew I was a little paranoid with most men, but I figured I was justified by past events. After a moment's hesitation, I stepped out of the shadows and dropped my lacing. If Breeohan trusted Rafan, the least I could do was give him a chance.

"Hello." Rafan said the greeting like some men said, "Hello, beautiful." Long and drawn out. He checked me out from head to foot, lingeringly. My face heated with anger, which only got worse as I realized it would look like I was blushing.

Breeohan was a little flushed as well. He gently pushed his friend back through the door, following him in. I came after and closed the door behind me. Inside, I was surprised to see a room furnished with bright red, purple, and blue rugs. The decorating was a mishmash, but the rugs looked to be woven well, with detailed designs integrated into the whole. They seemed expensive, and I wondered why Rafan looked so grubby when he was living in such comfort.

"You seem to be doing well, anyway," Breeohan said, indicating the rugs. "This room didn't look half so nice the last time I was here."

"I thought I would make the place more comfortable since I've had to stay here for awhile." Rafan turned to me. "I hope you won't hold my appearance against me, lady. I am not usually so ill-prepared to receive guests."

It was odd hearing such fluffy words from a raspy-voiced, grubby guy.

"Don't worry. I've looked worse myself," I said.

"I doubt that you ever look anything but beautiful."

He's certainly laying it on thick, I thought, stretching my lips into a courtesy smile. After Kelson, I didn't really care for flowery talkers. I looked him full in the eyes as I smiled, and his gallant expression faded at the sight of my golden irises, but he recovered quickly. Rafan's reaction made me remember that I'd been too distracted with trying to figure out who wanted Breeohan dead to ask him to explain why my eyes startled everyone.

"Why do you look like something that's been dragged through the sewers?" Breeohan asked. His arms were crossed, and he appeared to be in a foul mood.

"I'm undercover." Rafan winked at me.

"Well . . ." Breeohan reminded me of a schoolteacher who had just caught his student in the middle of a wrongful act.

"There have been reports of several attacks against magicians. The king wanted me to blend into the background—find out a few things," Rafan said.

"Have the attacks happened to specific mages, or are they directed toward all magicians?" Breeohan asked, eyes sharp.

"That is what I am trying to find out. So far the attacks *seem* random, but all the victims have been masters, key political figures in the court. It's a good thing you came to me instead of walking through the city tonight. Now that you are a master, you might be attacked too."

"We've been ambushed twice now."

"Tonight?"

"In the last town and in the Klio Wadi. What have you discovered?"

"Nothing definite, and I've been a beggar for weeks. We have caught a few of the attackers, but none of them know who hired them, only who they were supposed to target and where to get the promised pay. We have tried hiding guards around the rendezvous points, but no one ever shows. It's as if whoever is behind the attacks knows his thugs have been found."

"Magic?" Breeohan asked.

"I don't know. There has never been a lacing found that could do such a thing."

The two men looked thoughtful. I stood near a wall, happy to be overlooked. I thought Breeohan and Rafan were ignoring a simple explanation as to why no one ever came to the rendezvous point. There could be someone on the inside, feeding the mastermind information. The person behind the attacks could even be the insider.

"If you're going to the king," Rafan said, "I think I'll go with you and tell him what has been happening lately. It's been a while since I last reported to him."

"We can't go to him quite yet," said Breeohan. He turned to look at me, and Rafan followed suit, intensely interested. I took an involuntary step backwards, stumbling on a rug before catching myself.

"I need your help, Rafan. Since you're already in disguise, I need you to go to the docks and bribe sailors to say they saw a grand passenger boat that came and left this evening. Then—"

"Wait." I said quickly. My stomach was churning uncomfortably. "I don't feel comfortable lying. If you introduce me this way, you'll have to come up with lie after lie, and it might lead to trouble. I don't want to pretend I'm a princess. The story has too many holes, especially if you have to bribe people. I would much rather just go to the palace as myself. The less said the better. I'll just try to blend into the background or something. Why don't we just say that I'm a foreign magician studying abroad?"

"And who are you really, lady?" Rafan asked. He had a debonair twinkle in his eye. I shifted uncomfortably.

"I *am* a foreign magician," I said stubbornly. I didn't want to go into my whole story with Rafan. The fewer people who knew, the less likely the story would get back to Kelson.

"I think you are right, Mary. The simpler the explanation, the less likely people are to question it. But there is a problem."

"What?"

"Your gold eyes."

"What does that have to do with anything?"

I heard him mutter, "Fool," under his breath and was about to get offended when he said, "I was so worried with what was happening, I forgot to tell you."

"Tell me what?"

"That only nobility have gold in their eyes. You've seen that my eyes have quite a lot of gold? Well, the more gold, the more royal, supposedly."

"Well, that's stupid. What if a noble kid gets a recessive gene and ends up without any gold? Does that make him a commoner?"

"I don't know what a recessive gene is, but occasionally there are commoners with gold flecks, and there are a few nobles with no gold. However, if someone has totally golden eyes, he or she is never just a commoner. They are from a royal line, always."

Apparently my eyes were unusual everywhere. "Is this golden eye rule true in other countries too?"

"For some of them," he said. I was uncomfortably aware of Rafan's eyes on us as we talked. They were blue-green without a trace of gold. Was Rafan a noble or commoner? I hated to even have to worry about such classifications.

"I still don't want to pretend that I'm a princess. Anyone would be able to see through it in a second, and you said that people with golden eyes come from a royal line, not that they are a prince or princess," I said.

"I don't agree about your inability to act royal. I have certainly seen you acting royal enough on occasion." Breeohan's serious expression relaxed into a smile.

"A royal pain, you mean." I smiled back.

"You said it." He laughed.

Suddenly, Rafan took my hand, and Breeohan's smile faded. "I would have no trouble believing you royalty," Rafan said as he bowed over my hand. I was glad he didn't kiss it. *Maybe they don't do that here,* I thought hopefully.

"Whatever we decide, it is too late to start tonight," Breeohan said. "I think we should wait until morning before organizing a plan or trying to reach the palace. We might as well sleep."

"I agree," I said. I tried to get my hand back, and Rafan let go after another bow.

"I shall sleep in the far corner so you will not have to breathe in my unfortunate stench," Rafan said.

"That's very kind," I said and meant it. He smelled like rotting tomatoes. Close proximity was making me queasy.

I wanted to talk to Breeohan alone, but there was only one room, so I settled down for the night. Breeohan was quiet as well. He looked deep in thought, and I wondered if he was still trying to come up with a plan. I really hoped we wouldn't have to lie if we could avoid it. The phrase "The truth will set you free" kept running through my head. I knew it was pathetic to always use books as my life guides, but as a loner I'd had to do something with all that time spent without friends. In a book, a character's lies usually create complications that eventually lead to some big catastrophe. I had a feeling that I was already going to be in for a wild ride, even without some made-up story to trip me up.

When I awoke the next morning, both Breeohan and Rafan were gone. "Great!" I muttered. "What am I supposed to do now?"

I practiced a few lacings, contemplating possible magical defensive maneuvers. This was hard since it depended on what was around me. I did think of ways to disarm someone with a weapon and was mulling over the possibility of a magic alarm system when Breeohan and Rafan returned.

"Finally. Where were you?" I sprang to my feet. "You know you could have at least told me you were going somewhere."

"Sorry, we didn't want to wake you. We had to get some things," Breeohan said.

That was when I noticed Breeohan's clothes. He wore a shiny purple coat that came to his hip. The coat clasped at the side as my vest did, but around its edges golden embroidery glittered in frilly designs. His dark purple silk pants were also embroidered. The effect of the whole outfit, rather than looking feminine, highlighted and accented his broad shoulders and catlike grace. I had to stop myself from staring.

Then I saw his bulging bag. Suspicious, I asked, "What things?"

Rafan had been partially hidden behind Breeohan, so when he came up and bowed over my hand, I was too shocked to do anything but gape. He was not only clean, he was dressed in richly designed aqua-colored clothes that brought out the brilliance of his eyes. I hardly recognized the guy. With his hair tied back in a ponytail, I could see that his face, now clean, was attractive, though his nose was too hawklike for my taste.

"We have been gathering the articles that you will need for your presentation at court," Rafan said. His mischievous blue-green eyes stared into mine, but the rasp of his voice made me clear my own throat involuntary.

"I thought I was going to stay in the background," I said to Breeohan.

Breeohan looked sheepish. "Rafan convinced me that no one would believe you were simply a traveling magician. I think our only choice is to present you as a foreign princess."

I snatched my hand out of Rafan's and backed up against the wall. "No way! You said that there were all sorts of bows that I would need to know, and I don't. And I'm sure that there are tons of other things that I would be expected to just know. Plus, where am I supposed to be *from*? What if someone knows about the place? They'll know there really isn't a princess there."

"You are the princess of Kirosan. It is far away, but I read about it, and I know that they have a princess there. Her name is Kasala Ramay I'Onaf. I don't know how old she is, but I doubt anyone else will either."

"I can't even pronounce her name, and just because you don't know how old she is doesn't mean someone else won't."

"Actually, Breeohan is the only one who bothers to read those silly travel tomes," Rafan said.

"We can stay here today and tutor you as quickly as possible on how you will be expected to behave." Breeohan was a little red. I guessed from embarrassment.

"Breeohan, I just don't think—"

Rafan cut me off. "My lady, I am sorry to say this, but with your eyes there is no way that you would be able to blend into the background. No one will question your authority as a princess, whereas if you simply say you are a traveling magician, many people will be curious, drawing even more unwanted attention your way. Besides, as a common magician, you would deprive the court of your beauty." He smiled sweetly.

I raised my eyebrows at Rafan and glanced to Breeohan for support. But he was holding out a dress, looking solemn. The dress was gold with intricate black embroidery on the hem, sleeves, and neckline. Tiny black jewels sparkled among the stitching. I wondered how they'd gotten the dress so quickly with no malls around.

"What if it doesn't fit, and wouldn't a foreign princess wear her native clothes?" I asked.

"It will fit, my lady. I have a talent for such things," Rafan said. *Yeah, I'll bet you do,* I thought rudely.

"I think it will simply look like a gesture of good will to wear our fashions," Breeohan said. "And if anyone asks, we will tell them our story." Cover story, huh? I wondered how plausible that would end up sounding. Breeohan dumped the dress into my arms. The golden material was thick, smooth, and shiny like satin. My chapped hands snagged the fabric.

"Look. I don't have time to learn how to be a princess. The longer I take to find my mother, the less chance there is that she'll be okay." I ignored Rafan as I spoke, pleading directly with Breeohan.

"If you go to the palace as a simple mage, it may take days for you to see the king yourself. If you go as a princess, you will see him immediately.

I think that is worth sacrificing one day for learning, don't you?" Breeohan said.

"I thought you said you would be able to get an audience with the king quickly, and I have a letter from Ismaha. She said the king would help if she told him to," I said suspiciously.

"I would be able to tell him in a day or so, but he would be less free to act on my news if you were at court as a simple magician. You didn't tell me about the letter from Ismaha." Breeohan sounded reproving but shook his head after a moment of thought. "But if you were a princess, no one would question his interest in your affairs. Fewer people would dare question his actions, and he could send out a search immediately rather than needing to go through a council decision."

"What you say seems to make sense, but it's probably only because I don't know enough to point out the gaping flaws. I'd like to go on record now as saying that I think this is a bad idea."

"I will remember." Breeohan looked directly at me, and I felt a curious tightening in my stomach, then a flutter. I put it down to nervousness.

"We'd better begin teaching you what you need to know then, Your Highness," Rafan cut in.

I looked toward the corner. "If I'm going to wear this, you two need to leave, so I can change."

"I am afraid we had to sneak back here as it is," Rafan said. "We cannot wait outside, attired as we are, in this part of the city. It would be a foolish right now with the attacks that have been happening."

"Fine, turn around then. And I will be watching your backs, so don't even think of peeking."

Breeohan smiled slightly, and Rafan bowed before turning away.

Just to be sure, I did my old sneaky dressing trick that I'd developed years ago to avoid stripping in the middle school locker rooms. I slid the dress over my head while removing my shirt under the gold fabric. I slipped my arms through the gold sleeves, and was about to drop my pants when I noticed a huge slit up the dress's right side all the way to my hip. In annoyance I left my pants on.

"There is no way I am going to wear this dress," I announced.

"What's wrong with it?" Breeohan asked, still turned away. Rafan turned around.

"It's okay, Breeohan. You can turn around." I glared at Rafan. Breeohan swiveled. He looked confused. "The slit is way too high. I wouldn't be caught dead showing this much leg in public."

"Didn't I give you the pants? Sorry, I thought I had." He reached into his bag, searched, and then pulled out a pair of golden pants. I was relieved to see that I wouldn't have to argue about modesty with them. They faced away again, and I pulled on the golden pants. They were a tight fit. They were also high-waters, but softly tinkling black beads hung from the embroidered hem and reached almost to my ankles.

The neck line slanted diagonally to fancy golden buttons, and the short sleeves dangled beads as well. It was like nothing I'd ever seen before, but it certainly made me feel like royalty. My straight hanging hair didn't really fit with the dress, however, and I wondered how I could arrange it better without hair spray, bobby pins, and other essentials.

"Are you done yet?" Breeohan asked.

"Oh, sorry. I was trying to think of how to do my hair. Do you have a mirror?"

"Don't worry. Rafan and I will do your hair."

"A couple of guys are going to do my hair? How many times have you done a girl's hair before?" I teased.

"Never." Breeohan blushed.

"I have, my lady. It will be no trouble," Rafan said.

"You seem to be an expert at all sorts of odd things," I said to Rafan, keeping my eyes wide and innocent. Rafan's face didn't redden, but he looked a bit discomfited.

"First, we will teach you how to bow. For now, you need to put this headdress on to practice with." Breeohan pulled out a golden object that looked like an art piece, not a tiara of any sort. He came over and twisted several strands of my hair into parts of the golden weaving, and it miraculously didn't fall off. It felt funny having Breeohan's face inches from mine, so I kept my eyes down.

"Since you are a princess, there are fewer bows you need to worry about," Breeohan said. Rafan and Breeohan spent the next several hours showing me the various bows for the different nobility. My head started to hurt after an hour, and I wished for the heavy tiara to fall off. It stayed firmly put, however, so I gritted my teeth and tried to remember which bow went with which title.

I learned that a second-born princess cannot pass her title on. Her children would be Zefas or Zefans and only the firstborn Zefa could pass on that title to her children. A second-born Zefan's children would be

Dolns or Dolnas. If a second-born Doln had a second-born, then he or she would be a Kav or Kava. When noble blood thinned below Kav level, they were too low to be found at court.

After an hour of purely verbal learning, I called a halt. "I can't remember this stuff if I can't write it down."

I reached into my backpack and got out my spiral notebook. Flipping to an empty page, I got out one of my pens.

"Okay, tell me again who is descended from whom. I'll make a pedigree chart."

Rafan and Breeohan looked curiously at my notebook and pen. But I ignored them, scribbling a little with the pen to make sure it would still work. Before I could draw more than two lines, they began speaking over each other.

"How does your strange quill make marks without an ink pot?" Rafan asked.

"Who drew such straight lines on your paper?" Breeohan asked

"Whoa, calm down. It's just a pen. The ink is on the inside. My paper was made in a factory, so the lines were drawn by machines." The words "factory" and "machines" didn't translate, so I tried again. "In my country, we've created contraptions that can do things for us, so people don't have to do it themselves. It would take too long to explain. Can we just get back to the nobles? I'm afraid I won't remember them all without a study chart."

Breeohan, used to unusual things about me, pulled himself back to lessons without further trouble. But Rafan kept distracting me from my chart with questions about machines and quills. I had to use several sheets of paper in order to accommodate the increasingly branching pedigree chart, and Breeohan finally commented on my waste of precious paper.

"I forgot. You probably don't have much paper around here, do you?" After that I tried to write as small as possible. Rafan then marveled about how small I could write with my quill and still have it be legible. *Really,* I thought. *It's not that wonderful.* Finally, I got too fed up with his constant breathing over my shoulder.

"How do you know if it's legible or not, Rafan? You can't even read my writing." I think he saw how frustrated I was because he backed off and stayed silent. When we reached the end of the pedigree line, up to present people, I was interested to learn that Rafan was a noble after all. He and

Breeohan were actually cousins. Rafan was Aria's brother, which meant that if anything happened to Breeohan's mother, Breeohan, and Aria, Rafan could become the heir.

One thing confused me. "Breeohan, why isn't your mother the heir? She's the closest in line."

"She made an agreement with the king to name me as heir instead." Breeohan's voice sounded funny, so I looked up.

"Is she all right?"

"Oh, she's quite all right. She wants me to rule because she thinks it would make me more responsible."

"I have been traveling with you for a while now, and I can honestly say that aside from your bad shortcut choices, I've never seen any irresponsible behavior. Have you been holding out on me, Breeohan?" I smiled.

His shoulders relaxed. The corner of his mouth twitched up. "What makes you think that you would be a choice judge of responsible behavior?"

"Only the fact that I've had a job ever since I was old enough to mow lawns and tend bratty kids. Someone had to help my mother make the bills every month."

Rafan cut in, and I suppressed a twinge of annoyance. He always seemed to cut us off when I was having fun teasing Breeohan. "I could tell you some stories about Breeohan's character that would shock such an innocent young lady like yourself. At magic school he was always getting into trouble."

I was interested in spite of myself. "What did he do?"

"I think we need to get back to studying," Breeohan said.

"Well, I'd like to hear what you did that was so terrible. Go on, Rafan."

"There was one time Breeohan snuck into the experimentation chamber at school. He nearly blew himself up playing around with the half-formed patterns written on the parchments there. The Masters gave him cleaning duties for a month after he was finally well enough to walk again."

Breeohan was blushing, but I was so disappointed by Breeohan's bad boy story that I couldn't help myself from blurting, "That's it? That's the big embarrassing story? I'm sorry, but you're gonna have to do a lot better than that to convince me that Breeohan is irresponsible."

I thought Rafan looked put out, but Breeohan smiled. "You chose the wrong story, Rafan. Mary has been fooling around quite a lot with untried lacings, and so far she has managed to stay unsinged, so she doesn't understand how dangerous it is to experiment."

We went back to the pedigree chart. After a while I asked, "Breeohan, I don't understand something. Didn't you say that only the firstborn passes on their title? Well, I'm confused about what happened with the third generation back, third-born Princess Rikah's children. Her oldest son is Zefan Kelteon. You said he's still alive, so why do his younger brother's children have the Zefan and Zefa titles? Shouldn't they be Dolns and Dolnas?"

"Kelteon was stripped of his title and exiled from Iberloah many years ago for trying to kill King Verone," Breeohan said.

"Why would he do that? It wouldn't have made him king. He'd still have to kill your mother, you, Rafan's father, Aria, Rafan, and Rafan's brother Temr, wouldn't he? That's a lot of people."

"He planned to kill all those who stood in his way to the crown. We only just discovered his plans before he could poison my mother." Breeohan's expression unnerved me. This quiet, contained anger was more dangerous than the sudden bursts of petty fury I frequently inspired in him.

I had never in my life had anyone want to kill me or Mom. What was it like to have to constantly watch for that sort of deceit? I decided to change the subject. "So the title will now pass on through Zefa Avana's line, regardless of any child Kelteon might have?"

"Yes," Breeohan said.

A thought struck me. "This Avana wouldn't happen to be the same one you claimed as your sister when you wanted to buy my book, would it?" I smiled mischievously. He blushed. Amazingly, I felt a little stab at his reaction. Suddenly, I didn't feel like teasing him about Avana anymore.

"Well, anyway, I think I have most of the people memorized." I handed the sheets to the two men. "Quiz me." They asked me who was related to who until I wanted to tear the pedigree chart into shreds. But I was fairly certain I had it down pat by the time we quit for the night. I fell asleep dreaming of trees stretching ever upward, splitting into branches that jutted newer, littler branches from their tips until the twigs were a huge latticework of never-ending lacings.

Chapter 10

I felt a touch on my arm and came instantly awake. Breeohan stood over me. "Mary, you need to get in your dress, and we need to do your hair so we can arrive at the palace on time."

I felt like I hadn't slept, but I sat up anyway, pulling the princess dress over my head. Breeohan turned hurriedly around. Rafan still watched, but I was too tired to care. I was good at changing in hiding. The little voyeur would see nothing but cloth. When I got to the pants part, though, I turned so he wouldn't see my leg through the huge slit in the dress.

Breeohan had me sit on the floor while he and Rafan put on the headdress. I couldn't see what they were doing, but I felt them threading hair through parts of the golden metal. When they were done, all my hair was firmly twisted somewhere, without a loose strand in sight. I admired the look in a little mirror they handed me. The golden headdress now looked like an extension of my head. It would be hard to get off, but it certainly made me feel royal.

"Pretty impressive for a couple of boys," I said.

"Now for your face," Rafan said, looking pleased with himself.

"Wait. It's one thing for you to do my hair. It's a totally different matter with makeup. I'll do it myself."

Breeohan handed me the packet he was holding. I found a vial of thick golden liquid with a paint brush. There were also vials of several colors of red, black, and bronze, and two different powder containers. They looked more like art supplies than a makeup kit. I decided to put the makeup on the way I normally would at home, though I never would have chosen gold eye shadow before. I did so now, however, using the little mirror to see my work. With the brush, I felt like I was painting myself instead of applying makeup. It was an odd feeling, putting on a golden mask.

Even the powder that I used for blush was golden. I decided to combine part of the powder on my eyes for eye shadow with the liquid gold so it would create a shiny but softened effect. I used a brownish-red for lipstick, and black for eyeliner. That part was tricky, and the eyeliner ended up thicker than I normally wore it. After close scrutiny I decided that it didn't look too bad, but when I was done I hardly recognized myself. Breeohan and Rafan had started going through their bags as I painted myself, so when I announced I was done and they looked up, both were shocked by my appearance.

"Do you do it differently here?" I asked, thinking about how wide a variety of cultural makeup there was in the world.

Rafan spoke. "You have applied the paints differently, but I much prefer your way. It accents your beautiful eyes, lovely cheek bones, and full lips. I am sure you will start a new fashion."

Even though I wasn't too sure about Rafan, it felt nice to have my features complimented by someone besides Mom. I hoped Breeohan would say something too, but he was silent, and I wasn't going to fish for compliments.

"We should go now," Breeohan finally said.

"We have one problem," I said.

"What?"

I flipped the slit in the dress open wide, exposing my golden pants. Then I wiggled my feet. "No shoes."

Rafan turned and pulled out a thin-soled pair of black beaded sandals. I could tell that they would be too small. Rafan was not as good at picking out shoe sizes as he was dresses.

"They won't fit. I wear a size ten." They looked confused so I tried again. "I have big feet for a woman, even in my country." I put the shoes on to prove my point. My heel stretched beyond the sole by a good two inches. Both Breeohan and Rafan assumed expressions of panic.

"We don't have time to find any more," Rafan said.

"She can't go barefoot," Breeohan shot back.

"Why not? We could say it is a custom of hers," Rafan said.

"Hello, I'm here too, and I'd rather not go barefoot, if you don't mind," I said.

"You'll have to. There is nothing else we can do at this point." Rafan kept looking around as if he would suddenly see the answer somewhere in the room.

"Hold on. Let's think about this for a minute." I looked closely at the sandal. The sole was plain black leather. I wondered if I could stretch it, and what kind of pattern would do so. The pattern of leather flashed in my mind, and I felt rather than saw the way to tweak the lacing to stretch it. With a mental tug, the soles sat before me two inches longer than before. They were also thinner—I doubted they would be much better than bare feet. But at least I would look respectable. I heard a gasp and glanced up to see Rafan's dark face go white.

Breeohan was unmoved. "I told you my meddling at school is nothing compared to what Mary tries every day."

"Did you know what you were doing?" Rafan asked shakily.

"Mostly. I'm getting better at telling what parts of a lacing can be tweaked."

"Do you know what you could have done to us all?" Rafan's voice was suddenly loud, and his face had gone from white to brownish red.

"I was pretty certain of what to change." I started to feel defensive.

"Look, we are all fine, Rafan. Mary just helped us solve our problem," Breeohan soothed. "We'd better leave now before we miss the entrance time."

The red in Rafan's face faded, and he seemed to get himself under control. In the silkiest courtier's voice ever—which, considering his raspy voice, was quite an achievement—he said, "Forgive me, Mary. I was merely shocked for a moment. I had no idea that you were such a talented magician." He bowed low. I noted that it was a bit lower than it should have been for a princess, and I felt an uneasy twinge. Would it be bad or good for Rafan to know about my ability to figure out lacings?

"It's all right, Rafan. Let's go then, shall we?" I picked up my bags.

"Please, allow me, Princess Kasala. A princess should never carry her own baggage." Rafan took my backpack and bag from me. I knew he was right, but I didn't like parting from my backpack. It felt wrong to hear someone else's name addressed to me, but there was no helping things now.

Breeohan asked me to use the unnoticeable lacing so I could slide into the streets unseen. Breeohan and Rafan followed carefully because they were still visible. I noted right away that I was going to miss my sneakers. On top of that, I'd been wearing the headdress for only an hour, and already it pressed down, promising a headache. I hoped the pain wouldn't fully descend until after my court presentation.

We slid through the streets quickly. It was early morning, and bright sunrays were just peaking over the three-story buildings we passed. The streets were cobbled more evenly than the last towns I had visited, and the trash in the gutters decreased as we traveled closer to the palace. It took a few hours to get to the upper-class buildings. Without Breeohan and Rafan, I'd have been hopelessly lost, despite the streets being less winding than in Cibar or the other towns I'd passed through. I noticed something else as well. People had plants everywhere—and not cactus either. Real green-leafed bushes and trees. I realized the city must have some sort of irrigation system running from the river to water so many plants.

Long before we were near enough to enter, I saw the top of the palace and its huge surrounding wall. It was the strangest building I'd ever seen. It looked like a cross between the Taj Mahal and a fairyland castle. Out of the building several turrets jutted, shaped like crystal, coming to sharp points. Bigger towers rose to tops swirled like soft ice-cream. The palace was whiter than all the bland city houses surrounding it, and the whiteness seemed to make it glow, though that could have been the morning sun striking it at just the right angle. Our plan to present me as a princess felt more stupid than ever.

My feet started to hurt from the thin-soled sandals, and the nearness of my headache was palpable. As we neared the palace, the buildings became grander, with engravings on the walls and doors and sometimes gated gardens.

Finally, we reached the gateway leading to the palace. Men in gold and purple uniforms questioned us, but then allowed us to pass through the huge entrance. The wall was at least two arm-lengths thick. Once through, we entered a huge, smoothly cobbled courtyard with decorative potted plants grouped in clusters to make the space look less forbiddingly vast. The palace loomed ahead, every inch of its white walls carved with animals, scenery, and symbols. It had to have taken years to create such detailed friezes. To the right of the palace, strangely colored horses roamed in a huge enclosure. I assumed a building next to the fence to be the stables. Next to the stables was another large square building where more men in gold and purple moved in and out.

We walked up to a wide marble staircase, leading to an enormous door. One side of the door was open to admit newcomers. I was trembling, so I held my dress to hide my shaking hands. Reaching the door, I saw that five people could walk through the open side together and barely brush shoulders.

We walked into a large marble-floored room tapestries and paintings hung on the walls. I admired the artwork, but thought they'd gone a little overboard on the decorating. There wasn't any free wall space anywhere. The room was well-lit from a large skylight in the ceiling. I wondered how they had managed to make the domed ceiling out of all windows.

A man wearing what I guessed were the royal Iberloahan colors bowed respectfully.

"Please announce the arrival of Zefan Breeohan Irat Ahasan, Princess Kasala Ramay I'Onaf of Kirosan, and Doln Rafan Isat Diosa," Breeohan said. The man bowed again and walked quickly across the length of the room to two large carved doors. These doors were not quite as large as the outer doors, but they were more ornately decorated, with gold inlay on and near the door knobs. The servant pushed the doors open, bowing as we passed.

I found myself at the top of another marble stairway, this one of green stone. It was only about ten steps to the bottom, but the height displayed the whole of a large ballroom, filled with people in vivid silken dresses and suits. At the sight of Breeohan, Rafan, and me, the nobles stopped their loud talking. It was nerve-wracking to have so many faces turned on me. I wasn't perspiring yet, but I felt my confidence sliding away like sweat. Through the silence, the doorman's voice rang out.

"Presenting the heir to the throne of Iberloah, Zefan Breeohan Irat Ahasan, accompanied by Princess Kasala Ramay I'Onaf of Kirosan, and Doln Rafan Isat Diosa." When his name was called, Breeohan stepped forward down the marble stairs, so I followed suit when my name was bellowed, fighting the urge to look at my feet, but fearing that with my head up, I would trip.

Across the large room on a raised dais, the king sat in a purple stone chair with gold cushioning. He looked to be in his forties. His frame was lean, and his dark brown hair was fashioned in the traditional ponytail, but he wore no crown. Across his shoulder he wore a gold jewel-encrusted sash that fell to his waist and, I assumed, looped back up his back to his shoulder.

He looked at me as I looked at him, but he was too far away for me to see his eye color. I was interested to see how much gold his eyes contained. I reached the floor without incident, following Breeohan across the suddenly clear path to the king's throne. My nerves were doing acrobatics, and I had to fight not to look back and forth at the people we passed. Their stares felt like heat on my face. When Breeohan reached the foot of the dais, he moved to the side, so that I stood in the center. I guessed Rafan was somewhere behind but didn't dare look back. As one, Breeohan and I bowed low to the king.

"Please rise," King Verone said. I straightened and looked up into his face. Our eyes met. His were mostly golden with just the hint of brown at the outer edges. He did not react in the least to the color of my eyes, and I couldn't help but think that he was the first person since coming to this country who hadn't shown shock at my eye color. I knew it was probably because he expected as much from royalty, but the lack of reaction steadied me somehow and gave me confidence.

"Princess Kasala, what brings you to my kingdom without even a forerunner announcing your arrival?" I heard a rebuke in his tone, though his voice sounded kind.

Breeohan opened his mouth, but I felt instinctively that I should answer. "I beg you will forgive me, Your Majesty. If I could have sent a runner, I would have, but I come to you under strange circumstances. In fact, it is a miracle that I am here at all and not at the bottom of the sea."

One of the king's eyebrows rose.

"You see, Sire, my ship was set upon by pirates as I traveled from Kirosan to Biopa. My maid managed to distract the pirates so I could escape onto one of the longboats. It drifted for a day before coming to your shores. I didn't know I was in Iberloah, however. I thought I was on Reksa, so I traveled inland, thinking I would reach the capital. Instead, I became increasingly lost. Then I met Zefan Breeohan, who aided me in reaching you." I stopped, worried that if I blabbered on, I would sound neither convincing nor princessy.

King Verone studied my face. I was suddenly afraid that he knew more about Kirosan than Breeohan did. There was no real reason for my fear. His gaze was steady, not slit in suspicion, but I couldn't help feeling he could see the lie in my face. What if he knew what age the real Princess Kasala was, and what if she was ten or something? I knew this was a stupid idea. I felt my face turn hot with the beginnings of panic, and I tried to breathe calmly. Strangely enough, his steady gaze reminded me of the one Mom gave me when she knew I was hiding something.

My fears, however, must have been imagined because the king said, "I am distressed to hear your sad tale. We will do all we can to help you." He looked pointedly toward Breeohan. "Zefan Breeohan, I will be interested to hear the tale of your Master journey and kind service to the princess. We will meet during the sixth portion in my study." He nodded to us all, which I assumed meant we were dismissed. We backed away to fade into the crowd of shiny skirts and tinkling beads. As soon as we did, the room roared with the jangle of too many voices talking at once.

I found myself separated from Breeohan and Rafan by two women. One wore a crimson gown, one a green in a style similar to my own, but with more jewels sewn into the embroidery. They were both almost a head and a half shorter than me, but I was intimidated nonetheless. The girl in crimson satin looked like a living version of Queen Nefertiti. Where many of the courtiers had intricate designs painted on their temples and foreheads, she had a dark red garnetlike jewel on each side of her face, next to her eyes, with one more in the middle of her brow. Her eyes were a brilliant emerald green, with just a few flecks of gold, and the look in those eyes was anything but friendly. She smiled politely and bowed the proper depth to me, but her smile did not reach her eyes.

Nefertiti said, "It is an honor to meet you, Princess Kasala. I am Zefa Avana, and this is my sister, Zefa Dora."

I bowed the height required for a Zefa and looked more closely at them. So this was the girl that Breeohan had blushed over, huh? I tried to suppress my immediate dislike. Maybe I was just imagining the unfriendly look in her eyes. Maybe she was as sweet and intelligent as she was gorgeous. I decided I'd better give her a chance before totally hating her.

Zefa Dora's eyes were a muddier green, though she also had flecks of gold near the middle. She was less beautiful than her sister, on the plump side. In her gaze I felt a warmth not present in her sister, and my body moved toward it as one would move to a fire away from the cold. Dora wore no jewels on her smooth dark skin, only green leaf fronds painted on her temples and forehead. Poor girl. She would have looked much better with simple makeup.

"I'm pleased to meet you," I said.

"We are happy to hear that Zefan Breeohan was so fortunate as to find you in your distressed state. Think of what might have happened if someone less kind had found you first." Avana sounded disappointed that they hadn't.

"Yes, I was lucky," I responded.

Avana wasn't put off by my short answer. "Were you able to rescue any of your possessions?"

"Unfortunately not."

"How did you survive without any money or servants?" Avana asked.

I almost laughed. Avana seemed to think it was impossible to survive without paid help. I glanced at Dora to see what she thought and saw a slight smile on her lips.

"It was difficult." I tried to give a "poor me" look, but I don't know if I succeeded because Dora was still smiling.

Avana's little frown suddenly turned into a look of delight. I looked over my shoulder to see Breeohan approaching and sighed. At least I wouldn't have to talk to Avana anymore. Obviously, she wasn't going to be bothered with me when Breeohan was around. He came to stand next to me. Avana angled her head to look up flirtatiously from long dark eyelashes.

Could she be more obvious?

"Zefa Avana, Zefa Dora, it is such a pleasure to see you again," he said, bowing.

"Please, Breeohan, you haven't addressed me with my title since we were five. Don't start now. Are we not closer than mere acquaintances?" Avana batted her gargantuan eyelashes.

Breeohan's cheeks flushed red-brown, and I felt suddenly warmer than the room merited.

"You are quite the hero. Rescuing a damsel in distress. If I had known all I needed to do to get you alone was to be in trouble, I would have done it ages ago," Avana said.

I guess obvious is her style.

Breeohan, still red, said, "I would never wish you in any danger."

Luckily Dora came to the rescue, because I sure wasn't going to say anything—I was too busy feeling annoyed. "How did your Master trial go?" Her voice was surprisingly low and soothing. I thought she would have made a good therapist.

"I almost didn't make it, but I accomplished the journey without loss of limb, as you can see." He gave another elaborate bow, I guess to prove that he could, and the two girls giggled. I pasted a smile on my face, wishing just to leave. My headdress was starting to feel like lead. Avana and Dora wore headdresses that looked even heavier than my own, and I wondered how they endured it.

"We shall watch for you at the jova courts then. Many are eager to spar with you. They feel you might have lost your edge from so much travel. I hope you will prove them wrong," Avana said.

"They may be right, but I am grateful for your confidence," he said.

I had no idea what they were talking about, and wondered if, as a princess, I should. I decided to say nothing in case I was supposed to know.

"Do you compete, Princess?" Avana asked, a gleam in her eye.

Her cocky demeanor spurred the worst of my bullheaded characteristics, and I found myself saying, "Yes." It was then that I noticed Breeohan's ever so slight shake of the head warning me to say no. *Oh well, too late.*

"Really?" Her eyes were wide in surprise, but there was a wicked curve to her lips. "Then I will be happy to see you on the courts as well. I am sure we would all be interested in seeing what Kirosan is capable of."

"Avana, Dora, I don't wish to be rude, but the princess has had a trying journey. I promised that I would see her to her rooms. If you will excuse us?" Breeohan bowed. And then I bowed, and we walked away to a different exit on the side of the chamber. As soon as we were out of sight from the throng, Breeohan grabbed my shoulders.

"Do you realize what you just did? Oh Mary, why can't you think before speaking?" His voice came out in a strained hiss.

I shrugged his hands off. "I'm sorry, but she was so smug I couldn't help myself."

"She was not smug. She was trying to include you in the conversation. She won't be able to help being shocked, however, when she sees that you don't know anything about what goes on in the jova courts."

Had he really not seen Avana's honeyed condescension?

"How do you know I don't know how to do whatever it is?"

"Mary." He made an aggravated grunting noise. "Do you realize how unstable is the sand we tread? Too many mistakes and people will start questioning your verity."

"Look, Breeohan, I told you I thought this was a stupid idea. Don't start blaming things on me, especially since nothing bad has happened yet." I wanted badly to punch him, but I restrained myself. What had happened to the easygoing guy I'd traveled with for so long? It was like *Invasion of the Body Snatchers* or something.

Breeohan was taking deep breaths. After a minute he seemed to sink back into his old self. "I'm sorry I spoke harshly to you. I'm more worried than I thought I would be."

"Well, it's not like this is my favorite day ever either. I wish this whole thing could be over already. I just want my mother back." A knot formed in my throat, but I held my tears in check.

He took my arm and gently led me down the wide stone hallway. "We'll find her. I'll mention it to the king as soon as I see him."

"I want to go with you when you meet with the king," I said.

"He did not invite you to come with me."

"Please, Breeohan. I could wait outside the door until you're done talking, then you could ask him if I can come in for just a minute to speak with him."

He looked at me suspiciously. "Why? What do you plan to say?"

"The truth. I think he deserves to know what's really going on. I think he suspects that I'm not a princess anyway. Something in his look made me decide that it would be better to come out with the whole story."

Breeohan sighed. "I was going to tell him everything. I don't know if your telling him would make much difference."

"Hello? Did I just hear you say you can tell my story better than I can?"

"You have a tendency to say too much sometimes. I could keep it simple."

I started to get angry again. "So now you're telling me I would say something stupid?"

"No, I didn't say that. You . . . Very well, just wait outside, and I will see if I can convince the king to see you also."

"Thank you so much for the concession," I said dramatically.

We started walking, but there was one more question I'd been distracted from asking. I tried to sound casual. "By the way, Breeohan, what do you do at the jova courts?"

Breeohan rolled his eyes up at the sky.

Chapter 11

I waited outside the doors to the king's study as Breeohan walked in at the sixth portion, which I translated as twelve o'clock. Breeohan had told me that time was divided up into twelve portions for the day and twelve for the night, with the first day portion at sunrise and the first night portion at sunset.

I paced, clutching Ismaha's letter, but there were two guards in purple and gold watching me, so I finally forced myself to stand calmly and smooth out the wrinkled paper. As I did this, the study doors opened and a doorman—the same one from that morning—said formally that the king wished for me to enter.

I walked through a hallway of bookshelves full of fancy gilt and leather bindings before reaching the octagonal chamber where the walls seemed made of manuscripts and leather-bound volumes. The shelves stretched two stories high, and there was a sliding ladder along the wall that could roll to any side. A little further out from the wall, away from the ladder's path, was a large wooden desk. It was oval except for where a half circle bit out one side, and in that depression the king sat looking at me. Breeohan sat in a chair opposite the king. Two more chairs sat empty next to Breeohan.

I wasn't sure if I should sit until the king gave me permission, so I waited for some signal. A shaft of sunlight hit the center of the desk's stained wood, making it a deep blue brown, and illuminating the dust particles so that they looked like tiny floating fairies. The beam of light also made it harder to see the king's face from my position.

"Please be seated, Princess Kasala," the king said. So Breeohan hadn't told the king anything yet. I'd sort of hoped he would do it, so I wouldn't have to, but I'd asked for this chance, and I wasn't going to back out now. Once I sat down I could see the king's face more clearly. He looked much more approachable in his study than seated on a throne, atop a three-foot-high dais. Here he looked less dazzling, more of an everyday kind of guy, despite his richly embroidered clothing.

"Forgive me for asking, Princess Kasala, but I can't seem to remember if perhaps one of your parents ever came on a diplomatic voyage to my country?" Verone asked.

"No, Your Majesty." I didn't know how to begin, and I was confused by the bewildered concentration on the king's face. He looked as if he were trying to remember something. "I don't know where to start. The thing is, Your Majesty, you could never have met my parents because I'm not really Princess Kasala. I'm not a princess at all. I'm a high school student from Oregon—well, Arizona. I really am in trouble, though, and Breeohan thought that you wouldn't be able to help me if I came to court as myself. Plus, Breeohan and Rafan seem to think that my eye color was a royal give away, but in my country it isn't. We don't even have royalty. I hope you aren't too angry at my lying to you because I really didn't feel right about it at all, and I can't tell you how much it relieves me to be telling you the truth . . ."

The king held up his hand, looking stunned. "Did you say you were from Oregon?" he asked.

"Yes," I answered, expecting him to ask where in the world that was.

"Oregon in the United States?"

I was too shocked to reply. He knew where Oregon was. A quick look at Breeohan showed me he was surprised as well. A rush of relief coursed through me in a tidal wave. Then the wave broke, and I started to cry.

"I'm so happy you know where that is. I've been so afraid I was on some other planet or an alternate reality or something. I even thought that maybe I . . ." I couldn't finish. It was as if the tenuous bit of hope that I'd been afraid was severed forever was suddenly cast out again. I caught at that hope with a grip of steel. My breath rasped in and out until I forced myself to breathe more deeply. The king offered a handkerchief, and I dabbed my eyes. My makeup was probably ruined. I was sure I looked a mess.

"Ismaha wanted me to give this letter to you." I thrust the crumpled letter at him. It was all I could do. I was too afraid to ask the king about what he knew of the United States. He might say that he had only heard of it from a fantasy book or some equally dreadful thing. I think I shocked the king too, because he hesitantly took the letter, his eyebrows almost in his hairline. He broke the seal, and then his eyes flicked back and forth across two pages. I wondered what Ismaha had to say for two pages.

"Ismaha says that your mother was taken by a man named Kelson. Is this right?"

"Yes."

"He is older?"

"Well, he looked my age when I first met him." I felt my cheeks going red. "But when I drew him one time in art class, he looked about forty. He may not actually be old. I may have just drawn him like that to sort of expose his nature to myself."

"It's possible, but that means we know even less than I'd hoped." His brow furrowed.

"Will you help me, then?" I hardly dared hope for a positive answer.

"Ismaha says I must, so I must." He smiled for the first time since I'd met him. It changed his face wonderfully, transforming him from cool-cut magnificence to warm sunshine. I felt a huge weight lift from my shoulders.

"Please, Your Majesty, no one else seems to know about America. How do you?"

I held my breath when I saw the king's smile vanish. He looked more majestically unapproachable than ever. Then he shrugged. "I went there once."

"You did? Well then, do you think, once I find my mother, you'll be able to help me return? I'm not sure if the pattern that I copied would get me back. I don't think I got the whole thing right, anyway, since I definitely didn't end up where Kelson did."

"In that case, you are lucky you didn't end up in space somewhere. You see, Iberloah and America are on different planets, and the one record of the pattern was stolen. There are magicians who know of it, and even those who have gone there, but I thought no one ever would again."

The contents of my stomach dropped like an anchor and then rose to my throat. I wanted to throw up. I glanced at Breeohan. A look of disbelief was plastered on his face.

The king's face softened. "I am sorry." He glanced at the letter. "But you sense the truth of what I have said. Yes?"

I nodded dumbly, but I wanted to scream. I couldn't be stuck here. I just couldn't. There had to be a way back.

As if hearing my thoughts, the king said, "There is still hope. If this Kelson was able to get to Earth, he must have found another record of the lacing. It could even be the one lost so many years ago." His words cheered me a little, but my stomach still churned when I realized that I would probably have to get the pattern from Kelson himself, and he wasn't likely to just say, "Why sure, Mary, I would love to give you the means to get back to your world."

"I think that you should maintain your identity as Princess Kasala for now. If this Kelson is among the magicians at my court, or has contacts from the palace, he may not realize that you are in Iberloah at all. I'm not sure what Kelson would want from either you or your mother, but we shouldn't make things any easier for him. I will talk to my counselors about sending out search parties and will ask my most trusted mages to help you in your search. However, it may be difficult to get much help from magicians at the moment, due to the attacks directed toward them. I will do all that I can, but you must realize that it may take some time," King Verone said.

"I appreciate anything you can do, and I can even help with magic stuff if you show me what to do. Breeohan has been teaching me, and I think I'm getting the hang of lacings if you need an extra person on the job."

"You really have magic abilities?" He seemed surprised, despite my earlier mention that I brought myself to Iberloah, but I didn't blame him. I'd been shocked myself. "I would be glad of your help," the King continued, "but I am afraid I will not be able to spare anyone to continue your training."

"She learns quickly, Sire. I don't think you will find her a burden at all. She sees complete lacings," Breeohan interjected.

The king's eyebrows flicked up once more. "For now, I suggest that the two of you rest for awhile. I will have much for you to do later."

That was plainly a dismissal. Breeohan stood. I was a little slower than he, wishing I could look around at some of the books lining the walls, but the king was studying the letter from Ismaha again, and I didn't want to annoy him after his kindness. I also wanted to ask him about his trip to America, but he had seemed reluctant to talk on the subject. Questions teemed in my head as I followed Breeohan toward the door.

"Just a moment." The king looked up from Ismaha's letter. "You failed to tell me your real name, and Ismaha doesn't mention it either."

"Mary Margaret Underwood," I said.

King Verone sat still in his chair. "And your mother?"

"Fiona."

The moments lengthened uncomfortably as the king stared at me.

I started to wonder if he had forgotten Breeohan and I were even there, but then he said softly, "Breeohan, I would like you to stay for a moment, if you wouldn't mind waiting outside, Mary?"

"Sure." I flashed a glance at Breeohan who returned it with a shrug.

I sat outside, studying my hair lacing, wondering what it would take to change it some other color. I thought I knew which thread to tweak, but I couldn't quite work up the courage to do it after Rafan's reaction that morning. My royal interview bothered me, but I couldn't focus my thoughts very well. Why hadn't the king talked more about America? Had he felt it would be kinder to steer clear of the subject since the lacing to get back to Earth was lost? I couldn't figure it out.

Finally Breeohan came out of the room, looking unnerved, which only increased my feeling that there were important facts flitting away as quickly as I reached for them. He turned to the king's servant. "The king asks that you fetch Prince Sogran." He turned to gaze beyond me down the hallway.

"What happened?" I asked. "You look like you've seen a ghost."

This threw Breeohan from his train of thought, and he pulled himself back from wherever he had been. "What are you talking about?" He looked exasperated, but he also seemed intensely confused.

"You seem a little overwhelmed. What did the king say to you?"

"He said a few things." He looked in my direction, but his gaze focused beyond me, puzzling something out.

"Well, that's helpful." I sighed. I didn't feel like pulling teeth to get the details, so I started walking.

Breeohan walked with me in brooding silence. He showed me the door to my room and was about to leave when a man wearing dark red silk approached us and challenged me to face him in the jova courts. I stood dumbfounded, watching the man's face glow with malicious intent. *How could he have known to challenge me?* I wondered. The image of Avana's glowing face floated back from memory. No doubt this had been the slimy little suck-up's idea, but there was no way I was going to mention that to Breeohan.

"I will meet you there at the seventh portion," the man said as if there was no question of me declining the challenge. He strode away, and Breeohan muttered something that sounded suspiciously like a curse. It was already about three quarters past the sixth portion, so I quickly entered my room to put my traveling pants and shirt on since I didn't have anything else. All the time I dressed, I wondered what I had been challenged to do.

As soon as I emerged from my chamber, we began walking back through the palace, and Breeohan pounced on me. "Do you have any idea what you're doing?"

"No. You were going to tell me, but it must have slipped your mind."

"Well, let me tell you now. You are going to have to fight Doln Baro."

"I figured as much." I tried to sound casual, but my stomach gave an uncomfortable lurch. "What kind of fighting?"

"The art of jova includes all manner of weapons. There is one blessing. Since you were challenged, you get to choose the weapon." His brows knotted in worry. "I wish I could stand in for you, but there is no way. Perhaps if you claim an injury? That could work. No, everyone saw you this morning. They will think you are a coward without honor if you refuse to fight."

"No one gets hurt, right? I mean it's not to the death or anything?" I held my breath.

"Not usually. There are judges to keep track of points. Whoever reaches five first wins. People are often injured, however. That is the blessing and the curse of having so many mages around to heal you. The nobles take advantage of that privilege by ruthlessness in the jova court challenges."

I was starting to panic, so I stopped and took a few deep breaths. I'd been a fool to let that silly Avana goad me into pretending I knew what a jova court was. "Okay, let me think. What if I choose no weapons?" I asked.

"I don't think it has ever been done before, but there is no rule against it."

"Good," I said as we stepped outside. "Maybe if no one is used to hand-to-hand combat, I'll have a chance." We were about to enter a crowd of people surrounding a circular structure.

"Oh, and don't use magic," Breeohan said. "It is forbidden within the court, and the mages in the crowd will be able to tell if you do."

My stomach lurched again, but I forced myself to focus on possible fighting strategies. I walked into a structure that reminded me of a small Roman Colosseum where gladiators had fought and people had faced off against hungry lions. It was an uncomfortable likeness. There were weapons of all kinds on the wooden racks that lined the outer wall. Most looked similar to what I'd seen in barbarian movies, but there was something about seeing a staff with razor-sharp jagged metal jutting out of both ends that squeezed my heart into terrified thumping in a way the movie weapons never had. I was directed to the middle of the circular court. Six feet up from the wall of weapons were benches filled with nobility wearing bright colors and hats with enormous brims. I wondered for the sixteenth time why I couldn't have kept my big mouth shut.

Doln Baro walked from the arched entryway to the open sky of the round court and faced me. He wore thick, nut brown leather that shone in the sunlight. I wondered if the material would hamper his movements enough to help me get away with certain moves. Seeming to be on the verge of a yawn, he asked, "What weapon do you choose?"

A disbelieving grunt burst out of my mouth. He was trying too hard to look uninterested. "None. I choose hand-to-hand combat," I said.

Baro looked startled, and it was nice to know I could upset his mask of boredom just a little. "Are you afraid of a sharp edge?" he sneered.

"Are you afraid of not having one?" I countered.

"It makes no difference to me. I will beat you either way." He did his best to look exceedingly bored.

I wasn't sure how we would get started, so I kept a wary eye on him, noting the spectators settling into seats. How had word spread so quickly? Perhaps Baro had declared his intention to challenge me right after the court assembly.

"I find your attire quite appropriate. A beggar's outfit will certainly crown the moment when you beg me to spare your life."

"No one is allowed to kill on the jova courts," I said, hoping he didn't note my slight quaver.

"I certainly could not be blamed if something were to happen accidentally."

As Baro and I talked, the crowd chatted excitedly. I scanned the group quickly for Breeohan but couldn't see him anywhere. At some cue I couldn't see, a hush fell. I didn't get a chance to think of a reply to Baro's threat. A deep horn sounded, and Baro attacked. I almost didn't sidestep his attack quickly enough. I wrenched my body to the right of his charge, out of leg range. He bulldozed forward again, and I could tell immediately that he was not used to fighting without a weapon. His lunge was off-balance. This time as I sidestepped his punch, I caught and pulled his arm as I swept his leg from under him. The momentum of his punch sent him tumbling forward onto his face.

He got up quickly, growling, transformed from the bored courtier to an enraged hornet. I had to give him credit, though. He was smart enough not to charge me again. I waited on the balls of my feet for his next move, every nerve tense, ready to spring. Instead of trying to run me over, Baro tried to slide in close enough to punch me in the face. I front-kicked him, then continued my momentum, sweeping down his arms and punching his face instead. I felt the numbing tingle of fist hitting flesh as I again sidled away from his recovery blow.

I didn't like that I was actually hurting Baro. A longing for my dojo swept through me. With my thoughts distracting me, I almost missed blocking Baro's next punch to my face. Because of that, his other fist struck my stomach, and I staggered back. Baro gave me no time to recuperate but came flying at me as he had at first. Even winded, I managed to step to the side and sweep his feet from him using his own momentum. But I was panting, and I felt a sharp jab of fear. I wished the fight would just end.

Baro got up, his face turnip red. If he'd been mad before, he was positively raging now. He didn't seem to know how to do anything but punch. I blocked him with determined concentration. Sweat on my brow trickled into my eyes, making me blink constantly. One blink lasted too long, and he hit my jaw hard enough to blacken the world for an instant. I struck out blindly and was blocked, but it gave me enough time to be able to see again.

Rage built off the fear inside me. I focused on Baro as if he was the only thing that existed. My sensei had often remarked that it took getting hurt before I woke up enough to start fighting well. Baro had just woken me up. I attacked, striking with quick combinations of punches and kicks. He tried to block, but I hit more often than he blocked. I hardly heard the low bellow of the horn.

"Stop." Baro shielded his face with his arms. "It is over. For pity's sake, stop."

I recoiled from him as if hit. His face was bloody, bruises already blossoming on the sections of his skin not shielded by his leather outfit. I looked at my own hands to see them covered in red. Bile rose up my throat, and I came perilously close to regurgitating chunks of food all over the arena. A temporary fighting frenzy had taken over. That had never happened to me before. My fear from the fight turned inward; I was afraid of myself.

I looked around the crowd, feeling lost, looking for something I couldn't identify. The crowd was standing, clapping politely as if I had just performed a piano concerto, not beaten a man's face in. I stumbled stupidly toward the archway that led outside, tripped through it, and ran like wildfire to my room. Once I got there I used the cleaning lacing on myself, but I still felt dirty. I dipped my hands into the water basin and scrubbed until my already raw knuckles bled. At that point I was shaking too much to continue.

"Stop having conniptions, Mary," I told myself. "It's not as if you killed him or anything. He'll be healed in two seconds. Won't even get scars. So why are you acting like a two-year-old?" A drop rolled down my face. I was shaken, not because I had hurt Baro, but because for a split second as I had been attacking him like a crazed maniac, I had almost enjoyed it, reveling in the feeling of fist squarely hitting face.

There was a knock on my door. I jumped from guilt but stayed quiet.

"Princess, are you in there? You need to let someone see to your injuries." It was Breeohan. I would know his smooth baritone voice anywhere. I stayed silent. "May I come in?" he asked. Then in a lower, quieter voice, he said, "Mary, please let me in."

My eyes were glued to the door, wishing he would come in but also wishing he would go away. After a few minutes I heard his steps as he walked off.

I woke to the sound of knocking. A glance at my window showed a brilliant orange and red sky against the few clouds hovering overhead. I lay on top of the soft feather mattress and all the covers, still dressed in the outfit I had fought Baro in. My knuckles stung, and my jaw hurt, so it took me a few seconds to get my mouth to creak open.

"Come in," I said, still too groggy to form any coherent thoughts.

"Princess, I was pleasantly surprised to see you fight so well this afternoon. It was amazing. I haven't ever seen jova matches where the weapon is no weapon."

I couldn't see him, but Rafan's gravelly voice wound around the bed curtains like a saw to my ears. He walked to where I could see him, smiling broadly.

"Can I help you with something?" I tried to sound as if I hadn't just woken up, but I was still feeling groggy and wasn't sure I pulled it off.

"I am here to help you. There is to be a formal dinner tonight held in your honor, and I wanted to make sure you made it to your feast."

I didn't want to go. I was sure I would be gawked at, talked at, and just plain stressed out by trying to act royal rather than rural.

"What's this? Your jaw is bruised, and your hands .... Let me heal them for you."

"No thanks, I've got it," I said, and with a swift twist, I healed myself.

Rafan's frown almost looked like a pout. "I brought you another dress for dinner." He threw a dark blue gown onto the bed next to me.

"How did you get these dresses so quickly?"

"I can't reveal all my secrets. If I did, I would have nothing to keep your interest." He was back in charmer mode.

I tried not to roll my eyes. "Well, thank you, Rafan. I'll put it on right away." We regarded each other for a minute, me pointedly, he obliviously.

Finally, he shifted his feet uncomfortably. "I shall send in Sentai to dress you and will wait outside to escort you to dinner."

His eyes looked expectant, but I had no idea what he wanted. "Thanks."

A woman in a plain purple and gold outfit entered as Rafan left. "Good evening, Princess. I have been assigned as your maid here in the palace. Would you like to dress now?"

"All right." I eyed her warily. I was in uncharted territory when it came to servants and what I was supposed to do with one. "Are you Sentai?" I took off my outer clothes and quickly pulled the dress over my head. It was embarrassing to be seen in my undies by a complete stranger.

Instead of answering, the maid made a funny noise, something between a gasp and a sob.

"What?" I looked around the room quickly. "What's wrong?"

"I am sorry, Princess, that I displease you. I will inform my superior that you desire a different servant." She backed toward the door.

"Why? You haven't done anything. What would I be displeased about?" I felt flustered.

"I am sorry for speaking without permission." She ducked her head to stare at the ground.

What in the world? "Look, Sentai, in my country everyone, including servants, can speak whenever they want to. So I would feel a lot better if you would just tell me what you usually do. I think we would both avoid a lot of confusion that way."

"Yes, Princess." She still looked at the ground.

I waited again, hoping my silence would make her crack. She was much better at staying silent than I was. "So, are you going to tell me what I did wrong?" I asked.

"Princess, you are always correct in whatever you wish to do."

"What's that? When you look down and mumble to the floor, I can't be sure if I hear you correctly. I thought you said whatever I do is right, but you couldn't have said that. I am the queen of blunders. Believe me, once you get to know me a little better, you will take back your words."

My speech was odd enough to make Sentai look up, her eyes filled with confusion. I gave my goofiest grin. "Now would you please tell me what I did to upset you? This place is confusing to me, and I could really use your help. That is, if you wouldn't mind."

She pointed hesitantly to my dress, which was still unbuttoned. "If you please, it is usually the maid's job to dress her mistress."

"What is wrong with these nobles? Can't they even dress themselves? They have to get someone else to do if for them?" I burst out in frustration.

At my words, Sentai backed up and fixed her gaze to the floor.

"Hey, look, I'm sorry. I'm not mad at you. I'm just feeling a little overwhelmed. Some things here just don't make any sense to me. Forgive me?"

"The lady may do whatever she wishes," she said to the floor.

I sighed, suddenly tired. *Me and my stupid tongue*. I decided to give up for the moment. "Would you mind helping me button my dress? And you wouldn't happen to do hair and makeup would you?"

She nodded, still not looking into my eyes, and moved to help me with the buttons I could easily have done up myself. I felt silly having Sentai do it, but I gritted my teeth and bore it.

She motioned for me to sit at the curved desk with a framed round mirror attached to it and then began to comb out my hair. The next thing I knew, she was looping strands into curly-cues, somehow making the hair stay. I caught the flash of a pattern and realized that she was using magic to do my hair. I turned around mid-curl.

"You're a mage," I said, making a note of what she'd done.

"No, Princess, I can only do a few simple lacings on my mistress's behalf." She kept her eyes lowered.

"Well, I think it's great. I didn't even think of using a lacing to *curl* my hair, just to color it. Sorry for the interruption." I turned around again to face the mirror. In the reflection I saw Sentai looking baffled. I must be acting really odd for a noble, but I wasn't sure what they normally acted like, other than snobbish, which I didn't want to do. I decided to just keep acting like myself. Maybe Sentai would get used to me and learn that she didn't have to be so guarded all the time.

It didn't take her long to make my hair look like a work of art. She had woven a small blue tiara into my hair, using part of my own locks as padding so it would be less uncomfortable than Rafan's golden headdress. Next was makeup. I was a little wary about this part since no one at court seemed to know what subtle meant.

"Do you think we could just do a little makeup? I don't feel comfortable in a mask."

She nodded, turning me away from the mirror. I fidgeted and then felt bad about making application even harder for Sentai, so I concentrated on sitting still. This was so unlike going to the hairdresser. I missed the meaningless chatter of the salon at home, even though I had always hated having to think of things to say to the stylist. Silence was worse.

Finally, Sentai turned me back toward the mirror. She had brushed on blue eye shadow, but mixed with the blue was some brown, making it seem featherlike rather than garish. At the corner of my eyes she had drawn graceful flowers, which were mirrored in reality throughout my hair. My rouge was brownish red, and my lipstick a neutral color. I felt transformed.

"It's wonderful, Sentai. Thank you."

Sentai ducked her head.

This dress had white embroidery and white beads hanging from the pants and sleeves, contrasting sharply with the midnight blue of the fabric. Rafan had left white sandals on the bed. These fit, but I couldn't figure out how to lace the leather up my ankle. Sentai came to my rescue.

"I guess I'm ready to go." I felt a strong reluctance to leave my room. Sentai made it impossible to loiter, however, for she went straight to the door and opened it. There, leaning against the door frame, Rafan waited to escort me. I sighed.

"Are you ready, Princess?" He held out his hand, palm down. I put my palm on his as he and Breeohan had taught me, and we walked, elbows stiffly squared, all the way to the banquet hall.

The doorman from that morning was waiting for us. *Man, that guy is everywhere,* I thought. He repeated our names as we walked into another huge chamber. Everything about the palace seemed to be super-sized. A table snaked around the room in a half circle, and everyone was already sitting down. Apparently, I was a little late. Why hadn't Rafan told me to hurry? I felt my cheeks go hot from all the staring—it was what all these people seemed to do. They stared at me in the reception hall, in the jova courts, and now from their secure seated positions at the table. It was hard to bear, considering that I had spent my entire life avoiding notice from strangers.

The king stood from the center of the curved table, and everyone else followed suit. "Princess, be welcomed. We are honored to have you in our kingdom and hope that you will stay for as long as you like." His eyes were intense in their nearly all-golden hue. He gestured to a place at his left. Breeohan was sitting on the king's right. Rafan bowed to me flamboyantly, then walked to a seat slightly further down the table.

I felt exposed. Walking slowly, I kept my head up, trying not to imagine what the courtiers were thinking about me. Did they think me barbaric because of my episode in the jova courts? Had I already blown my cover? If so, would the king be forced to publicly denounce me once I reached the table? My thoughts kept whirling, but I tried to keep my face calm. They certainly *would* suspect something fishy if I looked like a frightened rabbit.

When I reached my chair, I stood, waiting until the king sat. When he did, there was a wavelike motion as everyone sat again. I stared at my golden goblet, unsure what to do. The king blocked Breeohan from view, and the curve of the table was so gradual that I couldn't see Rafan, despite his being only a few seats away. I glanced covertly to see who was on my right, but saw only a dark orange dress before the woman shifted to look in my direction. I swiveled my gaze to my hands, hoping the woman hadn't noticed.

Several servants holding huge trays of food dispersed themselves evenly along the empty inner curve of the table. One stood before the king, set his tray down, and bowed as he backed away. It wasn't till that moment that I noticed how quiet the room had been. With the appearance of the food, the noise level increased to a low roar as courtiers chatted with those close to them. I was startled to hear my "princess name."

"So you are Princess Kasala. I didn't have the opportunity to see you earlier, though I heard you were quite busy displaying your talents."

I looked to the woman on my right. She smiled as if to assure me she meant no harm. Though she wasn't a particularly gorgeous woman, her smile lit her face into prettiness. The dark orange silk of her dress hung loosely on her twiglike frame. I was glad to see that her makeup was subtle in comparison to the vivid orange fabric of her dress. She'd used mostly browns to complement her dark chocolate skin, with just a hint of orange in her eye shadow and two small citrine gems at her temples. "Baro deserved a lesson in humility, if you ask me. He is always trying to humiliate people in the jova courts. He often succeeds, but I hear you surprised him," she said.

I had been dividing my attention between this woman and the king's movements, finding it disconcerting to be sitting so nonchalantly next to the ruler of an entire country. At the mention of the jova courts, I felt a sudden stillness to my left.

"It was really stupid of me to accept his challenge," I said quickly, focused on the king's lack of movement, but not daring to actually look at him.

"Oh, but you must accept a challenge once it has been declared, or you would be labeled a coward," the lady said.

"Perhaps that would have been better than acting like a barbarian. Where I come from, we do not take hurting people as lightly as you do here. My behavior today was unacceptable, and . . ." I hesitated, not sure if I should say anymore. "I think if anyone else challenges me, I will decline from now on."

The lady's eyebrows rose. I heard a cough on my left and turned to the king.

"I was surprised to hear of you participating in the jova courts today, especially knowing where you come from. But it would not be wise to decline all challenges from now on. It gives ill-wishers a means to discredit you. You are allowed only one challenge a week, however, so it shouldn't monopolize your time."

My eyes flitted back toward the lady on my right. The man on her other side had distracted her with a comment, and she had turned to talk with him. "Sire, I took karate for ten years. Have you ever heard of it? Well, we only sparred without weapons. I don't think I would be able to use any real weapons against an opponent without getting seriously hurt."

"If you wish, I can have you work with my training general, Prince Sogran. I need to introduce you to him anyway."

"Will he cut me up?" I asked apprehensively.

"You might get a little bruised, but Sogran is a very good teacher. He will only hurt you if the pain will teach you a lesson. And you will have to overcome your squeamishness if you want to fight well. Healing yourself is not difficult," he said.

"I forget how easy it is for people to suddenly be well again without even scars. I wonder if it's always a good thing." I clamped my mouth shut, remembering belatedly that I was talking to a king.

"I agree with you. We get too comfortable with injuring each other, knowing that there will be no permanent consequences. But there are things we cannot fix. It is next to impossible to cure someone who has been poisoned because we have to exactly determine the poison before we can fix it. We also lose people to illnesses often. No one can figure out how to cure colds."

"I can see how it would be harder to find the patterns for those things. Viruses mutate constantly."

"It's been a long time since I have heard anyone talk as you do," the king murmured, smiling.

His comment reminded me of his earlier confession, and I was ready to burst with all the questions I wanted to ask him. But the king shook his head, warning me not to say anything about Earth at the table. He was right. Too many people could overhear us. But I was starting to feel that I was never going to get any answers from the king.

I wondered how long the king had stayed on Earth. How much of what I said would King Verone understand? Who were the other magicians who had gone to Earth? A thought finally popped to the surface that had been just beyond my grasp before. If magicians had gone to Earth before, could that mean that my father was one of those magicians? No one on Earth had magic like I did. It made sense to leap to the conclusion that I got it from Esa. For all I knew, the king himself could be my dad. He had gone there, after all. But the thought was too ridiculous. I would ask the king later which other magicians had gone to Earth.

"In honor of your presence, I think we will have to have a ball." King Verone raised his voice a little, interrupting me from my wild musings.

I saw Breeohan's head poke around the king and look at me. But before I could smile a hello at him, he turned to the king. "Your Majesty, perhaps we should wait for Princess Kasala to feel more at home before planning such a big event."

"Breeohan, are you trying to offend her? You know that to not have a ball in her honor would be a grave insult." The king raised his eyes in the same kind of look Mom gave me sometimes when I was being particularly difficult.

The lady next to me spoke up. "Did I hear you say we were to have a ball? It would only be proper to formally welcome the princess into our midst." She gave me a nudge. "And I would love to be able to perform the musical pieces I uncovered from the palace's archives. It would be wonderful."

Breeohan's lips pressed tightly. "Why don't you perform the pieces here at the banquet?"

"Oh, don't be silly. I am not ready tonight. But I will be in a few days if the king will allow it." The lady looked at the king for consent.

"We will be honored to hear what you have uncovered," King Verone answered. His lack of inflection made me think that perhaps he wasn't really looking forward to the performance.

But the lady didn't seem to notice. "Wonderful. I will tell my players of our luck as soon as we are dismissed from dinner." Her eyes brightened with excitement.

"You must be Lady Aria," I said, suddenly putting her comments together with what Breeohan had told me about her.

"Yes, oh, I am sorry for not introducing myself. It completely slipped my mind." A huge smile lit her face. I found it hard to think of her as Rafan's older sister. Her manner was so uncomplicated, and even as I talked to her, Aria's eyes unfocused, looking above my head. She spaced out for almost a minute before she jerked her head back toward me, remembering that we had been talking.

"I hope you won't be offended, but I am a bit scatterbrained at times. I guess I spend too much time in the archives and not enough with people. That's what my husband tells me anyway. Oh, this is my husband, by the way, Zefan Kree." She indicated the man to her right whom she'd been talking to before. He nodded in my direction after Aria tugged on his shirt.

"Nice to meet you, Zefan Kree," I said. He nodded again and turned back to his food. I wondered if Zefan Kree spent a little too much time in the archives as well.

"I can't wait for you to hear what we have been preparing. Some of the music I have uncovered hasn't been played in generations. I have been recopying all the old manuscripts so that they will not be lost to decay. Do you play an instrument, Princess?"

"No, not since I was little."

"That's too bad. I would have loved to hear what Kirosan had to offer. Do you sing at all?"

"Unfortunately not." I felt no guilt for lying.

"Oh well. I suppose I have enough to do as it is without getting involved in studying your country's music."

"I am sure that is quite a task." I was starting to run on autopilot, having lost most of my interest in the conversation. Aria was nice, but I was worried about the ball, and it was hard to concentrate on the topic of music when questions like, *How do they dance here?* and, *What will be expected of a princess at a ball?* kept popping into my head.

I chatted pointlessly with Aria as food arrived and was carried away again, the whole time wishing I could talk to the king or Breeohan about what I'd need to know for this ball. However, the king was busy whispering to Breeohan, and it turned out Zefa Aria was anything but scatterbrained when discussing finding and restoring old music manuscripts.

I was having a hard time keeping my eyes open when the king finally stood to dismiss the courtiers. "I would like to announce that we will have a ball in honor of the princess in five days' time. I hope you will all join me in making the princess feel welcomed," King Verone said.

Chairs screeched against the floor as all the courtiers stood to leave. The king strode off with Breeohan, dashing my hopes of conferring with either of them. I stood slowly, not wishing to talk to anyone on my way out. Everyone seemed to be in a hurry to leave, so I didn't have to wait long before the room was mostly empty. I waved good-bye to Aria and her husband as they walked off, then slowly slunk from the room, avoiding the few groups of people still gathered.

I had no energy to talk with Sentai as she helped me undress and take down my hair. I activated the cleaning lacing on myself, relieved to feel a makeup free face, then I toppled into the feather bed and fell asleep.

Chapter 12

I woke well before the sun rose, having gotten used to little sleep on the road. I dressed in my peasant shirt, vest, and pants, since the only other pants I had were the ones that went with the dresses. There was no way I was going to wear a dress if I didn't have to, so I settled for my familiar traveling clothes. I wandered around the palace for awhile, passing through one high vaulted hallway to another, occasionally glancing into open doors and stopping at particularly interesting wall hangings.

Several people in what I recognized as servant garb passed me once in awhile. I smiled and said hello. They looked startled and walked away without answering. I figured I was probably committing another Iberloahan social faux pas, but I didn't care. I was in a good mood. My jaunt through the palace was invigorating. After awhile, though, I started to get hungry. I was just getting really lost when a servant passed by, toting a big tray of food.

"Could you show me the way to Princess Kasala's room?" I asked. He nodded, glanced at me knowingly, and signaled for me to walk ahead of him. I wondered how he knew I was someone of importance in my ordinary travel clothes. His walking behind me was a nuisance because I couldn't tell if he wanted to turn until I had gone too far, and he politely coughed at me. I would then have to wind my way back to him and walk ahead before he would start moving again. His coughs were just becoming the Pavlovian signal for me to attack when we reached my door.

"Thanks a bunch," I said as I hurried inside, but he coughed once more. I controlled a sudden urge to hit something. "Can I help you?"

He held up the platter of food and nodded his head toward the inside of my room. He seemed to want to get it inside without actually giving it to me. But by this time I was fed up, so I just took it from him and shut the door. I felt a little guilty afterwards, but when I opened the door again to apologize he was already gone. Sentai was at my side by then, taking the platter from me. She ushered me to sit at a little table at the north side of the chamber, where she set the tray down. I plopped down, still feeling a little like a heel but famished from my morning's activities.

"Do you want to join me?" I asked Sentai, restraining my hand from snapping out to the juicy fruit on my plate.

"It would not be proper."

I shrugged, unwilling to argue. The food looked strange but tasted surprisingly good. It was a nice change after the breakfasts I'd experienced so far in Iberloah. I saved the strange fruit for last and savored every sweet morsel.

I couldn't help feeling uncomfortable with Sentai just watching me as I ate. The silence seemed strained. I wiped my fingers. "So, what are your plans for today, Sentai?"

"I will do as you wish me to do."

"What do you *want* to do?"

"Whatever my mistress wishes."

My headache, brought on by the male servant and dispelled by food, started to reappear. "Well, I would like you to do whatever you want. I think I will go find the training general so I can start my lessons. Take a break, talk to your friends."

"I will have the seamstresses make more clothes for you, if that is acceptable."

"Don't approve of my outfit, eh?" I had noticed Sentai's look of dismay when I walked in with breakfast. "Well, I guess clothes are a good idea, but you don't have to do it. I could go. Do I need to be measured or anything?"

"Forgive me, but it would not be proper for you to go. I will take your measurements now and order the clothes, if you will allow?" She gestured with a string.

I shrugged then stood, arms stretched out as she took my measurements. She knotted the string at each different length, and then bowed. "Do you require anything before I go?"

"Nope, I'm great. Thanks."

She bowed again and left the room. I headed out the door as well, in search of the training general. Even though I didn't want to get beat up, I was curious about what sort of weapons he would train me in, and I had nothing better to do.

I didn't get quite as lost as I had earlier, but I still had to retrace my steps three times to find my way out of the palace. I walked from a dark hallway into searing brightness. The sun wrapped me with soothing fingers, and the open sky made me realize how good it felt to get out of the palace's inner webwork.

I decided to go left along the outer wall of the palace since all I could see were palm gardens and cobbled walkways. I soon reached the entrance where I'd first entered the palace, and from there I could see the building I thought most likely to be a barracks. That place seemed as good as any to find people bashing each other, so I headed in that direction. I was hoping the sound of grunts and yells would assail my ears as I got closer so I would know which part of the huge building to walk to, but the place seemed eerily silent. Finally, I literally bumped into a guard in purple who was kind enough to show me the way to the barrack's door, though I had to put up with walking ahead of him.

We walked in to a melee of shouts, grunts, the cracks of weapons, basically the sounds I had been listening for but wouldn't have heard through the thick stone walls. There was no way I would hear any polite coughing to tell me if I was headed in the wrong direction once inside, so I just strode toward the practice court, looking for someone who had the air of a teacher.

I found him in the third practice ring of five spread throughout the building. There were narrow walkways to the side of the training platforms where wooden and metal weapons were stacked against the walls. The man I assumed to be the training general was wearing a loose version of the purple guard livery, as were all the other fighters, but he stood watching a pair of fighters with a commanding air. When one man hesitated with his long curved blade, he yelled an order to move faster. When the other man failed to strike properly, the broad-shouldered watcher commanded the offender to clean up his moves or risk losing an arm.

I turned back to see the guard still behind me. "Is that the training general?"

"Yes, Princess. I will fetch him for you."

"No, don't interrupt him. I'll talk to him when he's through with the pair . . ." It was at this point that I noticed he hadn't heard me in time and had already rushed off to whisper in the training general's ear.

The general looked sharply at me, his mostly golden eyes lined with a smidgen of brown around the rim. Their shape and color were very much like the king's eyes, and I tried to picture the pedigree chart in my head to remember where the training general fit. He had gray in his hair and a few crow's feet extending from his eyes, but this only gave him a look of weathered steel. I felt intimidated, despite my efforts at nonchalance. I took an unconscious step back, wishing I'd found some other activity to occupy my time.

He shouted a halt to the pair he was observing, and they dropped their swords to their sides with the speed of exhaustion. The training general dismissed them and walked over to me.

"You really didn't have to do that," I almost yelled so I would be heard over the crashing.

"You are Princess Kasala." It was a statement. His look had none of the deferential behavior I was begrudgingly starting to get used to, but instead of comforting me, it made me even more jumpy. It was far too intense.

"Yes," I said too quietly to be heard, but he shocked me by bowing at my reply. It was the bow of a prince to a princess, and I remembered hearing the king mention that he was Prince Sogran. I bowed back, awkward in my movements, and had to straighten up quickly so I wouldn't embarrass myself by stumbling.

"Come with me to a private training room. We will be able to hear each other better there," he said. I knew his wish for more quiet was to spare my own voice, for I could hear the training general perfectly despite the noise. He had the kind of voice that carried without effort. It boomed with authority without being deafening. I turned, unsure of where I was supposed to be hierarchy-wise in the leading/following tradition of Iberloah. The training general relieved my worry by taking the lead in a brisk manner. Had the king told him who I really was? There were so many things that I didn't know yet. I felt panicky.

He led me through a door at the end of the building into another room with a lone practice area. The door shut, and I was shocked by the sudden silence. I wanted to scuff the floor to make some sort of sound, but I didn't want to do the wrong thing. So I stood, hands behind my back, staring at his purple shirt rather than at his face, feeling stupid for acting so cowed. I remembered that the king had called the training general "Sogran," but I doubted anyone else dared call him by anything but his title.

"The king has informed me that I am to help you prevent a ride with the winds by training you to fight with weapons. I saw your fight yesterday."

I looked up into his face and was shocked to see a slight smile form on his lips. I wondered if he always regarded people with such intensity. It was as if my face was a foreign text he intended to decipher.

"You did well. I have never seen a style of fighting quite like yours. I will teach you because the king has asked it of me, but I would hope that you may show me some of your methods as well." He still had a slight smile on his face, and I couldn't decide if it made him look less formidable or not. I was leaning toward not.

"Um, sure," I said.

"Let us start then." He lifted one of the wicked-looking curved long swords I had seen the men in the practice arena using.

"Could we maybe start with wooden swords, or something a little less sharp?" The words popped out before I thought about how the steely man would react. He laughed. I almost jumped.

"Verone mentioned that you were unused to our ways. You will need to learn to adjust if you want to survive here."

I was still getting over the shock of someone in this culture calling the king by his name when the second part of what he said struck me. "Survive? I thought the mages could heal any injury one might get from fighting in the jova courts."

"Not everything."

That sounded ominous. "What can't mages heal?" I asked.

"Sometimes when a weapon bites into the skin and a mage heals the wound, the wounded man gets a high fever and dies. No one knows why, other than it has something to do with old or dirty weapons. Sometimes weapons are poisoned. There has been nothing found that can heal such cases unless the mage knows what poison was used and the pattern of that poison. So you see, you must be better than your attacker and not get cut. In order to overcome your attacker, you must practice with the actual weapon. If we practiced with a wooden sword, you would not learn to handle the heft of the real blade. You would misjudge your moves."

I thought of the stab wound I had suffered from the thugs who attacked Breeohan and me. If that knife had been infected, Breeohan wouldn't have been able to save me. I would've died despite all his efforts. It was a chilling thought, and one that didn't inspire me to take the long sword from the training general's hands.

He thrust it into my palm anyway and immediately attacked. I was so stunned I barely brought the weapon up in time to defend his snakelike strike. He struck again, and I awkwardly moved the sword to block, fear running like ice through my body. It was like the fight with the thug all over again, except this time my opponent really knew what he was doing with his weapon. I was scared into block after block. The only thing keeping me from getting diced into little pieces was adrenalin. I was simply incapable of anything but frantic counters to his powerful strokes. All my years of working with that wooden samurai disappeared into a fog as I barely avoided death strokes to my body.

Finally he put down his sword. "You have some skill, but it only shows in bursts. You are too afraid."

My arms shook as I warily lowered my weapon. I wanted to say, "What do you expect me to do when a huge guy I barely met comes charging at me with a sword?"

"We learn differently where I am from," I said. *We don't charge the person before teaching them anything,* I thought sourly.

I must have been glaring or maybe he caught the criticism in my voice for he said, "It is not for the student to teach, but the master."

"That's strange. My mother always told me that a good teacher often learns more from the student than the student does from the teacher." My near-death experience had done a funny thing to me. I found myself feeling bolder with the training general. I must have disconnected a wire in my brain during my struggle because I felt like egging him on.

At the mention of Mom, Sogran's expression softened so that steel seemed suddenly transformed to flesh. It was over in an instant, but it left me confused. He raised an incredulous eyebrow. "You speak strong words against an opponent who could kill you if he chose."

My confusion fled in the heat of my frustration. "Is everything about being mightier than someone else?" I was so sick of the stupid power struggle here. It seemed to go on everywhere. It irked me that Sogran thought he was better than me just because he had more fighting skill. *Big whoop. I could dance circles around him in human anatomy.*

"That is an unusual question from a princess." His face was unreadable.

"What can I say? I'm an enigma." I jutted my chin into what Mom called my "no longer capable of reason" face.

"You may want to watch what you say around certain people. They might decide that you are more trouble than a visiting princess should be."

My mouth, about to say something else, clamped closed. *Was that a threat?* The hand gripping my sword twitched as I heard him chuckle. "So, you *can* learn. That's good. You will need to stay sharp to survive this country."

Now I was really confused. It was impossible to make heads or tails of this guy. His responses were so foreign to me. I felt like I was still speaking English and had never learned the language lacing that made it possible for me to speak and understand Iberloahan.

The training general walked over, took my sword, and adjusted my hands on the hilt the way he wanted them. My confusion made me feel oddly like silly putty as he shaped my position. He then stood next to me. "Follow my movements." He swung his sword up in a block to his head, and I copied him as he swung from one move to the next.

He started slowly, but I found that the blocks were only slightly different from what I had learned in karate class, so he didn't often have to halt and correct my angle. When we were moving at a quick pace, he suddenly stopped. I hesitated as well. "Keep moving," he commanded. He moved opposite me and struck as I moved through the blocking routine he had shown me. It was much harder to stay in the flow of the movements when there was a sword clashing against mine.

I felt myself reacting a little too slowly. Any minute I knew that the training general would whack me. "Could we stop for just a second?" I panted.

"Do you think your attacker will stop if you ask him to?"

He wasn't even sweating. Perspiration poured from my face and soaked my shirt. "No. But if I go much longer I'm going to vomit all over you." It was too much effort to say anymore.

The training general stepped back suddenly. I thought maybe he was averse to vomit, but when I dropped my sword with a thud and looked back up at his face, there was the hint of a smile. "You are a strange girl, Mary."

My mouth dropped open, and I plunked to the floor, panting and looking up at him dumbfounded. "You knew the whole time. The king told you?"

"Yes."

"Then what was with all that stuff about princesses, huh?"

"I wanted to learn some things about you, and I have."

"What, that I'm tactless and don't really act like a princess?"

"Yes, as well as other things." He didn't say any more, and I didn't really want to hear how many deficiencies I'd revealed in one sword lesson.

"I guess I'll go wash up now." I used the sword as a crutch to help me up and walked stiffly to the door I'd come through.

"Don't go that way. This door will lead you outside rather than through the training courts. Be here tomorrow during the third day portion."

I had been hoping he wouldn't say anything about another lesson, so I could just pretend that I didn't know I was supposed to come again. But it would be a lot harder to plead ignorance of daily lessons now that he had set a time. *Drat him.*

I'd turned to go, when Sogran's voice stopped me. "Verone said he told you that he had been to Earth. Did he also tell you that I have been there?"

I spun around as if hit from behind. "You've been there, too? How many others have gone there? When did you go?"

"I know of only two others who have also gone to Earth, though there could be others from other countries. The king and I went there together some years ago." He stared at me in the same way the king had in his office. I could tell this was all I was going to get out of Sogran. As if to confirm this, he turned and walked out of the training room without another word.

I headed back to my room slowly, dragging my feet at every step.

When I returned, Sentai informed me that she could only find one outfit that would fit me immediately. I would have to wait for the rest to be sewn.

"It's because I'm so tall, isn't it? Sorry about that. I always had a hard time finding long enough clothes at home, and there were hundreds of options to choose from." I stopped, remembering that I was supposed to be from a country that also lacked clothing stores.

Sentai opened her mouth as if about to say something and closed it again. I tried to look politely curious in order to draw her words from her, but she kept her mouth shut.

"What's next for today? I'm hungry. Do you think I could get some food?"

"I will bring it immediately." Sentai stood quickly.

"Thanks. Sorry to make you work so much. You know I could get it myself if you want to keep sitting." Sentai looked at me again as if she wished to say something but couldn't decide if she should.

"What? Please tell me. I'd rather know."

"You asked me to help you to adjust to Ismar's social etiquette." There was another long pause, and I tried to keep a look of eager interest instead of frustration. Why was she so reluctant to talk to me? "There are those here at court, powerful people, who do not like you. They will look for ways to hurt you, and I'm afraid if they see how you treat servants, they will use that knowledge to accuse you of not really being a princess." She watched my face intensely as she spoke, seeming to search for some sign that she had gone too far.

"And what would happen then?" My stomach gave a nervous flutter.

"Their words have power, and they could make your life more than difficult. If they claim you are an imposter, you would no longer be around to bother the natural order of things." Her eyes were earnest, and I realized with a chill that she meant I could be killed. She must suspect I wasn't who I claimed to be either. What I really needed was to get out of Ismar as fast as possible, but I still had no idea where to go.

"I'll try to be more discreet. Thank you for your help, Sentai. I really appreciate it."

She nodded and looked around, as if trying to remember something, and then slipped out the room. It hadn't occurred to me that I could be killed if someone found out that I wasn't a real princess. However, it made sense from all that I had seen of Iberloah so far. If they thought I was really someone of a lower class, they might become afraid that other lower-class people would realize that there was no real difference between them and royalty. It would ruin the nobles' cushy set up. There was no way anyone of the upper class would stand for that.

I was in a deeper hole than I had realized and for the first time since coming to Ismar, a shroud of Freon-numbing fear gripped me. I felt close to shattering. My breath whooshed in and out for a few minutes before I could think straight again. No wonder Breeohan had seemed so tense since coming to the palace. I suddenly felt angry at Breeohan for getting me into this situation.

There was a knock on my door, and I jumped. I had to clear my throat before I could manage a feeble, "Who is it?"

"It's Rafan."

I rolled my eyes and reluctantly went to the door, opened it a little, and then stood wedged between the door and the wall. "What can I do for you, Rafan?"

"Princess, I was hoping you would join me for a stroll in the gardens. But if you are busy . . ."

"I'm sorry. Sentai was just going to bring me some food, and I'm really hungry. Maybe we could go for a walk later." I edged back through the door slightly, but didn't want to close it in his face.

He didn't take the hint. "Ah, may I join you? We can take a walk after your meal."

I didn't really feel like company, but I couldn't think of any excuse to get rid of him that wouldn't be rude and dangerous, considering he knew

I wasn't a real princess and could use that knowledge against me. Rafan was a wild card. I felt like he wanted something from me, but I had no idea what. I decided it'd be better to humor the guy than to let on that I thought of his flattery as gilded hogwash.

"That would be nice. Come in, Rafan. Have a seat." I smiled and moved so that he could enter. I opened the door wider and left it that way as I motioned him toward a chair at the table in my outer chamber.

"So how's your day been so far? Done anything interesting?" I asked, trying to be conversational.

"Nothing of much importance. I have been resting up from my trying time in the city."

I had no response to that. Did he want me to ask about his adventures in the city? I nodded, trying to look interested.

"You really have no idea of what it is like to have to be dirty all the time."

I thought it was kind of forgetful of him to say that since he knew I'd traveled for a week without being able to wash most of the time. I smiled though and tried to look sympathetic, not even tempted to show him my cleaning lacing.

"That must have been hard for you." I hated these kinds of conversations. It was difficult to keep looking interested.

"The whole undertaking was worth the effort since I was able to meet you at the end of it. That is a handsome reward I had no way of knowing I would be given."

My cheeks ached, and my smile felt ironic. I tried a smaller one hoping to look more sincere.

Sentai came back at that moment, saving me from having to respond to his remark. She hesitated before setting the food on the little table before Rafan and me. Then she faded into a shadow against the wall. I remembered not to thank her. It was probably a good idea to start acting more princesslike, even in front of someone who knew I wasn't a princess. The tray was obviously made for one person, but I offered Rafan part of my food anyway.

He refused politely and sat watching as I gnawed on bread. The bread was soft in my hands, but it stuck in my mouth and refused to go down. It was unnerving to have him watch me eat. Though not full, I couldn't clear more than a third of the plate. His gaze stuck to me until the taste of the delicate fruit turned sour.

"I'm ready," I said, pushing my plate away with regret.

"Good. I will take you to the south garden since you couldn't have seen it as we came in." He held out his arm, and I took it with a mental shrug.

We walked through more hallways, past embroidered hangings and stone carvings, until I was hopelessly lost again. When we finally reached a large archway with the doors wide open to the outside, I saw green, broad-leafed plants defying the heat of the sun by looking almost junglelike. Trees and flowers grew in a wild tangle, only kept at bay around the sand-stone cobbled paths by dedicated gardeners, or so I was informed. It was a remarkable inconsistency in the dry and hostile land. Rafan led me to the shade of the path, keeping my arm in a stiff square at our sides. My muscles started to ache from the strain of holding steady after wearing myself out that morning with the training general, but I didn't want to be rude by ripping my hand away from his.

When I couldn't stand it any more, I tried a lame diversion trick. I took my hand from his and pointed at a purple vine twisting up one of the trees. "What do you call that plant? I've never seen anything like it before." I quickly reached for one of the strange purple leaves before he could reclaim my hand. The leaf was rubbery with large black veins weaving its surface like embroidery.

"It is a dorkee plant. They grow best in places where there is almost constant shade, though there is a tougher version of the plant that is a horrible muddy brown-purple. That variety grows almost everywhere you don't want it to."

I walked ahead of him to the next plant, trying to look engrossed at the little yellow flowers growing in a clump next to the path. I heard indistinct chatter ahead and looked at Rafan to see if he still wanted to go on. He showed no sign of being deterred, however, so I continued on with him, touching a leaf here and a flower there so that I wouldn't have to strain to keep my arm placed on his.

The path widened, and Rafan and I came upon people. My fists clenched as I saw Avana sitting on a rock bench, purple skirts fanned perfectly about her, with one panted leg artistically peeping out. Next to her sat Doln Baro. She was laughing daintily at something Baro said. When she noticed Rafan and me, her lips tightened, all traces of laughter gone. Baro's eyes narrowed, and his brown face turned reddish brown.

"Zefa Avana, how lovely to see you. You look like the sun itself," Rafan said smoothly. He smiled broadly as if at a secret joke.

"Doln Rafan, I am always pleased to see you." She stood and took his hand. Her head stayed fixed on him as she spoke, her eyes never wavering to include me in the welcome. "You know Doln Baro, of course." She waved her hand at Baro who was staring fixedly at me.

"Of course. We used to spar together to keep fit for the jova courts," Rafan said.

Baro's eyes swiveled toward Rafan, his face turning a deeper shade of puce.

"Well, it was so nice seeing you both again," I said pointedly. "Doln Rafan was showing me this fascinating garden, and I would really love to see more of it, so if you two don't mind we will let you continue the conversation we so rudely interrupted." I put my hand on Rafan's and walked us quickly away. The corners of Rafan's mouth curved skyward. I removed my hand again and reached out to pluck a leaf off the closest dorkee plant, shredding it into tiny pieces so that I wouldn't say something I would regret.

"Be careful. The dorkee plant stains," Rafan said, and sure enough purple sap was dyeing my fingertips. I dropped the leaf and tried to resume my former act of interest in the plants rather than looking agitated. After an eternity we reached the path's end. It was a relief to see the entrance to the palace.

"Thank you for taking me on the lovely tour of the garden. But I'm feeling a bit tired. I think I'd like to go to my room to rest now, if you don't mind."

"Not at all, I shall escort you back to your room. Shame to me for not realizing you were so fatigued." He flashed a solicitous look and then took my stained hand in the courtly gesture that seemed so possessive to me.

I really was tired. Despite all the toughening up I'd gone through on my journey here, the workout with Sogran had been arduous. I felt the need to take a catnap. Sentai wasn't in my room as Rafan led me through my door, but I didn't doubt she was off doing something else to help me seem more like a real princess rather than the imposter that I was. Thanking Rafan rather shortly, I closed the door on him before he could utter a sappy good-bye. I flopped on the bed and tried to get my brain to stop going a hundred miles an hour. Despite my fatigue, I couldn't stop thinking, so I finally gave up and got out my anatomy book to study the lacings of the human body.

Soon there was another knock on the door. I unraveled myself from the bed sheets and book images to answer it. This time it was a servant in the royal colors. I tried to look unconcerned rather than nervous by straightening my shoulders.

"Yes?"

"The king asks if you would join him if you are not already engaged." The servant looked all the time at the ground rather than at me.

"Of course. I'll come with you now." He nodded to the floor, turned, and then waited until I'd passed so that he could follow me through the corridors. I was glad there were so many people to help me figure out which way to go, but I so wished they would just lead the way. Instead, I led him through another merry chase full of polite coughs to redirect my course.

Finally we reached a spacious room with only one or two chairs against the wall. Nothing obstructed the beautiful marble floor, laid out in circles and diamonds in coral and off-white. I looked up from the floor to see the king in one of the chairs. He put down a stack of papers he was reviewing and stood, motioning the servant to close the door. The man bowed out, leaving only the king and me in the vast and empty room.

"Princess. It's nice to see you." His voice and facial expression made his words sound surprisingly and comfortingly sincere.

"Please, Sire, there is no one here but us. I would prefer you call me Mary when no one is around. I'm starting to dread the word 'princess.' "

"Mary, then." He paused as if mulling the sound of my name over, then shook his head. "Since we are having a ball, and a princess is expected to dance, I thought I would teach you as quickly as possible. I could have forced Sogran, but he would make me suffer for it. It is one thing to have him teach you weaponry—he likes that, and he likes you—but it is like digging for water in the sand dunes with bloodied hands to get him to dance at all, much less teach it."

I was glad to hear that Sogran liked me. I hadn't been sure by the end of our training session. "I'm sorry to trouble you, Your Majesty," I said.

"No trouble at all. Not much, anyway. I like to dance, though you will find many a better dancer. Besides, teaching you will give me a break from some of the more tedious tasks of the day. It also helps Breeohan learn to handle the repetitive drudgery of being a king." He smiled mischievously, which made him look very unkingly. I much preferred it.

"So how does one dance at an Iberloahan ball?" I bowed dramatically.

"It is similar to ballroom dance, but more stylized."

It felt so wonderful to hear him refer to ballroom dance that I couldn't help giving him an enormous grin. I could feel it stretch through my body, the kind of smile Mom usually inspired in me. He smiled back, eyes crinkling, sensing I think, what had made me so happy.

He held out his hand and led me to the center of the floor. "We can't risk asking for musicians while I teach you, so I hope you have a good imagination and at least a passable sense of rhythm."

"I played the piano as a kid."

"We don't have those here, though I hear they have something like it across the ocean in Krio. Now, let's get started. Right hand to right, and left to left. Left is high, and right is low in opposite arches like so. Next you step right, then forward with your left, right again forward, forward to the side." I was now at a right angle from the king. We repeated the steps so that my back was to him as he held my hands over my head, then to the side again. Finally, we faced each other once more.

"Now that is the simplest dance. It has a few variations." He showed me the more complicated steps one could do. I found them much easier to learn than I'd feared. Much of the ease, however, had to do with the king's ability to make it seem natural and fluid. He explained things very well. He was also patient when I stumbled, showing me the sequences I messed up on until I got it right.

"Do you know anything about Kirosan?" I asked as we moved around in the dance patterns.

"I know that Princess Kasala is twenty-five years old. You didn't appear to me to be twenty-five."

"I could tell you knew I was lying."

"Is that the only reason you and Breeohan decided to tell me the truth?" He sounded stern, and his smile vanished.

"No. Breeohan was going to tell you no matter what, and I didn't want to pretend to be a princess in the first place. I don't know why Breeohan thought it would be a better plan than just being me."

"Your eyes do create a problem."

"But why would it be so bad for an ordinary person to have gold eyes?"

"Our world is not quite like yours, Mary, as you have begun to discover. Equality is slow to emerge and there is only so much I can do to encourage that trend. You may think that kings are all powerful, but even a tyrant cannot have complete control, and I hope that I am not a tyrant. I walk a dune that constantly shifts under me so that I must hurriedly and repeatedly pull up my feet from the falling edges. I have tried to promote the notion that those who are not courtiers are worthy of the same respect, but it is like telling a sandstorm to turn its course.

"Even should you behave strangely, most would rather believe you an eccentric or heretic princess than a commoner. Gold flecks in courtier's eyes have stood for generations to mean that one has a superior heritage. If you had come to the palace with your royal golden eyes and claimed to be merely a commoner, you would be saying that the color doesn't mean anything. There are those who would have killed you on sight to stop that idea from spreading."

"I can't believe a whole culture would be so obsessed with eye color."

He smiled indulgently. "It is no stranger than the white men of your history who thought people with darker skin a subspecies."

I flushed, thinking of my grandfather and the discomfort my own darker complexion had brought me within Mom's family.

"They were stupid, too," I said bitterly.

"Yes, but such beliefs take years to undo, as you also know from your history."

"You certainly know a lot about my world."

His eyes became instantly distant. He turned me in the dance so that I could no longer read his expression, his silence a sudden weight.

I'd been feeling more comfortable with King Verone, but his reaction reminded me that he was still the king of an entire country, and I was simply a girl. He'd said he hoped he wasn't a tyrant, but did that mean he wasn't? Was there something to fear from him? I stumbled in my worry and almost stepped on his foot.

"I'm sorry, Your Majesty." I nervously looked to see if he was angry.

He must have read something of what I was feeling. "You must excuse me, Mary. I'm not angry, and I know you want very much to speak of Earth. You are far from home, and Sogran and I are the only ones you can talk to about it. But I am not sure what to say to you, and Sogran is sometimes difficult to decipher." He smiled ruefully. "Perhaps we have learned enough for today. I shall send for you tomorrow." He bowed the bow a king gives a princess, and I dipped into the bow reserved for a ruler. He went to the door, opened it for me, which surprised me once again, and asked his servant to show me the way back to my rooms. I turned back before going around a corner to see the king slumped against the side of the door frame, looking at nothing. I decided that Sogran was not the only person who was hard to understand.

Chapter 13

I wasn't required to go to dinner in the ballroom, so I stayed in my room. It had been a long day and after eating I went straight to bed. The next day I rose just in time to get dressed and meet the training general. He scowled at me as I entered the private sparring room. "You're late."

"I thought I just made it."

"To just make it is to be late. You should be waiting here for me to be free. I should not be waiting for you."

"I'll try to get here before you do next time," I said, exasperated.

"See that you do or I will work you so hard you *will* vomit, and then I will start all over again."

I shivered. What a stickler! I wasn't even late.

"Let's begin," he said.

We started out with the sword that he had used yesterday, but after awhile we switched to knife-work. I did worse with this because I had never worked with knives in karate. He had to show me how to hold the knife as well as explain the differences in body movement to compensate for using a shorter weapon.

Sogran finally got frustrated enough that he stopped me mid-stroke. "I think I will teach you only a few blocks and strikes with the knife. You are too used to working with weapons with longer reach. I will cure you of that later. For now, you need to learn at least two different weapons. I think I can work with you on the sword. You seem to have some background knowledge. Is there any other weapon we have that you would know how to use?"

"I practiced with staffs, sais, and nunchucks."

"I know what a staff is, but the words 'sais' and 'nunchuck' mean nothing to me. Could you show me if we have anything like them on the rack?"

He swept his arm over the rack of weapons against the wall.

I looked but didn't see anything similar. "I guess I will have to work with a staff."

"It would seem so. Grab those two staves, and we will begin."

The strikes were slightly different, but they were related enough that I was soon able to spar. I had to watch my hands. We had to stop a few times to fix bruises, and once my finger broke. Despite the quick healing, the pain taught me better than words. I swiftly learned how to protect myself.

By the time Sogran called a halt, I was gasping, my face so hot I could fry an egg on it.

"You are making too many mistakes. I don't want you to unlearn all that I have been trying to teach you. Come again tomorrow." He walked out of the room without a backward glance and without me ever getting the chance to ask him anything about his visit to Earth.

The sun outside struck me with a singular spike of heat as I walked slowly back to the palace's inner coolness. I was too exhausted to even feel satisfied when I reached my room without any wrong turns. A bath was waiting, for which I was grateful. I didn't have the energy to magically clean myself.

The king's servant came a half hour later to herd me toward another dancing lesson. All this cattle wrestling was forcing me to learn the palace layout more quickly than I otherwise would have. This time I only had to suppress my desire once to grab the servant's shirt front, shake him in frustration, and wrench him in front of me.

When we reached the dance room, the king was again going through papers. He certainly liked to utilize his time to the fullest. His brows furrowed in concentration over the paper he was examining, so he didn't notice me approach until I was standing right next to him. He looked up with the air of one whose mind is still mid-thought, but then his gaze focused on me. A smile blossomed.

"Mary, you are here. I'm starting to get a headache from squinting."

"What are you reading?"

"Oh, just some diplomatic dribble from the country next to us. Since we are mostly a desert country, we must watch our relations carefully with the surrounding countries so that we can import and export freely."

I leaned a little to get a look at the writing. It was all scribbles to me, and I realized that Breeohan had never taught me the lacing for writing. I hadn't needed to look at my map once Breeohan joined me in my journey.

"Do you know the lacing for your writing?" I asked.

"Yes, I can show you if you wish." He began constructing the lacing strand by strand in the air, each string a swirl of golden brown light. Though he did one piece at a time, he built the pattern quickly so that the lacing formed in a matter of seconds. "This is the thread you must change," he pointed. I studied it carefully for a moment and then performed the lacing. Instantly the words on the paper made sense. My eyes skimmed the flowery language until Breeohan's name popped out at me.

"We congratulate Zefan Breeohan on his recent attainment of Master's class, and await Iberloah's request of Tisimony's presence to impart of our esteem personally," I read aloud. "Who's Tisimony, a person or a country?"

"A country bordering ours. What that statement is really saying is that they wish to send some of their suitable young ladies in hopes that they can negotiate a marriage."

"Would you do it? Doesn't Breeohan have any say in the matter?" I massaged a sudden cramp in my stomach. The king's eyes dropped to my hands, and my palms stilled.

"I will not pretend that an alliance would not be unwelcome, but I have already told Breeohan that he may marry whomever he wishes. I will not force him. Shall we begin today's lesson?" He stood, dropping his papers onto the chair. His hand was warm and firm in mine as he guided me to the middle of the floor.

He took me through the steps we had learned yesterday as a review, then began to elaborate on those steps as well as teaching me the beginning steps of a new dance style that was much more flowing. It was harder to do, considering that much of it was done without touching the other person. I had to learn the steps thoroughly since the absence of a lead increased the probability that I might turn the wrong way.

We finally halted. I worried that I wouldn't remember it all for the ball, especially if I had to learn more. I mean, how much can you really learn in five days? I expressed this concern to the king.

"There isn't too much more to learn, and Sogran, Breeohan, and I will make sure that you are otherwise occupied during any dances you do not know."

That was a relief, though I thought the attentions of the king, the heir, and the training general might be in demand, which would make keeping an eye on me much more difficult.

There was silence for a moment, and I shifted nervously. "Have you found out anything about my mother or Kelson yet?" I asked in a rush.

The king looked me in the eye. "I am sorry, but we have found nothing yet. You must admit that there is little information to help us in locating this Kelson."

I looked away to the marbled floor. "I know." What was I doing here anyway? How was staying at the palace going to help find Mom? No one but me knew what to look for. I felt a great yearning to just leave the palace and search for Mom on my own, but I knew that would be fruitless. It was a big country, and I had no idea which direction to look.

I glanced up again and found the king watching me intently. "I promise you I am doing all that is within my power to find your mother."

"Thank you."

I was tired and starving, not a good combination for exuding pep. I got lost once on the way to my room, but found my wrong turn almost immediately and was grateful to see Sentai had lain out a meal. I tucked into the food, hardly noticing what it tasted like. As I started to get a little fuller, I realized this probably was a good thing. It was one of the stranger Iberoahan dishes that, once my hunger lessened, my stomach had trouble handling. I stopped eating before I was full just to make sure I wouldn't throw everything back up again and then went to lie down on the bed.

The next thing I knew, I was being gently shaken awake. The morning sun streamed through the window in brilliant orange rays, though the air from the open shutters was still cool. I groaned and tried to shrug off the hand disturbing my slumber.

"I am sorry to wake you, but if you sleep any longer you will be late for your lessons with the training general," Sentai said.

That brought me up with a start. "What time is it?" I grabbed the clothes Sentai held out for me and stuffed myself in them at sonic speed.

"It is nearly the third portion, Princess."

"Holy cow, Sogran is going to kill me." I grabbed a piece of bread from the table and dashed out the door, flying through hallways. I got to the training room breathing hard, but still before the third portion gong, my piece of bread mashed in my hand.

Sogran walked in the instant after I did. He regarded me with raised eyebrows.

"I assume that you haven't yet eaten." He looked pointedly at my hand. "It will be much harder to train winded and on an empty stomach."

I nodded to save breath, my hopes that he would let me eat the bread plummeting.

"Well, sit down and eat while you recover from your harrowing journey here," he said, surprising me.

My bottom hit the floor, and I tore into the soft bread in case he decided to change his mind. After I finished, I stood slowly.

"Thank you." I wondered if he was having a good day to be so lenient.

"I am not a monster, Mary."

I felt my face go hot. "Why did you and the king go to Earth?" I asked in a fit of daring.

Sogran stood looking at the weapons along the wall for so long, his granite face especially unreadable, that I thought maybe he wasn't going to answer. *Great job, Mary. Make him mad so he can kill you off in practice, why don't you?*

"Verone and I both had our reasons for wanting to leave Iberloah. When Verone discovered the lacing to travel across great distances, we both decided to test the untried lacing and see where it would take us, knowing we could explode just as easily as travel anywhere. I went first to make sure that wouldn't happen to Verone, and ended up in a farther, stranger land than I had ever imagined the lacing would take me—America."

I opened my mouth to ask more, but Sogran stopped anything from getting out. "Since you have already warmed up, we will go straight into man-to-man weapons practice. Get the staff." He turned away and got a staff of his own, then came to the middle of the floor, waiting.

I sulked over to the rack and retrieved my staff slowly. Why was it like pulling teeth to get any information out of the king and the training general? Why would they both want to leave Iberloah in the first place? Granted, Iberloah couldn't be very appealing to the lower classes, but both the king and training general were pretty high up on the Iberloahan food chain.

I was so involved with my thoughts that I didn't notice I had reached the middle of the floor until I felt a whop strike my stick and send it clattering to the ground.

"Pay attention. You're fortunate I decided to hit your stick instead of you."

I picked up my staff more warily and blocked his immediate thrust just in time. He kept a running commentary of what I should correct, or when I blocked well, but I had no breath or free brain space for any replies.

We switched staff for sword after about an hour. The next hour I was far more stressed, consumed in focusing on every move Sogran made. A slice from a sword would be much more painful than a whack from a staff. I was doing pretty well until he got past my guard and nicked me under the arm. Pain lanced through my body, jolting my mind off my counter-strike.

Sogran pulled back millimeters before touching my abdomen. "You must learn to block out the pain and keep fighting. If you lose your concentration, you will be dead."

"Why? Why do I have to fight at all? I should be at home with my mother." I sank to my knees, the words coming out in great gasps as I struggled and failed to hold back the sobbing. "I shouldn't have to fight and if I ever have to kill someone, I'll have that on my conscience forever. I shouldn't be here. Mom and I, *we* shouldn't be here. Our biggest worry should be getting the bills paid on time, not death from barbaric weapons." It was funny how being out of breath combined with a bloody slash on my arm knocked out the flood gates of my suppressed emotions.

I was looking at the floor, vision blurry from the copious tears springing from my eyes when I felt a hand press my shoulder. I waited for the reprimand. None came. Sogran stood silently next to me while I cried.

When I got myself under control enough to breathe properly, I sucked in the air deeply. Next, I fixed my arm with a lacing. The absence of pain helped me stop crying all together. Still, I slumped in embarrassment. Sogran removed his hand and sat next to me in one fluid movement. His poise made me more aware of my bad posture, so I straightened and looked at him.

"You are right that things here are much less safe than your home on Earth in some ways, and that Iberloah might require of you things that you would never have had to face there. But know this, Mary, if you are trying to do what is right, you will never be given more than what you can handle. I believe you are here now for a reason and that you are meant to be here. You are needed, Mary."

It was strange to hear Sogran waxing motivational on me. He hadn't really struck me as the encouragement-speaker type, but his words did something to me, loosened something I'd been holding back. I no longer clung to the bare hope I'd hidden deep down that being in Iberloah was all a dream or that I would wake to find myself strapped to some new state-of-the-art virtual reality simulator.

I stood up. "Okay, I'm ready to spar again."

Sogran nodded. He stood waiting across from me. And this time I struck first.

Chapter 14

I left the training room more tired than yesterday. I'd put new energy into my attacking and blocking. Knowing that my life could depend on my skill or lack thereof spurred me on when I felt ready to drop.

Sogran nodded approvingly at the end of practice. "All you needed was a little nick in the arm to get you to concentrate more fully. If I would have known that, I would have done it the first day." At my look, granite man actually chuckled. "You can't deny that you focus better once you have been hurt. Baro is a good example of that. You didn't put your whole attention into fighting him until he had hit you in the stomach."

"You mean I didn't go berserker until then," I said.

"No, it wasn't a lack of control that I saw. You transformed into another fighter altogether—one who saw more quickly what strikes were coming and blocked them before the strike had full power, giving you time to counter. Did you notice how many more times you were able to move offensively rather than defensively after you were hurt? The difference was significant." He must have read my look for he added, "I was not going easy on you. What you need to discover is how to tap into that focus before you are injured."

"I can see your point, but *doing* is harder than *saying*."

"That is why we train. I will see you tomorrow," he said. Then he walked through the door into the larger training ground. I hobbled slowly outside, feeling the blast of the sun's heat as a throbbing in my skull. A lacing fixed my headache, but I felt a different kind of pain as I saw Zefa Avana heading toward the training grounds in a pair of elaborate green pants and a shirt. They looked new and expensive. I wondered why she was coming this way.

"It seems we are developing a habit of running into each other, Princess."

She elongated the word "princess" so it sounded like a joke rather than a title.

"It does seem that way." I stretched my lips into a smile and bowed only after she bowed to me.

"Dear me, what has happened? You look as if you've been set upon by thieves." Her eyes projected concern while the quirk at her mouth spoke more loudly of scorn.

I looked myself over nonchalantly, taking in the torn and blood-stained sleeve of my shirt, and the sweaty wetness of my clothes. I shrugged. "I've been working hard."

"The servants must have mistaken you for a peasant worker. How unfortunate, but what can you expect in such attire?"

"You'll have to ask the training general, though I wouldn't mention the part about thinking of him as a servant. I don't think he'd like that." I'd stumped her for the moment, so I pressed my advantage. "I see you are heading to the training grounds yourself. Are you going to practice for a jova court match?"

Avana jerked straighter. "I am a lady of noble blood, not some wench to be seen sweating, dirty, and bleeding like . . ." She looked at me disdainfully.

"Like me perhaps? But you forget, Zefa Avana, I was challenged. You could be challenged as well."

"You told us you compete, so of course you can be challenged. I, however, don't compete. I would never so disgrace myself."

"And yet you were begging Breeohan to get back in the game. It didn't seem so loathsome to you to insist the heir fight in the jova courts."

"*Zefan* Breeohan is a man." She accented the "Zefan" as if to further emphasize my unworthiness to call Breeohan by his name only.

"How observant," I said sarcastically, gesturing over her shoulder to Breeohan approaching.

Avana's manner changed instantly to sweet gooeyness. She turned a brilliant smile toward Breeohan. "Breeohan, it is so good to see you here. I was just taking a stroll and found Princess Kasala on her way back to the palace." She turned to me. "It was so nice to talk with you again. I find our encounters quite charming."

This was obviously a dismissal, so I decided to stay where I was. It was gratifying to see an instant narrowing of her eyes before she turned her glorious seductress face back to Breeohan.

"Zefa Avana, Princess Kasala, it is a pleasure to see you both." He bowed, and we bowed in return. I was sure Breeohan was being so formal because of my bedraggled appearance. I rolled my eyes at him behind Avana and performed the cleaning lacing as well as the lacing to fix my clothes, as he rose from his reproving bow. I saw the corner of his mouth twitch upward before Avana cut off any possible response by talking.

"Are you on your way to the training ground, Breeohan? I was hoping I might catch you there and view your practice. You're always so amazing to watch."

Gag me.

"You may watch if you wish, Avana, but I fear you will soon be bored." Breeohan didn't look too comfortable with the idea of Avana ogling him from the sidelines as he was bashed and tossed around the practice arena.

"I could never tire of watching you," she said.

Boy, if Breeohan wasn't embarrassed, I sure was for him. He darted a look at me, and I shrugged. Avana followed Breeohan's glance. I was happy to see shock in her expression when she took in my suddenly altered appearance.

"I won't intrude on you two little love birds any longer. Lovely to see you, Breeohan, Zefa Avana."

Breeohan's head shot up at "love birds," startled. But Avana looked triumphant as I nodded my good-bye and walked past into the palace.

I hurried to my room where a filling meal of stew, bread, and various fruit awaited me. It was almost normal. Sentai stood in the corner watching me eat. I ate hungrily, feeling a wave of sleepiness as my stomach signaled me to stop eating or face the consequences. Since I still had about an hour before meeting the king, I lay down and dozed, asking Sentai to wake me when it was time to leave.

It felt like only an instant had passed before she gently shook my shoulder. I let her dress me in something fancy, feeling like a baby the whole time, and gritting my teeth since to not let her clothe me would hurt her feelings. Then I walked quickly to the ballroom where the king and I practiced.

I stopped short when I saw not the king, but Breeohan.

"Where's King Verone?" I asked in surprise.

"Don't act that way, Mary. I'm sorry for what happened."

"I am not acting any way, I just wondered where the king is." I realized I'd sounded huffy, though I honestly hadn't meant to.

"He has business that only he can attend to, so he asked me to help you in your dancing lessons today."

I was speechless, and he didn't say anything more. Finally, I said, "We should probably start dancing then." I held out my hands stiffly. He moved toward me and took my wooden limbs gently, hesitantly. I felt that funny tingling and tightening of my stomach again. I looked at him sharply, remembering the enchantment lacing, but was unable to detect any trace of it with my inner eye.

I found it difficult to follow Breeohan's lead and messed up much more than I would have with the king. We hardly talked, except when Breeohan corrected my mistakes. I kept my eyes locked on our feet. Finally, he stopped, but I continued to look at his feet.

"The king told me you were getting quite good."

That brought my head up in a flash. "I mess up a lot less with him than you," I said defensively.

"I wonder why that is." The corner of his mouth quirked as his purple-gold eyes looked into mine.

"You make me nervous." The words came out before I could stop them. I felt somehow caught but unsure why. I jerked away in alarm, once again searching for evidence of the enchantment lacing. Nothing. This time Breeohan noticed that I was searching for something magically.

"What are you looking for?" He sounded worried.

I could sense him doing a magical search as well. "Nothing, I . . . Look, are we done for the day? I'm kind of tired."

"If you'd like, but I wanted to talk to you about Avana before you go."

"Want a girl's opinion on the most romantic way to pop the question?"

"Pop the question?"

"You're right, you're still a little young for that. I say wait awhile before deciding on forever. You know what I mean?" I smiled, seeing his look of confusion.

"I have no idea what you are talking about."

I was starting to feel more comfortable again, so I decided to have more fun. "You know . . . Breeohan and Avana sitting in a tree, K-I-S-S-I-N-G," I sang. The G didn't really rhyme with tree in Iberloahan. It sullied the effect slightly, but I still saw a satisfactory red spread on Breeohan's cheeks.

"You're impossible," he said in obvious frustration.

"Aw, come on, Breeohan. You know you love me." I grinned hugely. He blinked, and his head jerked slightly.

"You are welcome to Avana," I continued. "Just please don't ask me what gifts to buy her. I know you like her, but she seems to think I'm some sort of threat. I really don't think she'd like it if she knew I recommended her newest token of love. I'll see you at the ball." I breezed out of the room feeling winded.

I arrived at the training ground early the next morning and decided to stretch while I waited for Sogran, something that even the training general had not thought essential since he hadn't had me stretch once.

I was sitting in the middle splits, head down, arms outstretched, when I heard a muffled sound of sympathy for someone else's pain. I looked up to see Sogran and King Verone wincing at me.

"What's the matter?" I asked.

"We didn't realize you were such an acrobat," the king said.

"That," Sogran said, pointing to my position, "should be banned."

"I will make the law right away," King Verone said. "Now would you please do us both a service, Mary, and sit normally?"

I was enjoying their looks of discomfort, but I folded my legs into a cross-legged position.

"Breeohan told me that your dancing lesson yesterday didn't go quite as smoothly as it is wont to with you and me. I thought that might be partially due to the fact that you are only used to my cues, so I have enlisted Sogran's help with dancing this morning."

"I thought you hated to dance," I said to the training general.

"I avoid it when I can, but it seems today is to be especially trying," he replied.

"The ball is today," said King Verone.

"What? I thought it was tomorrow. Did I lose track of the days or something?" My stomach tightened and tied into knots.

"No, it was moved due to unforeseen circumstances that must take place tomorrow. As hard as a ball date is to change, the other event proved impossible to move, so I decided to cancel your fighting lessons today," Verone said.

"Couldn't you have delayed it?"

"Alas, no. I am sorry, but it would look like a slight to you if I delayed the ball rather than giving it sooner."

"I don't mind, really," I insisted, though I knew it would do no good.

The king smiled, and even Sogran looked a little less grim. "I know *you* wouldn't mind, but Princess Kasala would."

My shoulders slumped. "Fine, let's dance," I said glumly.

Sogran laughed. "Anyone would think you were me."

I looked up sharply, wondering if there was something implied in that statement. Both the king and the training general regarded me with equally unreadable expressions, and I suddenly wanted to scream in frustration.

Sogran's arms extended in invitation, his eyes locked with mine in a look that seemed to say, "Stick with the dancing, kiddo—and no questions or you're a burnt bagel." I clenched and unclenched my fists before extending them to Sogran.

Sogran moved me through the dances without any hitches while the king watched our progress. But it felt strange to be dancing so properly in a room lined with weapons.

"You know, you're very good for someone who avoids dancing whenever possible," I commented.

"I am not bad at dancing, I merely prefer to do other things," Sogran said.

"Why?"

King Verone laughed. "It is because Sogran is a very eligible match, and women will not stop pestering him at balls."

Sogran gave the king a look that stopped the king's smile immediately. Verone even looked a little contrite.

"I'm certainly not the only one who is sought after at balls, Your Majesty." Sogran spun me out with more force than necessary.

I caught myself, but suddenly felt I was in the middle of a battleground. "Please, gentlemen. I'm sure you're very desirable to women. It must be hard on you both." I lay on the sarcasm as thickly as possible. "And there is no need to argue over who is the more pitiable for being the most charming."

That got both men to smile a little, but the smiles were sad. "It is a hard thing to be sought after not for yourself, but for what you represent, especially when you've made it clear that you will not marry," King Verone said.

"Wait. By 'you' do you mean you the king or both of you?" I asked.

"He means us both," Sogran said.

"Why? What do you two have against marriage?"

"Nothing," they said in unison.

"You are stumbling, Mary. Stop talking and pay attention," Sogran said.

"I am *not*. Well, not much anyway. I think you just don't want to talk about marriage. Besides, won't the people I dance with expect me to talk to them?"

"I think it would be better if you said as little as possible to your dancing partners," Sogran said.

My face grew hot. "So I'm supposed to be like Eliza Dolittle and only say small phrases like, 'How do you do,' so no one will suspect I'm a fraud, is that it?" I felt miffed.

"I think it would be best," the king said mildly.

"Fine. I'll try to curb my loquacious tongue." If Mom could've seen the look on my face, she would've said I was pouting.

"Good. It is better to be mysterious. Let people fill in the gaps of your silence with their own expectations of what a princess should be like," King Verone said.

Sogran passed me off to the king. We danced in silence for awhile with Sogran looking on. I noticed they had skillfully changed the subject on me, but I let it go, not sure how much I could safely aggravate a king and a training general.

"My biggest fear is that I won't be able to do this with music. I'm so used to dancing in silence that I'm afraid the music will throw me off."

"I think the music will help more than hinder," said the king.

The training general and the king traded me through each different dance style. I felt like a ping pong ball, but it helped to have two different leads to work with.

"There is something I've been wondering about," I said as the training general spun me through a particularly dizzying maneuver. He gave me a wary look but nodded as the king looked on.

"The king called you Prince Sogran. Since Breeohan said he and his mother are the closest in line to the throne, does that make you from somewhere else?"

"Yes," Sogran replied shortly. I looked at the king in appeal.

"Come, come, Sogran. No need for reticence," the king said mischievously. Sogran scowled at him but stayed stubbornly silent.

"Sogran is the second son of King Korh and Queen Dokra of Zephti, one of our neighboring countries," the king replied helpfully.

"Then why are you here?" I asked Sogran.

Sogran spoke simply but with the air of one who wishes the discussion over. "Queen Dorka was born in Iberloah as a Zefa here, and since I am a second son with my brother already married, it wasn't necessary for me to be there. So I was sent here many years ago as a diplomatic gesture of good faith. I have remained here because it is my wish to do so." As if to ensure that I would cease to ask questions, he stopped me mid-turn. "I think she will do well enough, Your Majesty. I don't know why she and Breeohan had trouble yesterday. Perhaps you should avoid dancing with him for the evening."

I felt a funny sense of disappointment mixed with relief.

"You know we can't do that, Sogran," said the king. "It would certainly look odd if the princess never danced with her rescuer."

"I suppose. Just remember to stay focused. I don't want you to have to get hurt before you concentrate," Sogran said.

I rolled my eyes. "Dancing is hardly fighting, Training General."

"It has similar elements," he said stubbornly.

I grinned mischievously and grabbed my leg, straightening it in the air in air splits. "Like flexibility, perhaps?"

He bumped me so that I had to let go of my leg to catch myself. "No, like balance and fluidity of motion. Now leave. I'm sure your servant is worried about getting your dress ready in time for the ball."

It struck me in a surreal sort of moment how casually I'd been conversing with a king and a prince, but I shook it off.

Sentai flung the door to my room open the moment I reached for the handle.

"Wow, Sentai, you made me jump out of my skin." I put my hand to my rapidly beating heart.

"We must get you ready, Your Highness. We must make sure that the dress fits you perfectly. Then we will need to start your hair and makeup preparation."

"But the ball isn't until this evening. We have hours and hours, I mean portions and portions," I protested, thinking that portions and portions did not sound as convincing.

"We will need all the portions before the ball to make Your Highness into the most stunning figure present, if Your Highness permits. It would not do for you to be outshone at a ball in your honor," Sentai said with unusual briskness. I was so impressed, I let her boss me onto the little stool she had moved to the middle of the room while she called in the seamstress from outside the door. I had no idea where the seamstress had come from;

I hadn't seen her on my way into the room.

The seamstress was a petite woman, short and thin, with an outfit that fit her form perfectly. It had no laces or frills, but had an elegant economic cut that made her seem gracefully efficient. I could only see her clothes from the back, however, because she carried yards of fabric in front of her, all of which—I soon found out—were my dress.

She managed to bow, despite the heavy load of cloth in her arms, and then waited patiently while Sentai undressed me. I felt myself going red when Sentai indicated that I should take off even my underwear, but no sooner were they off than the seamstress slipped a golden filmy undergarment onto me almost as if by magic. Scissors, needle and thread appeared in her hands. She snipped off the bunchy parts of cloth and sewed seams back together with amazing speed. I stood as still as I could, wondering if the garment would come off again after such snug adjustments.

Next Sentai and the seamstress had me step into silky golden pants with swirling, dark purple embroidery, which started out sparse near my thigh, but became more dense as it twisted toward my ankle. At my ankles, Sentai clasped bracelets made of a dark purple metal, making it seem to come out of the end of the pants and extend toward my foot in one continuous flow until they reached the golden slippers on my feet.

Over the pants went the dress, split into four sections in the front, but solid in the back. Unlike the pants, the dress was a deep purple material with golden stitching. The golden design started sparsely near the bottom, but became a great tangle of gold in the bodice so that very little purple showed near the top. A diagonal strip of solely purple material was stitched tight to the bodice in the front, but flowed free in the back like a scarf to mid thigh, with golden tracery near its end. The sleeves extended just past my elbows, but were designed for the twisty golden bracelets Sentai clipped into the fabric as a metallic extension of the material winding down the rest of my arm.

As the seamstress sewed me into the dress, Sentai put gold and amethyst rings on my fingers. I started to feel slightly overdone, but I wasn't even close to finished. I stood for what felt like an hour as the seamstress finished sewing. By this time I had determined that I would, in fact, have to be cut out when the ball was over.

Finally, I was allowed to sit. I plopped into a chair and the seamstress squeaked in horror. I stood, fanned my dress and sat down carefully. Sentai sighed. I couldn't see a mirror and so was unprepared for the tremendous weight crushing my skull as Sentai lay something upon my head.

"What is that?"

"It is your headpiece, Your Highness," Sentai replied.

"You mean I'll have that weight on my head the whole night?" I asked in horror.

"Of course, Your Highness. It is a headdress befitting your station."

I thought there was a warning in her tone, but I said anyway, "Isn't there a lighter headpiece that would befit my station?"

"I hope that Her Highness will not be displeased with me, but there is not," Sentai said firmly.

Where had this bossy Sentai come from? "It's your fault if I topple over," I muttered but sat still as she wound hair through the headpiece and worked lacing magic on my hair to make it into a Sentai original. The seamstress took her leave, but I stayed glued to the chair for several hours as Sentai finished my hair and started on my makeup.

Knowing the way the Iberloahans tended to match their makeup to their clothes, I pleaded with Sentai, "Could I at least not be forced to wear purple lipstick? I don't really feel in the mood to look like a gothic golden pin cushion."

"Point out the color that would please you, Your Highness," Sentai said in a voice that indicated she was granting me a huge boon. She was getting much bolder with me despite the constant "Your Highnesses."

I pointed to a red lipstick with a brown undertone that I thought would work with my skin and was rewarded with an approving nod. Sentai ordered my eyelids closed. She painted several shades of purple onto my lids, used a thin brush for the golden eyeliner which she extended to my temples in the same loopy, twisted vine design on my dress, and then glued several purple stones amid a few golden loops. She applied golden brown rouge and the lipstick, and pushed twisty golden- and purple-jeweled earrings through my earlobes. They dragged at my piercings. I wondered what she would have done if I hadn't had pierced ears. Probably stabbed the earrings through.

Finally I was finished and allowed to look in the mirror. The person who stared at me in the glass was not Mary Margaret Underwood, that much was certain. It was strange to look at myself, knowing it was me, but seeing someone so totally unlike me. The makeup was like a physical mask, but it didn't look cheesy. Sentai had done a good job using the different purples to make my golden irises all the more vivid. The web work of golden and purple metal on my head, with hair interwoven throughout, added a regalness to my facial structure I had never detected before. Sure, I felt like I would topple over at any minute, but the feeling of the royal disguise made me straighten my shoulders and hold my chin up to compensate.

"So, when am I expected?" I asked.

"Even now, Your Highness."

My middle squeezed in nervousness. I didn't want to leave the room. What if I messed up in the dancing, showing everyone that I was a fraud? I would be toast for sure.

I swallowed a suddenly dry throat. "I'm ready to go." It was a lie, but I knew it would be even worse if I didn't show up at all. I stood, wobbled, caught my balance, and walked out ahead of Sentai toward the right, only to have Sentai cough me in the other direction. *I guess a regal mask can only do so much.*

My heart thumped in panic. I'd never gone to any dances, but I was pretty sure that if you showed up without a date you'd be branded a loser. I almost asked Sentai, but decided not to as there were other servants in the hall.

We reached the giant doors to the ballroom and waited, just short of being seen by the guests below. I had a horrible feeling, similar to when I first pleaded my case to the king. Was it only five days ago? Time had slowed and stretched out, filled with the many things I had learned since I'd faced King Verone on his throne.

Music drifted through the doors, as did the deafening murmur of many voices. The music sounded vaguely medieval, but with strange instruments. I felt a gentle nudge in my back from Sentai, urging me forward, but I took a few deep breaths before plunging past the door to the top of the steps. The roaring murmur died to a low buzz as the king's announcer rang out my princess name in a clear, carrying volume. My chin up, I descended the marble steps, trying not to look like my whole concentration was centered on not tripping. Even though it was.

King Verone was waiting at the bottom in an amazing outfit of gold and blue. He wore a golden jewel-encrusted chain that fell from his left shoulder to his right hip and back. Breeohan and Sogran stood next to him, Breeohan in a dark purple and golden outfit strangely similar to my own, with a smaller golden chain around his shoulder. Sogran stood stiffly in grey and silver. Trust Sogran to find the most boring color to wear to the ball. He looked regal, however, and I thought the simplicity of his hue actually made him look more distinctive than all the other brightly clad ball-goers.

"Princess Kasala, in the name of Iberloah, I welcome you to this ball in your honor," King Verone said loudly so that all might hear.

The king looked at me as if a response was required, so I said, "I thank you for your kindness. I am honored to be here." Sogran nodded slightly, and I sighed inwardly at finding I hadn't botched my answer.

"Now that you are here, the dancing may begin. Would you further honor me with the first dance?" King Verone asked.

"I would be glad to, Your Majesty," I replied. I was immensely glad when I saw other dancing partners line up along the floor. This would not be like the king and queen's dance at prom, where the couple danced alone at the beginning of the song. The music started. King Verone's familiar lead helped me relax enough to realize that it *was* easier to dance with the rhythmic beat of the instruments. I actually felt confident enough to take a brief glance around at the other dancers, but immediately regretted it when I saw Breeohan dancing with Avana a few people away. She wore a gorgeous maroon gown with green embroidery. Her headpiece was only slightly less elaborate and huge than my own. She looked like Aphrodite come to life.

I hurriedly looked back toward the king, who appeared amused. "You are doing very well, Princess, but I would advise keeping your attention on your partner," he said as I risked another quick look in Breeohan's direction. I zoned back in on my own dancing, narrowly avoiding a stumble. The dance finished, and King Verone and I bowed to each other in thanks.

I thought perhaps I would get to sit out the next dance, or maybe even the next few, but Sogran approached. "Your Highness, may I have the pleasure of a dance?"

"Of course, Training General. I would be honored." I tried not to smile. But once the music started, I couldn't help but whisper to him, "I thought I would never hear you utter 'pleasure' and 'dance' in the same sentence."

"It is a ball. I must observe the pleasantries. Besides, if I don't dance with you, I must dance with one of the schemers." Sogran tilted his head to the side where a gaggle of women gossiped, glancing often in our direction.

"Isn't it the guy who asks the girl to dance?" I asked.

"Not always. It is acceptable for a woman to ask a man, and they do, believe me." Sogran sounded aggrieved. His face was the most emotionally expressive I'd ever seen on him. I had to concentrate on my steps so I wouldn't laugh or trip. At the end of the dance, the training general and I bowed, and I tried to slip to the wall but was stopped by a young man in a dark green and light purple outfit that made him look remarkably like a peacock.

"May I have the extreme honor of this dance, Your Highness?" He bowed low with flourish. Normally, I would have smiled, but I wasn't sure if I could say no, and I was nervous about dancing with someone new.

"I would be honored, uh . . ." I trailed off, not knowing his name or what bow to give him.

"Doln Zemph, Your Highness," he supplied, bowing again. I gave the appropriate bow back and let him lead me back to the dance floor. The dancing went surprisingly well. Doln Zemph turned out to be a good dancer, easy to follow. After I bowed my thanks to him, he was quickly replaced by an older man in orange, then a young man in red, then green again. I gave up trying to remember their names. They all started to blur together. Dancing began to be painful. I had a stitch in my side. My head became heavier with each step.

The king or the training general always managed to snag me away from the dance floor during the dances that I didn't know, so I was spared having anyone discover my ignorance, but the dancing still seemed endless.

I bowed to another colorful fabric, looking more at my feet than the man, and wondering if it would be worth the energy to perform the lacing to fix the ache in my soles when the man's voice caught my attention.

"Princess." Then softer, his breath touching my ear, he said, "Mary."

I jerked my eyes from the ground and found my face inches from Breeohan's. The music began. We moved apart in the graceful flow of the dance's steps. Breeohan kept his eyes on mine.

"You seemed absent," he said.

"I'm sorry. I've danced with so many men. Everyone was starting to blur to me."

"You don't have to accept every offer. If you like, we can stop, and I'll take you to the refreshment area. There are tables and chairs there. You could sit down and rest for awhile." He looked concerned.

The dance steps brought us close again, our cheeks a breath away. For a moment I forgot my pounding head, the stitch in my side, and my aching feet. I felt an unreasonable desire to keep dancing, to bring my cheek the fraction closer that would . . . I pulled away quickly.

"I *would* like to rest. Thank you, Breeohan." I was shaking. Breeohan noticed. "I must be more tired than I thought," I added.

"I should have noticed before. I am sorry, Your Highness." Breeohan bowed. He offered his arm, and I took it, dreading the need to hold my arm up, but Breeohan whispered, "Put your weight on me; I won't bow under it." So I did. His arm flexed in response to my weight.

We soon reached an unoccupied scrolled metal table that looked like patio furniture. I sat with a sigh while Breeohan left to get me a drink and some food. The table area reminded me of a French café. The people at the tables scrutinized those who were standing and dancing from the comfortable obscurity of seats while sipping their drinks and nibbling their food. Across the room were the entry stairs and adjacent was the throne dais, leaving only the area directly opposite the throne's platform out of sight. The tables were small, with only two chairs each so that couples could converse.

I watched the ebb and flow of the dancers, enjoying the view from a seated position. My serenity was shattered, however, by the sight of Aphrodite Avana looming before me with hatred on her thickly painted and jeweled face.

"I hope you have no intentions toward Breeohan," she said in a deadly tone.

"Get a grip, Avana." I didn't feel like saying more because my head was throbbing again. I fixed the headache with a lacing. It wouldn't be smart to get into a battle with Avana when I already had a headache.

"What does that mean? That makes no sense," she said contemptuously.

"It means you're a head case. I'm not trying to steal Breeohan from you, so stop blaming your insecurities on me." I hoped to make her mad enough to go away.

"I am not a fool, Princess. I saw how you looked at him on the dance floor. But you will not have him. I will expose you for the fraud you are, and then the only thing that will touch that pretty throat of yours is the kiss of steel as it cuts through your neck." She turned with a whoosh of fabric toward a young man a few feet away. I watched as she batted her eyes prettily at the man, as if she had not just threatened my life, or as if life threats were common, not to be dwelled on. A chill ran down my spine in a trickle of sweat.

I had no idea her malice ran so deep, and I knew that she could prove me to be a fraud because I was one, and all the magic in the world would do me no good then.

When Breeohan finally returned, I had no appetite for the food he laid before me, though the water was a welcome balm to the desert sand lodged in my throat. He sat and furrowed his brows. I knew he was concerned, but I couldn't look at him.

"What's wrong? What's happened?"

"What time can I leave the ball without offending anyone?" I asked.

"Not for portions yet. I'm sorry," he replied.

"I don't know if you should hang around, Breeohan. Go ask your love to dance or something. She needs some reassurance that you're hers." I watched Avana twirl in the dance with the other young man. She kept darting glances in my direction.

"She's not my love and has no claim on me." His anger made me glance at his face in surprise. "Why do you do that?" he asked vehemently.

I was confused. "Do what?"

"Push me at Zefa Avana," he said.

"I don't. I mean, I got the impression that you two were pretty close before, and I certainly know that she wants to be closer to you. You like her, or you wouldn't have blushed when I teased you. I really think it would be best if you let her know that you like her, so that . . ." I stopped myself just in time. He wouldn't believe Avana had threatened me.

"So that what?" he demanded.

"Nothing. Hey, is this chocolate? I have been dying for some chocolate ever since I got to Iberloah." I looked carefully at the plate of food I'd ignored before.

"No. I don't know what chocolate is, but that is not going to work, Your Highness. So that what?" He glared at me so hard I could feel it even as I studied the plate of treats.

"Are you really telling me there's no chocolate here?" I asked in misery. He just kept staring, not answering.

I sighed. "Fine. Avana just threatened to expose me as an imposter so my head would be chopped off."

"She did not. Avana doesn't have a malicious bone in her body."

I was suddenly furious. "See, I knew you would never believe me! I'll have you know your little cream puff of perfection can be quite cruel to those she dislikes."

"I can't believe it. I have never seen her be cruel." He sounded confused.

"I'm sorry, but if you can't see how completely stupid that statement was, you deserve what you get. I hope you two have a happy life together." Though I had serious doubts that they would ever be happy once marriage forced Breeohan to see who Avana really was.

I stood up swiftly and headed to the nearest young man. "May I have the honor of the next dance with you?" I asked him. Breeohan was too proper to yell at me to come back, but I could feel his gaze on me. I looked up and noticed Avana looking toward me as well. She had a slight smile on her face. My anger burned hotter, and I had to force myself to concentrate on the proper pleasantries of beginning a dance with someone.

One young man blurred into the next until I found myself facing the king again. As soon as we were a little more isolated, I asked, "When can I stop, Your Majesty? I'm really afraid that I'm going to collapse if I don't take this torture device off my head."

"You're hiding it well," he said.

"I figured it would be a good idea to hide my discomfort, considering what's at stake."

"It is true there are some dangers, but you are under my protection. Don't worry too much, just stay alert," he said.

"That's what I am trying to do," I said, sighing.

The dance ended. "Just dance three more dances and after the performance given by Zefa Aria and her musicians, you may bow out gracefully." It was all he was able to say before a mob of eager young women swallowed him up.

I turned to find another partner, or if I could, escape to a table, when Doln Rafan approached in a resplendent outfit of gold material with aqua embroidery that made his eyes flare. His lips curled upward as he held out his hand in invitation.

My responses were by this time automatic. I smiled pleasantly, bowed, and took his hand as he led me to the dance floor, all the while thinking, "Only three more dances then I am done, done, done."

"You look lovely this evening, Princess," Rafan said.

"Thank you." *Almost done, done, done.*

"I couldn't help but notice that you and Breeohan seemed to have some unpleasantness between you this evening. He is a fool to discard such exquisite beauty."

Done, do— What? Thrown from my chant, I tried to recall what I'd missed.

"I hope you will not think all Iberloahan men are such brutes," he added.

"Oh, I don't. I think it's bad policy to judge an entire people on the few I've met," I said. I could see he wasn't sure how to take that statement.

"And are we all so bad?" he asked coyly.

"Of course not." I knew what he was fishing for, but I didn't feel in the mood to flirt. It was too much work.

"Poor princess, you have had a rough time here, haven't you?"

I deemed that unworthy of a response, but he took my silence as acquiescence.

"I see you do not wish to complain, but it tears my heart that I can do nothing to ease your burden. Perhaps . . ." He trailed off, baiting me.

I was actually a little curious about what he was up to, so I took the worm. "Perhaps what, Doln Rafan?" I batted my eyes in what I thought was obvious sarcasm. I guess not.

"You must know how much I love you, Princess," he said.

I was floored.

He continued. "If you married me, you would be protected. You would have real status. No one could hurt you," he whispered in my ear. He actually sounded and looked sincere. I didn't know what to say. All I could do was open and close my mouth like a fish.

"Don't answer now, just think about it, and know I will come whenever you call for me." The dance ended, and Rafan gave me a yearning look before disappearing into the crowd. But his gravelly words stayed with me. What was with this guy? I didn't understand him. Did he really love me? I had been pretty sure he was just a lady's man, a courtly flirt full of flowery nonsense, but had I misread him?

I accepted the training general's next invitation in a haze of confusion, too deep in thought to pay much attention, so when the dance ended, it took me a moment to understand that he was asking if I needed to sit down.

"You seem dazed, Mary. Can I get you a drink or lead you to a chair?"

"What? I'm sorry, Training General, I'm not quite feeling myself. It would be nice to sit down."

He led me to the same table I had sat at with Breeohan, but I stopped him before he could leave. "Would you mind sitting with me?" I didn't want to be trapped into any more odd or unpleasant conversations this evening. "How goes the search for my mother?" I asked, hoping desperately for a breakthrough so I could just leave the palace and not have to worry about death threats or marriage proposals.

"We continue to search." He avoided my eyes. That was weird. In the little time I'd known him, he had never sounded so shifty before. But then, it had been a long night. I was already on emotional overload, so there was no trusting my observational skills at the moment. We watched the dancers in silence until the music ended.

There was a sudden hush as the king stood on the dais and announced, "Zefa Aria and her faithful troupe of musicians have prepared a special musical number for your enjoyment." His expression was carefully neutral.

Everyone turned to the musician's stand in expectation. I heard a few titters, and then stunned silence hit the crowd as a large drum boomed in syncopated rhythm, followed by the wail of a bassoonlike instrument that flew over the scales in a wild manner, barely staying with the drumbeat. Next, a plucked instrument entered the musical fray, twanging away while a rattle shook in opposition to the drum.

I loved it. It was so unlike the stuffy, flat music I'd been listening to all evening, but the people around me went rigid with alarm and embarrassment. A woman near me winced when Zefa Aria started singing in a controlled wail that jumped and flowed with the instruments. I thought it was beautiful and intriguing but quickly saw that I was the only one. I felt sorry for Aria and her band; they were playing to the wrong audience.

When the song finished, a collective sigh spread through the room. No one clapped. I wasn't sure if people clapped here so I didn't either, but my sympathy for Aria rose a notch. I decided to stay just a little longer so that I could tell her how much I enjoyed her performance. I wanted more than anything to leave, but no one deserved such a cold reception to what had obviously taken a lot of preparation.

I excused myself from Sogran and stood to look for Zefa Aria. Halfway to the musicians someone stepped in front of me, blocking my way.

I sighed. "Leave me alone, Avana. You saw the fight Breeohan and I got into. Isn't that good enough for you?"

"How could you think I would be happy about that? I feel so horrible and responsible somehow, though I truly don't know what I did to make you two fight. Will you please forgive me?" Avana asked.

What? That didn't sound like the Avana I knew and loathed. I looked around and, sure enough, saw Breeohan within hearing range trying not to look like he was listening. What a little snake. If I told her off now it would look like I was making the whole thing up. She was certainly a sneaky devil, and I was at a loss as to what I should do. Finally, I decided I didn't care.

"You feel guilt? I didn't think it was in your nature, especially during moments of triumph. Now if you'll excuse me," I said. Avana's eyes glinted happily before she moved aside and began a brilliant performance of the poor, snubbed maiden only trying to be kind and loving to those who, for no reason that she could see, hated her. She even shed a few tears. Breeohan, of course, strode to her side to lend comfort, but not before a brief hesitation when he looked from Avana to me in confusion.

I strode on toward the musicians, who were carefully packing up their instruments in hard leather cases. Zefa Aria was with her husband, putting away the large plucked instrument. But she turned when she noticed my approach.

"I just wanted to thank you for your beautiful music. I thought it was wonderful," I said.

She looked close to tears. Her husband rested a soothing hand on her shoulders. At my words, however, her face glowed. "Did you really? It took us ages to find the manuscripts that described the instruments' original forms, and then we only had fragmented music to work with, so we had to do some guessing and arranging to get it to what we think was the principal sound of the music. But," her face fell again, "no one seemed to like it."

"Well, I did. I could tell you put a lot of work into the performance. It was the best thing I heard all evening." I acted over-enthusiastic to make up for the lack from everyone else.

"Oh, thank you, Princess. I can't tell you how much it means to hear someone of your superb lineage say something like that to me."

"Yes, well." A stab of conscience smote me. "I hope to hear you again." I bowed and headed for the stairs and door as fast as my aching feet allowed.

Once in my room I couldn't wait for Sentai's slow and careful ministrations. I tore at my hair until the crown headpiece came free, and performed the lacing to fix my headache. Only then did I feel well enough to let Sentai finish undressing me at a slower pace.

After I was disrobed, I tried to perform a cleaning lacing, but was too tired to complete it. In my emotionally fatigued state, this fact almost brought on a melt-down and made me realize how dependent on lacing magic I'd become. I had to wait for Sentai to draw up a bath, all the while wishing to just fall asleep, but not wanting to wake up with the mask of makeup still smeared on my face. I crawled into bed after the bath and fell asleep the moment my cheek touched the pillow.

Chapter 15

The blanket of warm light that fell across my eyes the next morning was an unwelcomed and unwanted alarm clock. However, I didn't want to incur the wrath of the training general if I was late, so I got up and had Sentai dress me. I hardly had to remind myself not to fidget as Sentai administered to me. That didn't mean I liked it any better. Such coddling seemed like a horrible waste of time and energy all around, but I gritted my teeth and bore it to satisfy Sentai's sense of propriety and avoid any more rumors about my commoner behavior.

My body fought wakefulness even as I meandered to the training grounds. The sun's gentle warmth so early in the day was like a soft massage on my shoulders and head. I walked even slower, closing my eyes every few steps. So when I entered the practice room to find Sogran still not there, I was rather surprised and relieved. I'd taken longer on my way than I'd intended and was, in fact, late to the training grounds.

I decided to stretch while I waited, then after he still didn't come, I did some sword warm-ups. Twenty minutes passed. I really started to wonder, so I went through the door into the main practice area. The noise level in this area was substantially different than when I'd first entered. There were only three pairs sparring, with a few hangers-on watching the bouts. I couldn't see Sogran anywhere.

I walked up to a man watching one of the matches. He was concentrating on the fighters, and even my "excuse me" didn't merit more than a flick of his eyes before he trained his bug-eyed orbs back on the sparring.

"Could you tell me where the training general is?" I asked.

He was silent for so long I thought he hadn't heard me. But just as I was about to ask again he said, "He's gone somewhere with the king. Took a few soldiers with them and gave the rest a half day's break." He never took his eyes off the fight.

Weird. I did remember the king saying something about moving the ball up because he had to do something today. But Sogran hadn't said anything about canceling our practice. I shrugged and watched the fight for a few minutes.

After leaving, I wandered back to my room and plopped myself onto the bed. The sudden absence of activity made me think again of Mom and things I could do to find her. There had to be some sort of lacing I could discover that would help.

A knock at the door interrupted my musings. "The king wishes to see you, Princess," Sentai informed me. So he was back. I was curious as to where he and the training general had gone. The king had said it was something that could not be delayed, but he hadn't said what, so I doubted I was on the list of people he would confide in.

I found myself standing in front of the guarded doors of the king's study once more, but I didn't have to wait. The two guards swung the door open for me. The smell of old books and dust tickled my nose as I walked past the shelved hallway that opened into the study. The king looked up from a paper he was studying and gave me one of his unreadable looks.

"Thank you for coming, Mary. I think we have solved the mystery of who has your mother," he said, his eyes intense.

I felt like I was missing something he expected me to know. "Who?" I almost shouted, but managed to keep my voice from rising too much.

"Kelteon."

Something about that name sounded familiar. It took me a second, but then I had it. "Wait, isn't that the guy Breeohan told me about who tried to take over the throne but was banished when he failed?"

"Yes."

"How do you know it's him?" I still felt like I was missing an important piece of information.

"He sent a letter."

Now I was really confused, why would Kelson—no Kelteon must be his real name—send a letter to the king about my mother? What did either of us have to do with anyone in this foreign place? A suspicion formed in my mind, but it was too preposterous to be true. Besides, there were at least four people that I had heard of who had gone to Earth and could be my father, and that was only the people from Iberloah.

There was a whole world here. If indeed, as I suspected, my father had come from this world, it was unlikely he was the king sitting so inscrutably before me. Studying my face again, he looked like he was going to add more. But then his eyes dropped to his desk, and he shuffled through some documents until he pulled a map from beneath the papers, set it on top of them, and turned it toward me.

"When Kelteon was banished, we know he went over to the country of Zephti. But my spies lost track of him some time ago. It's uncertain where he is now, but we will search for him and your mother."

I stared at the map as if I could get it to tell me where Kelteon was if I just concentrated hard enough. Nothing spoke to me. I sighed and looked up at the king, who was staring at me. It made me nervous. "What can I do to help?"

"Nothing. You can stay here while I send others to search. I don't want to give Kelteon the chance to get his hands on you."

I grew a little annoyed. "Why would it even matter? It isn't like I'm a real princess," I said, baiting him. "I don't see any reason why this Kelteon person is even interested in holding my mother and me. It doesn't make any sense."

I almost thought the king was going to say something, but we were interrupted by the king's servant who came through the hall into the study. "Sire, the council has assembled and is waiting for you."

"I will come immediately." The servant bowed out again. "I must address the council about this, but we will talk again later. For the present, I would ask that you confine your movements to your room and the training area. It seems you are already making a few especially rigid nobles feel threatened, and I don't want things to get more disturbed than they already are." He hesitated a moment, glancing swiftly at me as I seethed with resentment, and then he walked around his desk, past my chair, and out the door.

So now I was a prisoner of sorts. What in the world was going on anyway? When I finally got enough control over myself to huff out of the king's study, I found the same servant who had led me to it ready to take me back to my room again. I preceded him in huffy silence. Not that he noticed or cared. I felt more lost and trapped than ever. But I was powerless to do anything about it.

In my room I sat at the table and simmered like sauce left too long on the stove. "Sentai, I will have dinner in my room tonight, and if anyone asks, I am not feeling well."

She must have noticed the storm cloud drooping over my head for she didn't comment, just nodded and slipped out quietly. I stared at the table without seeing it, thinking about what the king had said. Why was he suddenly restricting my movement, and how had he found out it was Kelteon? Had that been the purpose of his little trip this morning?

Had Kelteon really written a letter, telling the king he had some foreign woman? I couldn't imagine what Kelteon would say in such an epistle. Something like, "How's it going, King Verone? I know I tried to kill you, but I just thought I'd write to bring you up-to-date on what's been going on with me lately. I've been busy with my plotting. How 'bout you? Any new schemes in the works? Oh, yeah, I remember you knew something about Earth, so I thought I'd tell you about this lady I recently kidnapped. Aren't Earthlings funny? Hope to see you six feet under. Sincerely, Kelteon."

The absurdity of my mock letter made me laugh, and the raincloud over my head lifted a little. I sat up straight. The training general had been acting a little funny last night; maybe they had found something even before today. For the moment I was powerless, so I lay on the bed to rest my eyes while I waited.

I must've rested in reality, for when I opened my eyes again, a candle illuminated the dinner Sentai had laid out. She, however, was nowhere in sight. She had an uncanny ability to appear and disappear. I walked through the shadowy room to the door, opening it a crack. Light streamed in, and a man to the side of the door turned.

"Is there something I can do for you, Princess?" he asked, giving me a bow. A sword hung at his belt. I forced a smile as a shiver of fear and rage ran up my spine.

"Yes. Would you be so kind as to send for Zefan Breeohan? I need to see him as soon as possible," I said.

"Of course, Your Highness. I will have a servant fetch him at once."

The door slid shut. I stood for a moment getting reaccustomed to the darker shadows of my room before moving to the table of food. So I was truly a prisoner. The guard knocked that truth into me like a sledge hammer in a way the king's subtle command had not. My insides tumbled with fear and frustration.

Like my shadowy room, I had little light to see by lately. Even though I now knew the name of the person who had Mom, I felt no closer to finding her than before. I had to either get more information, or get out, preferably both. But I needed Breeohan's help for both these things and considering the state of affairs between us, I wasn't at all sure I could trust him to help me either.

I chewed my food mechanically, hardly noticing it as I mulled over what I should say to Breeohan. A light tap on the door made me aware that my food was gone.

"Come in."

The hinge creaked slightly as the door opened to reveal Breeohan's silhouette. He stepped in, and hesitated to let his eyes adjust to the small candle before sitting opposite me. The tiny flame made his amethyst eyes richer, and I wished for a better light so that I could read his expressions more clearly.

"Do you enjoy being in the dark?" he asked.

"Not at all. That's why I sent for you." His eyebrows rose questioningly, but even in the dimness of the room Breeohan was not good at hiding his emotions. I could see he knew something. "What do you know, Breeohan?"

"About what?"

"Please don't play with me. How does the king know Kelteon has my mother?"

"From a letter."

"From Kelteon?" I asked incredulously.

"Yes." Breeohan looked up to the ceiling and performed a fire lacing to light the chandelier above. A dozen candles burst into flame, lighting the edges of the room and brightening the purple of his eyes.

His tactic didn't distract me, however. "Why would Kelteon suddenly write the king a letter and mention my mother?"

"It was intercepted. It was not meant for the king."

I narrowed my eyes and studied the set of Breeohan's jaw. His teeth were clenched though he tried to stare at me innocently.

"I see. And for whom was the letter intended?"

"I don't know. I only know that the king is sending out men to find him."

"Did the letter say where Kelteon is?" I asked, feeling excited.

"It didn't specifically mention the place, but the king was able to determine where the letter came from."

I slumped back in my chair, thinking. "Something doesn't seem right about all this. It seems a little convenient. How did King Verone find out about the letter?"

"I don't know. He doesn't tell me everything, Mary, and I didn't ask. What does it matter? I would have thought that you would be happy to know we are so close."

"I am. It's just . . . Why am I suddenly confined to the palace?"

Breeohan wouldn't meet my eyes. "The king thought it would be safer for you."

"To be stuck here where people want me killed? The king is the only one with enough power to stop them from taking me down," I said angrily.

"That is why you have a guard."

"Why can't I just go with the king?"

"He has his reasons," he said.

"What 'reasons' could he possibly have?" I held my breath, waiting to see if Breeohan would tell me anything.

Breeohan studied the table. "That is for the king and the training general to say." We sat in silence for a while as I struggled to suppress a yell of exasperation. The king and the training general. Again those two. Did that mean one of them was my father or just that they knew something about who my father was? Breeohan knew something, but it was obvious he wasn't going to say.

"I am glad you called for me. I wanted to say good-bye," Breeohan said.

I sat up straight. "Where are you going?"

"I am going with the king and his troops."

"I see. So you're allowed to go look for my mother, but I'm required to sit here like a good little fake princess." I barely held my voice below a yell.

"It's for the best."

"It is not for the best, and you know it. Please convince the king to let me come. I can't stay here. I don't belong here, and with you and the king gone, I . . ." This part was hard. "I'm afraid something will happen to me." I couldn't say more.

Breeohan put his hand on mine across the table. I concentrated on not pulling away. "Nothing will happen to you, Mary. The king has made sure you will be protected while we're gone."

"The training general is going too? That means the only one left here who knows who I really am will be Rafan." The thought was not comforting.

"Actually . . ." Breeohan looked sheepish.

"Rafan?" I asked in astonished resentment.

"It's necessary," he replied.

"Just let me go with you," I pleaded, feeling extremely exposed.

"I can't," he said.

I pulled my hand away slowly, my head bowed. "I think you should go now, Breeohan." I watched his fingers curl into his hand.

He sat for a moment more and then finally stood and walked to the door. "Good-bye, Mary." He waited for a moment but I sat silently until he finally opened the door and left.

I lolled in a muddle of depression, thinking about Mom and wishing I could find her, wishing I could leave.

I got out the map Ismaha had given me and looked it over again, wishing that the intensity of my gaze had the power to pull my eyes to the right spot. The king had said that Kelteon was banished to Zephti, but when I spoke to him as Kelson, he had said he was from Michigan in Iberloah. No, that wasn't right. When he'd started to say Michigan he'd said it funny before correcting himself. Could he have been saying a name in Iberloah before stopping himself? I started reading all the names on the map, looking for a name similar to Michigan. The place jumped out at me: Mitigan. It was in the mountains before Zephti. That had to be where he was, I was positive. But there was nothing I could do about it.

I went to the window to see how far up my room was from the ground, but found that though I could probably get down without injury if I hung from the window and dropped, there was another guard sitting far too alertly at the foot of my shutters. I went back to the dresser, put on my peasant clothes, and packed one nice outfit in my backpack with my map. I couldn't bear to leave my backpack behind. Also, it was the only bag in my room. I tied my hair back and took the golden comb on the dresser. I felt horrible for taking it, but I only had a little money left from the sale of my schoolbook to Breeohan. My money wouldn't last long, and the trip would be a long one. I'd have to pay the king back somehow. Staying here was not an option.

I went to the door and peeked out of the crack. The guard turned.

"Could you send Sentai to me? I need her for something."

When Sentai came in, I was sitting on the bed waiting. She saw the bag next to me and how I was dressed and immediately pleaded, "Please, Your Highness, don't do anything rash."

"I have to, but I need your help. Please? I know I'm asking a big thing of you, so if you don't think you can, I'll understand." My heart was in my throat.

"I will do whatever my lady wishes," Sentai said in her best neutral servant voice.

"I can't afford to have you acting on orders. I need to know you will do this favor not as a servant, but as a friend. Otherwise, I'll just say good night and ask that you talk to no one until you must."

"I will help," she said with the hint of a sigh.

"It won't take much. All I ask is that when you leave, you hold the door open a moment so I can get through. Will you do that for me?"

"As you wish, my lady," she said.

I sighed sadly. "Thank you, Sentai. I want you to know, if I never see you again, that I really appreciate all your help. You didn't have to be nice to me, and I am grateful for it. I wish there was something I could do for you, but I have nothing, and I have no power. I'm so sorry."

"You were kind, my lady. That is more than most servants can say of their mistresses."

I looked at her in sympathy. "Okay, let's go," I said. I created the unnoticeable lacing in my mind and tapped the strand that would activate it. Sentai nodded and turned toward the door.

"I have fulfilled the princess's desires," she said, opening the door wider than necessary to get out. I followed as close behind her as I dared, but still came perilously close to getting my foot stuck in the door when the guard unexpectedly shoved it closed behind Sentai. I followed her a few more meters before whispering good-bye and heading to the huge palace wall.

The air was still and thick with the hoarded heat of the day as I walked quietly through the courtyard, past the well-manicured entrance plants and smooth, cobbled road. I felt like a shadow, unreal and not quite solid. When I came to the huge gates blocking my way, my substantiality returned to me in a jolt as I realized I hadn't thought of how to get past the wall. Indecision gnawed at me as I watched the men on the upper walkway pace and then stand silently a while before moving off in the opposite direction.

I scanned the darkness of the wall to find the door leading to the walkway, wondering when the watch would be changed. The door was near the large gates, but in a recess. Pulling on the handle as quietly as I could did no good. It was locked. So I settled down to wait for the change of the guards, still not sure what good that would do; even if I did get through the door and up to the walkway, I'd still be stuck on the top of the wall with no way down the other side.

As I waited, I mulled over the problem. In order to descend the wall, I would need hands and feet that would stick like a lizard's or, more realistically, a rope. But where would I find one? Suddenly my mind got caught on my first thought. Why *couldn't* I have hands and feet like a lizard's? It wasn't hard to heal my skin. Would it be much harder to change it? I felt the smooth rock of the wall and wondered if even a lizard would be able to find purchase. It seemed doubtful. What else would be able to stick, suction cups?

Then it hit me. An ordinary lizard might not be able to climb the sheer face of the wall, but I was positive a gecko could. I tried to remember all I could about geckos, recalling part of an article I'd read, explaining why geckos were able to climb across ceilings and absolutely smooth surfaces. They had a million tiny hairs that became so small at the tip that they bonded to the molecules of the surface where the gecko stood.

I concentrated on what I knew about gecko's feet, trying to remember every detail about the article that I could. Finally, a golden lacing formed in my mind. I studied it alongside my own hand lacing for quite some time before I saw what part of the gecko lacing I needed to modify, what string of golden light I needed to change. Just as I took my sneakers off to try the lacing, I heard the sound of laughter and footsteps.

Melting further into the wall's shadow, I waited for the newcomers. As I'd hoped, it was the next guard shift. Standing as close behind the last man as I could without alerting him to my presence, I slipped in after him. My toe scuffed the first stair, making a sound like thunder in my ears. I winced in pain, and clamped my mouth closed, hoping the sound of the other men had drowned out the noise. After locking the door, the last guard simply turned and bounded up the stairs on the heels of his companions.

Breath puffed out of my mouth in relief . . . a little too soon. The man stopped mid-bound and rotated back toward me. I quickly slunk to the darkest part of the stairwell. He studied the darkness for a moment, but the torch was several feet up from him, leaving me in deep shadow. Finally, he turned and climbed more sedately after his companions.

I waited, still as a statue until I could no longer hear him on the stairs, then I cautiously followed him up, worried he might detect me if he were still actually looking for someone. I wasn't exactly invisible, after all. At the top of the stairs I peered around the bend cautiously. But the two different shifts were reporting to each other, so I slipped by to the outer wall on tiptoe and looked down to the ground below.

Ever since Rafan's comment about blowing things up, I'd been a little nervous every time I tried something new with my lacings. But the gecko feet and hand lacing worked without any explosions. In the dark I couldn't even tell any difference to my palms or soles—at least, I couldn't until I tried to move to the ledge and found myself stuck to the ground. It took several yanks and a silent scream of panicked frustration until I remembered that the gecko article had also said the molecular bond became too weak when the gecko tipped his foot past a certain angle. Cautiously, I angled my foot away from the ground rather than pulling it straight up. My iron lock on the floor released.

I sighed and moved slowly over and down the edge of the wall, getting used to putting my hands and feet straight down, then angling to release their tenacious hold. The wall was dizzyingly high, but each time I moved a limb, I stuck like super glue, so I didn't feel as frightened as I would have otherwise. It was actually rather exhilarating. That is, until I looked up at that same rear guard peering down on me with a furrowed brow, as if he wasn't sure he was really seeing something or not. I froze and tried to pretend to be a rather large bump in the wall.

"Hey, Ero," the man called. "Would you come over here and look at something for me?" His form disappeared for a moment, and I decided to get down fast so that I could retreat to a more shadowed place. I moved as quickly as I could. Straight, angle down, straight, angle down, straight, stuck, remember to angle, and down. My foot hit the dirt. I quickly changed my feet and hands back to normal and ran to a nearby bush just as the two men reappeared at the wall.

"I could have sworn . . ." the man said before turning to apologize.

"Seeing mirages, Tentr?" the other man asked.

"I suppose so. It was certainly strange," he answered. They moved away again, and I sprinted for the cover of the nearest house. Though all the mansions in the area were walled as well, I walked in their shadows until I was sure that I wouldn't be seen from the palace wall. I then stopped to put shoes and socks back on my abused feet.

I was a little disoriented, but I headed in what I thought was a southerly direction. The mansions changed to un-gated houses, then shops, and then much more rundown buildings. A few people moved about. The dark blue sky was lightening, and the stars beginning to fade. I'd have to hurry and hope that I was heading in the direction of the river. If I was wrong, there was a chance I'd be discovered missing and dragged back by my ear before I even left the city.

The air began to feel more humid and everything smelled of fish and damp. I breathed a sigh of relief and trotted in the direction of the smell. There were no signs, and the men loading the ships didn't talk much beyond short phrases such as, "Ware!" or "Haul away." Fatigue washed over me as I undid the unnoticeable lacing. Lack of sleep seemed to affect the stamina I had laboriously built up with Breeohan. Shucking off the chameleon lacing had been difficult. I'd have to be careful so another lacing wouldn't be necessary.

I eased out of a shadowy corner, trying to look as unimportant as possible. No one seemed to pay much attention to me as I headed purposefully toward the first ship loading cargo. A potbellied man stood watching as crates were loaded onto the ship. From a distance he looked unkempt. As I neared, the stains on his clothes stood out in all their crusted and splattered glory. I had to stop a few feet away to keep from gagging at the smell of him.

"Pardon me, but are you the captain of this ship?" I asked, trying to fight my body's natural reaction to dry heave and instead keep a pleasant expression on my face.

"I am. What do you want?" he asked in a sharp, deep voice.

"Are you heading upriver?"

"Yes, in about a portion, so if you don't have anything useful to say, leave."

I was tempted to do just that, but traveling by foot would be much too slow. "Can I book passage on your ship?"

"Not unless you can work. Do you know anything about sailing?"

"Not much, but I learn quickly."

"How are you at cooking?"

My eyes were partially cast down to hide their color, but this man seemed to interpret the movement much differently, for I saw him leer at me through my lashes. I repressed a shudder. "I'm a fairly good cook, but I may not know the recipes you're accustomed to."

"Good enough. My last cook just left me without a cloud of warning, so you'll have to do. You won't get paid, but I won't charge for your passage. Got anything to do before getting aboard? If not, then get inside and acquaint yourself with the kitchen. My name's Captain Hior. I am sure you and I'll have a good time getting to know each other while we're aboard."

"Thank you." I hurried away as fast as I could without being obvious.

The thought of the captain made me nervous. What could I do if he wanted to take advantage of me? I certainly wouldn't let him, but it would make my situation much more difficult. I'd just have to find another boat as soon as I could.

The boat's galley was a mess, and I kept myself busy cleaning and cooking for the crew. They ignored me, and I returned the favor. Captain Hior shot some disturbing glances my way during the meals, but it wasn't until late in the afternoon of the second day aboard his ship that he confronted me. No one had directed me to a cot on board, so I'd slept on the kitchen's floor. I was napping as the soup for dinner stewed when something sharp kicked my shin, jolting me awake.

I looked up, disoriented, to see the captain's form leaning menacingly over me. "What? So you're a lazy one, are you? Sleeping while you should be cooking. I've a right mind to reprimand you good and proper." His voice bellowed in anger, but his eyes were slitted slyly. I stood up quickly.

"The soup is cooking. There's nothing more for me to do but wait for it to be done," I said quickly.

He stood for a moment, leering at me, and I moved to the pot both to stir the soup and to get farther away from him. But I kept my body angled toward him so he couldn't sneak up on me.

"We'll be another two days getting to our next port. You decide whether the rest of your time on this ship will be uncomfortable," he indicated the kitchen floor with a sweep of his hand, "or comfortable," he stepped toward me to stroke my cheek with his sausage hand and my nose was swamped with the stench of unwashed human. I backed up hastily, feeling a mixture of fear, anger, and nausea.

"I choose the floor," I said, barely remembering to keep my eyes downcast.

He followed my retreat with another firm thunk of his boot-shod foot, effectively trapping me in the corner. "Oh, now don't be shy. I insist." His voice turned hard. My insides churned from the smell of body odor and my own fear. "If you're good, I'll make sure no one touches you but me."

Though the floor had been hard and sleep difficult, I felt much better at this point than when I'd entered the boat. I knew that I would be able to fight, be it with magic or fist, and suddenly my fear was dispelled by a wave of anger.

I looked him straight in the eyes and saw him gasp before his eyes narrowed again in lustful speculation. That was not what I wanted. "Step away, Captain Hior, and leave me alone or you will regret it."

"Come, come, a little thing like you? And with me surrounded as I am by my crew? I am sure you wouldn't be so foolish," he said. Had he really missed the fact that I was half a head taller than he was? The thought of the crew backing him up did give me a chill, however. Everyone had ignored me up to now, but that could quickly change.

He saw me hesitate and smirked as he snaked his hand toward me. "Stop!" I yelled, but he didn't listen. I blocked his arm and punched him in the gut. Then I kneed him in the groin before slipping past his bulky form to stand, with a table between us, near the stairs leading out of the galley. He crumpled in pain and shock but recovered himself with a roar of fury, taking the table in his hands as if to fling it aside to get to me.

"Stay where you are or I will make sure you never harm another person ever again." He paused, hands gripping the table, but a smirk spread over his face.

"And how would you do that? If you haven't noticed, you're on a boat full of my men on a very wide, croc-filled river. One shout and my crew will come rushing down to carry out my orders. Jump out of the boat, and you'll be food." Would the men really obey an order to rape me? Were they all as horrible as Captain Hior—and did he say crocodiles? What was I thinking to get on this boat in the first place?

I was thinking of getting my mother back. That hadn't changed. And it wasn't going to change now. "Call your men, and you will all find yourself having a very uncomfortable voyage for the next two days," I said, making a sphere of light jump to life in front of me.

The captain recoiled as if struck, and I curved my lips up into a smirk as an added bluff, even though I was quaking inside.

"I don't allow magic on my boat," the captain said. He looked afraid.

"But you do allow rape? How convenient for you. I'll make you a deal. You and your men stay away from me. No one comes down to the galley for any reason—other than food at the regular times—and I will refrain from using my skills to strip you of what little manhood you may possess." I snuffed the light in front of me.

"You will still make the food and you are not to go above deck," he said in a blustery voice meant to show me he wasn't cowed. My eyebrows rose incredulously.

"I will make the food because that was our agreement, but I will not agree to imprisonment," I said.

"My men will make mistakes if they have to worry about a mage up top. I don't want them slipping at the ropes, causing accidents because of you."

"Well, then don't tell them. Just order them to keep their hands to themselves, and we'll all be fine."

"Get back to work," he said, storming past me. His cloud of stench trailed behind him as he headed up the stairs. I noticed that he made sure not to touch me as he passed, however. I walked back to the soup, stirring it with gusto to calm my trembling.

The men were unusually quiet at dinner. After dinner I heard the roar of many voices upstairs, mixed together in argument. But I couldn't make out what they were saying. I started to ascend the stairs to find out what was going on. A young man sat at the top of the stairs. He dashed off at the sight of me, and by the time I reached the deck, all the sailors were silently about their business. I felt a chill creep up my neck and down my arms as I slowly went back to the kitchen and piled all the pots in the doorway.

I set the broom next to me as I lay down to sleep, but though I was tired, sleep was elusive. I couldn't stop thinking about possible lacings to use if I was attacked. I thought of a kind of shield lacing, but I wasn't sure it would work. Questions circled endlessly in my mind until I forced myself to stop and relax. If I got no sleep at all, I would be even more likely to mess up if I ran into trouble. I tried not to think until I finally drifted into a light doze.

I swam in and out of wakefulness until a clank startled me into full awareness. I grabbed hold of the broom and listened in tense concentration. Another scuff sounded against the floor boards, but no more pots rattled, so I was unprepared when a man loomed in front of me and struck my head. The world swayed. The already dark room faded further.

Rough hands dragged me up from the floor as light struck my closed eyelids. My head was on fire with pain, and my mind refused to focus clearly. Many hands carried me up the stairs into the soft glow of dawn.

"Is she unconscious?" I heard the captain ask.

"Yes, sir," someone holding me muttered.

"Good. You men have done a great thing. We are fortunate I discovered her plan to poison us all as we slept so that she could use dark magic to enslave us to her will. I can't believe a dark mage came so close to the palace. But these are perilous times, men. We will be doing the country a service by throwing her to the crocs."

The men surrounding me murmured assent. I used the distraction to perform a healing lacing on my throbbing head. Then I lay as still as possible, trying to maintain the illusion of a comatose state. *The slime.* So this was to be Captain Hior's revenge for my refusing his advances. Boot-shod feet approached me. I heard the other men fall back as the clop of boots on wood came nearer.

"Yes, we have averted a great disaster today," said Captain Hior. His smell strengthened, and in a whisper so quiet I knew only I would be able to hear, he said, "No one makes a fool of Dirro Hior." His meaty finger traced the contour of my cheek. I found it hard not to wince and give myself away. A sudden pain burst to life in my stomach. I gasped, but kept my eyes shut. The blackguard had kicked me.

Hands lifted me roughly from the floor. I risked slitting my eyes open to see where I was so I could judge what my next move should be. The far bank would be a long swim in unsafe waters, but staying on the ship was not an option. I could never overpower that many men. And I had a better chance surviving in the water if I wasn't beaten to death before going in.

"One," yelled the men as they swung me almost over the edge, then back.

"Two." I braced myself for the fall.

"Three." They heaved me forward. My body froze for an instant before plunging into the cool murky liquid of the Kazik River. I stroked underwater away from the boat for as long as my breath would hold, then burst out of the wet murk to look back. Men pointed as they spotted me. A few fingers were indicating something beyond me. I spun around and caught sight of two pairs of eyes making a small wake in the water before the crocodiles sank beneath the brown water. They were headed for me.

I created the steel shield lacing I had thought of the night before to make my body as hard as if it were encased in impenetrable metal, but discovered the disadvantage to this protection as I began to sink. No amount of kicking would bring me to the surface. I was dropping quickly in water whose murk hid anything that was more than a foot away from me.

I had to undo the lacing, but the crocodiles were coming for me, and they probably saw much better through the muddy depths than I did. My lungs started to strain. My ears pressed painfully as I descended. I was about to undo the lacing when a force slammed into my side. Jaws clamped down, but rebounded harmlessly from my steely skin. The other croc I'd seen clamped onto my leg, and though its teeth didn't penetrate, it didn't let go. It tried to roll me in the water, but I was too heavy, so it released me and moved out of my range of vision.

Black sparks began to float before my eyes. Soon I would try to breathe and inhale only water. I undid the steel shield lacing and kicked toward the surface. It took almost too long, but I broke past the water just before the black of unconsciousness overcame me. I breathed in great heaving gasps, but I had only a few moments of air before I saw four pairs of eyes disappear into the water no more than ten feet from me.

Think, think, think, Mary, think, I screamed silently to myself. In desperation I created a water lacing in my head, focused on the water beneath and several feet around me and tweaked the lacing to make it freeze into ice. I felt slick cold touch my feet and rise with sudden force. My body started sliding off the ice, so I created the steel shield lacing again and struck my fingers into the ice with the power of pure fear. My hand wedged tightly as the last of the water rushed off. My newly created mini-iceberg bobbed crazily before the upper portion settled a foot above the water.

I looked down and jumped when I saw a crocodile no more than five inches down, embedded within the ice, teeth bared in readiness to crush my bones. Its tail stuck out of the side of the iceberg, and lashed furiously, loosening large chunks and rocking the iceberg. But the grip of the ice proved too strong, and after several minutes its struggles ceased. I almost felt sorry for the creature despite the chill that shuddered through me when I realized how close I'd come to death.

The other crocodiles circled the ice a few times. One tried to scramble up the side toward me, but slipped. It succeeded in disrupting the iceberg's precarious balance, however, and I was in a state of sheer terror as I gripped my finger crevice and tried to stabilize the ice's swaying so it wouldn't tip over. One of the other crocodiles seemed to think he would give climbing a try too, and the ice dipped as I slid dangerously close to his open jaws before he lost purchase and slid back into the water. I pulled myself to the opposite side to counterbalance the wobble, and then back again, but each time brought me within snapping distance of a crocodile's teeth.

When the ice righted itself there was a lull as the crocs circled. I looked upriver. Captain Hior's ship was almost out of sight. No one would have seen me survive. I was floating in the opposite direction, back toward Ismar. Looking that way, I saw another boat about two hundred yards behind me, just coming into view around a wide curve in the river. But I didn't have any more time to worry or hope. Another croc, or perhaps the same one, scrabbled for purchase on my ice.

He almost made it onto the ice and a wave of water swamped me before I could scramble to the high side of the iceberg. The boat was only one hundred yards away now. I could see people coming to the front of the boat, pointing and yelling. Another croc came closer, so I created the ice lacing in my mind and extended the ice another three feet around the edges. Not expecting the sudden solidity, the crocodile ran full tilt into the ice and reeled away, stunned. The ice rocked, though not as strongly as before since the iceberg's wall was now a foot and a half high and its width was about ten feet across. The crocodiles circled once more, but moved away as the boat came closer.

I watched the predators slide off through the water before looking up toward the approaching ship. Then I went rigid as my gaze locked with familiar, intense aqua eyes. I wrenched my gaze away. Rafan stood motionless among a sea of scurrying men who were being directed by a person in well-tailored, brown clothing. Though he faced away, I knew him at once.

Breeohan.

Chapter 16

Somehow he had found me. He must have figured out where I'd gone almost right away, or he wouldn't have caught up so quickly. I came very close to swearing and felt a despairing sob rise before I could swallow it. He'd send me back to the palace. It didn't help that he was finding me in such a horrible position.

Breeohan turned to look at me with an unreadable expression. He was close now, only a few yards away, but he didn't speak. A sailor threw me a rope.

"Grab on, miss," yelled the sailor. I caught it awkwardly, undid the steel shield lacing, and was hauled ungracefully aboard the ship. I stood, dripping river water all over the deck. I looked like a drowned rat, but I didn't want to use so obvious a magical working as the cleaning lacing around the sailors. Using magic in public was part of what had gotten me thrown overboard in the first place. Straightening, I lifted my chin in a haughty manner as if to say, "How dare you disturb me from my morning swim."

Rafan pushed roughly through the men crowded around me and grabbed my hand earnestly. "My lady, are you well? Do you need a physician?" I could have killed him right there as the previously friendly sailors started to murmur uneasily at the sound of "my lady."

I let out a short bark of laughter instead. "Me? A lady? Hah!" I reclaimed my wet hand and caught a sailor's eyes to share the joke. He paled and bowed awkwardly. Curse my stupid, stupid eyes! Why didn't they have contacts in this horrible, flea-ridden, croc-filled . . . My mind went blank mid-insult as Breeohan stepped forward. His expression seemed to be a mix of anger and something more desperate and unsettling. But anger won.

"What were you doing?" he said, his voice loud, his eyes furious.

"I decided to take a swim," I said, wide-eyed and innocent. Wasn't he even glad to see me? I shrugged that thought away.

"You were almost killed. I had to save you again. Why can't you just do as you're told and stay where you're ordered?"

Fury swiftly replaced my dread. "First of all, you did not save me. I saved myself, which you would have noticed if you weren't so wrapped up in delusions of grandeur. Second, it's my mother. I *will* go after her, no matter what you or anyone else says. Third, who died and made you king? You aren't the boss of me." I heard gasps of shock and realized I might have gone too far on the king comment, considering that Breeohan would, in fact, rule after King Verone.

"I may not be king," there was an unspoken "yet" before Breeohan continued, "but King Verone himself ordered you to stay in the palace. Your actions could be taken as treason." The last was spoken in a whisper of anger for my ears only.

"I am not even a citizen of this country. I have done nothing wrong. Are your laws so corrupt that you would hold an innocent person prisoner?" I hissed this back and then felt a twinge of guilt as I realized that I wasn't totally innocent. I would certainly be in big trouble if anyone let slip the fact that I had impersonated royalty. Although, that wasn't entirely my fault either. It was another one of Breeohan's misguided ideas.

Breeohan's hand smashed down on the boat's rail, startling me. "It was for your own protection, which you obviously needed." His hand swept back to the iceberg, now floating a few hundred yards behind us.

"I told you I was fine. I don't need your help, and I don't recall asking for it."

"What were you going to do, float aimlessly, hoping to come to shore?"

"I would've thought of something," I snapped back.

"And just gotten yourself into trouble again," he retorted.

"Stop treating me like a baby. You're not my father, or my brother, or anything at all to me, so just back off."

Breeohan really did step back as if punched. I looked down in sudden confusion and guilt. "Nothing?" he whispered.

Rafan's raspy voice interrupted me. "My lady, you are soaked and tired. Why don't we let you bathe and get into clean clothes? It seems you've had quite an adventure, and after you've rested, perhaps we can hear about it."

That snapped me back into my surroundings. I looked around to see that the sailors had been watching the show between Breeohan and me. When they saw me looking, they quickly tried to act busy. I felt my cheeks grow hot, but I couldn't go below deck until one thing was settled. I spoke quietly, but firmly. "I am *not* going back to the palace. Breeohan, believe me when I say I'm not any safer there. I figured out where my mother is. How can I do nothing knowing—?"

"I won't stop you anymore." Breeohan turned and walked in the opposite direction as Rafan herded me belowdeck.

"You there, get a hot bath ready immediately," Rafan yelled at one of the sailors.

"No, don't bother," I counter-ordered. "I'm tired of being wet." I performed the cleaning lacing, ignoring any response it might create. I didn't really care what the sailors thought anymore. I felt drained and stupid, and with a shock I remembered that my backpack was still on Captain Hior's ship. A wrench gripped my stomach. I had lost the last link to my former life. I hadn't known how much I'd been relying on it for comfort. Even my sneakers were in my backpack. Nothing—I had nothing left. I had to find Mom soon, or I might begin to doubt her existence.

Rafan led me to a room below where a narrow bunk was nailed to the wall. I noted the bags and gathered that this must be Rafan's and Breeohan's room. I regarded the beds thoughtfully and wondered whose bed was whose.

"I'll leave you now and let you get some rest. You look exhausted, but let me know the moment you need anything." Rafan's eyes looked at me earnestly.

I felt uncomfortable as I remembered his sudden declaration at the ball. "I will, thanks," I mumbled. He hesitated, as if waiting for something else, but then slipped out of the cramped room, closing the door. Slumping to the bottom bunk, I squirmed around uncomfortably until I switched to the top bunk. It felt softer and cleaner, and I soon drifted into a deeper sleep than I'd been able to have in days.

That didn't stop me from waking when the door opened several hours later.

"It's just me," said Rafan. "I brought you some food. You missed the midday meal."

I swung my legs over the side and jumped down. Sharp pins jabbed my feet and legs as I landed. Rafan handed me a plate of grubby-looking soup. I stared suspiciously at some of the floating chunks. *I guess it's back to terrible travel food.* I sighed inwardly. Several forced bites later, as the rocking of the boat began to feel like ocean swells and Rafan's eyes stayed glued to me, I put my spoon down, unable to eat any more.

"Are you full already? You hardly ate anything." Rafan set the bowl aside carelessly. Some of the soup spilled, but he didn't notice because he was grabbing my now-empty hands and hunting my evasive eyes with single-minded purpose.

"Rafan, I . . ."

His finger lifted to my lips with catlike quickness. "Wait. I know it is too soon to expect an answer. I just wanted to ask if you would allow me to go with you on your search for your mother. I can be of help to you."

"I didn't think I had a choice."

"There is always a choice."

My hands started to feel sweaty. I didn't really want to promise not to ditch Rafan, just in case I had to for some reason. I was looking around for a distraction when Breeohan came through the door, saw my hands in Rafan's and froze, his hand still on the door. I quickly tugged my fingers out of Rafan's but realized that probably made it look worse. Rafan's smug smile didn't help either.

"Am I interrupting something?" Breeohan said in a neutral tone.

"Yes," Rafan said at the same instant I said, "No."

"No," I said again more firmly, shooting a dagger glare at Rafan. The curl of his lips lifted even more. I turned back to Breeohan. "Rafan was just trying to convince me to take him with me to where I know my mother is." A glance back showed that Rafan was no longer smiling.

"Rafan and I were already planning to take you to the king. You can travel on from there with the whole company if King Verone permits you." Breeohan sounded doubtful. The idea of meeting up with the king sounded bad for my chances.

"Are they on a boat too?" I asked.

"No. Boats cut time from the journey, but the king has too many people with him, and they will need quite a few horses for when the path splits from the river. Horses in the numbers they will need are hard to find at the river's turn-off, so they're traveling by horse from the palace. They're probably two or three days behind us," Breeohan said.

"So what will we do? Wait for them at the next port?" I asked as nonchalantly as I could, even though I chafed at the thought of turning around or waiting for so long, especially since the king might again decide to leave me behind. Maybe I could convince Breeohan and Rafan to continue ahead with me. If not, I could always try sneaking off again. That thought didn't sit well with me, though. I'd rather talk Breeohan into going on with me. I wouldn't feel so childish, like a spoiled kid who runs away every time she doesn't get her way.

"That's what we'll have to do since the captain has insisted that he cannot turn around." Breeohan scowled, jarring me from my thoughts.

I had to think for a second to remember what my question had been. "You can't blame him for wanting to keep his appointments," I said, trying to look innocent. Breeohan glanced at me suspiciously. It was time to change the subject. "You wouldn't know if there is any way of getting my backpack from the ship I was on when we get there, would you? They aren't that far ahead. I bet they'll still be in the next port when we arrive. The thing is, I don't think I should be the one to get it."

Breeohan sighed wearily. He sat and invited me to do the same. Rafan looked intrigued as he too sunk to a chair. "I would love to hear what transpired to leave you floating on ice in the middle of the Kazik," Rafan said, the edge of his mouth curling.

"So would I," Breeohan said. He didn't look as amused.

"I left the palace, got on the first boat out, was accused of being a dark mage, and got thrown overboard. Not much to it really," I said quickly, realizing I had chosen the wrong subject with which to distract Breeohan and Rafan.

"There is certainly much more to your story than you said." Rafan grinned.

"Don't think you're getting away with telling only that," Breeohan said. "I know how you slipped past the guard at your door. Sentai told me. But how did you get past the wall?"

"She told you? Just like that?" I felt betrayed. I guess she didn't think of me as a friend after all.

"It wasn't hard to make her see how perilous things could be for you on your own in Iberloah. She was worried for you," Breeohan said. I kept my eyes down, sad but not angry. Sentai had done what she felt was right.

"So, the wall? How did you get through it?" Breeohan repeated.

"You know, this and that," I said. *Yeah right, like I'm gonna tell him.* He'd probably just narc on me to the king so they could keep a better lock on me the next time they decided to protect me for "my own good." Breeohan glared, and I glared back.

"What happened on the boat?" Rafan asked to get my attention. He cocked his head impishly.

I leapt to answer the new question gratefully. "Captain Hior didn't want passengers, so I got on as ship's cook, only I found out there were stipulations to the job that I wasn't willing to pay." I scowled at the memory of Captain Hior's greasy, smelly body close to mine.

Breeohan's body tensed, and Rafan's smile had disappeared. "Did he ruin you?" Rafan asked in a rough growl.

"Ruin me?" I suppressed a surge of annoyance. "Uh . . . if that means what I *think* you mean, then no, but he did try. I made the mistake of thinking that a warning was enough, but I guess his pride couldn't take my refusal. He told the crew I was an evil magician planning to poison them, so they threw me overboard." I shrugged.

"That scoundrel. He won't get away with this," Rafan said.

I looked at him quizzically. Something about his words seemed fake, like he was pretending to be affronted rather than really caring. Breeohan said nothing, but looking at his face, I felt suddenly afraid. I could tell he was angry at the captain not me, but it was unnerving to see his eyes dark with rage. It was a different kind of anger than when we had argued, deeper and definitely scarier.

"I'm fine, Breeohan. Nothing happened. He couldn't touch me. See?" I held out my arms. "He couldn't even bruise me." The flame in his eyes dimmed, but his jaw was still clenched tight. Rafan looked offended that I'd addressed Breeohan when Breeohan hadn't even been the one to say anything. I sighed in frustration.

Breeohan caught the sigh and the look on Rafan's face. His lips curved up, and his jaw relaxed slowly. We shared a look like a private joke. It felt good, and I realized I didn't like having Breeohan angry at me. Why did he have to act so funny lately, all tight and reproving?

I looked away from him, sad. "So do you think you two could get my stuff back?" I asked the table. Glancing up I saw a slight frown on Breeohan's face. Rafan looked confused.

"I'm sure something could be arranged," Breeohan said quietly.

"Of course it can," Rafan said loudly, with a renewed coquettish smile. I wasn't sure if guys were really allowed to be classified as coquettish, but that was certainly the word Rafan made me think of at times.

"Thank you." I smiled equally on all. After all, I was grateful. Breeohan looked up and smiled back, wearily.

"So, where am I going to be sleeping for the night?" I asked.

"I asked the captain, but there are no more cabins. You can take my bunk," Breeohan jerked his head up indicating the top bed. "I'll sleep on the floor."

"You don't have to do that. I slept on the wooden floor of the galley for the past two nights anyway. I'm used to it," I said.

Breeohan's jaw tightened again. "Indulge me."

I noticed Rafan didn't offer to sleep on the floor. I guessed he was hesitant to give up his creature comforts. "Okay," I agreed. Then, feeling the desire to confuse Breeohan, I gave him a cocky grin. "You don't have to twist my arm too hard."

Breeohan looked puzzled. "I fail to see how twisting your arm will be more convincing to you, but if that is what you want." He shrugged, but there was an impish twinkle in his eye as his hand shot to my elbow and tugged hard. My bottom slid off the chair, but I managed to save myself from falling by grabbing the seat at the last second.

"Unfair!" I laughed as I clung to the chair. "I can't even retaliate." Breeohan dropped my elbow, and I scooted back to the seat.

Breeohan looked quite boyish as he laughed with me. "Are you convinced yet?" he asked, the devil still in his eyes. I tried to scoot the chair back but it was bolted to the floor. Breeohan made as if to catch my elbow again, but I jumped up out of the way, his hand brushing my thigh as I twisted away.

"Ha," I trumpeted, gloating in my successful evasion. Breeohan looked ready to pounce after me.

"Breeohan, I am surprised at your obscene behavior toward Mary." Rafan's caustic tones wiped the smile from both our faces. Rafan looked angry enough to tear through iron. "If you weren't the heir, I would challenge you to a duel for such mistreatment," he continued.

I suppressed a surge of irritation.

"Is that all that's stopping you, Rafan?" Breeohan said in a voice devoid of humor. "Because if it is, you needn't concern yourself on that point. Or perhaps it's something else that keeps you from engaging in anything more threatening than words. Or rather, a lack of something." Rafan's and Breeohan's eyes locked tensely.

"Hold up. Nobody's fighting anyone. You two are not going to brawl over a stupid joke. Rafan, I'm sure Breeohan didn't intend for his actions to seem obscene. He was just taking an expression from my country a little too literally." I tried not to roll my eyes. "Breeohan, goading Rafan certainly doesn't help solve anything. What is wrong with you two, anyway? I thought you came after me to help me, not snarl at each other like, like . . . I don't even know. It doesn't make sense. If you'll excuse me, I'm going for some fresh air."

I turned my back on them and slammed the door behind me. On deck the crew was moving about in a leisurely manner. The sun was low on the horizon, and the breeze was almost cool on my face. The water slid by, reflecting the light like a murky mirror. I shivered when I saw a crocodile slide into the water from the far shore. I would never look at crocodiles quite the same way after today.

Turning my eyes slightly, I saw a purple smudge of distant mountain peaks jutting close to the horizon. They seemed such a long way away, and the king was so far behind, traveling at a much slower rate. I remembered from my map that I could stick to boats for quite a while before the path diverged. How much more time would it add to the journey to go by horse the whole way? Would it make a difference to Mom's life? It had been so long already. It might not make much difference. My heart squeezed painfully at the thought. More time might not logically make much difference, but I couldn't stop the feeling that I needed to get to her as fast as possible.

It would be easy to get Rafan to go ahead with me, but Breeohan? How was I going to convince him to leave without the approval of King Verone? The sun sank as my thoughts churned on what to do. There was no way I was going ahead with only Rafan. I couldn't figure the guy out, and the thought of traveling alone with him gave me the heebie-jeebies. *I mean, who proposes so soon after meeting someone, especially someone he knows nothing about?*

Rafan couldn't actually be in love with me. He was either deluding himself or up to something. I didn't have any riches, and he knew I wasn't a princess. Maybe he hoped the truth of my humble origins would never be discovered, giving him the chance to rise in the ranks of Iberloahan society. As if I was going to stick around!

That thought jolted me as I remembered there might be no way to get back to Earth, even after I found Mom. More startling was the confusion that ensued when I thought of leaving. I felt a strange mixture of reluctance to go, juxtaposed by the desire to retreat back to my sometimes boring, but definitely safer and more comfortable existence. My stay in Iberloah certainly hadn't been a cookies-and-milk experience, but the desert had wrapped around me as the cool green forest and cloudy skies of Oregon never had. Though the sun was often blistering hot, it was also comforting in its cheerful consistency. I could get sun in Arizona, but this desert was different. I had discovered and been taught the wonders of magic here. There was still so much potential to uncover.

And as hard as I tried not to dwell on it, the possibility that either Verone or Sogran could be my father was never far from my mind. I wanted to find out the truth, but I was afraid of what that discovery would reveal. My thoughts veered away as they always did when I contemplated the troubling mystery of my parentage.

I heard steps behind me but didn't look over as a figure leaned against the rail beside me. A warmth spread through my middle as I thought of another reason I didn't want to leave Iberloah, but I slapped the feeling away, remembering that Breeohan wouldn't have much time for odd alien friends when he was king and married to the queen of all evil, Avana. She would make sure of that.

The two of us stared at the dark water for several minutes before Breeohan spoke. "I'm sorry," he said quietly.

"For which thing?" I asked, trying not to smile.

"For my crude behavior."

"What, the arm pulling? Do you really think that was crude? I don't think I'll ever understand this country of yours." I sighed.

Breeohan smiled at the water. "No, that's not what I meant. I was referring to when I yelled at you . . . and for making things more difficult between you and Rafan." Breeohan's smile dropped away, and his face became brooding.

Me and Rafan? What was he talking about? "He's your friend. I was just trying to avoid getting thrown off *this* boat, but thanks for apologizing. I'm sorry I yelled at you too, and I am grateful you pulled me out of the water." The last part came out reluctantly.

Breeohan glanced over, smirking. "With such sincere and lavish gratitude to be had, I don't know why I haven't been rescuing beautiful young maidens more often."

My breath caught on the word beautiful. Did he really think I was beautiful, or was he just being funny? He looked over quickly when he heard me gasp. "You didn't rescue me." I tried to say it as a retort, but it came out as a wimpy, rather breathy whisper.

Breeohan's eyes, locked with mine, seemed suddenly intense. "I know," he said.

Chapter 17

It was awkward getting settled in the room with Rafan in the bunk below me and Breeohan on the floor. But a relatively soft bed, combined with my interrupted sleep from the night before and my Nature Channel moment with the crocodiles, brought sleep swiftly. When I woke again, a single candle showed that Rafan and Breeohan were gone. Lack of sunlight made it hard to judge the time. I got up and performed the cleaning lacing on myself, then walked up to the deck where the day's brightness blinded me till my eyes adjusted. Looking around I saw Breeohan and Rafan talking quietly but venomously to each other. I was too far away to hear what they were saying but decided I'd better go break it up. They noticed me as I neared, and both their mouths snapped shut.

"You look lovely this morning, my lady, as usual," Rafan said, stepping forward and kissing my hand. Breeohan said nothing, just stared stormily as Rafan tucked my hand under his elbow. I tried to pull it out again, but I felt Rafan's hand tighten around mine, locking me in place.

"So what are you two arguing about?" I asked as I studied my bound hand and tried to devise a way to free it.

"Shipping. Breeohan thinks that certain families have too much power on the river, while I think that they have earned their right to higher prices," Rafan said.

I looked at Breeohan for confirmation and could tell from the quickly covered look on his face that shipping was *not* what they had been arguing about. But I let it drop. "Did I miss breakfast? I was thinking of heading down for some food." I gave another tug on my arm, but it was held fast.

"First meal was served two portions ago, but I know they will find you something if I ask. Let me escort you there," Rafan said.

"No really, I'll get it myself. It's no problem." I gave a no-nonsense yank to free myself.

Rafan just grabbed me again. "It is no problem at all. My discussion with Breeohan was getting dull anyway."

Breeohan's fists clenched, but he remained silent, so I let Rafan lead me to the galley. There Rafan made a few sharp and, I thought, somewhat rude commands to get me a bowl of lumpy stew.

Rafan sat to watch me eat, but I was hungry so I tried to ignore him and the taste of the food. Despite stuffing my face as fast as possible, I was still left with a sourness in my mouth and an irrational desire to scratch Rafan's eyes out so I could rest from his single-minded attention. I knew most girls dreamed of someone as good-looking as Rafan mooning over their every move, but my experiences with Kelson and Joe were still too fresh in my mind. Mom and I seemed to have a talent for attracting bad apples.

As I set my empty bowl down, Rafan's eyes caught mine. I furiously tried to come up with ways to ditch him on a small boat. My prospects were not looking good.

"You know, that is the first time I have seen you finish your food," Rafan said with a flirtatious grin.

What do you say to that? Apparently nothing, as Rafan continued.

"Can I assume this means your nervousness caused by my presence has receded a little?" My eyes went wide in surprise. "You don't have to worry, Mary. I know you are a shy person. I won't press this point any longer. Just know that I'm glad you're losing some of that reserve." Rafan suddenly scooted closer to me on the bench and moved his face to within an inch of mine. "Though I hope you won't lose all those flutters."

Too flustered to speak and afraid he might kiss me, I turned my face away quickly.

Rafan chuckled. "Still shy, I see. I can wait."

As I studied the wood grain of the table, Rafan quietly left. The good news was that I was free of Rafan breathing down my neck, and I hadn't even had to try. The bad news . . . my insides were broiling in confusion.

I climbed topside slowly, unsure if I would be left alone long, and undecided about if I wanted to be. It was moments like these that made me miss Mom the most. Talking with her had always seemed to make my confused thoughts click into place.

Breeohan stood by the rail, looking across the river, and I found myself heading to him before my brain remembered I'd craved solitude.

"Hey." I leaned against the rail and looked to where Breeohan's eyes were fixed. A crocodile's head poked above the murky water. I shivered. "So what were you and Rafan really arguing about earlier?" I asked.

"You, of course," he said simply.

"Me, of course? You make me sound like a force of destruction. 'There was an argument? Well, of course it had to be about Mary, the source of all conflict, don't ya know.' "

Breeohan's mouth quirked, but his eyes were still troubled.

"You were arguing about letting me go with you to find my mother weren't you?" I asked, my light mood vanishing.

"Yes and no."

"What does that mean? Look, I don't know exactly why the king decided to leave me behind before, but I'm here now. It would be silly to send me back now."

"It would be for your own protection."

"Don't I have a right to decide what's best for me?"

"Not when you're ignorant of so much."

"Of what, the culture? I'm just as ignorant there as here, and my ignorance there was making my stay even more dangerous than traveling to find my mother."

"More dangerous than superstitious sailors throwing you overboard and crocodiles snapping at your limbs?"

"Okay, just as dangerous. But I would rather be doing something constructive than sitting on my behind since I seem to be in trouble no matter where I am anyway."

"That's certainly true." Breeohan smiled wryly.

"Then we're agreed," I said triumphantly.

"No."

"What? Come on, be reasonable."

"I am being reasonable. It's you who can't see the whole picture. You'll just be a liability if you come along with the search party," he said.

That was the last straw. "Well, at least now I know what you think of me." Ice dripped from my voice. I turned to leave, but Breeohan grabbed my arm before I could step away. "Let go," I said, violently shrugging off his hand.

"That came out wrong. I didn't mean you're useless, I just meant . . . I can't say," he trailed off.

"Wow, that's some apology. You should go into business." I walked away before he could make me feel worse.

We reached the city of Tois at the sun's last flare. The wooden dock was still crowded with workers, and it wasn't long before the ship was roped securely and a plank bridge had been connected from the ship to the floating wooden walkway. I searched for Captain Hior's ship and found it, tied closer to land. Only one man was visible on deck, and I decided to forego Rafan's and Breeohan's help in retrieving my backpack. I didn't really want to be around either of them anyway.

As soon as the plank was in place, I jumped to the bridge and descended to the wharf.

Breeohan's voice stopped me. "Wait, my lady, don't go anywhere without Zephan Rafan and me, if you please," he yelled. I considered several snotty quips, but with such a large audience around, I decided to keep quiet. Instead, I waited until the workers' attention was back on their jobs and then pretended to trip while two men shielded me from Breeohan's view. It took only an instant to activate the chameleon lacing. Then I stood and began to weave my way, unnoticed, toward Captain Hior's boat.

I heard a curse behind me as Breeohan discovered my absence, but I ignored him as I analyzed which would be the most discrete way to board Hior's ship. For time's sake, I decided to chance the boarding plank as soon as the man on watch looked away. It wouldn't take Breeohan long to figure out where I was going.

I threw a rock to the far side of the ship and scuttled up the plank as the lookout's head turned. Then I flattened myself against the rail when he looked back. It was unnerving to have someone look so close to my exact spot and yet not see me. I waited with bated breath until he looked away. When he turned, I ran past him to the stairs.

The ship's inner rooms were as empty of people as the deck, so I had no trouble getting to the kitchen, but my backpack wasn't there. I searched the storage rooms with no luck, and even ventured into the sleeping area. The only place left to search was Captain Hior's quarters. I had a strong feeling that my backpack was there, but I didn't want to enter the nest of such a loathsome man.

I tried the door. It was locked, but before I could think of how to break in a yell sounded from inside. "Who is fiddling with my door?

Either knock like a man or go away," he bellowed.

My hand poised, undecided, then descended in a loud knock. I slid to the shadows just as Captain Hior opened the door, his miasmic odor sweeping out with the whoosh.

His lungs filled with what I could tell would be a loud roar, so I knocked him in the jaw three times in quick succession, and amazingly, he crumpled to the floor. His breath let out in a repulsive but noiseless blast. I gagged but stepped around him into the mother lode of disgusting aromas. My backpack lay in plain sight on the blackened floor. My clothes and books were strewn near it, but Ismaha's map was unrolled on the captain's food-encrusted desk. Something sticky smeared one edge, but I didn't dare use the cleaning lacing in case it erased the ink too.

I settled with wiping if off as best I could with one of Hior's cleaner looking shirts, then checked the bag's front pockets. The granola bar and several pens were missing, and I couldn't see my shoes anywhere.

A twitch of movement from the corner of my eye snapped my head toward the prone form of Captain Hior. He jerked again, and my eyes were drawn to his legs where I gazed in horror at my shoes on his feet. Who knew what kind of disgusting fungal cultures dwelled on those sausages? I yanked my sneakers off in anger and performed the cleaning lacing on them before stuffing them back in my bag. Then I jumped over Captain Hior to the hallway. I ran up the stairs and crouched in a recess until the thundering roar of Captain Hior's voice brought the lookout streaking past me down the stairs. Then I sprinted over the boat, down the plank, and smack into Breeohan.

"Mary? I can hardly see you. Would you please release the chameleon lacing?" he said with clenched teeth.

"I don't think that would be a good idea right now." I slid to his other side so that he would shield me from Captain Hior.

Rafan came up to Breeohan just as an earsplitting blast erupted on the deck of Captain Hior's ship. "Thief, there's been a thief on my ship," he yelled as he searched the dock below for someone suspicious.

"What's going on?" Rafan asked. He didn't seem to have noticed me yet.

"Just move casually," Breeohan said to him.

Breeohan and Rafan began to stroll past the ship with me sandwiched in between.

"I thought you wanted us to get your pack," Breeohan hissed.

"I was tired of being useless," I snapped in a whisper.

Rafan jerked to a stop, so I grabbed his shirt to drag him back into motion. "Mary? What happened to you? I can't see you very well."

"I get that a lot," I said.

"She decided to get her pack alone, despite agreeing to let us handle it."

"My lady, you should have let us retrieve it for you," Rafan said sternly.

"Too late now. It's done. Let's just get out of here." I glanced nervously behind me where Hior was still creating a racket, stopping everyone who passed. He searched unlucky passersby roughly for evidence of my shoes and backpack.

Four city guards passed us to deal with the commotion, and Rafan, Breeohan, and I walked as quickly as we could without seeming to flee. "You do have a way of attracting trouble, my lady," Rafan said.

Breeohan snorted agreement. I chose to ignore both of them. Once we were far enough within the city for the smells, sights, and sounds of the river to have disappeared, I dropped the chameleon lacing.

"That's quite a trick. I would be honored if you would show me the lacing, my lady," Rafan said, his eyes intense with desire.

It made me uneasy. "Would you please stop calling me 'my lady,' Rafan? There's no one else here."

"I think it would be best if we kept up appearances just in case. Don't you?" Rafan asked around me to Breeohan.

"It would be safest," he replied.

I was annoyed at being talked over. "I don't see how. What reason could Princess Kasala have for going to a river port four days inland?"

"Why *wouldn't* the princess wish to sample the sights along the river of Kazik? We have some of the most beautiful cities in the world here," Rafan countered smoothly.

"But I didn't bring my servant. I've gathered going without servants is a major faux pas." "Faux pas" didn't translate. "Oh brother!" I groaned. "How am I ever supposed to make my point when no one can understand me?"

Rafan ignored my tantrum. "We'll tell them I charmed you away with promises of all the servants you could desire." He grinned lasciviously.

I sidled away an inch. "I'd really rather keep a low profile," I said in as no-nonsense a tone as possible.

"It is a bit hard to stay unnoticed with eyes like yours," Breeohan replied.

"I'll keep my head down," I said firmly.

"If that is what you'd really prefer," Rafan said doubtfully.

"I would." We were to a section of the city that looked clean, but unadorned, so when Rafan suggested that we stop at the building with the sign saying "Crown's Rest," neither Breeohan nor I argued. Thinking it might not be a good idea to let people see my backpack, I cast the chameleon lacing on the bag itself before we entered, earning a look of approval from both men. Rafan's face showed he would not wait long before peppering me for details about how to do the lacing, but I looked away and kept my eyes downcast as Breeohan paid for supper and two rooms for the night.

The food was edible, and I wondered if I was starting to get used to the odd cuisine—just a little. We sat cross-legged on the floor and spoke very little before I retired to my small room with a narrow cot. The straw-stuffed mattress was a little lumpy, but it smelled fresh rather than musty, so sleep came quickly.

A knock woke me at dawn. I rolled slowly to my feet and unlatched the door, rubbing sleep from my eyes. Rafan and Breeohan stood outside looking far too alert and immaculately dressed for so early in the morning. "Going somewhere?" I asked in sudden hope, coming instantly awake at the thought that Breeohan had changed his mind and had decided to travel ahead of the king with me.

"I am. You and Rafan are not," Breeohan said shortly.

"Breeohan, as much as I respect your ability to barter for the goods we'll need, don't you think it would be better if I go rather than you?" Rafan asked. "I seem to remember you coming to Tois before in your role as heir to the crown. You may be recognized."

Breeohan's brow furrowed. "That's true, but it's been several years. I doubt any would remember me."

"It's better to be safe, don't you think? If Mary's wish is to stay unrecognized in the city, the best person to acquire our goods would be me." He turned to me. "I'll regret missing time I could have spent with you, but this will be the best way to fulfill your wish of anonymity." He bowed and raised his eyes flirtatiously to mine.

"Why don't we all go? We could get supplies and be on our way," I said.

"We're not going anywhere until the king gets here." Breeohan glared reproachfully.

Refusing to comment, I slumped onto the bed, my back to both men.

Behind me I heard the door open then shut. Wanting to feel a connection to my old life and my purpose in this new place, I started to lift my shirt to change into my T-shirt and jeans, but a strangled yelp stopped me. I spun to see that Breeohan had not left the room after all.

Smoothing my tunic back in place, I growled. "What are you still doing in here?" Breeohan's face was a dark umber, and my face felt warm as well. I thanked everything I knew that he hadn't seen more than a sliver of my back.

It took a few moments for Breeohan to recover. "I'm here to make sure you don't run off again."

Anger quickly swamped my embarrassment. "So I can't even be in my room by myself, huh? I'm to be under constant guard."

"I will sit outside, if you wish." He turned toward the door.

I jumped up from the bed and grabbed his shirt to stop him. "Why are you doing this?" I asked in exasperation.

His own eyes had turned angry as well. "I'm trying to protect you. Why are you so determined to kill yourself?"

"I'm not suicidal, just in a hurry. Waiting around for the king is a waste of time—time my mother may not have. And I don't need your protection," I stated emphatically, my face only inches from his as if that would prove my point better.

"Mary," he said quietly, his voice strangely persuasive and gentle.

I suddenly felt awkward and confused with my face so close to his. I wanted to back away, but then he would know how unnerved I was, so I froze, unsure of what to do. "Yes?" I tried to say it sharply, but instead it came out in a timorous breath.

Breeohan's eyes seemed to be boring holes into mine. I had to use all my strength of will not to squirm and look away. "Why do you *think* I'm doing this?" he asked so softly I wouldn't have heard if I weren't so uncomfortably close to him.

My insides quaked in unexplainable fear. I stepped back and looked frantically at the small window and then at the door past Breeohan, contemplating an impossible escape. "I don't know," I said. I looked down at my hands. They were trembling.

Breeohan's dark brown hand hung inches from my own, and I watched in fascinated terror as it slowly rose toward my face. The tips of his fingers traced my cheek as lightly as butterfly's wings. Then he started to raise my face, so I would look at him.

"Mary, I—"

There was a tap at the door. Breeohan and I jumped apart as though scalded.

The gravelly voice of Rafan came through the door in an urgent whisper. "It's me. We have trouble." Breeohan unlatched the door and opened it only enough for Rafan to slip in.

"What's wrong?" I took in the sheen of sweat glistening on his face, the way his hair was slightly mussed, and his ripped sleeve.

"I was attacked. I managed to subdue the man, but I discovered from him that I wasn't the real target. You are, Mary." He locked eyes with me. "He said more men would be coming for you. We have to get out of here."

"Who could know she is here?" Breeohan asked.

"I don't know, but the man I questioned seemed to think there would be more than one person coming after her. We should leave now."

"You're right." Breeohan turned to me. "I think it would be wisest to make our movements as little known as possible."

"So we're leaving the city?" I asked hopefully.

"Immediately," was Breeohan's short reply.

Much to my digruntlement, Breeohan slowly and carefully showed Rafan my chameleon lacing. I didn't know why I felt so possessive of it, but the idea of others besides Breeohan and me knowing it made me feel edgy. I told myself I was just being selfish.

It took about twenty minutes before Rafan felt confident enough about the lacing to use it. I chafed at the delay now that I knew we would actually be in motion. I was only a step away from convincing Breeohan to keep moving until we reached Mom.

The three of us finally applied the chameleon lacing and moved out of the inn, holding onto shirttails to keep track of one another. No one noticed us slip by, nor did anyone but a small child even look in our direction as we slid through the streets of Tois. We didn't head back to the river dock, which I regretted, though I realized it would not be smart to get on a boat in a city where someone seemed to be looking for me. Instead, we headed toward an area of town that smelled increasingly of manure.

"Since you were attacked, I think you should buy a horse first. We will come after to see if anyone is following you," Breeohan commanded as we neared the first of the corrals at the horse market. Rafan made himself visible and went to barter for a mare whose ordinary dun color melded into a disconcerting burnished gold at the horse's fetlocks and again at the strip on her head.

Breeohan and I followed in silence after he finished, darting glances in all directions for anyone who seemed interested in Rafan's movements. After we passed two more corrals without noticing anything extraordinary, Breeohan whispered, "I will wait until you two have walked on for a few minutes and then buy another horse. We will meet one kenar outside the city on the road to Kospa. Mary, you ride with Rafan, but keep the lacing active."

I tried to recall my Iberloahan map in my head. "Kospa is in the wrong direction," I said.

"We are going back to meet the king," Breeohan said sternly, grabbing my shirt for emphasis.

"Don't you think that is just what someone would expect us to do?" Rafan whispered mildly.

"Not if they know Mary," Breeohan said with a little too much sarcasm.

"Yes, but not that many people here actually know me, so if they're after a princess rather than an American teenager, I think they'd plan on me fleeing toward the king, don't you?" I asked persuasively.

"Unless they do know you are a sirista foreigner," Breeohan mumbled almost inaudibly. His mouth turned out in what looked suspiciously like a pout. I wanted to ask what "sirista" meant but didn't dare.

"Fine, we will meet one kenar outside the city on the road to *Cardo*," Breeohan huffed before letting go of my shirt and fading into the background of the next horse corral to wait until Rafan and I were out of sight.

Rafan kept walking the horse until we passed the horse market and reached a building corner where we were mostly blocked from view. He mounted and held out a hand, looking blindly at a spot a few inches to the right of me. I viewed the horse with trepidation, never having actually ridden one before. But a man with his arm extended to a wall was bound to attract attention, no matter how secluded a spot, so I grabbed his hand and let him haul me up behind him, feeling the mare's warmth beneath me as she shifted to accommodate the new weight on her blanketed back. We had no saddle, though Rafan used a bridle to steer her. My arms shot around Rafan's waist and squeezed like a vise. He chuckled annoyingly, but I didn't dare let go, even if he was interpreting my embrace as something other than fear.

The horse moved at a slow gait, but I still felt that any wrong shift could leave me flat on my back in the road. I concentrated on keeping my balance until Rafan had safely negotiated the mare out of the city. When the road straightened, making the fear of falling less intense, I slackened my hold around Rafan's waist.

"That was quite a passionate embrace, my lady," Rafan rasped.

I loosened my arms as much as I dared before replying, "I've never ridden a horse before. Where I come from, there's usually a saddle to help a rider stay on."

"A saddle would have been nice, but it's not needed. It's better to save our funds for other things, such as food. Feel free to keep your hold on me as tight as you wish."

I took care to keep my limbs as loose as my nervous stomach would allow, but my care was foiled when Rafan suddenly urged the horse to go faster, forcing me to hang on tightly again.

"I don't think I will slow at all until we get there. It seems the only way I can get you to hold me." He laughed. I gritted my teeth, but couldn't let go.

About a kenar outside of town, Rafan rode to a small hill that hid us from approaching travelers coming from the city. He swung down from the horse and turned to help me, but I slid quickly to the ground. The horse startled, and Rafan was forced to calm the creature. I retreated to a rock, still in my near invisible state, and sat quietly.

"Come, Mary, there is no need for you to stay unseen now," Rafan said. "I'm sorry if I offended you earlier. I know how shy you are," he said contritely.

A loud "ha" burst out of my mouth. Shy!

Rafan didn't interpret my outburst in the way I intended, however. "I really am sorry, Mary." He sounded more sincere than before. "I promised I would wait for you to come to me, but I can't help loving you. Waiting is more difficult than finding water in sand dunes."

"You don't love me, Rafan."

"But I do. I've loved you since the first moment I saw you." The familiar glint of mischief shone in his eye as he headed toward where he'd heard my voice.

"I don't believe in love at first sight. I believe that to love someone you must know them." I moved to a different rock as Rafan slunk toward the sound of my words.

"And you don't think I know you well enough to love you." His lips curved up.

"No. You don't know anything about me."

Rafan turned, confused by my move. "I know more than you think." He took tentative steps toward my new spot.

"Oh yeah? What's my favorite color? What do I like to do most in my free time? What ideals and thoughts are most important to me? Do you know any of those things, Rafan?"

He sauntered much too quickly in the right direction so I moved again.

"I know you are loyal and beautiful and adorably shy and afraid."

Again with the shy; it was really starting to tick me off. Plus, afraid? If I was scared, it definitely wasn't of him. I could tell he expected me to challenge the scaredy-cat accusation, but I wasn't falling for it. Okay, maybe I was. "I'm sorry, but I don't love you, Rafan." I couldn't help but go on. "I'm not shy, and I'm not scared of you. I don't want to hurt you, but I can't help the way I feel," I said, trying to be nice despite my fury over the accusation of being afraid to love him.

After an awkward silence where he stood unsure, he continued in his normal bravado manner, "You're afraid of letting someone love you, and you're afraid of letting yourself love, but you don't need to be. I will always protect you and keep your heart safe. I love you."

I was glad Rafan couldn't see the expression on my face because I was sure it wasn't the flattering look he would expect after such a speech.

I didn't know what to say, but I didn't need to say anything after all when Breeohan's voice, huskier than usual, said, "We should get moving. I think someone followed us out of the city." Breeohan's eyes were cast down, his stance tense. I didn't know how much of Rafan's words he had heard, but I was pretty sure he'd at least heard the "I love you" part. I felt my face flame and was acutely glad of my camouflage.

"Would you mind retreating for just a moment, Breeohan? Mary and I were in the middle of a private conversation." Rafan's purr had transformed into a harsh growl.

"I do mind, and if you really cared about keeping Mary's 'heart safe,' you would be more concerned with getting as far from the city as possible than with forcing your attentions on her. You also would have been watching the road," Breeohan snapped at Rafan. I guess he'd heard a little more than just 'I love you.' Breeohan seemed to notice for the first time that I wasn't visible. He swiveled his head in confusion.

"There has been no forcing here," Rafan spat.

"Is that so? Then why is Mary hiding from you?" Breeohan demanded.

I had an intense desire to be on an island surrounded by molten lava rather than here watching Breeohan and Rafan's snarling match. Instead, all I could do was become visible again. "Guys, can you please calm down? Breeohan, didn't you say there's someone following you? Shouldn't we leave right away?" I asked reasonably.

"Yes. Let's get moving." Breeohan turned and remounted his horse as Rafan did the same. Then as if choreographed, Breeohan and Rafan reached their hands out to me at exactly the same moment. I stared stupidly at the two hands, thinking of the joys of lava-encircled islands. What kind of suicidal girls ever really wanted to be in this sort of situation?

"I really don't feel comfortable on a horse. I'll just run," I said hopefully.

Neither man thought that worth a reply, but Breeohan's hand slowly dropped back to his side. "Why don't you ride with Rafan first, and we'll switch when his horse starts tiring," he suggested in an emotionless voice, his features smooth sandstone.

No wait, I thought desperately. I wanted to be as far away from Rafan at the moment as possible, but the identical *Swan Lake* gesture had stumped me for a critical second.

"Uh, okay," I said unenthusiastically. I wasn't looking forward to riding with Rafan, but it would be worse than insensitive to say so, especially after he'd gushed his heart out to me in a sloppy mess. And Breeohan would probably think me a huge dirtball if I cruelly told his friend I'd rather hop across two car roofs heading in the opposite direction than ride behind Rafan on a horse.

I mounted up behind Rafan and relaced the chameleon pattern so only two riders traveling together would appear. Rafan refrained from commenting on the joys of my embrace, for which I was grateful, and Breeohan avoided even looking in my direction. Not that he would have seen me, but it was still somehow nerve-wracking.

After what seemed like days, but was really only a few hours of exhaustive riding, where I tried to hold onto Rafan as little as possible while still avoiding an embarrassing and painful drop off the horse's back, Breeohan stopped to pour water into a large shallow bowl. He placed it in front of his horse to drink while I slid to the ground, my thighs throbbing in agony. I stayed nearly invisible until sitting on a nearby rock so that the two men would not see my penguinlike waddle.

When I undid the lacing, Rafan handed me the water flask with a flourish while Breeohan scowled and transferred the beast's water bowl to Rafan's horse. We didn't rest long. Breeohan mounted and held his hand out to me. Rafan shot a parting wink while managing to glower at Breeohan at the same time. I couldn't help but let out a groan as my legs swung into place behind Breeohan. The chameleon lacing back in place, I put my arms tentatively around Breeohan's waist. He sat ramrod straight until the horse forced him to sway with its bouncing gait, a gait that made me wince and hiss at every step. Though I tried to keep the cursing internal, I hissed aloud.

"Do you need me to heal you?" Breeohan asked.

I felt like hitting myself. How could I forget about the ability to heal myself? "No, thank you. I'm glad you reminded me, though." I quickly made the lacings to heal myself.

The road to the next city swerved away from the river, putting well-ordered farms between us and the murky water. The land to my left was sparse desert with gnarly, hardy-looking trees here and there that squatted close to the ground, as if growing tall in such heat was too exhausting. Sagebrush speckled the landscape, occasionally blocked by white and orange-red sandstone jutting out of the ground in swells.

Breeohan's horse stumbled. I was almost thrown before a quick clutch at Breeohan's clothes saved me. I must have pinched skin as well for Breeohan hissed.

"You would be much less likely to fall if you scooted forward a few inches instead of relying totally on your legs and my shirt," Breeohan said, his tone cool. He was looking straight ahead so I couldn't see his expression, but he certainly didn't seem too happy. Had he heard my part of the conversation with Rafan where I turned his friend's love down? Had he been insulted by it?

"Sorry if I hurt you." I tentatively closed the distance that I'd been keeping faithfully. It was remarkably difficult to make myself do so, but I felt guilty for pinching Breeohan. I slid forward until I was like a barnacle sealed to a rock. I was uncomfortably aware of every portion of my body in contact with his. It felt too much like an embrace, a very intimate embrace. I leaned back so that at least my upper body would be free, but my torso kept bouncing into him with the rhythm of the horse if I wasn't constantly thinking about keeping a cushion of air between us.

Breeohan was also stiff. Whenever I accidentally bumped him, his shoulders would jerk, and I could picture the accompanying wince on his face. I did, however, feel more secure on the horse than I had before, and my legs felt sweet relief.

Rafan rode ahead several paces. I wondered if I should talk to Breeohan about what he'd overheard, but I wasn't really sure what to say or what good it would do anyway. Any subject would be better than dwelling on the awkward uncomfortable movement of our little "don't touch me" game, however, so I cleared my throat to speak. Breeohan cocked his head a little.

"How far to the next city?" I asked.

Breeohan's shoulders winced again even though I hadn't touched him. "About four portions. It's probably best if you stay on my horse since Rafan's has already carried you for more than five portions." His tone was sharp, defensive.

"Okay." I shrugged, though inside I had to admit that I would rather have the discomfort of riding with Breeohan than the agony of riding behind Rafan. Breeohan relaxed a little at my obvious neutrality.

"Are we going to ride past the city, or are we going to get on a boat?" I asked.

"I haven't decided yet."

"I vote for the boat."

"Then we should probably trade our horses for new ones and keep riding." His head was cocked toward me with a hint of his old mischievous grin.

I cuffed him lightly on the shoulder. He reeled in exaggerated pain. This was the Breeohan I liked the best. I found myself relaxing, the space of air between us becoming smaller as he sat up more normally and I relaxed forward.

"I seriously don't think I'll be able to ride after four more portions. I'm having a hard enough time now," I groaned.

"Never ridden bareback before, have you?"

"More like never ridden before at all."

"What? How is that possible?"

"Not many people ride horses where I come from. It isn't necessary. We have cars. These days the only people who have horses have them for fun or competitions, not really for travel."

"What kind of animal is a car?"

"It isn't an animal." I tried to think of how I might describe a car to a three-year-old. "People make cars from metal and other materials, and use this substance that is really combustible called gas to make it go." It wasn't too great an explanation, but I was no engineer. "That really doesn't help much does it? Sorry, I just don't have the knowledge to explain it to you. I can tell you that if we had a car here we could probably get to the next city in a portion rather than a day on horseback."

"That's impossible."

I just shrugged. "No more impossible than magic was to me a few weeks ago."

Breeohan was silent for a minute. "It must be frustrating for you to have to travel so slowly then."

My back stiffened at the sudden deluge of emotions that rushed through me. Breeohan's unexpected sympathy for something that had been eating at me for so long almost undid me. But I managed to hold back and simply gulp out, "Yes."

He was silent again until I regained control of myself and relaxed a little.

"We'll get on a boat at the next city," he said quietly.

"Thank you."

Chapter 18

By the time Cardo's buildings came into view, the sky had turned deep purple and the hanging street lamps cast the walls of the houses into strange relief. Rafan and Breeohan had a brief argument over which inn to go to, but finally settled on Breeohan's choice when he pulled rank on Rafan.

The place seemed anonymous enough, but Breeohan insisted that we all sleep in the same room so that I couldn't be attacked while alone. I was too tired and too sore to care. I just managed to perform a cleaning lacing on myself before dropping into the lumpy bed.

The next morning I rolled stiffly out of the cot, legs aching, until I remembered ruefully that I'd once again forgotten I could fix the pain in an instant. It was still hard to keep the concept in my head. Breeohan had already sold our horses and booked us passage while I lay sleeping, so after meeting with the boys, we all moved quickly and unobtrusively to Cardo's dock. The boat sailed upriver almost immediately after we alighted on deck, and I was quite impressed. What sort of motivation had Breeohan employed to inspire such quick action?

I had my own room in the ship, so I assumed Breeohan and Rafan weren't as worried about me being spirited away on water as they had been on land. The room was only a foot wider than the narrow cot it held for sleeping, but I didn't really care. It would be nice to have at least a little privacy if I needed it.

The boat was smoothly gliding upriver by the use of sails when Rafan again sidled up to me at the boat's rail. Breeohan was only a few feet away, but that didn't stop Rafan from leaning against my shoulder. I slid away from him, disguising it as a stumble with the roll of the ship. Rafan just moved again once I recovered, and I discovered that I couldn't stumble away further because I had sandwiched myself between them.

"I am glad that we'll have so much leisure time on the ship. It will give me a chance to prove my words to you," Rafan pretended to whisper. I saw Breeohan stiffen out of the corner of my eye.

I suppressed the urge to snap like a cornered wolf, but before I could make a scathing reply that I would later regret, Rafan spoke around me to Breeohan. "Breeohan, this would be the perfect time to write that apology letter to Avana. I know how you've missed her. I've seen the way you've been tearing yourself up for running off so suddenly without even a good-bye. Why don't you write her a little love note so you'll feel better and soothe any hurt on her part?" Rafan suggested genially.

Breeohan opened his mouth.

My stomach plummeted in a gentle sway of the ship. "You guys will have to excuse me. I don't feel very well. I think I'm going to go lie down." I backed away from the rail, feeling panicky and nauseous. Both men regarded me like a strange new breed of insect, though Rafan smiled a little as if the insect was a particularly fascinating one. As I turned away, I saw Breeohan swivel to Rafan with narrowed eyes and a tense jaw.

We sailed for four days with little incident, and I avoided talking to either Breeohan or Rafan as much as possible. Instead, I struck up conversations with the crew when they weren't too busy working the sails or the oars, which were only used when the winds were unfavorable. The crew put up with me, but I didn't find anyone really interested in friendship, so my interchanges with them remained fairly dull question-and-answer sort of affairs. It was enough to make me want to talk to Rafan and Breeohan again, but whenever I saw either one coming, my need to flee overrode my boredom, and I ducked away to hide in my pea-sized room.

The landscape turned more uneven the further upriver we went, starting with baby hills that seemed to grow until the huge mountains, once a small purple blur on the horizon, crouched high above, waiting for the right moment to pounce on us.

The morning of the fifth day heralded the end of our voyage by boat. The sailors informed me that the city of Boparra was the last port for any ship of such size as theirs, or any ship at all for that matter. To go any further would risk ripping a larger boat's bottom on jagged rocks, and smaller vessels would be helpless against the upper river's currents.

As we ascended in altitude, the temperature cooled, and the farmland, despite the rugged landscape, increased remarkably. I wasn't surprised to see that Boparra's size rivaled that of the capitol's. The eighty-five-degree weather had to be a big draw considering everywhere else I'd been so far was lucky to get a low of ninety-five.

It was possible to dock the ship on either side of the river, for the city ballooned out from both water edges like a large mushroom cut down the center. Breeohan directed the captain to the right, and I stepped off the boat with some relief even though we would have to ride and hike from here on.

Keeping with the pattern I'd set over the past few days, neither Rafan nor Breeohan said anything to me as we twisted our way through the curving streets of Boparra. Even the buildings bowed outward in semi-circular shapes, sliced through by occasional straight alleys and broader throughways leading to the city's next loop. I really wished I could view the city from a helicopter to see if each ballooning layer created a true orb or if it wavered in its spherical accuracy.

We had sailed through most of the city's diameter before docking, so Rafan, Breeohan, and I didn't have to struggle through too many rounded roads before reaching the edge of the city's circuit. Despite the swiftness of our route, I was starting to feel uncomfortable walking next to Rafan and Breeohan in silence.

It was one thing to feign sickness or fatigue in my cabin in order to avoid the two men; it was quite another to be standing beside them and feel suddenly that all my attempts to seek solitude had convinced them to actually ignore me. I was especially surprised that Rafan made no overtures. The absence of his usual flirting made me twitchy. It felt as if he was waiting for the absolute worst moment to drop another love bomb. But paranoia aside, I hoped he had finally gotten the message that his come-ons were truly unwelcome.

As we reached an inn on the outskirts of the metropolitan area, my only assurance that I was remembered at all was when Breeohan handed me a key to my room, though his concentration seemed to be fixed on the food being served at the tables. I was impressed by this little bit of metal as the first evidence of a lock I'd witnessed in any inn. Up to now it had been thin wooden latches on the inside. There'd been no way to lock a door from the outside. The strangely twisted key's teeth were curved instead of straight, like the rectangular teeth I'd seen before on antique skeleton keys.

"Am I in my own room then?" I asked. I wasn't sure if I'd be acknowledged. Rafan was already at a table and hadn't heard my question, but

Breeohan turned to me. I was unprepared for the raw emotion that flickered in his eyes before his eyebrows rose in polite regard. The expression had been potent, but it was gone before I could name it.

Had I hurt Breeohan by my silence of the past few days? Now that I thought of it, it wasn't a good way to treat a friend. I suddenly felt like a royal heel. I might have been confused, but avoiding Rafan and Breeohan had not been very mature. I stuttered a repeat of my question.

"Rafan and I thought it best that way. We will take turns sitting outside your door tonight."

I did favor being alone to having Rafan and Breeohan in the same room, but I didn't want them staying up all night guarding me on the other side of the door while I blissfully slept either. "You don't need to do that."

"It's easier than chasing through this maze if someone were to steal you," he said with a shrug. He made me sound like some sort of bothersome possession.

"Oh, gee. Well, when you put it that way . . . no. It still doesn't make sense." I was starting to feel testy, but instead of getting angry in return, the corner of Breeohan's mouth twitched upward. "Look, if you're really worried about me getting kidnapped, why don't you two just sleep in my room? That way we can all rest."

"We have already discussed this and decided our solution would be most proper." His jaw was starting to take on what I dubbed his won't-be-swayed-for-anything look.

"Proper? Is it just me or is my memory deceiving me? I seem to recall all of us sleeping in the same room in Cardo. And what is this 'we' stuff? I don't remember being consulted about this plan." I was pretty sure my face showed the same stubborn-as-a-mule symptoms. Did they even have mules here?

"Cardo was different. We were all too tired to plan ahead. This situation being what it is . . ." He regarded me coolly.

What? He must have heard me at the rocks telling Rafan that I didn't love him. Was that the problem? I realized I'd just answered my own question. If Rafan really did love me (which I still highly doubted) and was finally getting it through his head that I didn't like him, he could be feeling pretty torn up. I could see how sharing a room would not be the most desirable thing in that situation.

While I was still grasping for some sort of reply, Breeohan turned away sharply and headed to Rafan's table. I followed mutely behind.

We ate in silence broken only by our server asking if we wanted refills of our drinks, which tasted a little like cranberry juice. Rafan gave me soulful looks that I couldn't decipher: painful or hopeful or just creepy. I tried not to meet his eyes, and instead let my gaze wander to a man and woman lounging close together at another table, ignoring their food as they gazed with silly sappy expressions into each other's eyes. Their fingers wove together in and out in an intimate caress. I looked hurriedly away, embarrassed.

When we finished, Breeohan announced that we would all go to the city's marketplace for supplies. I was surprised that he hadn't demanded I stay in the inn all day with one of them as guard. But going to a market bazaar sounded much more interesting than staring at walls all day long, so I tried to deflect all attention from me as we headed back into the streets, lest Breeohan and Rafan remember their paranoia.

The market was near the outskirts of town, so we simply had to follow the last curved, orange cobble road until the sounds of vendors shouting and shoppers gabbing became more distinct and then overwhelming. When the carts became visible around the bend, I saw the path on the road narrowed so only four people could stroll abreast. This made it easy for vendors to snag shoppers caught in the congestion.

Though the weather was only in the high eighties, the salesmen had spread large swaths of bright and colorful fabrics above their stalls to create shade. The fabric snapped in the warm breeze like plumage from a hundred colorful birds in flight. As Breeohan, Rafan, and I walked into the melee of sound, odors, and colors, I saw bracelets and necklaces of twisted gold with inlaid gems in one stall, while the cart next to it sported wicked-looking blades of jagged steel and delicately carved leather sheaths.

A stall holding brass and glass knickknacks caught my attention momentarily. The little contraptions looked almost mechanical, but when the eager-looking vendor behind the counter asked if I wished to buy a magelight guaranteed to work twice before needing a mage to re-lace it, I realized that the connecting brass pieces had been melded together for added effect rather than for any mechanical reason.

I was so absorbed in the mage items, looking intently at each gadget to find the lacings, that I didn't realize Breeohan and Rafan hadn't stopped with me to gawk at all the objects that I found so foreign and intriguing. I glanced up just in time to see the blue of Rafan's vest disappear through a group of people who were choking the pedestrian traffic. I hurriedly set the mage item down and jostled my way through the human roadblock as fast as I could.

Part of me thought sourly that for two guys who were so insistent upon guarding my room at night, they weren't overly concerned about me being easily snatched away in a crowded and confusing marketplace. Still, I wasn't too worried until I came to a section of the market that branched out in two directions. I couldn't tell if I should go straight along the same outer round road or turn right onto one of the intersecting streets that led deeper into the city. The connecting road had stalls crowded just as tightly as the main thoroughfare and seemed to have a few stalls I thought we might need to visit.

As I stood uncertainly, jostled from all sides, I turned back in the direction I'd come and noticed a man staring at me. He looked away as soon as I noticed him, pretending to gaze at a flowered swath of fabric in the stall where he lurked. My heart jumped and sped up. Though I'd inwardly griped at Breeohan and Rafan's inattentiveness, I hadn't really thought anyone would be looking for me in Boparra.

I pushed past the people in the street, deciding that I would be less likely to get lost if I stuck with the main road, rather than turn into the city. Every few feet I looked behind me to see if the staring man was following me or if it had just been a figment of my overactive imagination. When I caught a glimpse of his tan peasant shirt and brown gee-like vest through the jumble of brightly colored shoppers, my heart hopped faster, and doubt faded. I elbowed through the grazing customers more forcefully, hoping I'd chosen the right direction.

I was craning my face to the rear when I ran into someone in front of me. This hadn't been the first time I'd done this, so I apologized absentmindedly, still looking back and sliding to the side to move past. Strong fingers gripped my shoulders and stopped me. My head snapped forward to see that the hands belonged to Breeohan. Relief washed through me. Before my better sense could stop me, I clutched tightly to the back of his vest, and buried my head into the scratchy green fabric at his shoulder.

"Thank goodness. I'm so glad I found you," I said into his shirt. Breeohan released me in surprise, but then encircled my shoulders as I gripped his back. The pressure of his arms sent a warm tingle through me. My grasp relaxed, and I felt a delicious desire to burrow my cheek even more deeply into his shoulder. The intensity of my craving to snuggle with Breeohan effectively knocked me to my senses. I tried to step back, feeling my face glow with heat. Breeohan's hold tightened briefly, then released as he backed away. I firmly shoved off a terrifying wish to step back into the warmth of that hug.

"What," Breeohan began, but had to clear his voice. "What happened?" he asked. His face seemed to have a tinge of color as well.

"Someone's following me." I glanced behind me again but couldn't see the tan and brown clothes of my pursuer. "I don't see him now." I turned back. "Why didn't you wait for me?" I was annoyed to hear that my voice sounded whiny. I hoped the rose of my cheeks had faded.

"Rafan said you were right behind him. By the time I figured out we'd lost you, we were well into the marketplace. I'm sorry."

Was Rafan paying me back for rejecting him? "Where is Rafan?" I tried not to sound angry.

Breeohan looked around him in surprise. "He was right behind me. We must have gotten separated coming back for you. Why don't we wait at this booth until he catches up to us? We can keep an eye out for the man you saw at the same time." Breeohan swiftly began scanning the crowds, carefully avoiding a glance in my direction.

The owner of the cart containing the karate gee-like vests, so common in Iberloah, did not appreciate Breeohan and me blocking his wares when we so obviously weren't even browsing. When he complained for the fifth time, Breeohan spun around, grabbed a puke-colored orange-brown vest and reached into his pouch under his shirt for money.

I grabbed the arm holding the nauseating vest. "Not that one. If you're going to buy something, at least get one that doesn't resemble the spewed contents of someone's stomach." I snatched a bright yellow vest with black swirling embroidery.

"This one will look great with your eyes." I held the fabric up to his face to see how the yellow fabric made his purple eyes pop until I realized that those amethyst eyes were fixed on me. I shoved the vest at him, flustered. "Anyway, it's better than the other one." I quickly turned back to watch the people passing through the narrow pathway.

Out of the corner of my eye I saw Breeohan pass money to the vendor. By the man's sound of pleasure, I guessed that Breeohan had paid more than the item was worth, probably to keep him from grumbling further. As he turned around, I caught sight of tan and brown to my right. My breath caught, but the hint of fabric disappeared before I could be sure it was the same man who had been trailing me.

Breeohan noticed my whoosh of air. I explained what I'd seen, giving him the pursuer's description. He nodded, and we continued to scan the passing crowd. A familiar blue vest and startling white billowing sleeves peeked into view, but coming from the opposite direction than it should have.

When Rafan's face came into view, I saw that his eyes sliced from one stall to the next as if looking for someone. The look in those eyes was not worry, it was calculation. My body took a half step further into the stall before I checked myself and called out. "Rafan."

Breeohan's eyes flicked first left, then right, eyebrows high when he saw I was not looking in the direction that Breeohan had come from.

Rafan strolled up to us, and his look of calculation morphed into one of relief. "I was so worried about you, Mary. I'm glad to see that you're safe," he said with a trace of his old sappiness.

"How did you pass me without my seeing it?" Breeohan asked, cross.

"I must have gotten ahead of you without noticing in one of the particularly crowded areas. Maybe we should hold onto each other's shirttails from now on as we buy what we need," he suggested with a carefree smile. Something struck me as strange about his explanation, but I put it down as nerves when I couldn't think of what it was.

"We are not buying anything. We are getting out of here right now and getting passage on the next boat back to meet the king," Breeohan said firmly.

"What?" I was too flabbergasted to come up with anything more intelligent.

A scowl appeared on Rafan's face, surprising me. "People lose each other in throngs like this all the time. You're overreacting and treating Mary like a child." His rough voice made the words seem singularly menacing. My own anger was momentarily checked by shock at Rafan's defense.

"She was being followed," Breeohan snapped back. "I don't know why I got myself talked into coming closer to Kelteon in the first place. I should have taken you back to the king," he said to me, self-recrimination etched into his features. I was again thrown into confusion by Breeohan's blatant emotional display.

"How could you tell she was being followed? Are you sure you didn't imagine it?" Rafan gibed.

"Mary saw him watching her and caught him trailing her," Breeohan shot back.

Rafan raised his eyebrows in doubt. "You'll forgive me," he said with a nod in my direction and a little smile that I think was supposed to look apologetic but didn't quite qualify, "but Mary is probably about as familiar with marketplaces as she is with riding horses. Don't you think it is possible that her mind invented a pursuer as a natural reaction to being left behind?"

Wow, first he says Breeohan is treating me like a child, but then he turns right around and accuses me of the same thing. "What a hypocrite!" I must have muttered the last bit, because Breeohan coughed and quickly covered his face to hide a smile. Rafan regarded me with narrowed eyes before widening them to a look of polite inquiry.

"You should never assume, Rafan." My voice was dripping icicles. "I've been in places where I was surrounded by hundreds of people who were jammed together so tightly there was hardly room to turn. This little market is nothing to that."

"I stand corrected, my lady, but you must admit that you may not know the customs and behavior of this people as well as you do your own. Do you think it possible that the man was simply admiring you?"

"If he was just looking, why did he follow me?"

"There aren't many paths to walk in this bazaar. Perhaps he was just shopping in the same direction as you," Rafan replied.

My eyebrows were tense in an angry glare. Rafan's explanation sounded entirely plausible. It also made me look like a silly girl with an overactive anxiety complex. I opened my mouth to defend myself but snapped it shut again. If I argued further with him, it would just make me seem more childish. I wasn't sure what Rafan's motivations were, but it occurred to my surly self that even if I did convince Breeohan that I wasn't imagining things, it would only make him more inclined to head to the first boat sailing back to the king rather than continue on toward Mom.

"It is possible he could have just been admiring you." Breeohan looked at me apologetically. "Could you tell he was specifically pursuing you rather than just following the same road?"

"There isn't any way I can prove it." I gritted my teeth.

"Then I think we should wait for the king here. To go any closer to Kelteon would be foolish," Breeohan said.

"Not necessarily. We are a small enough group that we could scout out the area for the king. With our help, he will be better prepared to deal with Kelteon when he comes," Rafan said.

"And if we are caught, what then? We would be handing Kelteon more leverage on a platter," Breeohan said, hissing the words. I noticed the vest vendor wasn't even pretending to not listen anymore. Breeohan shepherded Rafan and me in the direction of the inn, but in our slow huddle, we were more a roadblock than moving traffic.

"So long as we keep the chameleon lacing active, there won't be any question of us getting caught," Rafan assured.

My personal humiliation was forgotten in the intensity of my desire to find Mom. I prayed that Breeohan wouldn't remember that the chameleon lacing didn't make you completely invisible nor did it stop you from making noise.

"That might be true, but it isn't necessary for us to be the scouts. We can wait for the king and his men and teach them the lacing," Breeohan retorted.

Grrr. Why did Breeohan always have to be so difficult? If only he were a little less sharp, I thought morosely. But wishing wouldn't accomplish anything. I needed a plan. "Let's think of this logically, Breeohan," I said in a rush, trying to come up with something as I talked. "Let's say we get straight back on a boat and head for the king. How are we to know exactly where he is at this point? We know he's coming our way, but not what route he's taken. What if he decided to put the horses and his men on several ships to save time? We could pass right by them without even meeting him."

Breeohan opened his mouth, but I held up my hand to forestall him. "We could, as you suggested, just wait here in Boparra, but that could be as much of a problem as heading back toward the king. I might have just imagined I saw someone following me, but what if I didn't? That would mean that my location is known. The longer we stay here, the more opportunity someone will have to kidnap me, right? So the only thing to do would be to move on to the next place where we know the king will be, but this time be careful that no one sees exactly where we go." I gasped in a much needed breath after that barrage, hoping Breeohan wouldn't find any flaws in my reasoning.

Both Breeohan and Rafan were silent. I looked up to see a smirk of satisfaction on Rafan's face and a scowl of concentration on Breeohan's.

"You're right." The words dragged out grudgingly from Breeohan's lips. "I left a message for the king at Cardo, but there's no telling how close to us he is right now. We will have to get our supplies and move on as we'd planned," he finished reluctantly.

"Good. Let's go shopping." A small sigh escaped my lips, and Breeohan's eyes narrowed suspiciously, but he said nothing more.

I didn't think Breeohan completely dismissed my stalker because though we didn't hold each other's shirttails, he did keep me firmly in front of him.

By the time we purchased everything we needed for traveling, the sun was close to setting. My head was starting to ache from the jabbering crowds and the pervading scent of too many unwashed bodies crammed closely together. I knew I should be starving, but the occasional whiff of cooking meat or roasted sweet root—an Iberloahan sweet—combined with powerful B.O., churned my insides.

My arms were loaded with provisions, and Breeohan and Rafan were equally weighed down. Despite my fatigue, I was on high alert, considering we were practically labeled with fluorescent signs reading, "Easy pickings this way." I might have said the man in tan and brown was a figment of my imagination, but I didn't really believe it.

Breeohan seemed to feel more nervous too. He set a brisk pace out of the market and an even more rapid one through the empty city streets. Our worry seemed pointless, however, for we reached the inn without mishap. We stashed our goods into packs, and I was surprised to find that Rafan was the best at making everything fit. I had an Iberloahan pack that I would carry as well as my faithful backpack, making me the only one who would be shouldering two bundles.

That night I lay on my mattress, unable to sleep, listening to the soft sounds of uncomfortable shifting against my locked door. I was finally floating on the edge of slumber when I heard the murmur of voices. My eyes fluttered open. I couldn't distinguish words, but I picked out Rafan's rough rumble followed by a mumbled reply. It was not Breeohan's smooth baritone. This voice had a whiny edge.

The exchange was quick. When the hall settled back to silence, I drifted slowly into slumber, wondering absently who Rafan had been talking to.

A knock at my door woke me. I performed a cleaning lacing to derumple, then unlocked the door and admitted Rafan.

"Ah, Mary, you are looking lovely this morning, as usual," Rafan said, bowing.

"Rafan," I warned.

"Not to worry, my lady. I will not speak of the subject you found so distasteful before," he replied, flatly. His face was a study of pleasantly raised eyebrows warring with the steely aqua glitter of his eyes.

I was torn between feeling guilty and nervous. "Where's Breeohan?" At the moment Breeohan's presence to diffuse the awkwardness between Rafan and me was very high on my wish list.

Rafan glanced to the partially open door as if hoping for the same thing. "He should be here soon. He went to buy the horses."

"Oh." The silence stretched unbearably.

"Who were you talking to last night?" I was relieved to find some way to push back the disconcerting quiet.

Rafan stiffened before relaxing into nonchalance. "The innkeeper came to ask if I needed anything."

"That was nice of him." I was out of conversation ideas.

There was a light tap on the partially open door before Breeohan slipped into the room. "We're ready to go. I suggest we don't use the chameleon lacing until we've left the inn and started traveling on a decoy route," he said.

"That's fine with me." I smiled at him gratefully.

We ate a quick breakfast in the inn's low-tabled dining area before leaving. At the door, I remembered the key.

"You guys go ahead. I forgot to return the key." I rushed to find the innkeeper.

I had to ask one of the serving maids to point him out, because I hadn't been paying attention to who Breeohan talked to when we'd arrived. When I reached him, I handed the beautifully twisted key back to him with a twinge of regret.

"Thank you for your business. I hope you have a good journey," he said in a melodious bass. I froze. Rafan had said that he'd talked to the innkeeper last night, but there was no way that whiny voice could have come from the man standing in front of me. He'd lied. But why? The innkeeper shifted uncomfortably, so I thanked him and walked back outside to Breeohan and Rafan.

They were waiting in the street with three earthy colored horses who all had white around their hooves, like socks. One of the horses had a lead rope tied to the saddle of another. I was happy to see that all three horses had saddles this time, though I felt nervous flutters at the thought of riding alone. Breeohan helped me awkwardly mount the third beast, then efficiently mounted his own as Rafan waited astride his mount.

We rode directly out of the city and headed down a road that curved loosely away from the mountains. I held the saddlehorn tightly, wishing it wasn't necessary to ride away from the direction that we would really travel. I wanted my pony ride over with as fast as possible. After about twenty minutes, Rafan doubled back to make sure we weren't being followed. When he returned and informed us that no one was on our tail, we turned the horses around. Breeohan threw another rope for Rafan to tie to his horse, and then we performed the chameleon lacing on ourselves and the horses.

The animals whickered fretfully, and for a dizzying moment I had to cling to my saddle as my mount jerked on his lead and side-stepped almost out from under me. But the horses soon adjusted to the fact that they couldn't see themselves, and then nothing but the soft clop of hooves indicated our passing.

Whenever someone neared on the wide dirt road, Breeohan veered his horse off the side of the path and halted. Rafan would reign in his horse as well, but all I could do was wait for my horse to bump into the lead mare. It was jolting, but my stallion didn't seem to get too upset, and he soon learned that a detour off the path meant he should stop. We would then stay quiet until whoever was coming had passed by.

We approached the town of Kerln by early evening. Its thick sandstone wall crouched darkly at the foot of the first towering monolith of the Ziat mountain range. Set against so grand a background, the city seemed small. Its wall was no protection from anything more menacing than paper. As we neared the ten-foot construction, the illusion of frailty shattered, and instead my heart quivered at the thought of being trapped inside such a solid barricade. Two guards stood at the wide gates regarding the people passing through with sharp attention. Rafan, Breeohan, and I rode through on the heels of a cart carrying hay, our horses' hooves completely camouflaged by the wagon's creaking.

We slipped through the gates just in time. The two guards braced their bodies between the door and the thick wall before tugging the heavy, thick, black oak doors shut.

Breeohan, Rafan, and I kept the chameleon lacing on until we entered the stables at an inn called "Good Rest." I looked around to make sure there wasn't a stable kid around before I undid the lacing. Then I unlaced my horse's invisibility as well before sliding carefully to the ground. Rafan and Breeohan did the same to themselves and their horses. They were already unsaddling their mounts while I was still wincing at the pins-and-needles feeling in my feet. I waited for the jabbing to stop, and then healed my sore legs. I glanced uncertainly at my own horse's tack.

"I'll get that for you, Mary," Rafan said kindly. I nodded my thanks and let him do the horse stuff while I watched, propped against the stable door.

When we came out of the stable, we surprised a girl coming back from the inn.

"I was having my supper, but I was watching the whole time. I don't know how I could've missed you," she cried in distress.

"We prefer handling our horses ourselves," Breeohan assured her. I was disturbed by her genuine fear of being beaten by her master. Even after we'd promised we wouldn't report her, she looked nervous. I slunk inside hesitantly, feeling suddenly depressed, but then decided to shake off my gloomy thoughts with a distraction.

"Are you going to insist on guarding my door again?" I murmured to Breeohan.

"Yes."

"It's dumb. We'd all have a better chance against any attacks if we were in the same room, and it would save money," I added practically.

"I'm not going to argue this with you, Mary."

I was stopped from further discussion when a sharp-eyed woman came toward us. The woman proved to be the innkeeper, and she and Breeohan bartered for two rooms right next to each other on the upstairs floor as well as breakfasts and dinners for the next two days. As they talked, the woman regarded us with a harsh stare, and I noticed uneasily that she had arms like a blacksmith. Breeohan, noting her glare and crossed arms, paid in advance. We sat cross-legged on pillows at the low table where I stared into a meatloaf soup that looked about as appetizing as dung. I wanted to reopen my discussion with Rafan and Breeohan, but as soon as I opened my mouth, Breeohan cut me off. "I don't think we should talk here. There are too many people."

I looked around. A man and woman sat across the room, arguing in a harsh whisper. Both looked lean and hard, as if they'd seen little luxury in their lives. At another table three rugged men cradled their cups silently, as if in deep thought. The table closest to us held a raggedly dressed, but muscular man, intent on shoveling soup into his mouth.

Nobody seemed to pay the slightest attention to us, but I felt intimidated by the atmosphere and so kept quiet anyway. If Breeohan wanted to keep acting pointlessly stubborn, that was fine with me. I wasn't going to feel guilty about it.

Upstairs I said good night to Rafan as he entered his room. He grinned back before he closed his door. I said the same to Breeohan as he settled outside my room, and he whispered a quiet return as I shut the door and slid the flimsy wooden latch into place.

The bed crackled as I lay on it, as if it was filled with hay, but even with a few uncomfortable pricks, it still felt better than the ground. I was tired, so sleep came quickly. I drifted in dreams until the sound of a soft scrape woke me. I twitched, and the mattress crackled loudly. The room was black as pitch but for a crack of faint light. I turned my head, still half asleep, to see that the light streamed through the partially-opened door where the ragged man from dinner stood staring at me.

I was tangled for a fateful second in my sheet. Then he launched forward and, as I wrenched my feet from the covers, he caught my arms with one of his and struck my head with the knob of his dagger handle. I knew no more.

Chapter 19

I awoke to searing pain in my head. Only gradually did I realize that I was blindfolded and that my arms and legs were tied behind me. It forced my back to arch achingly. I concentrated on forming the lacing that would heal my head. The release of pain was startling, but before I could think of some way to get free of my bonds, I heard a man's voice, muffled as if through a cloth, say, "She's healed herself. Quick!"

Agony exploded through my brain. The world turned black again.

When next I woke, I held absolutely still despite the furious throbbing in my skull. I heard the swish of fabric behind me as someone shifted, probably the person who would conk me again if I roused. I thought past the pain to avoid giving myself away.

It would have helped to see where I was, but the blindfold was tied tight, making my headache beat more painfully. Finding a way to convert the tight coarse rope around my wrists and ankles to stretchy bungee cord was relatively easy. I guessed the string that would change the give of the fibers without altering their appearance and tweaked it. A slight lessening of the pressure around my arms and legs told me my idea had worked. After my arms were free it would be an easy matter to pull the blindfold off.

A flash of golden lines, and I'd donned the chameleon lacing. I heard a gasp of surprise as I quickly rolled away. The now elastic rope slipped off easily. I concentrated past a burst of renewed cranial agony, tore off my blindfold, and healed the lump on my skull. The misery ceased immediately, but I had no time to enjoy it. There was a door to my left. My captor was groping around the room, his arms sweeping in wide gestures as if he were blind. His eyes belied the illusion, however, as they swiftly searched the room for movement. I bolted through the door as he was looking the other way. He cried out as I burst into the next room. Twenty heads turned in my direction. Some looked confused, seeing nothing but the man behind me.

"She's escaping. Look for movement," the man behind me cried. I cursed myself for not knocking him senseless when I had the chance. Twenty men and women started sweeping the room with flailing arms and keen gazes. I'd startled to the side of the door when coming through and stood flat against the wall. There was no chance at making it untouched across the floor, so I did the only thing I could think of. I activated my gecko lacing and climbed the wall to the ceiling.

Luckily, my searchers missed the ascent, and no one thought to check the ceiling. I carefully stuck and unstuck my hands and feet above them. As I reached the opposite side, I stopped, unsure what to do next. The door had been slammed closed. I secured myself to the edge of the wall, my weight resting painfully on the balls of my Superglue feet. I found, however, that sideways pressure was better than pulling my shoulder sockets out by hanging upside down.

"She couldn't have gotten out," someone growled in frustration.

"Everyone line up against this wall. We can do a sweep across the whole room side to side so that there will be no way of her getting past," another man said.

All twenty-one men and women lined up on the wall beneath me with their backs against the yellow brick. I held my breath, afraid that even the sound of breathing would give me away with so many searchers right under me. A muscle on my left arm twitched with fatigue, and I concentrated on holding absolutely still until my captors swept the first third of the room, then I painfully detached my feet and arms one at a time until I reached the ground.

My captors searched intently in front of them. I undid the gecko lacing and then slowly lifted the latch of the door so that the wood wouldn't scrape. I then curled my fingers around the handle and inched the door open. They were more than halfway across the room. My heart thudded like thunder in my chest. I was sure that at any moment someone would look back.

The door was almost open enough to let me through when the hinges squeaked. The sound, though slight, might as well have been a gunshot.

"The door!" someone shouted, and the temporary paralysis that had gripped the room lifted as my captors charged.

I flung the door wide and flew into a narrow outdoor alleyway filled with garbage. The smell was like a physical blow, but the motivation to move was stronger than my nausea. I turned right and twisted through a maze of refuse-strewn paths, my bare feet squelching through decomposing offal, despite my best efforts to place them carefully. I ran until my chest burned and my breathing heaved in and out in ragged mucus-filled gasps, but still my pursuers followed close behind.

Someone yelled as they spotted me, and I tried to increase my speed. My foot bore down on a piece of broken glass which embedded itself deeply. An involuntary scream escaped before I ground my teeth together to stop the sound. I leaned against the wall, breathing fire through my chest, feeling fire lance through my foot and up my leg. Twisting my leg up, I carefully pulled the large dagger of glass out of my flesh. I calmed my breathing enough to concentrate and then healed my foot. I started to run again, ignoring the pain in my side.

It was too late.

My scream drew my pursuers like spiders to struggling prey on a web. I heard the sure crunch of running boots behind me just as I reached a dead end in the alley.

Two men and a woman blocked my escape.

"There," the woman shouted and pointed me out. They rushed me. I barely had time to sidestep and kick the back of one man's knees so that he would fall. He caught at his companion's shirt to prevent the fall, which threw them both off-balance.

At their moment of instability, I kicked again and both went toppling. I didn't have the chance to run. The woman swung wildly and nicked my shoulder. I dodged her next punch with ease. There was a distinct fighting advantage in my chameleon state, but I was struggling for breath. As she stumbled, I roundhouse kicked her in the head. Her face snapped back, and she fell with a sickening little mew and lay still.

Air surged in and out of my lungs in strained gulps. My arms and legs trembled with fatigue, but I activated the gecko lacing. The two men jumped up to grab me just as I was convincing my aching muscles to carry me upward. Their vengeful vigor gave me the jolt of fear-laced adrenaline that I needed to start climbing.

"Where'd that cursed girl go?" snarled the man I'd tripped.

"There, on the wall. I see something moving," the other, shorter man said.

I was pulling upward as fast as my shaky muscles would allow, but the taller man caught my left foot just as I detached it to move out of reach. He tugged with a ruthless yank that made my hip ache, but nothing short of a bombing could make my hands and foot release the rough yellow sandstone, so I stuck fast to the wall.

I had no leverage to really hurt the man, since he was holding my foot above his head, but the position was an awkward one for him. Before the short guy could come to help, I kicked my foot back and forth in a vicious frenzy until he was forced to let go, then I quickly climbed out of reach. However, after only a few feet I had to stop to catch my breath before I could continue to the top.

"Where'd she go?" the man who had not been fast enough to grab me asked.

"She's still on the wall. You just can't see her cause she stopped moving," the other replied. "Come on down, girl. You might as well just come with us now. We'll find you one way or another." I saw him make a small gesture to his comrade before the other disappeared back around the corner. He probably knew a way around the dead end. I made myself keep climbing.

"Where're you going to go? There's nowhere you can hide. The whole city is on the alert to find you. We've got your boyfriends too."

I paused, almost to the roof. Was he telling the truth? Did he have Breeohan and Rafan, and was the whole city involved in this scheme? The city part seemed unlikely. But I'd been kidnapped, why not Breeohan and Rafan too? The man's sharp eyes noticed me hesitate, so he continued. "Come down now, and your friends won't get hurt."

I hadn't ever been in this kind of dilemma before, but though my heart ached with guilt, I'd seen enough movies and read enough books to know that bad guys who say they'll spare your friends never keep their word. I had no way of knowing if this guy was telling the truth. If I let him catch me, I would have no way of helping Breeohan or Rafan, assuming they really were captured. I climbed the rest of the way to the top of the wall and rolled over onto the building's flat roof just as the man who'd disappeared at the signal of the other burst through a door leading to the roof of an adjoining building.

He ran to the edge looking down at his partner. I started slowly crawling to a farther side. "Where is she?"

"She just made it to the top. Hurry," the man below yelled up as I rolled off the building's roof and stuck fast to the opposite wall. The short guy's steps pounded rapidly nearer. I slowed my gasping and stilled my muscles' tired trembling with monumental effort. I wished ruefully that I'd been an avid climber back on Earth so that I wouldn't be so near to collapsing now. But hindsight wasn't very useful, so I concentrated on holding still as the man stopped near my edge, sweeping the roof with focused determination.

As he moved further away to search a different part of the roof, I stealthily slipped down the wall to the ground. Once on the blessed horizontal dirt, I huddled in the corner of two buildings, shaking with tension and heat exhaustion. My strength reserves were starting to wane, and I wasn't sure how many more lacings I could do before I would be completely out of energy.

If I held still, I was pretty sure those two men wouldn't be able to find me unless they got close enough to hear my breathing. But now that I had a moment to rest, I wondered how my captors had known to look for the slight ripple my movement caused. Had we been discovered on the road after all? Maybe someone had seen us enact the chameleon lacing while we were traveling or perhaps someone had observed the waver of our passing.

Whatever the reason, I had to proceed under the assumption that the grungy man had been telling the truth when he said that the whole city was part of my kidnapping plot. Kerln was far smaller than Boparra, so it could be possible. I thought back to the people I'd observed here so far and realized that, with the exception of the frightened stable girl, I hadn't seen any children anywhere. There'd been no women gossiping on the streets as they beat their rugs or washed laundry. The road had only supported a few men and women with dull clothes and sure strides heading to destinations unknown. I hadn't noted anything as being strange before, but it struck me as odd now.

I jumped when I heard the man on the roof yell down toward my alley.

"I can't find her up here." The other man appeared at the mouth of my alleyway, and I suppressed a betraying shiver.

"We should hurry to the gate and tell them she can climb walls. We'll need to double the guard. We'll have to keep a sharp eye out."

"He said she was a tricky one," the man above me commented before I heard the clomp of his boots. The other man stared toward my resting spot for an agonizing minute before he turned and vanished around the corner. It was impossible to hear his steps on the dirt, so I stayed still as stone for a half an hour before I dared twitch, then I slumped into a more comfortable position.

Even if the whole city wasn't involved, whoever controlled the gates was, and they would be on the lookout for me. I wondered who had said I'd be a tricky one. Kelteon? It must be. He'd probably realized after showing me the light lacing that I could see whole lacings without anyone having to project them in front of me, string by string. He must have found out I came after him and had arranged all the kidnapping attempts. There really wasn't another logical explanation. There wasn't anyone else who had shown such a strange and strong desire to kidnap me. It was disheartening to know that I wouldn't be able to surprise Kelteon when I tried to rescue Mom.

Even though I had the chameleon lacing activated, I thought I might need to think of a better disguise since all eyes seemed to be peeled for my unusual flickering movement. I needed to think of a better way to stay unnoticed while I tried to find Breeohan and Rafan. I searched fervently for some way to become completely invisible, but couldn't figure out a lacing for it. I knew the lacings for all sorts of animals, but I was afraid to turn myself into an animal, petrified by the possibility of losing my thoughts, my magic, and myself. It was too much of a risk, so I discarded the idea with a little shiver of fear and a wisp of regret.

What if I hid in plain sight? I'd changed aspects of my body before. It wouldn't be that difficult to do a little painless reconstructive facial surgery. I explored the lacings for individual parts of my face, thinking I would do changes on several parts. But I wasn't sure if I could manage activating many more lacings before I would be tapped out, magically speaking. So instead, I thought of a woman's face and tried to find a lacing for the whole of it rather than parts.

The lacing was easier to ferret out when I pictured an actual person, so I concentrated on a woman I'd seen in Boparra with a hooked nose, small kewpie doll lips, and wide, kind, gray eyes. She'd caught my eye because of her infectious laugh. It'd been hard not to join in, despite the fact that I had no idea what she was laughing about. I thought her face would be ordinary enough to be safe.

I undid the gecko and chameleon lacings then snapped the string that would transform my face into someone else's. The lips felt strange, too small, as if I'd gotten lip liposuction. I ran my finger down the sharp ridge of my nose and across my lowered cheek bones and experienced a moment of panic. It was frightening to touch my face and feel unfamiliar curves. I quickly rechecked the lacing to make sure I could change back and took a few calming breaths. It was startling to discover that after years of bemoaning the tragedy of my facial features, I didn't want to permanently lose a single one.

There was no way to hide my bare feet, but I did morph my tender soles so they would be as tough as thick leather. Finding my way out of the maze of alleys required that I turn around several times, but I eventually found a wide road that led me within sight of Kerln's outer wall. I kept the imposing barrier in sight as I twisted through the streets, projecting the appearance of brisk purpose while really feeling hopelessly lost.

Eventually I found the entry gate. Backtracking through the streets, I came to the inn where Breeohan, Rafan, and I had stayed, but not before getting totally lost twice, having a terrible frozen moment when I thought a woman giving me a suspicious glare somehow saw through my new face, and discovering that my stomach had given up hope of obtaining food and decided to try eating itself instead.

The sun hid behind the mountains, casting a long cool shadow over Kerln. I held my hands held stiffly at my sides to prevent nervous trembling and I swaggered to reflect confidence as I neared the inn. A man stood outside the entry, glowering at my approach. The thought struck me that I had no money, no way to pose as a customer. I swerved away, pretending I'd intended to walk beyond the inn. After he was out of sight, I swung around and snuck into the inn's stable. Our three horses were still in their stalls. I cringed to see that the young girl was there too. She approached me with a look of confusion, noticing, I suppose, that I didn't have an animal with me.

"Can I help you?" she asked timidly.

"I was wondering if you had any horses for sale," I said, thinking furiously. "I plan to check elsewhere as well, but you never know . . ."

The girl looked at the ground with an expression of guilt plain upon her face. "My mistress bid me take these three horses to the guard's stables tomorrow, but she may be willing to sell one instead." She indicated our three horses. My stomach dropped sickeningly.

"I could go ask her if you want." She stepped to the door.

My hand shot out and caught her before she slipped out. "No. That's okay. What happened to the owners of these horses?" I asked gently. She backed up, eyes wide with fear and darted a glance at the door.

"I won't hurt you, I promise. It's just really important for me to find out if they're okay, and where they are." I tried to project friendly trust and calm, praying she wouldn't bolt. She glanced at the door again.

"I don't know what you're talking about," she said unconvincingly.

"Okay. That's okay. I don't want to get you in trouble." I remembered her fear at our first meeting. No matter how desperate I was, I didn't want to be responsible for getting the girl hurt. I sighed, pinching the bridge of my unfamiliar nose to prevent a headache from forming. I didn't have energy to heal myself.

The girl's sage green eyes regarded me. She shot a fearful look at the door but then darted forward, tugging the front of my shirt so that I would bend down.

"I don't know where they took the lady, but the two men are tied up in a room upstairs." She jumped quickly away and ran out the door. I slipped out after her. The dark of evening had spread, and the sky was a deep blue. It would be harder to see me with the chameleon lacing on, but I didn't want to waste any energy unless I had to, so I circled around to the back of the inn and watched for several minutes to make sure no one was near before I ran and flattened myself against the inn's brick sandstone. I redid the gecko lacing with a groan, wishing I could just float up to the open upper-story window. As I climbed, my arms pulsed with pain at each upward pull. Somehow, I made it to the windowsill and found the strength to heave myself through, after checking to make sure the room was empty. I slumped wearily in the dark, individual muscles twitching and cramping in a frenzied dance.

When the twitching died down, I got up and carefully walked to the door, my feet sticking and detaching as I went. I didn't dare undo the gecko lacing in case I didn't have the strength to activate it again. I opened the door a crack. A woman sat cross-legged in front of the door of the room Breeohan had rented for himself and Rafan. A dagger lay casually in her lap as she leaned her head against the wall. She wasn't asleep. Her eyes roved the hallway, and I quickly stepped back before she looked my way. I closed my own eyes and used the wind lacing to snap her head forward and then back into the stone. There was a dull smack, and the woman slipped sideways on the floor. My shoulders slumped against the wall. I wanted to sit but didn't dare in case I couldn't make myself get up again.

Finally, when no one came to investigate the noise, I found the will to move and crept to Breeohan and Rafan's door. It wasn't locked. When I pushed the door open, I saw that the reason it was unlatched was because

Breeohan and Rafan were gagged and tied. Breeohan lay still on his side, eyes closed. Blood matted his hair and purple bruises blossomed on almost every visible part of his skin.

Rafan groaned, opened his eyes, and looked at me with an expression of confusion. I hurried over, finally getting the hang of the strange gait required to constantly break the molecular bond my feet made as they fused to the floor.

"It's me. Mary," I whispered to Rafan as I untied his hands and feet. I left him to get his gag as I moved to Breeohan.

"Breeohan," I murmured, my throat suddenly tight. Breeohan's eyes fluttered but didn't open, so I gently tapped an area free of discoloration on his smooth dark cheek.

"Breeohan, wake up. You need to give me permission to heal you; I don't know how much I can do before I'll be useless." He winced and then slowly opened his eyes. But when he saw me, mistrust flickered on his face. I could see I'd have to waste some of my energy on changing my face back before he would trust me. I undid the mask lacing with relief, grateful to have my own features back.

"Mary," Breeohan croaked.

"Yes. Can you heal yourself, or do you need me to do it?" He was still too dazed to speak so I moved to his ropes.

As I analyzed the tight knots, Rafan spoke. "So it is you after all, Mary. You're always coming up with the most amazing lacing discoveries," he said in a volume I thought too loud. I turned to urge him to whisper, but stopped when I saw the menacing triumph on his face.

"Take your hands away from Breeohan's ropes, please."

I gaped at him, a terrible understanding bursting through my head like the rupture of a water balloon. "You slimeball," I spat, thinking furiously. I couldn't heal Breeohan, but I had strength enough to do one or two more lacings. I plucked the bungee rope lacing into life, hoping that Breeohan would be able to heal himself.

"I do so love your colorful Earth language, but before we chat further, there is a little matter that must be taken care of."

A lacing flashed behind my eyes, but it seemed to act as a shield. I could feel another lacing activated after the first one but, for once, I couldn't discern it. Darkness cloaked my vision in a thick, clinging veil, blinding me. My hands flew up, but I couldn't feel anything wrapped around my face. How had he done this? He shouldn't have been able to do anything physically to me without my permission. And somehow he had cloaked the lacing behind the first so that I couldn't undo it.

"Not to worry, Mary. You aren't blind. The mask of darkness is purely external, though you can't feel it," Rafan said. "It's not one of the most common lacings. Kelteon specializes in finding rare but useful magic. You'll get to see him again soon. He's almost to Kerln even now. As useful as it was to have you going to Mitigan yourself without even having to drag you there, he's concluded that Kerln is better suited to his plans and commanded me to keep you here."

"Why are you doing this?"

"Because I am not who I was. Kelteon is my—" Rafan's explanation cut off with a crack. I heard something thump to the floor. Then a lacing flashed, and the darkness cutting off my vision fled to show Breeohan crouching in front of me.

"I'm glad I knew how to undo that lacing. Are you okay? Did they hurt you?" He checked me over for injuries.

"I'm all right, but what about you? Do you need me to heal you anywhere? I think I have strength for one more lacing if you need it." I lightly brushed the back of his head, checking for the wound I'd seen earlier. We both stilled our gentle assessing at the same time.

"I healed it. Save your strength." He caught my hand in his and lowered it between us. "Mary, I am so sorry about Rafan. I know how you felt about him," he said in a powerful whisper of raw emotion. I pulled back, startled, hardly able to concentrate on his next words.

"I should have known something was wrong. He's acted strangely since we met in Ismar, but I didn't think . . ." He waved at the room around us in a staccato sweep. "I didn't trust my feelings of misgiving because he liked you, and I . . ." He trailed off.

"What?" It was hard to keep my voice pitched low. "I'm confused. I thought you heard me telling Rafan that I didn't like him, and that you've been mad at me for rejecting your friend. If anybody should be sorry it's me. He was your friend. He's never been anything more to me than that."

"Is this true?" he asked breathlessly.

"I'm sorry, Breeohan. I know what it's like to be deceived by a close friend."

Breeohan opened his mouth but froze when we heard a scrape outside the room.

"We have to go now," he mouthed.

I nodded and pointed to the window.

At Breeohan's incredulous look, I leaned in close, my mouth next to his ear and breathed, "I'll show you my gecko lacing. We'll climb down." He still looked confused, but he nodded. I projected the lacing for him, indicating which strings to tweak. I then had to show him how to angle his feet so they would detach from the ground. His eyes widened.

My descent from the building was anything but graceful. My arms were so tired I could only step down, move my limbs lower, then step down again hoping my sockets wouldn't jerk too much before I was able to jab my foot toward the wall and get a new suction-like hold. I still proved to be faster than Breeohan, however, who wasn't used to the strange angling involved in sealing and unhitching from the wall.

I collapsed to a sitting position and watched him carefully move one foot and hand at a time until he had reached the ground. He undid his lacing and then turned to pull me to my feet.

"Would it be too much to ask for you to undo my gecko lacing as well? I've only got juice for one more, and I should probably save it just in case. That is, if you're not too tired," I asked wearily.

"Of course," he said.

We crept forward, bare feet silent in the darkest shadows cast by the sandstone buildings. Breeohan seemed to know where he was going, and I followed, happy not to have to ferret out a direction on my own. By the time he stopped us in front of a nondescript wooden door in one of the narrow alleys, I was too tired to even jump at the scuttling of a rat in front of my feet.

No light slipped out of the broken shutters above the door, so Breeohan told me to wait while he checked to see if the house was occupied. He slipped up the wall with what appeared to my envious eyes as a tireless grace and disappeared inside the window. I waited in exhausted tension, listening for a crash or scream, something that would tell me that I needed to either go in to help Breeohan or run away. But no sound emerged.

The door opened, and Breeohan gestured me in quickly. "Lie down, Mary. I'll keep watch for awhile. You need the rest more than I do." He shut the door behind me.

"Thank you." I was too tired for pride. Lying down on the hard floor, I slept.

"You should have woken me," I said to Breeohan when I opened my eyes. The sun slanted through the slats of ill-fitted shutters in two round windows near the ceiling. The rays fell in stripes across my face. I sat up to stretch, and stopped mid-stretch when I realized that none of my muscles were shrieking with the anticipated pain.

"And did you heal me? You should have saved your strength." A surge of worry for him came over me unexpectedly.

Breeohan leaned against the wall, looking sheepish. "I may have. I thought it would be best if we were both able to move swiftly. I'm not tired though." He looked embarrassed. "After healing us, I couldn't help but fall asleep too."

"Oh, well good then . . . and thank you." I studied the dust floating in the sunbeams. The thought of silence was suddenly unbearable. "You've probably figured it out by now, but the city is full of Kelteon's people. I think the regular citizens are either hiding or were forced out. Oh, and they know how to look for the distortion movement in the chameleon lacing, so if we use it we'll have to be extra careful." I had started speaking just to fill the quiet, but I was starting to feel panicky.

"I guess Rafan knows about my mask lacing now, so they'll probably have passwords at the gate, if they're even letting anyone in and out with us on the loose. How soon do you think Kelteon will get here? Will he bring my mother with him, do you think? And the king, the king is coming here. We need to warn him, but how are we going to get out of here with a whole city trying to track us down? What if—?"

"Mary." Breeohan grabbed my hands, which were gesturing wildly as my agitation increased. "Calm down. We'll figure something out." I stopped talking, but Breeohan didn't relinquish his hold on my hands. The nervous turbulence that had been building up transformed into a flurry of soft and rapid wing beats inside my chest.

"You really never cared for Rafan?" Breeohan asked.

"No. I thought he was kind of creepy. No offense, but I didn't understand why he was your best friend. You two seem so different."

"The Rafan you are acquainted with is not the one I've known for so many years. I just wish I knew how Kelteon got to him. I would never have dreamed of Rafan changing so much or allying himself with Kelteon. I noticed that he was acting strangely, but I was too jealous to see that change clearly."

I gulped. "Jealous?" My mouth spoke against my brain's wishes.

Breeohan took a deep breath as if to fortify himself. "I was tormented with the thought that he loved you and that you loved him in return." Breeohan's eyes seared through mine until I felt at any moment I would burst into flames. "I know you may not care, Mary, but I love you. I fell in love with you the first time we met. You were alone, hurt, and scared, but you refused to let anything cow you. I'd never met anyone so full of determination. And then you looked at me with those defiant golden eyes. I was lost. I've been lost ever since," he whispered, reaching up to trace the curve of my face.

My breath stuck in my throat. The hand he'd freed trembled uncontrollably. Breeohan leaned forward into the striped sunlight between us. I watched in frozen fascination as the strips of light moved across his face, highlighting chocolate skin and refracting purple and gold as though his eyes really were crystal amethysts.

"But I thought you loved Avana," I stuttered while trying to fend off a cacophony of jumbled emotions. I wanted to bolt out the door. I wanted to never move. The thing I most feared was my wish that the four-inch gap between our lips would disappear.

"No," he said, his eyes grave and unwavering, and then his lips met mine in a soft, hesitant brush that tingled like fire through my frame. I shivered.

Breeohan noticed the shudder and pulled back. "I'm sorr—" he began, but I put my finger to his lips. His feathery touch had scrambled my brain, and it took me several breaths before I could form a halfway coherent thought. His lips had been like a drug, heady and intoxicating.

"I'm afraid," I said, my breath fast with more than fear.

"Of me?" he whispered.

"Yes. No. I'm scared if I let myself . . . You'll leave. Everyone in my life has either left me, used me, or been taken from me. I can't . . ." My eyes stared at my hand worrying the fabric of my pants.

He caught my fingers and turned my face to his. "I won't ever leave you." There was a tremendous pause where something was supposed to happen but didn't. "And I won't ask from you more than you can give." His right hand released mine, his left caressed my cheek before it dropped to his side.

No. No. I wanted to catch his hand and bring it back to my face, but I couldn't move so much as a finger. A scream of anguished frustration caught fast inside, all the more painful for being trapped. What was wrong with me? Why couldn't I just let go, let myself . . . But I couldn't even finish the thought. *They might as well take me to the loony bin right now—that's where I belong,* I thought angrily at myself.

Breeohan regarded the floor. I felt no better than slime oozing through the cracks in the brick. To see his pain was like being stabbed all over again, but every time I opened my mouth to say something, only silence emerged.

"We need to devise a way to escape the city and warn the king," Breeohan said quietly to the dust-layered ground.

I'm sorry, I'm so sorry, repeated in my head, but my mouth stayed cemented shut. He looked up and, seeing my anguished expression, curved his lips up in a pained but compassionate smile and shrugged. I was staked anew, feeling like a villain.

"It might be difficult to climb over the wall even with the chameleon lacing since, as you say, they know all our tricks," he said, smoothly keeping the conversation from uncomfortable territory.

I cleared my throat and tried to think rationally. "Just because they know all our old tricks doesn't mean they'll be able to stop us from using new ones," I suggested.

"Such as?" His eyebrows rose in inquiry, but I still couldn't quite meet his eyes.

"Well, the chameleon lacing isn't as effective as it used to be, but it's still useful if we don't have to move around much. So what if instead of climbing over the wall, we go through it? The wall is made of sandstone right? Sandstone's lacing is really similar to the sand lacing. We could make our own doorway through the wall. That way we could be virtually invisible, except for when we make a run for it through our new door."

"I think that could work. We would have to time our movements carefully, but it's better than what I was thinking." He sighed in relief. I wondered what he'd been thinking, but he leapt to his feet in one smooth motion and cracked the door, looking cautiously both ways before signaling me to follow him outside. I had a bad moment when I stood up and saw the world narrow into black before it gradually expanded back into Technicolor. I realized that I hadn't eaten for so long, my stomach wasn't even complaining anymore.

Breeohan led us through the narrow roads and alleyways. There was a tense moment when we both had to dart into the lee of a doorway to avoid a woman patrolling the streets. Until she passed, my heart did an Irish jig in my chest.

Breeohan whispered, "I think we'd better keep the chameleon lacings on, even if they know how to spot us moving. It's still better than being as visible as we are now."

I nodded in complete agreement.

"It will mean that we will have to hold hands. Losing each other here would be . . . dangerous." His eyes were fixed on the street where the woman had disappeared, but his voice was tentative, as if he expected a sound verbal slap.

My heart wrenched with guilt, and I shivered at the thought of being on my own again in Kerln. My hand shot like a bullet to connect with his, and I squeezed it tight. Breeohan turned to me with swift surprise before we both tweaked the chameleon lacing active. Then we moved again.

We had to stop five more times to avoid the eyes of patrollers, but we made it safely to some houses near a section of wall that seemed to be less crowded. For a long time we just sat in the shadows of the nearest building, observing how often someone passed by, above and below, for there were patrollers along the bottom of the wall as well as the top. We found that they spaced their walks to about every five minutes. It wouldn't give us much time, but I was hoping it would be enough.

After the ground guard made another pass, Breeohan and I scuttled quickly against the base of the wall. I focused on an area of the sandstone and tweaked the lacing in my mind to make the stone turn to sand. At first I thought it hadn't worked because the small archway I'd concentrated on looked no different, but then the sand shifted so that some spilled away from the wall. There was a slight indent at the top of the arch, but the sand still blocked our way. I kicked myself for not thinking my plan through. Sand might be less solid, but it was still very much in the way.

Breeohan quickly got on his hands and knees and shoveled sand as fast as he could. I followed suit. We managed to shift the sand so that a piece of sky shone through at the top. But there was no way we'd be able to make the hole big enough to crawl through before the next guard was due to walk by.

"Stand back and shield your eyes." My forehead dripped sweat, and I impatiently brushed it away before causing a concentrated wind to blast through the small opening, clearing the sand away in a whipping frenzy. Sand bounced back in our faces, clinging to my sweat in a gritty mask. Too late I realized that much of the sand was hitting the wall and shooting upward in a cloud, making a puffy yellow beacon in the sky. I stopped the lacing when I'd created a big enough space for us to crawl through, but guards were already running in our direction.

I cursed myself, pushing Breeohan into the opening.

"You go first," he insisted.

"We don't have time to argue. Just get moving." With protective desperation, I shoved him in the right direction. He followed my lead and began crawling quickly through the hole. I noticed that even with the chameleon lacing, the sand sticking to his face and body made him more visible. Looking down, I saw that I was in the same state. I crouched down to follow right at his heels.

I was almost completely in the shadow of the tunnel when someone grabbed both of my ankles and heaved. My hands scrabbled for something to stop my progress backwards but grasped only sand that slid through my fingers. Something between a shout and a scream emerged from my throat. Breeohan looked behind him, but there was no room for him to turn, so I watched his eyes track me helplessly during the second it took to drag my body out of the hole.

"Keep going," I yelled before rough hands flipped me by the ankles to my back. *Big mistake*, I thought as I bent my knees into my chest and kicked out savagely. The man holding me flew backwards and landed with a thud on the ground. I turned and tried to dive back into the tunnel, but a body slammed into my back and weighed me down before I could. Another man added his weight to the first, and I saw through my writhing struggles that a woman was trying to get past us and into the tunnel to stop Breeohan's escape.

Praying that Breeohan was already through the wall, I created a wind to catch the sand still in the tunnel and whirl it about, then changed the sand back into sandstone. The stone would be more brittle than what it once was, but it was solid. With that accomplished, I stopped struggling against my captors. My insides felt cold, remote. The people smashing against me became unimportant, not even worth the attention I would give a fly. When a sharp explosion of pain cracked through my head, I welcomed it with a near-hysterical relief. I fled into the dark oblivion that enfolded me.

Chapter 20

I woke to total darkness, feeling thoroughly tired of being repeatedly whacked on the head. But the thought of being unconscious again was a new and manic temptation. Such dark thoughts, so foreign to me, were enough to snap me out of my despair. I pushed the thoughts aside and held still, refraining from healing myself. I must have made a movement or noise, however, because I heard a ruffle of fabric. Instead of a blow, a soft hand stroked my face.

"Mary, honey, are you awake?" a sweet smooth voice asked. I would know that voice anywhere. I tried to sit up quickly only to fall back in a swamping wave of pain and nausea.

Swallowing down something nasty, I finally croaked, "Mom?"

"Lie still. I'm really worried about you. You've been asleep for a whole day, and I was starting to feel frantic," Mom's beautiful, wonderful voice said. Just hearing her made the shooting stabs in my head lessen.

"Don't worry. I'll be fine." I slowly brought the lacing required into the forefront of my mind and plucked the string for healing. The hand stroking my face twitched, then hesitantly brushed my hair back, a gesture that sent a rush of childhood memories through my mind. They were comforting, and I had to struggle to hold the waterworks at bay.

"So you can do this magic stuff too, huh? I guess that gives us a better clue as to why we're here." The hand brushing through my hair began to tremble.

"Kelteon hasn't told you anything?"

"Is that his name? I thought it was Kelson. He isn't a young man at all. Did you know? He changed from a boy into a middle-aged man right in front of my eyes."

"I know." I wished bitterly that I could see her face. I almost slapped myself when I realized that I had again overlooked a simple solution. I lit the room with a globe of golden light, or at least, I thought I had, but my vision stayed black. The blindfold lacing had been placed on me again, but this time, because of Breeohan, I knew how to undo it. The room's round contours quickly became clear, lit by my golden ball. The ground was sand, and as I lay looking up, I saw that the round ceiling thirty feet up had a square door. We were in a closed-up well.

I sat up to look at Mom. Wet streaked her cheeks. I found that the sand on my own face was being washed away in the same manner.

"Are you really all right, honey? I can't see you too well. It's like your face is only where the dirt is." Her voice wavered.

"Oh, I forgot." I undid the chameleon lacing.

Mom sighed in relief, and we hugged each other fiercely. I found myself sobbing into her shoulder, gulping out wet apologies. Mom massaged my back until we were calm enough for her to hold me at arm's length and look me over.

"Now, what's this about being sorry? You have nothing to be sorry about," she said.

"Yes, I do," I said, trying to get my breathing under control. "It's because of me you're here at all."

"It's not your fault, sweetie. It's Kels—Kelteon's fault. He's the one who tricked you, and he is the one who brought us here."

"He didn't bring *me* here," I said absently, distracted by the bandage wrapped around her arm. "Do you want me to heal you, Mom? I could fix that if you give me permission."

Mom sat back and regarded me steadily. "My arm is fine for the moment. I think you'd better tell me what's happened to you." So I told her about the first time Kelteon, or Kelson, had shown me lacing magic by making a ball of light, and how it had flashed through my mind so clearly, how I'd stupidly copied the magic to find that I could make the light too and revealed to Kelteon that I could see whole lacings, a feat almost unheard of in Iberloah. I told her how I'd tried to copy what Kelteon had done when he disappeared with her but had gotten the place in Iberloah wrong, making it necessary for me to travel to the capitol for the king's help to find her.

I skipped as many of the dangerous parts as I could, but I could tell my story was making her anxious by the way she clasped my fingers and unconsciously rubbed her thumb back and forth over the back of my hand. I watched especially closely when I explained how King Verone and Sogran, as well as at least two others, had been to Earth before the traveling lacing was lost to them.

"What do they look like, the training general and the king?" she asked, stroking her thumb faster over my hand.

I placed my palm over hers to stop her from scouring the skin off. "They both have similar looks: tall with cinnamon skin, dark brown hair, and light brown and gold eyes." She stiffened. I hated to get her hopes up only to have them dashed, and I felt a need to dampen my own hopes for the same reason. "I don't think we should assume one of them is 'him,' Mom. I don't know when they went to Earth, and others traveled there too. We're on a whole different world here. It's bursting with magicians. I'm sure there are people from other countries who've also traveled to Earth. For all we know, Dad could still be there."

Guilt swamped me for being such a cynic to my kind and sometimes flighty mom. I haltingly continued my tale until I concluded depressingly that I was once again a captive in what I assumed was Kerln.

"You've been through quite a lot, it seems," Mom said. She gathered me into a hug again, and we held each other in silence.

Finally I pushed away. "But what about you? It's been so many days, I've lost track. Have you been in a dark room by yourself the whole time?"

"No. I was put in a comfortable room with a light and given regular meals." She looked around at the small well, no more than five feet wide. "Well, until I was carted out of the mountains in a wooden box and brought here. The biggest problem was the boredom. Kelson—Kelteon didn't visit often at first, and all he wanted to do was taunt me with hints about capturing you. He also asked for permission to heal me, but I refused. Then he changed from looking like a boy into a man and tried to woo me. But I've had enough of men like Joe and Kelson. How could I fall for him when I've finally seen what my bad choices have done to you? Joe had to hit you before I realized how abusive and manipulative he was. And worse, you had a crush on the same type of guy yourself. I taught you that," she said sadly.

I felt indignant. "First of all, okay, yeah, you've made a lot of lousy boyfriend decisions, but I'd like to point out what you just told me about being brought here. You aren't responsible for other people's actions. And second, I'd like to state for the record that Kelteon was weaving an enchantment on me. I didn't really have a crush on him. Just so we're clear about that."

Mom's lips curved up slightly, her sad expression morphing into amusement. "Okay, we're clear. I'm so glad I have such a wise daughter."

"You're probably the only one in all of Iberloah that would express that opinion," I said, thinking of all my stupid blunderings since coming to this alien land. "So are you going to let me heal your arm or what?"

"Oh, it's mostly healed already. Don't trouble yourself."

"Mom," I warned.

"See for yourself." She unwound the bandage to reveal a scabbed-over gash. "I only keep the bandage on so the scab won't get scraped off."

"I can still heal it completely, scar and all."

She waved me away, and I gritted my teeth, but let it drop. If she wanted a battle scar, who was I to stop her?

Then I noticed there was bread, cheese, and water in the opposite curve of the well. My throat was instantly parched, and my stomach whined in hunger. "How often do we get food?" I forced myself not to snatch it up.

"Three times a day. Go ahead and take all that. You need it far more than I do."

Forcing myself to chew each bite ten times before swallowing, I tried to save some of the water for later. But everything disappeared more rapidly than was probably healthy as my hunger overpowered my self-control. Feeling better, I jumped up to look around and to determine the best way to get us out. I paced around the circle, looking up at the small door. It was a given that someone would be guarding above, possibly several people. I'd have to move quickly. Maybe if I got Mom to allow me to put the gecko lacing on her, she could climb as well.

I looked at her skinny limbs pensively, sure that several weeks of inactivity would not have improved her already nonathletic arms. She'd never been one for going to the gym. I'd have to go up myself and find a way to haul her up after overcoming the guards. I didn't like all the unknown variables.

I became aware that Mom was watching me with a look of pride, mixed with sadness. "You never give up, do you, sweetheart? You've always been my little problem-solver, out to save the world one paid phone bill at a time. You've been my rock whenever I've been weak."

I dropped to my knees. "You're the one who taught me to keep trying, to never give in to despair. You may have forgotten to pay bills on time, but you never stopped working, and you never gave up your dream to become a renowned painter, even when your boyfriends or our family told you to get a 'real life.' "

Mom wrapped her arms around me, holding my head against her chest as she smoothed my hair back. "I'm sorry. I guess all this time in captivity's affected me more than I thought. I've had a lot of time to reflect on my regrets."

I lay against her chest, feeling guilty and regretful myself. Suddenly Mom got up, and I had to catch myself from falling to the ground.

"So," she said, looking around the well and placing a hand here and there, hunting for handholds. "How are we going to get out of here? Any ideas?"

I stared at the ceiling. "I had one, but it's not very good. Kelteon would be expecting it.

"Well, it's better than nothing" she said. "I'm game." She turned up the wattage of her smile. Behind her grin I still saw a tinge of sadness, but it was almost wholly replaced by a new solidness and determination.

Mom and I had certainly had our share of battles in the past, but I loved her fiercely. And I knew that just because I was finally with her didn't mean that I'd saved her yet. A new resolve hardened in my core, driven by the need I'd felt my whole life to protect her.

"Okay, we'll try my plan. Sit tight and cover your face when I reach the top." I jumped up and hugged her shorter frame before I began climbing the wall. My muscles still ached, but all the practice I'd been doing lately was making a difference. I climbed to the ceiling without feeling as out of breath or as trembly as my previous expeditions had left me.

At the top, I took a deep breath, changed the solid wooden door to a more brittle wood, and kicked it. Splinters rained down to the floor as the door shattered, but I didn't have time to make sure Mom was all right. I followed the momentum of my kick and burst out of the opening, hoping to catch the guards off-balance.

I got no further than the well's rim. A circle of men and women surrounded me, standing shoulder to shoulder, each holding a loaded crossbow aimed directly at my body. I crouched like a cat caught in a car's headlights, knowing that at any instant I might feel metal-tipped arrows pierce my flesh.

The line in front of me parted, and Kelteon walked through. It was as if my two-dimensional pencil drawing had ripped from the page and gathered to itself depth and color. If I hadn't known already that Kelson and the man before me were one and the same, I would have thought this man was Kelson's dad. His ice-blue eyes crinkled, and his lips curled upward in a sharp hook of cruel amusement.

"Really, I'm disappointed. I thought you'd be out much sooner," he drawled.

"Yeah, well, it's kind of hard to come up with escape plans when you're unconscious," I said, trying to think of a way to overcome thirty people all at once. The situation was definitely looking grim.

He raised his eyebrows. "Such a touching reunion I heard below. I knew you'd like a little time with your mother. As you can see, she's alive and well, but that can change very quickly."

I felt a burst of rage at the thought of him listening to Mom and me, but my anger was swiftly overshadowed by fear. "You hurt her, and I'll—" I prepared to blast them all with hurricane-force winds, but Kelteon held up his hand.

"Think twice before you do anything rash, Mary." With a lazy flick, he pointed to the roofs of the surrounding buildings. More crossbows peeked over the edges held by men lying flat, nearly invisible.

"Attempt anything, and you and your mother are dead," he said with languid unconcern. "As juvenile as your behavior is, you have proven to be a bit slippery. I don't want to take the chance of losing you again." His grin felt like insects crawling all over my skin. My thighs started to cramp because of my half crouch, but I didn't dare even twitch.

"I have a proposition for you, which is quite generous, considering everything." His eyes flicked to his guards. As one, they straightened further and readjusted their aim to point at my head. "Have a seat. That can't be comfortable."

I sat on the well's rim, moving with exaggerated slowness so no bowmen would get trigger happy. I kept my eyes on Kelteon, feeling instinctively that he was a bigger threat than the plethora of snipers.

"What could you possibly want from me?" I worked hard to keep my voice from trembling and my face from broadcasting my fear. Kelteon's responding smile was sharklike, and I couldn't stop myself from shivering.

"Nothing so terrible. My proposal is this: you consent to letting me put an enchantment lacing on you, and I will refrain from killing your mother."

I felt the blood in my face drain away. "Never," I whispered. My throat had suddenly gone dry.

"Never? I thought you cared more for your mother than that."

My heart thudded painfully in panic; my mind flicked from one idea to another, as if I were some sort of crazed channel surfer. But I could think of no way to get myself and Mom safely out of Kelteon's grasp.

"If I let you enchant me, you could order me to kill my mother and there would be no way to stop myself from doing it. Your promise to keep her safe while still imprisoned means nothing." I tried to say this calmly, but my voice made a betraying squeak at the end.

The sun blazed down like someone pushing on my shoulders. A trickle of sweat slid into my eyes, but I didn't lift my hand to wipe it away. As the silence stretched, Kelteon regarded me coolly. He wasn't sweating at all.

"You really don't have a choice, Mary. You either agree to my proposal, or I kill your mother now." He signaled one of his bowmen to move to the well's open hole.

"Stop," I yelled before the man could take more than two steps. "You come any closer, and I'll blast you all into oblivion. I don't care if I'm killed too. And don't think I can't do it. I can," I said in manic fury. Kelteon held up his hand to check the bowman's progress, and the guard stopped, darting fearful glances my way.

"It appears that we are at an impasse," Kelteon said in his annoying languid way. No one moved. I blinked rapidly to get the sweat out of my eyes as flies buzzed brazenly around the heads of men and women who would not move their hands from their bows to swat the insects away.

"Send my mother unharmed back to Earth, and I will agree to the enchantment lacing." My insides wrenched in dread, but I couldn't think of another way to get Mom safely out of Kelteon's reach.

"As much as I would love to accommodate you, I cannot. The lacing to your planet was unfortunately destroyed."

"I don't believe you." I was beginning to hyperventilate. I forced the air to move in and out more slowly so that Kelteon wouldn't know the despair his statement caused me.

"Believe it or not, it is quite true. The traitor who destroyed them certainly discovered the mistake he made in crossing me." Kelteon smiled again, but the upward hooks on his lips made the gesture a nightmarish parody.

"Then it appears we *are* at an impasse," I mocked him in an effort to control my fear and hopelessness. Kelteon's creepy smile transformed to a scowl. I could see crossbows beginning to dip as the bowmen's muscles strained, and we all quietly fried in the sun for another minute.

"Sitting here doesn't do either of us any good," Kelteon snapped. Then he took a breath and smoothed his glower back to icy disregard. "Why don't we agree to a compromise?"

"I'm listening." I tensed and readied for treachery.

"King Verone is outside the city with his measly army of goons. I'll give your mother to them unharmed if you remain with me and submit to my lacing."

"I have to see her get to them safely. And you have to give me your word that you will never order me to hurt her or anyone else after I've been enchanted."

"Done."

Kelteon stared at me with lazy confidence, and I realized with a jolt of panic how powerless I would be to enforce my demands once I was under his will. Every nerve screamed at the thought of being in Kelteon's control, so I tried to focus instead on the fact that Mom would finally be safely out of Kelteon's hands, even if I wasn't.

If dying would have won her freedom and safety, I would much rather have died. But even if I managed to kill all the soldiers around me, there were too many others still in Kerln, and Mom would still be stuck at the bottom of a well.

Kelteon signaled two of his men to lower a rope with a woven seat on the end for Mom to sit on. I yelled down, "Don't worry, Mom. Sit on the rope chair. It'll be okay." I prayed fervently that I was telling the truth.

I heard an uncertain, "Okay," from below and darted my attention back and forth between Kelteon and the men hauling Mom up out of the well. When her head popped through the opening, I struggled to flash a reassuring smile while keeping one eye trained on Kelteon for any suspicious movements that might be signals.

He stood serenely still until Mom was standing solidly on the other side of the well from me. I moved toward her.

"Stop, Mary. I'm sure you'll understand, but I must keep you two completely surrounded until our transaction is complete, strictly to prevent anything from disrupting our business agreement, of course." Half of Kelteon's archers circled me. The other half surrounded Mom.

"I heard what you agreed to, and I won't stand for it." Mom's voice was furious. "You let my daughter go, and I will stay."

"I'm afraid you are of no further use to me." Kelteon signaled his soldiers to herd us forward. I heard Mom sob once before she got control of herself, and I realized that her furious demand had been a mask for desperation. I knew she felt as driven to protect me as I did her. I couldn't see her. Too many people were corralling around us, blocking my view.

"Don't worry, Mom. Everything will be okay," I lied. She didn't reply.

The trip to the front gates was frustratingly slow due to the difficulty of keeping a perfect formation around me while walking and pointing arrows at my face. I thought with a grim humor that if someone gave these people some gum to chew, they might all be undone. Kelteon strolled behind my circle, and I felt his sharp eyes glued to my back like a chilly breeze. I was sure he was watching closely for any magical moves.

When we reached the stairs to the top of the wall, several soldiers went ahead of me, climbing the steps backward so they could keep the bows aimed at my heart, while some came behind. As soon as we were out of the passageway and onto the wall, they molded themselves around me once more until Kelteon and Mom arrived in a circle of guards.

I couldn't see over the wall from my position because of the bodies surrounding me and the waist-high stone railing used to protect the defenders of the city from arrows and other projectiles. I wondered briefly if the true citizens of Kerln had even had the chance to use their wall to defend themselves against Kelteon before he and his army took over.

"Lower her over the side," Kelteon commanded. I tried to look through my captors as the ropes that were used in the well were brought forward and Mom was forced back into the woven seat.

"Mary, I'm so sorry," she sobbed as she strained to see through her guards and mine. My cheeks were wet, my vision blurry. I tried to wipe my eyes clear so I could keep track of her for as long as possible.

"It's not your fault, Mom. It's my choice. Run straight to the king's camp when you're on the ground, okay?" I tried to keep my voice steady as she was lowered out of my sight. "Tell them not to try and rescue me. It's really important that they realize I'll be a danger to them now." *If I live,* I added silently.

I turned to Kelteon in helpless anger. "Part of our agreement was that I would get to see my mother make it safely to the king, but I can't see a thing at this angle or through these people."

"As you wish. Just remember not to do anything rash. Your mother is still in my bowmen's range, as are you."

The soldiers moved closer *en masse* to the wall's edge, letting me see. Mom was out of the rope seat and moving away from the barrier as quickly as she could with bare feet. Beyond her, a group of about a hundred people were camped out of Kelteon's range.

They were too far away to distinguish faces, not that I would know anybody but the king, the training general, and Breeohan. But even as I thought of Breeohan, I realized he must have made it to the king in time to warn them not to walk blindly into Kerln

Mom had been pointed out by the group. As she got closer, I saw the men on guard act swiftly. With military precision, they formed a tight line, postures tense with bows at the ready. When Mom saw the hostility of the group, she slowed and put her hands up in the air.

One of the men in line lowered his bow. He must have called something to the other men because all the others followed suit. Then that man began to walk toward Mom. I didn't need to see his face; I knew that smooth gait. Breeohan approached her and bowed graciously before offering his arm to escort her the rest of the way to the king's camp. She must have said something as they walked because Breeohan suddenly whipped around to look back at the wall. For a moment I thought he saw me, but then I was dragged back out of sight by one of Kelteon's soldiers.

I jerked my arm out of his grip, but froze as crossbows swung in my direction.

"I believe I have held up my end of the bargain, Mary. Your turn," Kelteon said.

Bile rose to my throat. I couldn't control the shaking that coursed through my body. I shook my head and waited for the blow of an arrow to my heart.

"You wouldn't be thinking about going back on our bargain now, would you?" Kelteon asked. He nodded to one of his men. An arrow thudded into my thigh and pain shot through me. I struggled not to fall down.

"You may take it out and heal yourself if you like, but the longer you take to give me your permission, the more arrows will riddle your limbs," he said with the appearance of boredom.

"Kill me then. I'd rather break my word and die than be controlled by you," I snapped. Mom was safe. *That's all that matters now,* I thought.

A look of malicious glee replaced his boredom. "Oh, I won't kill you, but what I will do will make you wish for death, while ever keeping it out of reach. We had a deal, and I intend for you to keep it." He nodded. An arrow punched through the muscle of my other thigh.

I pulled out both arrows with a gasp and healed myself only to have another rip through my calf. A scream tore out my mouth, and I panted for a few breaths before I could concentrate enough to fix it. I waited for the next arrow to strike.

What happened next was no arrow. I saw the flash of the lacing that Rafan had used to hide the blindfold lacing from my magical sight, but this time there was no blindfold. Instead, pain lanced through my legs in waves of agony. I was burning. I saw my pant legs falling to ash and felt my flesh slowly crisping and melting away. I collapsed to the ground, screaming. The burning intensified, and my world narrowed to agony as my legs seared torturously, long past the point all nerve cells should have been destroyed. It was impossible to think beyond the pain. I tried to form the fire lacing in my head, but the cooking of my muscles shattered the pattern before it was fully constructed.

Finally, hardly thinking of what I said, I shrieked, "I'll do anything, anything! I give you my permission, please make it stop, make it stop!" My voice broke, and I sobbed silently through a throat gone hoarse. The heat ceased, but my legs still smoked.

"Very good." Through a haze that extended even to my mind, I saw Kelteon hide the enchantment lacing before he plucked it to life. My world narrowed and squashed, and Kelteon seeped into my mind like freon. Where his mind touched, my will froze, and was replaced by his. I fought for control, but the effort was as effective as pushing a mountain to make it move. In the end I scrambled to hide all that was left of myself, cramming into a small corner of my head. From my hiding place I discovered all I could do was observe through my own eyes as Kelteon directed my magic to heal my legs and then stand. I felt my face smile at Kelteon as his thoughts commanded it. He didn't even have to speak to order my every move. My will was his.

Chapter 21

I fought to shriek, to run, to make the smile on my face turn to a frown, but I found myself walking over to Kelteon and posing in a flirtatious manner. Kelteon slowly looked me over. My head moved down to survey my pants which were now no more than blackened mini shorts. My legs were smooth and unblemished with no sign that they'd been lumps of burnt flesh only moments before.

You pervert, I yelled in my mind. All the soldiers that had surrounded me were now ranged along the wall, surveying the king's camp and pointedly looking away from Kelteon and me. I noticed that one woman soldier didn't succeed in repressing a shudder, and I wished I could shudder too. But even subconscious physical responses were denied me.

"Come with me. We need to get you better clothing and some shoes. I also have someone I'm sure wishes to see you again," Kelteon said. He turned, and I watched from the little corner of my mind as my body followed Kelteon down the winding stairs to a building within sight of the wall. The door opened before Kelteon reached it, and we walked through to find Rafan holding the handle. He closed the door behind us. I wished heartily I could spit in Rafan's face, but I only stopped and stood meekly beside Kelteon.

"I believe you found out that Rafan has been on my side since your, let's see, second-to-last escape attempt. I thought it would be fun for my two puppets to face each other's strings, so to speak."

I struggled to understand Kelteon's meaning. He looked like a cat who'd succeeded in eating a pet fish from under its owner's nose.

"It's been such a pleasure spending so much time with you, Mary," Kelteon continued, "watching you struggle to understand the machinations of court politics, running to find me in the flesh while never realizing that I was by you at every turn, within Rafan."

Kelteon turned while Rafan and I stood, unable to do anything but stare at each other, our faces locked in masks of amusement while *my* mind, at least, was anything but. In all the time I'd know Rafan, I'd felt toleration for him, which had turned to loathing the moment I discovered he was working for Kelteon. Now compassion engulfed me. He had been trapped inside his mind as I was now. I wondered what Rafan was really like. I didn't get a chance to wonder long. There was a knock on the door and Kelteon's voice distracted me from my musings.

"Come," he commanded, and the door opened to admit a young man who was panting slightly.

"Someone approaches the gate, my lord. He holds the feathered staff of discussion." The young man spoke quickly, trying to get his breath back. He must have run all the way from the top of the wall.

"Who comes? The king?" Kelteon demanded impatiently.

The messenger shook his head helplessly. "We weren't sure." The man cringed as if waiting for a blow.

"Fine," he snapped. "I'll go speak with whoever has been sent. I want you to come too, Mary, but we don't want to give the king or his men the wrong idea. You, boy, tie her hands behind her back and gag her, then follow us up with an arrow at her back. Be very careful though. If you so much as knick her, your life is forfeit."

My hands moved obediently behind my back so the messenger could tie them. As he bound my mouth, my expression contorted into one more similar to what I really felt, despair and hopelessness. It appeared Kelteon didn't want it known that I was now his obedient android.

We moved to the wall and up the stairs at a pace that was quick but unhurried. When we reached the top, Kelteon ordered my body to stop out of sight while he moved forward to confront whoever had approached.

"Ah, Prince Sogran, it's been far too long," Kelteon drawled.

"That's certainly one opinion on the matter," Sogran yelled up the barrier to Kelteon. "Come, Kelteon, you know why I am here. What will it take to get Mary back? And I want to see her to make sure she is unharmed."

"You never did have any finesse." Kelteon grabbed my sleeve and made my body stumble artistically to the wall's edge. I looked down at the training general, my expression a mask of fear calculated, I'm sure, to anger Sogran. The training general bent his head up and watched with narrowed concentration. He sat comfortably on a horse that held so still under the general's hand it seemed a statue. In one hand Sogran grasped a tall staff with a multitude of brown feathers tied up and down the wood's length. The feathers fluttered softly in the breeze, a pointed contrast to the frozen horse and rigid training general.

"There is a crossbow at Mary's back, and many aimed at you, so don't try anything gallant. I shall tell you my demands for the princess's release."

The little bit that was left of me grabbed onto the word "princess" and gobbled it hungrily. Was I seriously a princess? Was King Verone my dad? I wondered in awe. I'd spent so much time contemplating the possibility but had always thrown it away as foolishness. It'd seemed too unlikely that a king would stoop to living a life as a common American. But he had. It was true. I wanted to jump and yip and dance around, but I could do none of that. My body stayed perfectly still, staring down at the training general with a new mix of confusion added in to the fear. I pulled my thoughts back from my daze to listen to Kelteon's demands.

"I wish my title reinstated and my status as exile dismissed. I also demand 4,000 shem and control of the lands from Kerln to the border. As my requests do not threaten the safety of the kingdom, I trust the king will grant them to see his daughter returned."

"There is a problem with your demand, Kelteon. You've made a mistake. You found Fiona on Earth, probably through the rumor that the king's refusal to marry was due to marrying a woman on Earth, but that rumor was only partially true. Yes, he fell in love with a woman from that planet, but he was not the one to get married there. I was. Verone was not the only one on Earth at that time. We made the journey together, and Fiona was not the king's love—she was mine. Mary is my daughter."

A stunned silence greeted the end of this speech. Kelteon's eyes widened in disbelief. I felt like reeling myself, but Kelteon was so preoccupied that my face expressed the same confused fear as before. I felt like I was spinning around in an emotional washing machine. I hadn't even had time to fully process the thought of King Verone as my dad before I discovered that Kelteon was wrong, and Sogran was really my dad all along. I was finding it hard to keep up, and my emotions sloshed around in a continuous rinse and repeat jumble.

"You lie," Kelteon growled. He looked furious.

"I assure you I do not. I suppose you believed Mary to be the king's daughter because of her eyes, but I am as royal as King Verone, though not from this country's line. I hope you will understand that it is not in my power to grant you your requests."

Kelteon stepped out of Sogran's view and made me step back as well. I posed, a breathing mannequin, while he paced back and forth like an angered lion. Sogran was silent below, waiting. Finally Kelteon's stalking slowed and stopped, and his languid mask of unconcern was back in place. He stepped confidently back to the wall.

"If it is true that Mary is your daughter and not the king's, then you will still need to meet my demand of 4000 shem. I also expect you to use your influence with the king to give me back my title and erase my punishment of exile. You and the king are close. Give me those things with the promise of no retribution for my actions here, and I will give you your daughter back."

"I can't speak for the king. I will have to confer with him before giving you an answer," I heard Sogran—my dad—say. The training general was my father. The thought was like an odd tang in my mouth that I couldn't identify. I heard horse hooves moving away. Kelteon turned to me with an expression of cool calculation.

"This changes things, but have no fear, you will still play an important part in my plan, if not quite as prominent a one as I had envisioned. I'd hoped to make you my queen, but now I suppose I'll have to marry Zefa Aria to cement my claim, once the king, Breeohan, and Aria's husband are out of the way. It's so much messier this way, but far from impossible. You will help." Kelteon smiled cruelly, and so did I, but inside I cried.

I knew Kelteon would not stick to his word to never demand that I hurt anyone, but in the agony of burning I'd forgotten the consequence of accepting the enchantment. *I should have let my legs fry. I should have dragged myself by my arms and thrown myself over the wall.* I chastised myself mercilessly.

Kelteon turned back to the wall to watch for Sogran's return. The smile stuck fast to my lips, and my cheeks started to ache. I wondered desperately if controlling two people at once was more complicated than Kelteon had bargained upon. It must be hard to divide his attention between himself, Rafan, and me. If only I could use that against him. I struggled to regain my own body, but found myself ramming into solid walls of resistance.

Without turning, Kelteon said, "I would advise you to cease, Mary. You will only tire yourself. You gave your will to me. You are mine until I release you or you die."

I retreated to my corner in a hurry, worried that Kelteon might annihilate the little part of me that still remained me. Kelteon decided to leave rather than wait idly at the wall, but my body moved forward to watch for Sogran's return.

"You need not point the crossbow at Mary until someone is here to see," Kelteon directed the man who'd fetched us and who'd faithfully kept me targeted through the negotiation performance. "You won't have to send for me when someone returns either. I will know as soon as Mary does."

Out of the corner of my eye, I saw the young man gulp as he lowered his crossbow. My hands were still tied behind my back. No one moved to untie the gag at my mouth. I watched the dimming view of the king's camp. The sun was setting behind the mountains, painting the clouds in oranges and pinks. But I could only view nature's canvas from my peripheral vision for my eyes were ordered to scan the camp.

I felt acutely embarrassed by my bare legs, but I wasn't sure if I should be grateful that Kelteon had been interrupted before he could order me to strip and change, or if Kelteon would have given me the illusion of decency and let me change in private.

My legs began to tremble as the sky darkened to a deeper blue. Despite the healing, being shot and burned had worn me down. It appeared that even Kelteon couldn't demand my body to obey beyond its normal physical limitations. With a whoosh of air and a sickening feeling of free fall, my legs lost the battle and collapsed beneath me. My bottom hit the floor in a painful thud.

My head swerved around to observe the reactions of the guards around me. When they saw me looking, they immediately suppressed all mirth and stood uncertain. Kelteon tried to direct me to instruct the soldiers, who were gaping in confusion, but my mouth was still bound and all that emerged was a muffled garble of sound. I gave a commanding, "umph," and someone moved forward to untie my gag.

"Kelteon instructs one of you to help me down the stairs to his rooms while the rest of you keep watch for the training general's return," I said. I wanted to stay where I was rather than go anywhere near Kelteon's room, but a guard helped me stand and supported me down the stairs to the room where I'd met Rafan. We moved past the entryway to a bedroom where Kelteon sat reading in a thickly cushioned chair by a large puffy-looking bed. A blue mage light floating above our heads made the bed covers and chair fabric appear tinted so that I couldn't be sure if they were purple or really red.

"Untie her. There's no need for disguise at the moment. I doubt Sogran will come back before dawn," Kelteon instructed. The soldier found it difficult to comply since it was necessary for him to simultaneously support me and loosen the knot at my wrists. Kelteon frowned impatiently, stood and grabbed me by the shoulders roughly while the guard finished removing the ropes. Then they moved me to the bed and dumped me unceremoniously on the sheets. I sank into the mattress.

"Sleep, Mary. I need you fully recovered for tomorrow's activities," Kelteon said ominously before my eyes shut unwillingly. There was nothing to do but sleep.

I woke suddenly to a windowless darkness, but I quickly realized that my waking wasn't a natural reaction to a full night's sleep since it was still dark. I made a globe of golden light above me and saw clothes draped on the back of the chair, and my body automatically put them on. The apparel was sufficiently scruffy-looking to accommodate the farce that I was a free-willed prisoner kept in less-than-desirable circumstances.

I stepped out the bedroom door and saw Kelteon and Rafan sitting cross-legged at a small circular table piled with breads, dried fruits, and the usual unidentifiable foods I'd learned to expect in Iberloah. I dropped to the empty space between the two men and began to eat without a word spoken between us. A few of the foods Kelteon made me jam in my mouth almost came back out again as my gag reflex kicked into gear. But Kelteon just had me clap a hand over my lips until the feeling passed.

He made me keep eating until I was sure I would throw up from being stuffed beyond capacity. Then Kelteon and I stood as one and climbed the wall to await a response to his demands. My hands moved behind my back, and Kelteon tied me once more and bound my mouth with rough cloth.

"Let's start the show. You there," he pointed to one of the guards keeping watch. "You keep your bow trained on my precious bargaining tool here until I can send her back to the dogs below," Kelteon instructed. Despite the pretense, Kelteon let me watch at the wall as we waited for movement from the king's camp.

The sun was just rising behind us, casting a long shadow from the wall onto the ground below. Metal glittered from the soldiers encampment, far out of the shadow of Kerln's imposing barrier. The reflections bounced around in a flurry of activity, and I surmised that we wouldn't have to wait long for Sogran's return.

As expected, a small group of armed men soon detached itself from the camp and came galloping toward the wall with the training general in the lead. He still carried the feathered staff at his side but seemed otherwise unarmed. When the group of soldiers reached the area just out of shooting range, Sogran signaled them to stop while he rode ahead. He came to a halt under the wall's shadowy embrace.

"Well, what do you have for me, Sogran?" Kelteon said with an insulting lilt.

"I have all that you asked for: the money, the writ made by the king to reinstate your title and cancel your exile, and the promise that the king will not seek retribution for your atrocities here, so long as you relinquish your hold on this city and agree to live always at court." Sogran's words were clipped and unhappy as he looked up into the mask of exhausted hope that covered my face.

"I did not agree to have conditions to my demands," Kelteon said carefully, but I almost imagined that he looked pleased.

"That is all I could do. Please take it and give me my daughter back," Sogran said, his face showing true fatigue.

"Very well, I agree. I believe you are an honorable man, but I wish to inspect the writs and money before I return Mary."

"You may inspect the papers, but I will not give you the money until Mary is safely with me," was Sogran's reply.

"As you wish." Kelteon signaled a guard to lower a rope with a basket attached. "Send the papers up."

Sogran skillfully maneuvered his horse to set the documents within the basket and then side-stepped his stallion to watch the rope slide back up the sandstone edifice. Kelteon looked the papers over carefully before seeming to reluctantly accept their veracity. I had to give him credit for his acting skills.

"Everything seems in order. I'll have Mary brought out immediately, and I will give back your city as soon as I have my affairs in order. I must disperse my people before coming back to the palace," Kelteon called down solicitously. He turned to his soldiers and spoke more quietly. "You eight take Mary down and surround her with your bows. Make sure the money is real before you hand her over to the training general."

I walked with the guards to the gate and stood, while those not assigned to me opened one side of the massive doors wide enough to let us out. Kelteon made me walk with a tired drag as I approached Sogran. The soldiers who accompanied him now approached with a chest the size of a large pig. It looked to be as heavy as an adult swine too.

"We must look at the money first," the guard next to me said. Sogran gestured for the two men who held each end of the chest to move forward, and the guard who'd spoken opened the lid to look inside. He nodded, and another of my guards stopped aiming at me to help take the chest from the mounted soldiers. I was pushed forward as Kelteon's men retreated quickly back to the gate. The door clanged shut behind them.

Sogran dropped the staff as if it were trash, dismounted from his horse with the speed of lightning, and caught me in a hug before I had stumbled more than two steps. I was oddly surprised, not having taken Sogran for the hugging type, even if he was my dad.

"Are you hurt? Quickly, get on my horse," he said in a jumble too fast to answer before he tossed me onto the saddle in an effort to move away from Kerln's snipers. Before we rode off, however, Sogran yelled up to Kelteon who still gazed down from above. "You have three days to surrender this city, disperse your men, and join the king's entourage back to the palace or your writs will be void." Then Sogran spurred his horse away from the walls in a mad gallop, surrounded by his armed soldiers.

I clung to Sogran with far more skill than I really possessed. If it weren't for Kelteon's horse smarts, I probably would have been bucked to the dirt. That didn't make me grateful to him, however.

We thundered into the king's camp through a sudden gap in Sogran's guards, which closed up again behind us. Not until we were all well within the camp did the training general pull up sharply on his horse's reigns. Despite Kelteon's expertise, the abrupt halt nearly threw my body to the ground. I felt a moment's regret that I hadn't fallen and broken my neck. I'd never before been a depressed sort or even remotely inclined to suicidal thoughts, but I'd never before been an unwilling assassin either.

Sogran dismounted and pulled me gently down after him. He gave me an awkward hug before stepping away, his eyes scanning the camp with an efficient gaze. But I thought his eyes avoided mine for a different reason than efficiency.

"I have to tell the king what's happened. Kirana, Shok, show Mary to her tent and make sure she is well protected. I'll not have her taken from us again," he directed two of his soldiers. My body stiffened as if in anger for a second before relaxing, and I felt a surge of private satisfaction. It would be much harder for Kelteon to make me do anything harmful if I was under a constant watch. Sogran turned back to me and finally met my eyes with a softened gleam in his brown-gold ones.

"We don't have the water for a bath right now, but you can at least scrub a bit of the dirt off with a cloth and a bucket of water. I'll get you clean clothes to change into."

I wondered with a stab of wild hope if Sogran knew about my cleaning lacing. Was he trying to find out subtly if the Mary in front of him was really me? My precarious happiness was dashed, however, when Kelteon had me reply, "Thanks. I don't think I have the energy to clean myself with a lacing yet."

I'd forgotten that Rafan—and therefore, Kelteon—had seen me use my cleaning lacing after fishing me out of the water onto his boat. My trapped self quaked with dread. My best chance was for Kelteon to mess up somehow, to do or say something that I would never do or say. But he'd been spying on me for a long time. It'd be easy for him to fake my personality.

"Why don't you go clean up and rest for awhile. I'll send Fiona to you soon," Sogran said. It was weird hearing him use Mom's name so casually, but they had been married after all. *Are they still married legally?* I wondered, *and according to whose laws?* Knowing Mom, it was entirely possible she had never filed for divorce.

I preceded Kirana and Shok, the two guards Sogran had assigned me, for although I was apparently a Zefa rather than a princess, it was still a faux pas for them to just lead the way to my tent. They did, however, tell me clearly when to turn right or left rather than coughing at me, and the camp wasn't incredibly large, so Kelteon didn't take any wrong turns as I traveled through the tall, tan-colored tents. Throughout the camp there was no hint of any bright-hued cloth other than the dark purple of the soldier's shirts.

Kirana and Shok took me to one of the centermost tents. It was wide enough inside to fit a cot in either direction, but no bigger. My head brushed the canvas at the edges, but if I stayed in the middle, next to the large pole that extended up to the ceiling, I could stand without my hair creating a static afro.

After Kelteon had me roughly scrub my arms and face of dirt, a purple soldier's gee top and a pair of loose desert pants were handed through the tent flap. I was still filthy and wished for a moment that he could do the cleaning lacing after all, but I'd never taught Rafan, and nothing could induce me to feel anything but fiercely glad that at least when it came to knowing my thoughts and memories, Kelteon was thwarted.

Once the new, clean clothes were donned, Kelteon had me lie down in my supposed extreme fatigue. I really did doze until a light voice outside my tent flap woke me. Before I knew what was happening, Kelteon had me jump to my feet and rush out the flap to hug Mom.

"Mother," he had me say ecstatically. *Don't fall for it,* I screamed uselessly in my head. *Notice something's wrong. I don't call you "Mother,"* I pleaded silently. You've got to see that it's not really me hugging you.

When Mom pulled away, there were tears running down her face, but Kelteon hadn't managed to pull that much off for me. "I'm so sorry I left you there. I will never forgive myself. Did he hurt you?" she asked, checking me over for wounds or bruises.

"It's okay, really. But do you think I could tell everyone everything at the same time? I don't want to say it more than once." My face was crumpled in a haunted expression, and Mom hugged me close again.

"All right, honey. Let's go find the king and Sogran. I know it's hard, but we really need to know what happened." She rubbed her thumb back and forth on my hand. Kelteon wouldn't know it, but Mom was troubled. I hoped it was about more than what'd happened to me after she'd made it to the king's camp.

Mom walked with me, her arm stretched up to reach around my shoulders while Kirana and Shok trailed behind us. Kelteon had me stoop into her, making my small mother take more of my weight than I ever would have. He was really playing up the pathetic victim role, and I wondered apprehensively what he was up to.

I knew when we'd reached the king's tent because not only was it big enough for a crowd to lounge around in without worrying about static hair, but the servant that always seemed to be wherever the king was when we were at the palace stood at attention outside the flap with two other soldiers beside him.

My head rose to catch the servant's eye. When he glanced my way my hand, tucked in close to my middle, quickly formed a symbol, kind of like a gang sign. And then my hand straightened my shirt as if that had been the purpose of the movement. No one else saw a thing. The two guards at the door were glancing at Mom, and my hand was completely shielded from the two behind me.

The servant moved his head so slightly that if I hadn't been aware of the hand signal, I would have thought he was only adjusting his rigid stance, rather than knowing it for the acknowledgment it was. I felt sick to think that Kelteon had a spy loyal to him so close to the king. The servant bowed to Mom and me, opened and held the tent flap, and then announced, "Zefa Mary and Fiona Underwood."

The dull canvas that blended so well with the desert on the outside was completely covered with rich and colorful silk swaths on the inside. Cushions lay randomly on the floor, on which King Verone, Sogran, and Breeohan sat with a stiff attention that made the comfort of the pillows seem wasted. When Mom and I entered, the three men stood and bowed before offering us cushions on which to sit.

The king looked genuinely happy to see me. I was expecting stern relief. I also expected a punishment for creating this mess. Breeohan's face was uncharacteristically unreadable. Sogran's lips quirked up, but that was all the greeting he gave before following the king and Breeohan back to the pillows and their uncomfortably tense poses.

There was a charged silence before my mouth opened and spoke. "I asked Mom to bring me here so I could tell you all what happened after she left, just once." My voice caught as I continued, "Please don't interrupt with any questions. I don't know if I can say it all if I'm stopped." My eyes were cast down, watching my hands clasp and unclasp as Kelteon made me pause.

"I don't know if Mom understood enough to tell you about the deal I made with Kelteon to get her free, that I consented to submit to an enchantment lacing." Kelteon looked up quickly to gauge their reactions. No one looked surprised. *That would explain the tension in their shoulders,* I thought with satisfaction. "Well, when she was safe over here, I refused to submit, despite what I'd promised. I felt I'd rather die than lose my free-will." Kelteon managed to make a few tears overflow from my eyes.

"He had his archers shoot me in the legs until I was too worn out to heal myself anymore. After he talked to the training general and I was out of energy for lacings, they dragged me to a room with a huge fire and used heated pokers—" My voice cut off with a sob.

Mom reached over to hug me. She was shaking all over. Kelteon didn't look up to see how the others were reacting. I really wanted to see if they were buying his performance, but I doubted even the great Kelteon could look them in the eye and still convince them of his version of events.

"I don't think Kelteon meant for me to pass out, but I'm glad I did. I was coming so close to giving in." My body shivered, and Mom rubbed my arm comfortingly. "When I woke up again, I was able to heal the burns, and you came before he could do anything else," Kelteon said with my mouth, gulping back sobs. "Thank you," he added before breaking down completely.

I felt like a traitor. His story could have been true if I had been a stronger person. The people I cared about were in more danger than ever because I was so weak. Kelteon's sobs were fake, but mine were real as Mom stroked my back and hugged me, and Breeohan scooted so close I could see his knees through my fingers, even with my face bowed low.

"It's over, Mary. You're safe now," Breeohan soothed. His hand rested on my shoulder and squeezed gently in compassion. After a while, Kelteon calmed my crying and looked up at the people around me. My head first turned to Mom, who looked guilt-stricken, then my eyes moved to Sogran and the king who shared expressions of rage, sorrow, and an almost imperceptible guilty relief, probably because they thought I was really me.

Breeohan still knelt close to me in a dark purple shirt that made the amethyst in his eyes seem of a deeper hue. Desperate sorrow and self-accusation marked his face. His fingers twitched up as if he wished to wipe my tears away, but his hands stayed in his lap. I prayed that Kelteon hadn't noticed the movement. It was funny how every person in the tent was riddled with guilt except one—Kelteon, the instigator of the pain who sat placidly spying from my eyes, unknown to all but me.

"Is it true then? Are you really my father?" Kelteon fished.

"Oh, honey . . ." Mom began but stopped when the king shook his head slightly. My head jerked in response, and I guessed that Kelteon was interested in the exchange. "Why don't we talk about everything after you've rested some more?" she continued. "I'm sure you've had your share of emotionally taxing events for the evening, and your father's story will take quite awhile to tell."

Kelteon could only have me nod reluctantly in order keep up the pretense of my harrowing imprisonment. Breeohan helped me to rise from the pillow.

"I'll walk you back to your tent," he offered. My head bobbed demurely. He held my arm in a supportive adaptation of the typical court hold as we walked away from the king's tent, Sogran's two soldiers trailing at a courteous distance. The silence stretched between us uncomfortably.

"You are justified in never forgiving me. I cannot forgive myself," he said.

"It would have done no one any good for you to stay," Kelteon had me say carefully. I got the impression he was trying to feel things out, unsure what Breeohan expected me to say. I was rooting for him to get some detail wrong.

"I might have helped you. Perhaps if I'd been there I could've stopped Kelteon."

I ached to comfort him, but instead Kelteon had me say, "Well, you didn't stay, and wondering 'what if' won't change anything." I saw the look of self-accusation on Breeohan's face intensify, and my hatred of Kelteon broiled to a fiercer pitch.

"Don't worry too much," Kelteon amended slightly when he saw Breeohan's tension increase. "You said yourself that I'm always getting into trouble. If you'd been there, you would have been caught too." I might have said something like that myself, but Kelteon said the words with ease. My body was relaxed, uncaring. I would not have been so blasé about those words, knowing that Breeohan was blaming himself for breaking his promise to me so soon after making it.

Breeohan was silent until we reached my tent, his face shuttered so that I couldn't tell if he had noticed something wrong with Kelteon's statement or not. He left with a polite good night and walked away, taking wide, slow steps. I entered the tent and lay down on the cot where my body went into a paralyzed stasis while Kelteon concentrated on other things.

My mind buzzed in a constant loop. It was a torture more refined than physical pain. I was glad when my useless thoughts were finaly interrupted by the sound of the tent flap swishing open. My body sat up. The king's servant stood outlined in the last light of twilight. Then he closed the flap and bathed the tent in darkness.

Kelteon directed my magic to light a small mage light. "Ah, Sirus, I trust the two keeping watch on the tent will be indisposed for some time?"

Sirus nodded warily. "They've just had their supper and will sleep for a portion, no more. Am I to assume that Mary submitted to the enchantment lacing after all?"

"Of course. She needed very little convincing to comply," Kelteon goaded me with my own mouth. "What news do you have for me?"

Sirus smiled nastily. It was creepy to see someone who had always blended in so well to the background look suddenly dangerous and menacing. "I have something that I know you will like. The training general's claim to Mary's fatherhood is false. It was a strategy to give you less power in negotiating. She is not only the king's child, but before he left to chase after his lost wife, he met with the council in secret and declared Mary his daughter officially, so that if any of the courtiers tried to harm Mary while he was gone, she would be protected by the fact that she really is the king's child and a true princess, if not the one she claimed to be. The council was not to tell anyone of her birth unless strictly necessary, so none but they know it still. But the king gave his seal to documentation declaring her legally his daughter."

"I suspected Sogran's claim was a ruse," Kelteon sneered angrily, my face contorting in fury. He had me stand and try to pace, but he soon found it was impossible in the small space and I sat back down. My emotions during Kelteon's little temper tantrum were twirling in their own confusing spin dive. I wished people would just make up their minds. *First, the king's my dad, then he's not, then he is.* It was enough to give me a headache and doubt Kelteon's spy, despite his apparent surety. Kelteon's scowl played on my face, curving my lips in a smile similar to that of Sirus', and I felt violated all over again to feel my face make such an expression of cruel delight.

"They think to have taken advantage of me, but King Verone will soon find that his scheme has failed. We will strike as soon as possible. Everyone has already eaten today, but I want you to add a sleeping herb to breakfast that will last the morning. I'll know when to move in with my men as soon as the training general's soldiers are asleep. Be sure not to get caught. It will be much harder to take the camp if the soldiers here are awake."

Sirus nodded once and left silently through the tent flap.

"It appears, Mary, you will have the pleasure of being my queen after all," Kelteon used my voice to whisper the news to me in satisfaction. Inside, I beat and clawed to take back control of my body, but Kelteon just chuckled and made me lie down to sleep. I resisted his command to close my eyes, but it was useless. Seeing nothing but the black of my eyelids, I sluggishly tried to figure out some way to warn someone. But answers stayed as far out of reach as the control of my body.

Chapter 22

I awoke in a panic, escaping the last of a series of nightmares that hounded me through my sleep. Awareness did nothing to calm me, however. Dread sat like a stone in my stomach. The tent flap swished, and my head turned to see a girl enter with a bowl of mush.

"Thank you," Kelteon said through me. He waited for the girl to leave before making me dig a hole in the ground and drop the food into it. I struggled desperately to make myself take a bite, but my body moved without pause, following Kelteon's orders.

He had me wait for twenty minutes before checking the state of the king's camp. My guards lay on the ground, drugged. There were a few people running around in confusion trying to rouse those who'd dropped, but I saw with dismay that those who lay senseless greatly outnumbered those still awake. My body moved closer to the edge of camp where the tents ceased, but before I reached the perimeter, a roar echoed in my ears. As the sound came closer, I heard men yelling and the clash of metal. Kelteon's brown-clad mercenaries rushed through the camp with the force of a riptide as they mowed down the few king's men still standing.

I wanted to look away, to hide, but Kelteon made me watch until the furor of the battle died down. Those still in a drugged stupor were dragged together and bound. My steps carried me toward the king's tent where I found Kelteon waiting.

"It's so much nicer to be with you in person, my dear. Come, let's say a final good-bye to your father." Kelteon reached out his arm in a courtly gesture to escort me within.

We brushed through the tent flap to the inside where the silken hangings were bathed in a bright blue magelight. It was too bright, making the hangings appear garish. The light accented the haggard bags beneath Mom's unconscious eyes. She hadn't been tied, but next to her the king lay bound and sleeping unnaturally. The training general had been tossed against the king and tied like baggage. To see the two men who'd always been so in control, so strong, and so assuring look so vulnerable made me crash and rage against the cage where Kelteon held my consciousness. Nothing happened.

Kelteon turned me to the far corner where Breeohan also lay tied and drugged. But even as I watched, his head twitched.

"Your friend is waking. He must not have eaten much, probably pining for you, as usual. I have to tell you, Mary, it was quite amusing to watch him through Rafan's eyes as we traveled together. He was such a sad little smitten pup, and you were so oblivious. It's funny really. I courted you through Rafan to keep you from getting too attached to the heir here, but I could have done nothing and still had the same result. You're quite cold toward men. What was that Earth term? A feminist man-hater?" Kelteon taunted. Breeohan twitched again.

"I know. Let's have a little fun before you kill him." He smiled with the terrible crooked hook at the corners of his mouth. My mouth felt dry at the thought of killing Breeohan, and despite Kelteon's hold over me, I felt my heart wrench and skip a beat before it painfully pumped blood through my veins once more.

Kelteon slipped a knife in the waist of my pants at my back and exited the tent, leaving me to kneel in front of a reviving Breeohan, my face a mask of concern.

"Breeohan," I whispered, shaking him lightly. "Wake up." His lids blinked slowly as if he was having trouble emerging from deep sleep.

"Mary?" he slurred groggily.

"Yes, it's me," Kelteon said through my lips, while I yelled *No, it's not!* and scratched at my mental prison looking for a weakness, a dent, anything that would give me a chance to break Kelteon's possession of my voice and actions.

"Something's wrong with me," he said, trying to lift his heavy eyelids.

"You were drugged. But everything's going to be okay now." My voice was pitched low, smooth and enticing. In my head I continued to mentally attack the bounds of my prison with vicious jabs. I felt a whip of pain as Kelteon gave me a psychic lash of chastisement. My thoughts went white with agony, but I fought the blankness and caught the end of his lash so I could follow it to its source.

"I'm tied," Breeohan pointed out with less of a slur to his speech.

"Let me help." Kelteon made me move around and pretend to work at the knots binding Breeohan. "There's something I need to tell you, Breeohan," I whispered softly, my face centimeters from his ear. Kelteon had my hand reach behind my back and grip the knife. Inside, I fought to hold the mental lashing of power as it bucked and crept painfully past my cerebral barriers to the power's nexus.

"Despite Rafan's betrayal, I still can't help but care for him." Breeohan stiffened, and I shrieked in silence, still pursuing the psychic whip. Kelteon made me lean until my breath gently touched Breeohan's face and bounced back to mine. "In fact, I think I've loved him since the first time I saw him clean and dressed for court."

The knife lifted and began its descent. I dug my psychic claws deep into the source of the mental lash and hung on, unable to do more than keep hold and watch as the knife started to descend toward Breeohan. It was going to pierce him. I was going to kill the kindest, noblest, most trustworthy man I'd ever known.

Something deep inside me snapped. A knowledge that had been hidden came into focus for the first time. The certainty of my love for Breeohan hit me in a surge of wonder. My doubt fled, and the fear that had held me constantly at a distance from realizing my feelings disappeared. A will more powerful than anything I'd ever felt before gripped me. In my mind I tore out the nexus of Kelteon's psychic lash with a fierce and desperate frenzy. There was a blinding flash of blue light. Then my mind slammed into my body as it too flew backwards, crashing into canvas. The knife jerked out of my nerveless hand at the moment of whiplash and arched in a deadly parallel to my body before puncturing the tent fabric an inch from my face.

My head felt like it was splitting open with the worst headache of my entire life. I reached a hand up to rub my forehead and then I stopped. I waved my arm around and stretched out my legs. I would have shouted with joy, but a groan was the closest I could manage with my head pounding like it'd been on the receiving end of a club swing. The blue light that had illuminated the tent was gone, leaving the tent shadowed but for cracks of light showing through seams and the flap.

I was still trying to convince myself to sit up, when a hand reached past me, grabbed the knife, and held it to my throat. I looked up to find Breeohan hovering menacingly over me.

"Kelteon. Give her back," he snarled.

"Wait, it's me. I got myself back." I winced. Talking hurt.

"How can I believe that it's really Mary speaking and not Kelteon?" Breeohan asked suspiciously.

"Kelteon controlled my body, but he could never hear my thoughts. He never knew you told me you loved me. But I guess you can't believe that either, not ever having been stupid enough to let someone enchant you. There is seriously something wrong with a world where someone can take over your body, but there's no cars, no electricity, and no chocolate!" I thought of the weeks of dirt and pain I'd endured with no chance to fix everything, and now to have Breeohan looking at me full of distrust was the last straw.

Tears leaked from the corner of my eyes and my head pounded with the rhythm of my heartbeat. "The story he told you about being tortured but resisting wasn't true. I'm such a wimp. I should've just burned to death. I almost killed you. It was so close. I'm so sorry, Breeohan. You were right. I'm like a walking curse, bringing pain wherever I go." I tried to keep from sobbing so that my head wouldn't explode.

"I didn't say that. I said you always seemed to get yourself into trouble," he replied softly, the knife still at my throat.

"Well, you were wrong. What you said was too mild. When I tore that blue ball of fire apart and broke the connection with Kelteon, I got slammed back into my own head with the force of lightning. You can tie me up or whatever you do to magicians—I don't care anymore. But would you just heal my head, please? I understand if you never trust me again. I wish I could prove that I'm me, but my head hurts too much. Stupid third world . . . world." My tears ran down my cheeks and dripped onto the hand that held the knife at my throat.

"You pulled apart a blue ball of fire?" he inquired.

"Yes. When I was trying to get my body back, Kelteon hit me with something, so I followed it and ripped it up, which seems to have worked, but I think death would be preferable to talking right now." I tried to concentrate on something other than the pulsating in my brain and the fact that Breeohan still had a knife against my neck.

"Where is Kelteon now?" he asked.

"I don't know. He left the tent so he could have some fun with you through me, but—" I jerked in surprise, and the knife nicked my throat. "Breeohan, you've got to get the king and training general and my mother out of here. The whole camp has been taken over by Kelteon's men. I don't know where Kelteon is right now." *I hope he has a whopper headache too,* I thought fiercely.

A purple lacing flashed through my mind, and then relief from the hammering pain washed through me like cool water. Another lacing and the cut at my throat vanished. Breeohan slowly withdrew the knife. "I choose to hope that you are telling the truth. If what you say about Kelteon's mercenaries is true, I'll need your help."

We scrambled over to the king, Sogran, and Mom and untied them. They were still unconscious, and I didn't know what drug was used so I couldn't figure out a way to heal them.

"What can we do? We can't drag them through camp." Breeohan paced through the tent's murky shadows.

I looked around and was struck with an idea. Reaching up I pulled down several swaths of the silk hangings that hid the tent's plainness, and performed the chameleon lacing on them, then I draped the cloth over the three sleeping forms on the ground. They vanished completely in the tent's dim light.

The tent flap folded back, illuminating the dark and catching Breeohan and me in its wide beam. Kelteon staggered in, clutching his head with one hand and pointing feebly at me with the other. Several armed men followed until the tent was crowded. Breeohan and I stood in front of the king, training general, and Mom so they wouldn't be stepped on accidentally.

"You wretched girl. What did you do to me? What did you do?" Kelteon snarled, his face a satisfying picture of miserable fury.

"My permission has been revoked. I guess I just needed a strong enough motivator to overcome your control."

"You'll pay for crossing me," Kelteon growled. He flicked his finger. An arrow loosed, heading straight for Breeohan's head. Time seemed to slow as I created a wind to knock the arrow off course.

"No. It's your turn to pay, Kelteon!" I yelled.

Another arrow was loosed and thrown off course. The soldiers, realizing that arrows would be useless, drew their swords and ran forward to mow Breeohan and me down. In one swift movement, Breeohan unsheathed his sword, blocked the leading man's sword and turned him into the other soldiers. The man behind the first accidentally skewered his companion, and three others were forced to swerve out of the way.

I used the distraction to grab the training general's sword that lay near the camouflaged cloth. I brought the heavy weapon up just in time to connect with the metal descending toward my face. The training sets that Sogran had made me repeat over and over moved my muscles without my brain's conscious thought, but I still barely held out against the much more seasoned soldiers that we faced.

The clash of sword on sword was loud in the tent. I blocked one man, only to find myself almost run through by another. Breeohan and I stood facing apart with the king, training general, and Mom between us. As more soldiers streamed into the tent, I started to worry about stepping on Mom and saw with tired desperation that we were losing. Already I had healed several severe cuts on my arms and legs. Then Breeohan cried out, and I turned to see him crumple to the floor, a man standing over him about to bring his sword down through Breeohan's middle.

The man I'd been fighting used my distraction to slice my arm, but I hardly felt it. A growl burst from my throat, and I loosed a wind lacing with savage glee.

The tent's stakes ripped from the ground, and canvas flew straight up so that we all stood in the open. Sand whipped around the soldiers who had forced their way inside as well as those who'd waited without. It thrashed around Kelteon and his men like a live thing but stopped short of the bubble of calm I kept around those I loved.

I focused, lacings flicking and activating through my head in a whirl as I freed each soldier's head from the sand, then condensed the remaining sand into dense sandstone encasing each of them. Several cried in horror, and some tried to escape, but none had time to do more than take a step before all but their heads were trapped in stone.

The wind died to reveal about twenty blocks of vaguely people-shaped stone with bare heads screaming and shaking atop stone shoulders. Kelteon's stone was planted in the middle of his men, trapped permanently in his position where the corner of the tent had been. He snarled, and I saw the flicker of a lacing begin to form, but before I could even warn him to stop, it winked out. Kelteon scowled and tried again, only to fail once more.

"I'm sorry to be the one to tell you, Kelteon," Breeohan panted painfully, "but from what Mary described to me, it sounds as if she tore the very center of your magic to pieces in order to escape you. It might take years for you to recover, if you do at all." He looked savagely pleased. I was elated to hear him speak at all and stepped to his side but was stopped by more of Kelteon's mercenaries running into the area, drawn by the sound of the screaming. When they saw the living statues, they halted fearfully.

"Don't try anything stupid," I said to them just in case. "I can encase you as easily as I did them." I pointed to their frozen comrades. "Drop your weapons and surrender."

"Attack them," Kelteon screamed. "I order you to kill them."

The free soldiers looked at each other uncertainly before dropping their bows and swords. I found rope and tied the remaining mercenaries securely while Kelteon yelled futile threats. I hurried toward Breeohan, but he waved me away.

"I'm fine. It wasn't so bad that I couldn't heal it myself," he said reassuringly.

"You stupid girl. This stone won't hold me for long. I'll make you regret what you've done to me," Kelteon snarled.

"It's not so fun being the helpless one, is it?" I quipped with immense satisfaction as Breeohan and I dragged Verone, Mom, and Sogran away from the encased soldiers.

It took us most of the morning to round up and subdue all the mercenaries who hadn't already fled. We also healed as many of the king's conscious soldiers as we could. Untying the drugged soldiers, we lay them out more comfortably.

I freed all but Kelteon from the stone. We took away their weapons and tied them up instead, and I found myself receiving bizarre sobs of gratitude as the stone encasings fell away. The soldiers stopped me from helping with the few burials that were necessary, and I was guiltily relieved that I could avoid looking at the dead.

When the few of us who were awake could do no more, we settled by the sleeping and waited for them to wake. Breeohan and I sat next to Mom, King Verone—my father—and Sogran. I still wasn't sure what to make of being daughter to the king.

"You must not have eaten even a whole bite of the food this morning—you awoke so quickly," I inserted into the silence.

Breeohan's milk chocolate cheeks reddened. "I wasn't very hungry. The thought of you being tortured turned my stomach."

It was my turn to redden. "I was weak. My legs were burning. All I could think about was the pain and making it stop. I put you all in danger because of my flimsy willpower," I whispered.

"Don't blame yourself. I defy anyone to have done better," Breeohan replied earnestly.

I didn't know what to say to that, so instead, I looked down at my lap.

"I wouldn't have had the strength to break the enchantment lacing if not for you. When Kelteon first hinted that he would make me kill you, I realized how glad I was that you had escaped, even if that meant leaving me behind. I knew that you were safe, and I was content, but I also knew that I would see you again as a possessed mannequin, and I wouldn't be able to stop my own hand from hurting you. I wanted to die."

"But you didn't kill me. You broke his hold on you."

"Yes." I hesitantly raised my eyes to Breeohan's. They reflected an intensity of emotion I'd never before seen on his face. My stomach knotted with a tension both unnerving and exhilarating.

I leaned forward, greatly daring, and touched my lips softly to his. His hands came up to cup my face and deepen the kiss. Then someone coughed. Breeohan and I parted, and I felt breathless and lightheaded.

"It's a good thing you're surrounded by chaperones. I'd hate to think what you two would do without anyone around." The king—my father—tried to speak reprovingly, but the effect was somewhat lessened by the drunken slur of his words. My face went beet red as I turned to see Mom, Sogran, and the king staring at Breeohan and me sternly, if somewhat sleepily. Breeohan looked just as red.

"Now you be quiet," Mom ordered the king of an entire country. "As far as I know, this is Mary's first kiss, and you're ruining it."

Thanks a lot, Mom, I thought unthankfully. The three adults were starting to look more alert.

"Your Majesty, please forgive me," Breeohan said. He quickly changed the subject, telling them of Kelteon's control over me and how Kelteon's men had taken the camp by drugging everyone, how I'd broken the enchantment lacing and broken Kelteon's magic accidentally at the same time.

"How did Kelteon get Mary to drug the food? She was watched at all times," the training general asked.

"Oh," I slapped my forehead. "I forgot to look for him in the aftermath. That servant of yours was Kelteon's spy," I said to the king. "He came into my tent and told Kelteon through me that you were really my father and had declared it before a council and everything. Kelteon ordered him to drug the food this morning. We've got to find him."

"Kreth, Zac, Johan come with me. We need to arrest Sirus for treason," the training general ordered.

Sogran left, leaving Breeohan and me facing Mom and the king in uncomfortable silence.

"So the secret is out," the king said hesitantly.

"I guess, unless you and the training general are going to switch the privilege again," I replied.

"No, Verone really is your father, Mary." Mom smiled shyly up at the king, and he smiled back goofily.

It made me instantly angry. "Don't smile at him, Mom. He abandoned us. He left you without even telling you why," I snapped. The smiles vanished, and I felt a stab of guilt but suppressed it.

"He had no choice. He was forced to leave," Mom said in a small voice.

"I was not supposed to be king. My sister ruled Iberloah before me quite well, but when she died in an suspicious accident, the people were worried. Revolts began to erupt, and nobles vied for the crown all within days of her death. I was on Earth when it happened with no plan of ever returning to Esa. But Dolna Zeva, the magician school's headmaster, knew where I was, and he knew where the lacing to get there was located. For the sake of the people, Dolna Zeva came to Earth and dragged me back with Sogran before I could even protest.

"Once I was in Ismar, the people calmed. The nobles scheming for the crown faded quickly into the stonework. But when I had things under control, I looked for the lacing, only to hear from Dolna Zeva that it had been stolen—I assume by Kelteon. I couldn't go back to get Fiona, though I searched for years for another copy of the travel lacing that would take me there," he finished sadly.

I was unsure how to feel. I'd grown up idolizing and hating my biological father in vacillating stages. Idolizing him because of the way Mom said he treated her when he was still around, hating him for running off and being the first man in a long line of many who had let me and Mom down. But if what he said was true, he really hadn't left because he wanted to. He'd practically been abducted.

"Kelteon said someone destroyed the travel lacing," I said, feeling awkward, at a loss as to what people should say in such situations.

"I'm sorry that you and your mother won't get to see Earth again, but I was hoping that you would decide to stay here with me," my father said. He looked quickly toward Mom, and she smiled blissfully back at him. There was no question about whether or not she wanted to stick around. It was nice to see that Mom's hopeless self-accusation had been replaced by a tentative happiness as she looked upon her long-lost husband. I'd seen for myself that King Verone was a good person, and really, where else would we go?

I glanced over at Breeohan sitting next to me and felt a thrill as he smiled.

"I think I'd like that. Mom?" I asked just in case.

"Yes. I'd like that very much," she said, still gazing at the king.

"I'm glad." I assumed the king meant to direct his comment to both of us, but his eyes were locked on Mom. Their faces drifted closer together, and I cleared my throat, feeling a strange mixture of happy uncertainty.

"Speaking of chaperones . . ." I said pointedly. Next to me Breeohan surreptitiously held up his hand to hide his smirk, but I caught it anyway and mock-glared at him. Mom turned to me with a mischievous glint in her eye, but before she could torment me further, Sogran returned, looking grim, and the sparkle died.

"Sirus isn't to be found anywhere in the camp." We all drew in sharp breaths. "There's more." The training general paused unhappily. "Kelteon's casing was smashed open. He's gone as well, probably with Sirus. I've sent men out to track them down. We'll apprehend them soon." Sogran said the words confidently, but they left a shadow on my previous ease. Why hadn't we heard Sirus breaking the stone?

"Continue the search, Sogran. We will break up camp and travel back to the capitol," ordered the king. Sogran saluted by grasping his left upper arm briefly, then strode off, bellowing orders as he moved.

While some soldiers broke up camp, the king sent a group into the city to make sure that all of Kelteon's mercenaries were routed out. I was trying to tie my tent canvas into a neat bundle but managing only a sloppy one when I saw the king's soldiers return. A prisoner marched miserably ahead of archers with nocked crossbows, his hands tied behind his back. I dropped the bundle and headed to intercept the king. By the time I reached them, Rafan was kneeling in front of the king, gazing down with a look of sorrowful disgust.

"There is nothing I can do," the king said in response to what Rafan must have said. "You are guilty of treason against the royal family. You must pay for your crimes."

"Wait," I said before my father could proclaim a sentence. "Rafan was under an enchantment lacing ever since he met me, probably before that. When I was under Kelteon's control, he showed me. I think when I broke Kelteon's hold, it released Rafan as well." Rafan nodded. I continued, "I really don't know what kind of person Rafan is since it was Kelteon the whole time. But I do know that the only thing Kelteon didn't control when I was under the enchantment lacing was my thoughts, so I think you should consider that when you pass judgment on him." I felt strange defending someone I had hated. But I hadn't ever hated the real Rafan. I'd never even known him, and being imprisoned in my own body had certainly been excruciating torment for me.

"Why did you submit to the enchantment lacing?" the king asked Rafan.

A horrible haunted look stole over Rafan's face. The voice I had only ever heard before as cockily confident trembled as he explained how Kelteon's agents had caught him when he'd been spying in the city. They'd tortured him until he agreed to submit to the enchantment lacing. "I held out against him for three days, but I broke," he rasped and hung his head in shame.

I dropped to the sand next to him and put my hand on his shoulder. "You lasted much longer than I did. I caved with hardly a fight. Don't torture yourself over someone else's wickedness." I spoke as much to myself as to him. He looked up at me, shame still spilling out of his eyes.

"I'm sorry for what I . . . what he made me do and say to you," he said in a jumble.

"No problem. I know it wasn't you. I'm not exactly sure who you are, but I'd be happy to find out," I said with a half smile. I looked up at my father. "I think Doln Rafan has suffered enough already, don't you . . . Dad?" I was unsure about calling the king "Dad." But when the word emerged hesitantly from my lips, King Verone's face transformed to a look of pleased surprise. I felt responding warmth grow in my chest.

"I think you are right, Mary. However, your explanation does make me worried. Kelteon has escaped. Is there any way he could regain control over you?" he asked.

"Never," Rafan's voice rasped vehemently. "I would rather die a thousand deaths than ever be possessed again, unable to even move my finger without Kelteon's command. I would kill myself first."

I vehemently agreed, but I was sure it would be awhile before Kelteon could even attempt such a thing.

Just then Breeohan appeared from around a tent corner. When he spotted Rafan and me on the ground, his face turned murderous. Breeohan's sword slid free of its scabbard. "I trusted you. How could you ally yourself with Kelteon?" he yelled while advancing.

"Calm down, Breeohan. Rafan was just as powerless as I was," I said. "He was tortured and put under the enchantment lacing." I looked up to the king.

Breeohan's sword drooped. He looked from me to Rafan to the king in confusion before sheathing the metal. I sighed in relief. Breeohan looked perplexed.

"I revoke my permission to Kelteon or anyone else to ever again control my will with the enchantment lacing. I vow death before submitting to such a vile and dangerous prison," Rafan's gravely voice rumbled feelingly.

"I am satisfied and am sorry for what you have suffered under Kelteon," King Verone said formally. "He will not go unpunished for his crimes. You are free to go, Doln Rafan. You may travel back to the capitol with us if you wish." The soldiers untied Rafan's hands, and I helped him to his feet.

My father and the soldiers walked off to various packing tasks, but Breeohan stayed standing in an uncertain but defensive stance.

Rafan murmured, "I'm so sorry, Breeohan, for . . . for how miserable I made you. I hope you know I would never . . ."

Breeohan held up his hand, shoulders slumping. "It wasn't you. I'm glad to know that my friend is still my friend in truth. We will bury that past and start anew." He briefly placed his hand on Rafan's shoulder, before turning away to help with the departure preparations.

As I watched him retreat, I realized that I'd been shamelessly watching a private moment. So I turned to go, embarrassed, but Rafan snagged my sleeve. He tried to meet my eyes but couldn't hold mine for more than a second before he looked away, coloring. It was jarring to see so many foreign expressions on Rafan's face, but also comforting, a confirmation that the man in front of me was not Kelteon.

"Thank you. The only me you ever saw was a womanizer, Princess," he said with the same rough voice I'd known since meeting him, but with a humility never before present.

"Yeah, well," I said, uncomfortable to recall my entrapment in Kelteon's will. "Kelteon would have been pleased if you had been declared a traitor. Also, I remember . . ." I couldn't finish my thought about how Kelteon's mind invasion had made my skin crawl. "I had to endure his will for a much shorter time." I shivered.

Rafan looked at me with haunted understanding. "Thank you, anyway," he said passionately. Then he blushed and strode quickly away. I watched him for a minute and shrugged, as unsure about what to make of this new Rafan as I had been of the old.

Chapter 23

The trip back to Ismar was slow because of all the people traveling in our party and the fact that the king had us parade through every city and town we passed in a royal display. Sogran sent soldiers to continue the search for Kelteon, but no trace of either Kelteon or his spy, Sirus, was found. The training general's men returned a few weeks later, frustrated by an unexpected blizzard in a high mountain's track leading out of Iberloah. We could only hope that Kelteon had been killed in the snow or at least trapped outside the country.

The uneasiness I felt about Kelteon's continued freedom was forced into a mild dissatisfied twitch at the back of my mind as Mom and I rode through the cities and towns seated in a cart, decked in brilliant-hued clothes, and waving like beauty queens in a parade. The king and Breeohan, also resplendently arrayed, rode horses ahead of us, and the training general trailed behind less conspicuously but always on the alert for danger.

Along the way, Mom and my father became reacquainted with each other and more than annoyingly gooey. I discovered that Mom had followed her nature and had never actually gotten around to getting a divorce from my dad, so they were actually still married. Despite that, they decided to get married all over again as soon as we reached the palace and to do it in the Iberloahan tradition, so that the people could feel secure. Villagers and townspeople alike cheered with an added frenzy that made me nervous after the news of Mom and Dad's upcoming nuptials was declared.

Word of the princess and the king's long lost wife burned through the kingdom like wildfire. By the time we reached the capital, the streets were packed with people tossing celebratory flowers onto the narrow lane between the crowds that was left open for us to pass through. The cobbled path was completely paved with petals. I wondered briefly where they had gotten so many flowers. People waved colorful strips of cloth as we passed and they all cheered like hard core celebrity fans.

When we got to the palace, servants descended in a whirl of action. I found that seamstresses had been working fulltime during our long return to prepare a glorious white dress ensemble for me, with gold and purple embroidery in curiously Celtic-like designs. The diagonal neckline slanted toward the side where jeweled buttons latched the bodice tightly. Large embroidered strips extended from the bodice, which made it easy to glimpse the white colorfully bejeweled pants underneath while still giving the outfit the feel of a dress.

As several women wove my hair into a heavy crown with swirling gold spirals and glittering amethysts and diamonds that perversely looked airy and delicate, I noticed Sentai at the fringe of the bustling workers. It was too noisy to speak, but I caught her eye and smiled and was gratified to see her smile and her eyes warm.

My makeup was painted on thickly in purple, gold, and white. I wasn't allowed to move or look in a mirror until the "artist" was done. When I finally saw what she'd done, I wanted to groan, but I held it in and smiled instead, wishing for the wedding to be already over.

Hours later, when I was deemed "done" and the time was at hand, I was politely coughed to a room where Mom stood waiting, dressed in a light green outfit in the same style as mine, just as heavily embroidered and jeweled but with silver and light purple. Her blonde hair twisted through a silver headdress and her makeup was a whirling canvas of light green, silver, and periwinkle paint.

"Hey, I thought I was the bride," Mom teased.

"I guess brides wear green here?" I responded uncertainly. We'd been coached in what to do for the ceremony, but I was still feeling a bit like a bird in a burrow.

The doors opened, and Mom was announced to the audience within the next room. She took a steadying breath and flashed me an excited schoolgirl smile before walking through the door. My announcement came next, and I followed close upon her heels into an enormous, circular room.

The audience, mostly of courtiers, sat on pillows in orderly lines from the furthest edge of the wall and continued inward. Only the path through which Mom and I walked, and an eight-foot-wide area in the middle were free of onlookers. In the center, four steps led up to a decorative table on which sat a gilded jeweled cup. King Verone stood next to the table, waiting for Mom. I stopped at the foot of the stairs but remained standing as Mom reached across the table and goblet to clasp my father's hands.

The crowd waited in silence. A shaft of light from the noonday sun streamed through the window in the ceiling onto the circular dais, illuminating my dad and mom in brilliant golden light.

"I, King Verone of the line of Oderfarst, do this day pledge my life and more than my life to Fiona Adams Underwood," my dad announced, looking joyous. "By the sun that shines faithfully on us, I swear to be loyal and true and will give my last drop of water to ensure her health and happiness."

Mom beamed. "I, Fiona Adams Underwood, do this day pledge my life and more than my life to King Verone of the line of Oderfarst. By the sun that shines on us, I swear to be loyal and true and will give my last drop of water to ensure his health and happiness."

Verone released one of Mom's hands to grasp the cup. It flashed in the sun as he handed it to her. She took a sip of the water within. Gold reflected in the light again as she handed it back for him to sip. Next, each drew out a bracelet, which they slipped onto each other's left wrists. A cheer went up as my dad and Mom clasped hands, raised them into the air and turned in a circle to view everyone. I found it ironic that an upper class society that spent hours donning complicated clothing and painting faces would have such a short royal marriage ceremony. The courtiers started to stand, but the king waved them back to their pillows and gestured to me. I climbed the stairs and jammed awkwardly between my parents.

"Though my wife and I have renewed our pledge today, it was really made nineteen years ago in a very far away land. I was called from her land to serve you without the option to bring her back with me, while my child grew in her womb. My daughter came to us under a different name, but she confessed to me her true origins as soon as possible. She herself did not realize what her story meant, but I knew and rejoiced. Today I present to you not only my wife, but my daughter and heir, Princess Mary Margaret Underwood of the line of Oderfarst."

There was a charged silence, followed by a spattering of applause as the courtiers remembered themselves. I shivered, not having realized before that my father would announce me as the heir to the kingdom. What did Breeohan think of this? I searched the room and found him clapping nearby with a huge smile on his face as if he couldn't be more thrilled.

"All may adjourn to the grand hall for dancing and refreshment," my father said, seemingly oblivious to any discord his announcement may have caused. He and Mom looked around me into each other's eyes, and I quickly decided to retreat from my unpleasant third wheel position.

I saw Breeohan looking up at me, smiling easily, and I aimed an interception course toward his comforting presence. It was harder to pick him out when I reached the ground, especially since a swarm of people surrounded him immediately, probably to ask him exactly what I wanted to ask, how he felt about being bumped out of the position of heir.

My walk toward Breeohan was interrupted by a soft hand on my shoulder. I turned to find Ismaha smiling at me, her eyes creased with kindness.

"I thought you didn't travel anymore," I blurted before thinking.

She laughed. "For this I made an exception. I knew after we spoke that you represented something extraordinary. I traveled slowly toward Ismar soon after you left, but it took me much longer than you to arrive.

"Thank you. Things could have been so much worse for me if not for you." I gave her a firm squeeze. As we parted my eyes.

She smiled. "Go celebrate. We will see each other soon."

"Only four steps closer to my goal and a sharp jab in my side knocked me sideways. I looked around to see who had struck. I looked around to see who had struck.

Avana wore a blood red dress with black pants, her face artfully painted to accent her high cheek bones and full red lips. I'd forgotten how stunning she was in the weeks I'd been away, but it hit me anew now with a worried pang. I wondered how Breeohan could love me when he could have had someone so beautiful. Then she turned, as if noticing me for the first time. Her eyes narrowed in open contempt.

"Princess, what is it now, Mare? You have so many names, it's quite confusing. But it's so good to see you again, whoever you are," she said carelessly while her eyes bored into mine, sending the clear message who she thought I was and that it wasn't anything near a princess.

"Court was ever so boring after you went away. I heard that both Doln Rafan and Breeohan went to rescue you again." She laughed, and a few courtiers close to us laughed nervously in response. "It's unfair of you to play the maiden in distress so often and take away our desirable young men. Not all of us are so fortunate as to have the freedom to ignore what such a scramble would do to our reputation."

A few more people tittered. My face grew hot with anger, but yelling or hitting Avana would convince people only that I was as crass as Avana suggested. Still, it was tempting. "I'm glad to hear you missed me, Zefa Avana. I was afraid you might be angry when my friends joined me on my journey and left you without so much as a good-bye. I guess you weren't as close to Zefan Breeohan as you thought," I drawled innocently with only the barest hint of sarcasm.

Avana's eyes narrowed. "If it is true that the king knew you were his daughter from the beginning, he likely told the heir of his discovery. Breeohan's sense of duty is such that he would have no choice but to trail you, despite his desire to stay. Did he have any warning that you were aiming for the position of heir, or did you snatch it from under him?" A few courtiers shuffled their feet nervously as if they wished to stay out of any trouble but couldn't pull themselves away from a good show.

Avana and I were glaring at each other so intently that we both jumped when Breeohan's smooth baritone said, "It is true that I knew Mary was the king's daughter, and I knew that meant I would no longer be heir. But you are mistaken to think that I was in the least bit disturbed by this discovery. Princess Mary will be a great ruler. I support her completely." He moved to my side and offered me his arm. "May I escort you to the Grand Hall, Princess?" He smiled sweetly at me without glancing once in Avana's direction.

My heart sputtered and then beat again with a fragile lurch. "Thank you, Zefan Breeohan. I would be delighted." I placed my hand in his as he walked us away from an astonished group of courtiers and a very angry Avana.

I cast a last glance back to see Avana's intense glower directed at me before turning away and exiting the room. I probably hadn't scored any points in the eyes of the surrounding nobility after my conversation with Avana. Avana would hate me more than ever now too. I would just have to deal with her venom as it came. Maybe I could ask my father to send her on a foreign relations trip to some distant country. That thought gave me a moment's happiness. But it faded as I thought of my newly acquired clout as heir to the kingdom.

"Uh, Mary, this isn't the Grand Hall," Breeohan teased after I veered us into an small, empty room to the side of the hallway where courtiers streamed past.

"Are you sure you don't mind not being the heir anymore? I didn't know that would happen. I mean, I guess it's stupid, but I thought you would stay the heir because you're from here and I'm not. You can have it back. I'll talk to the king—I mean, my father—and ask him to change it back." Fearful apprehension bloomed inside my chest at the thought of average teenage American me being required to one day rule a nation.

Breeohan put his finger to my lips. "I spoke the truth. I told you before I never wanted to be the heir. You've given me back my freedom—or at least the illusion of it." He smiled wryly. My foreboding faded as my insides tingled with the nearness of him.

We had been constantly surrounded by crowds and servants throughout the journey back to the palace and hadn't found an opportunity to be alone. I felt suddenly strange and disconcerted as we stood inches from one another with no one in sight. I tried to distract myself from my frantic heartbeat pulsing up through my throat. "Yikes. I guess that means I'm the caged one now. You're sure you don't want it back?" I laughed breathily.

"No, but I'll be happy to spend as much time as is needed to teach you all that is required of being the heir." The corner of his lips curved impishly.

"It might take me a while to learn it all." My mouth quirked.

His purple eyes snared mine, and my breath snagged. "That's what I'm hoping." The arch of his lips turned into a grin.

I remembered to breathe and retorted, "Fine, but I'm not calling you, 'Master.' "

He closed the scant space between us until I felt his light breath on my lips. And then he whispered, "I wouldn't dream of it."

Discussion Questions

1. What kind of problems do you think you would face if you were suddenly in a country without modern conveniences?
2. Why do you think there are class systems in so many societies? How does the class system in Iberloah compare to the ones you know? Is it better or worse or the same? Why?
3. How do you think Mary will handle being a princess in Iberloah's society after having grown up in a democratic nation?
4. Do you think that Mary is a passive character or an active character? Why?

About the Author

Alicia Buck was born in Salt Lake City, Utah, on a cold November day and has hated the cold ever since. Luckily, she now lives in much-warmer St. George, Utah, with her husband, Jason, and three children: Connor, Riley, and Elizabeth.

Alicia has wanted to be a writer ever since fourth grade. At that time, she felt sure her stories were creative masterpieces. When she was older, she reread her flashes of brilliance only to realize that they were nothing of the sort, but that didn't quash her desire to keep writing.

Alicia received her bachelor's degree from BYU in English and had to constantly defend her major when she had absolutely no desire to teach. Who said all English majors have to be teachers?